NOTHING MORE

To Lisa,
Thanks for all
your support!
xoxo *[signature]*

Janine Olsson

To Lisa.
Thanks for all
your support!
xoxo

Nothing More

Copyright © 2017 Janine Olsson

ISBN: 978-0-9911495-3-7

Edited by: Alison Duncan

PART 1: FALL

CHAPTER 1

LIV

The morning birds outside my window wake me with a desperate love song composed of sharp whistles, chirps, and tweets. Hugging my pillow, I focus on one particular song and imagine it's a male bird pining for a female's attention, declaring his heart's promised devotion through a beautiful melody. The way he carries on and on makes me believe the female is playing hard to get.

The thought makes me giggle.

In my younger years, my inability to grasp how birds look when flying caused my mind to spin with wonder and bewilderment. It was such a mystery to me. Being born blind, it was difficult for me to imagine what I couldn't experience through my sense of touch, so I tried to get my hands on all that was incomprehensible to me.

My fascination with birds led me to a petting zoo on my seventh birthday. There I had the pleasure of holding a young owl. I remember the pinch his powerful claws made through the thick protective glove I wore and how wonderfully soft his feathers felt as I stroked his chest. I can still recall his weight bouncing on my arm as a great gust of wind blew through my hair and flapping filled my ears. I can also recall how sad I felt when his weight pushed off my arm as he left me. The zookeeper said the owl was flying back to his post. I remember the *ahs* uttered from everyone around me and trying so desperately to imagine how glorious he must have looked.

I'm seventeen now and still completely blind. Although I can now imagine many of the things I once questioned, there is still so much I have yet to get my hands on.

With an exaggerated yawn, I stretch out of bed and wiggle my toes the moment my feet hit the soft carpet. I'm enjoying the sensation the thick weave provides when the mood outside suddenly changes. Two squirrels engaged in a heated argument steal the limelight as they chatter back and forth, firing what I imagine to be insults at one another. Amused, I make my way to the window and rest my forearms on the sill. The bickering continues as the September morning sun warms my face. I lean my forehead against the screen and inhale the rising smell of dew from the grass as a warm breeze passes through my long hair. I'm easing into a deep sigh just as a wet nose presses against the back of my bare arm. It doesn't startle me—actually, I was expecting it.

"Morning, Hank," I sing. This dog makes me sing—not well, but he's brought out the best in me ever since he entered my life five years ago. I was sitting in a sterile-smelling room when a nice lady with a high-pitched voice brought a few well-trained guide dogs out to meet me. They all seemed the same—big and soft, friendly and obedient—but one stood out. One made my heart expand with love. Hank. My diamond in the rough ... or ruff. There wasn't a doubt in my mind that we were meant to be together. I hugged his thick King Shepherd neck and didn't let go until the sensation of falling in love was complete—it took all of ten seconds. Love at first ... encounter.

No one has ever had the ability to brighten my day as easily as Hank. He offers me comfort and security like no other. He's my eyes and I trust him completely.

The commotion outside reaches another level, causing Hank to stiffen beside me. Jumping up, he rests his front paws on the sill and pants against the screen. The next breeze that comes my way isn't a pleasant one. "Ugh, Hank, you need a breath mint." The bugger licks my face. "Yuck! Seriously, Hank?" He barks—I swear he understands everything I say. Leaning my head on his, I pause to enjoy the serenity he provides. Bad breath and all.

Heavy footsteps walking down the hallway disrupt our peaceful moment. They stop at my door and light breathing follows. Hank turns his head to greet the silent man, his tail wagging happily, hitting my leg with every back swing.

Okay, I'll admit, I'm a tad jealous of how much Hank likes my stepfather, Gary. He's a nice guy, it seems, but Hank was all mine until Gary came along. I say "it seems" because Gary and I barely say more than a few words to each other a day. We are kind of stuck in an awkward stage. I think he's just uncomfortable around me. He doesn't know what to

3

make of me or how to treat me. And since I feel the same, we hang in limbo. But Mom is happy and that's all that matters to me. She married Gary almost four years ago—that's when we moved into his house here in Hardy, a small, middle-class town in northern New Jersey.

"Morning, Gary," I finally say.

"Hey, Liv," he replies. "Need anything?"

"No, thanks."

"Ready to eat, Hank?" At Gary's invitation, Hank races from my arms like a traitor.

I get up and walk to the bathroom. Being familiar with my surroundings gives me independence and living in this house for four years has given me the confidence to move around without aid.

There is no doubt that being blind has its fair share of challenges, but since I was born blind, it's my normal, and I'm very conscious of my surroundings. My hands, ears, cane, and Hank play the role my eyes can't. Maybe I can't see a perfect sunny day, but I can feel it. I can experience it—lie in the grass, smell the flowers, hear the birds sing and bees buzz, enjoy the warm breeze and the sun against my skin. I can experience the day in my own way.

I learned at a young age that you can't just want something; you have to go after it. Nothing comes to those who sit and wait. And there was one thing I really wanted—independence. So I made a choice to always push myself, try new things, experience as much as I could, avoid focusing on the things I couldn't do, and never hide behind fears. It wasn't easy, but the alternative would have been to let my challenges beat me, stay dependent, wallow in self-pity, and sit and wait for things to come to me. That's no way to live.

Don't get me wrong, there are times I wallow—I'm a teenager after all and I know how to wallow—but for the most part I'm happy. Like it says in the bible, "As a man thinketh in his heart, so is he." I love that saying. It offers such power. There is such hope in those words. I do my best to live by them and make a conscious effort to think of myself as capable, independent, and limitless.

I choose to think these things; however, sometimes the beliefs of others place many limitations on the blind—and the handicapped in general—and there are many days I'm reminded of the limits the outside world has placed on the blind.

When I was younger, I was very dependent on others. The more I grew, the less I wanted to rely on them. School, and Mom, taught me how to be self-reliant. They taught me the skills needed to step into society alone, from walking across a busy street to keeping my head up. I used to hold my head down, thinking what did it matter where my eyes were pointed, but they taught me how to carry myself as the sighted do. They said it's polite to face others when in a conversation, so I learned to follow voices, and I learned many other things so I could . . . fit in?

Even so, learning these skills didn't exactly cause everyone to trust my independence. There were times when neighbors would tell me in my own backyard to go inside until my mom was with me. I'd walk inside wondering if I had done something wrong, and Mom would say, "Some people think the blind should be guided everywhere they go. They think of the blind as helpless. The only way to shut them up is to show them you aren't. You want to ride your big wheel in the driveway, ride it. You want to climb the slide at the park, climb it. You want to skip through the sprinkler on the front lawn, skip. You know the safety precautions needed, follow them and your instincts. I'll deal with the neighbors and their narrow-mindedness. Don't give anyone power over your life, especially people who don't know you or what you are capable of."

Stepping into the shower, I think of Mom's love for me. It's profound. I can feel it in the air around me when she's near. She's a fighter—strong, loving and kind. Thank God for her strength. Without it, she may never have taught me such independence. If not for her strength, I might not be strong myself.

It's crazy to think that neighbors and strangers would actually admonish my mom for letting me play in our yard alone or allowing me to walk into things when I'd refuse to use my white cane. Having me deal with the consequences of not using my cane was a great lesson to learn. Others didn't understand how hard it was for Mom to give me that space or teach me those lessons. And they didn't understand the great service she was providing me. As mad as some of her lessons made me at the time, I tell you, I couldn't have asked for a better mom.

It was the lessons taught by society that I wish I never learned. Lessons on how they perceive the blind, lessons on ability and worth. I have come to understand that those sad lessons are learned by anyone born with a challenge, anyone born different.

Many people think that everyone should fit the same mold. Differences make some people uncomfortable, so the different, the mold breakers, are supposed to work harder to fit in—how sad is that?

Just think, babies aren't born believing they are different. They adapt and survive with what they are given. It isn't until someone points out that they are working with less than the person next to them that they develop insecurities and doubts.

That peeves me to no end. And also makes me wonder if I'm really the one working with less or if it's the narrow-minded who are.

After turning off the shower, I dry off, slide into my robe that's always hanging on the back of the door, and brush my teeth. I don't bother with makeup and my hairstyle . . . well, long, straight hair doesn't really require much attention. Brushing it and twisting it in a bun on the top of my head is good enough for me. I make my way back to my room and check the time by pushing a button on my clock at the left corner of my dresser. It announces that it's 6:40. I've always been an early riser. I have twenty minutes to waste, so I lie back down on my bed in my robe and find my iPod on the nightstand, right where it should be. Finding a good song, I ease onto my pillow as the music blocks out the nature show outside.

It sounds like that darn bird is still getting nowhere with his love interest and the squirrels are still arguing.

CHAPTER 2
LIV

"Liv, I've been yelling your name for five minutes!" Mom shouts through my earbuds, startling me. "Why aren't you getting ready?"

"I'm ready. Almost. I just need to get dressed," I say while pulling the buds from my ears and realizing I'm shouting too. Hank pushes his nose under my hand, whimpering nervously. Patting his head, I say, "It's okay, Hank." He barks, and my smile comes easily. "My sweet boy."

I wrap the earphone wire neatly around my iPod and place it on the nightstand before getting up. Opening my dresser drawer, I find underwear and a bra and socks.

"You want your hair braided?" Mom asks. She loves braiding my hair. And I love when she does. I pull my desk chair out and plop down.

Let her go wild.

Her fingers work quickly as she talks to me about school. When she's done, I go back to the drawer and find my things. Still in my robe, I ask her for some privacy. She walks out and shuts my door without an argument. Since I developed pretty substantial mounds on my chest a few years back, it's been awkward to be naked in front of her, even though I know I inherited my huge boobs from her, and my hips too—*thanks, Mom.*

My mother gave me curves and my father gave me height. I'm five foot eight, so I guess he gave me something good before he left. At least the height counters the hips and mounds. Mom's Italian and all the women in the family are five foot five or shorter, and large breasted. I'm talking *enormous.* When I was younger, they'd practically suffocate me in their welcomes. Just when one would let go, the next would pull me in, smothering me in her cleavage. I used to think they were secretly trying to kill me, until my cousin Dominic, said, "Try being a boy trapped in their welcomes. I'll be scarred for life." I love that guy, he's always good for a laugh, and yes, he is scarred. Poor guy is twenty-three now and refuses to date anyone who's larger than a B-cup.

Moving to my closet, I find the braille labels on the shelves to pick clothes that match. Organization is how I stay sane. Everything has a place and I never change it. I settle for light-blue jeans and a yellow T-shirt, then slip them on and find my Converse sneakers in the cubby marked "blue Converse" in braille. Understanding color is tricky for me. Like chartreuse—*what the heck is that?* The only thing I understand is that colors should coordinate. Some work well together and some don't. I follow that rule. There's no reason to stand out any more than I do already.

After slipping on my shoes, I find my laptop on my desk and allow the smell of Mom's coffee to lead me to the kitchen. I love the robust scent, not the bitter taste. I'm a tea drinker. Hank walks close to my leg, turning me at the door, and around the table. I pat his head.

"You have plans after school?" Mom asks from her seat at the table.

"Nope."

Gary's heavy steps announce his entrance into the room. He and Mom share a lip smacking kiss. "See you later, baby," he says, his smile easily detected in his voice, then he stomps to the back door. The guy's fit, but he walks as if he weighs three hundred pounds.

"Love you, you sexy thang," Mom replies, and I pretend to gag. Actually, there's no pretending. I gag.

"Have a good day, Liv!" Gary calls from the back door with laughter in his voice. There's no doubt they love each other. They're still stuck in the honeymoon stage. I truly am happy for Mom. She deserves the love they share.

"You too," I say over my shoulder.

The door shuts and the crinkling of the newspaper lets me know Mom went back to reading. I go about my routine. My backpack is right where I left it, on the hook by the back door, and I slide my computer inside. Moving to the counter, I find a banana, lightly press it between my fingers to see if it's to my liking, and then eat it before kissing my mom's cheek and walking to the front door.

Outside, I slide my aviator sunglasses on. Mom says they look really awesome on me and not all faces look good in the style. I guess it's kind of cool they work for me. I walk down the driveway to the mailbox with my white cane.

Knowing Mom is watching from the door, I turn and wave. She doesn't have to be at work until eight, so this is her routine—coffee, paper, seeing me off. She's about to say, "Have a good day, sweetie," and she does, right on cue.

"You too." I blow her a kiss and turn to search the front pocket of my backpack for my strawberry lip gloss. Finding it, I slide it over my lips. Yum! This stuff smells so good, I'm tempted to eat the tube every time I use it.

After one more swipe over my lips, I slide it back in the pocket and wait for my best friend, Catherine Binoche, to pick me up. It's the start of the third week in September and school has only been in session for eight days, but since she's arriving later and later each day, I have a feeling we will be on the tardy list by next week.

It's finally our senior year. I have high hopes for this year. Even though so far it's been a whole lot of nothing special, I still hold onto hope that it's going to be great.

Hardy High isn't a school for the blind. I had attended such a school before we moved in with Gary, but that school is hours away now. Even though I'm the only blind student in Hardy, I am comfortable here. I may be different, some say disabled, but that's their word, not mine. Never would I use the word disabled to define my academic abilities, or even my physical capabilities. I'm confident in myself. Yes, sometimes I walk into things, but so do the seeing. Students bump into me all the time. And yes, the faculty thought it best I be

11

guided when the halls are busy—teenagers don't pay much attention to their surroundings, and like I said, they bump into me all the time—but when the halls are empty, I can get to any room in the building without a problem. And my grades ... well, I'm in honors classes and I'm very confident in class. I have a superior memory—I was tested. I remember everything I listen closely to. I remember terms, definitions, formulas, and facts. Albeit, there are many things I can't grasp or even begin to explain, but tell me a fact and test me on it, and I'll ace it. I struggle with numerous things in school—as most teens do—but the work isn't one of them.

Screeching car tires making the turn onto my street too fast alerts me of my friend's arrival. Cat's a haphazard driver. No, wait, that's being too nice. She's a complete menace to everyone on the road. And sidewalks.

"Tell that lunatic to slow down or I'm calling the police myself!" Mom bellows over the squealing.

The car stops with a skid in front of me; the engine's heat hits my legs, the smell of burning rubber assaults my nose, and the creak of the passenger door swinging open fills my ears. "Get in, Liv, we're gonna be late." There's impatience in her tone, as if she was the one waiting.

Finding the door, I slide into the seat. Cat gives me little time to settle before squealing the tires while yelling both "hi" and "bye" to my mom. I fasten my seatbelt as she speeds around another corner.

"I can't believe I voluntarily get in your car. You're out of control." I chastise her with laughter in my voice. Truth is, I love that Cat's a bit reckless around me and never acts as if a porcelain doll just got in her car. And I have to admit I wish I could drive—better than her, of course. The freedom it must bring.

"Oh, you love it," she snickers.

"How did the talk with your mom go?" I ask after settling in the seat. She was supposed to ask her mom about aid for college. She hasn't seen any significant scholarship opportunities come her way yet and needs her mom's help, although her mom isn't exactly on board with the fact that she's even a mother who has a seventeen-year-old daughter.

"Did you talk to yours?" Cat deflects, and I know that means she hasn't yet.

Cat and I have been planning our future together since we met freshman year. We both dream of going to an out-of-state university and sharing a dorm room and eventually an apartment. Mom has reservations about me living in a dorm, especially coed. She's open and encourages college in general, but dorm life? Drunk eighteen-year-old boys who finally have freedom to make bad choices? She's not a fan. Though, if I go to college out of state, then some kind of dorm life is necessary.

"Yeah." I tell her about Mom's concerns and hear her sigh.

"We'll figure it out," she says, startling me with a smack on my knee. "Although your mom will find a way around whatever we come up with. She always does."

Cat complains about my mother's rules often, but I know she envies my relationship with Mom. She once told me that if her mother showed her a quarter of the love mine showed me, she wouldn't be the basket case she is. Cat's home situation is different than any I've known personally. Like I said, her mom doesn't seem to realize she is a mom. She works nights at a bar and sleeps all day. She never makes dinners—or breakfast or lunch—or comes to any of Cat's field hockey games, or shows any proof she knows she has a kid, but somehow she finds the time to entertain men often. And since Cat doesn't know which one of her mother's many conquests produced her, all she has is her mother, and that's like having nothing at all.

Cat is loved—by me and my mom and others—but I've come to realize that when you don't receive love as a child, you grow up not knowing how to recognize it or even how to accept it as an adult. She's desperate for love but also scared to death it won't last and foolishly thinks she isn't deserving of it. It's like a vicious battle between heart and mind, and oddly they seem to take turns winning. When her heart finds stability in someone else, her mind throws a grenade. When her mind finds safety alone, her heart retaliates with an aching longing for love.

I hope she finds a balance soon. I'm really worried about her.

I know Cat *safely* gets us to our destination when she says, "I can't wait to get out of this miserable pit of despair. Senior year. It's supposed to be awesome. So far it sucks sweaty balls."

This is the first year I finally feel comfortable in school, but Cat, she can't wait to throw that graduation cap in the air and never look back. She's been planning her exit since the first day she walked through the doors freshman year. Cat believes life doesn't start until college and she can't wait to live.

After an abrupt stop, she kills the engine. "Oh balls, this will be ugly," she says, sighing.

"Evan," I presume. Evan Tully is Cat's boyfriend. Correction, ex-boyfriend since last night. It seems

14

her mind threw its infamous grenade at her heart's happiness yet again.

"Yeah, and he's not alone. Tannon, Sparks, and Teddy are with him."

I reach out and grab for her arm, hitting the target, and I pull her upper body over the center console. "I don't understand why you did this. Evan's completely in love with you . . . Trust that. Tell him you had a bad night. Plead temporary insanity." The desperation in my plea causes my throat to tighten. "Does your crazy inner voice let you hear any of this? Are you listening to me?" All is silent. "Jeez, Cat, you're making a huge mistake." I let go of her arm, almost throwing it back at her.

What's she thinking?

Evan's the nicest guy I know and she's the lucky girl who gets to be loved by him. He's sweet, compassionate, understanding, and also my best guy friend. And from what Cat tells me, his sweetness comes in an attractive body—tall and muscular, with a handsome face, dark eyes and hair. He's the captain of Hardy's hockey team and well liked. I have no idea why Cat dumped him so unexpectedly. Even with the knowledge I have of her, I still can't for the life of me understand why she would hurt herself this way. She's blissfully in love with him, he makes her laugh, and yet she ended it for no good reason.

They were together for six months and it was the happiest I'd ever known her to be. Then, out of nowhere, something snapped in her head and she laced up her running shoes. I wish I could wave a magic wand over her to turn off the inner voice that's repeatedly telling her to sprint, but I can't, and there is no getting through to her. I hate the way she treats herself.

"Just get out. I'll come around," she says, and I don't bother scolding her anymore.

Sighing loudly, I adjust my aviators and open the car door, taking a moment to calm my emotions before placing my feet on the pavement. Just then, a strong hand wraps around my elbow. "Hey, Boo," is all he needs to say and I know it's Tannon Keaton, aka TK.

"Hi, Tannon." I smile despite my sadness. This boy always makes me smile. From what Cat tells me, though, he makes all the girls smile.

Tannon is also on the hockey team. He plays a merciless brand of defense—earning the nickname, Crusher. Cat says the boy has the looks, personality, and likeability factor of an athlete that can make millions off of endorsements alone—*if* he keeps his teeth, she teases. To which I retort, "I thought hockey players didn't need teeth."

And according to every girl in school, Tannon has an unbelievable body; irresistible dimples; sexy, hazel eyes; awesome, brown hair, sometimes styled in a faux hawk or left messy on top depending on his mood; kissable lips; a devilish grin; and a walk that has more swagger than any teenage boy should possess. I think what they're trying to say is—the boy is hot.

I know he's built bigger than the other high school boys—he's hugged me against his strong chest many times. And he definitely has charm—the girls are constantly pinning for his attention. Honestly, I like his attention too—he's nice to me, I enjoy his humor, and he's fun to be around. Only problem is, he acts like he knows how gorgeous he is and conceitedness isn't an attractive quality to me.

"Good morning, ladies," Harry Todd says, aka Teddy, being he's a giant, cuddly teddy bear.

"Morning, Teddy!" I say, smiling. He has the sweetest voice.

Tannon hugs me to his side. "Your smile is contagious," he whispers in my ear. The words trickle down my neck like warm water. His ability to cause unfamiliar reactions in my body amazes me, and confuses me, because, like I said, the image in my mind exposes a cocksure teen on a mission and I'm not attracted to that image.

I snap out of my bewilderment over Tannon at the tail end of a quarrel between Sparks and Teddy. I must have missed something significant. The name-calling has started, but then again, it could be nothing at all. Guys get along so differently than girls. I don't think I'll ever understand the banter between boys who call each other friends—they sound like enemies half the time.

"Whatever, lard-ass," Sparks snaps. "I'm right, you're wrong. End of story."

"We'll see, cheese face," Teddy retorts.

Sparks curses. Supposedly he has bad acne scars and the insult always hits home. The guys—his so-called friends—use the dig whenever they want to shut him up.

All goes quiet and I become conscious of Tannon's hard body again. I try to step away from him, feeling awkward in his arms this long, but he's not having it. He slides his hand down my arm, leaving a trail of goose bumps, and laces his fingers with mine. I'll admit my hand in his comforts me. He lifts mine up to his chest and I can almost sense him looking at it.

What's up with him? His touch is so different since the school year started.

The sound of skateboard wheels rolling over pavement echoes from behind me. I'm guessing it's Tucker Jenson. He enjoys riding his skateboard to school, even though he has a Jeep. There's a tap on my right shoulder as he skates past my left before he screeches to a stop. "Hey, sweets, how you doin'?" he says in that upbeat way of his.

"Hi, Tucker. I'm good, thanks."

Tucker's a skater—a rebel without a cause type. He got his first tattoo at thirteen by his tattoo artist cousin and now has seven tattoos covering his slim torso. Many of the girls in school say the tattoos are sexy and make him desirable because without them he's nothing much—their words, not mine.

My peers and I *see* people differently. Not to make them sound superficial, but they care about looks. I've come to realize most people do. I'm sure I'd be the same if I had been born with sight. Since I wasn't, I don't understand why so much attention is put on appearance and looks. I only *see* what's on the inside and, on the inside, Tucker is more appealing than Tannon. Tucker's one of those guys who's friends with everyone. He's charismatic and wild, and he doesn't care what anyone thinks about him. Or what anyone thinks about anything, really. He's just out to live a fun life. Yet somehow they consider him an average guy with hot tattoos and Tannon—the cocky guy—is considered appealing.

Go figure.

"So Cat, since you're single now, how 'bout a date?" Tucker's smile and amusement are clear in his voice and I know he's asking her out to get under

Evan's skin. Again, why do guys treat each other so contemptuously?

"I'll think about it," Cat answers, and I frown with disappointment.

Why's she doing this?

"Wow, Cat, seriously?!" Evan exclaims, full of sadness and shock. She doesn't respond to him. I want to reprimand her for it, but she doesn't give me enough time, her slim hand is already wrapped around mine and guiding me toward the school. Tannon doesn't let go of my other hand, and he keeps up beside me while Cat leads the way. I wonder why he continues to hold my hand—why they both do, actually. I normally use my walking stick to get into school.

"Hey, Cat. I'll walk with her," Tannon says, and it sounds like he wants to be alone with me.

"No. Leave us alone," she snaps, seeming to hate all males at the moment. Tannon walks with us a few more steps before reluctantly letting go of my hand. Cat wins again. She's so tough. Most don't bother fighting with her. "Boys suck," she mumbles.

I'm about to respond when suddenly someone pushes between us. "I'll walk you both," Tucker says. "Sorry guys, but when you got it, you got it, and I got two," he calls over his shoulder. "Now c'mon, how 'bout a date, Kitty Cat."

"Where's your loyalty?" Tannon shouts from behind us.

"I'm a teenage boy. It's in my pants," Tucker says, causing my jaw to drop.

"If that's all you want, then you know you're hanging with the wrong girl," Cat states firmly. She finds no amusement in his joke having made a vow freshman year that she would graduate a virgin. I really had no reason to make the vow; I've never had a boyfriend. And even if I did, the thought of being intimate scares the heck out of me. But I decided to make the vow with Cat, for her. She's adamant about keeping it. Her mother's loose reputation in this town seems to have attached itself to Cat. Guilty by association. Granted, Cat refuses to allow any truth behind the rumor. I respect her for it; she stays true to herself and sticks to her word. With her luck, she believes she'd end up a teen mom, just like her mother, and then the town would really talk. So Cat put a lock on her chastity belt and threw away the key. Evan knows it and still wants to be with only her. I guess she's proof that if a guy likes a girl enough he will wait.

Tucker groans before saying, "I know you're all locked up, baby, but maybe I hold the right key. A boy can fantasize, can't he?"

"Just keep your fantasies to yourself," she grumbles. Tucker laughs at her mood and bear hugs us tighter. The clumsiness of his step makes me trip over his foot and I stumble out of his hold.

Landing on my right knee, I fall forward with a groan. My hands skid across the pavement and my backpack slides up my back, the computer inside slamming against my skull. The terrifying feeling of free falling into the unknown causes my adrenaline to spike, overpowering any pain.

"Liv!" Cat shouts. "Are you okay?"

She takes my shoulders and helps me roll over. "I'm fine," I lie, waving my hands for her not to fuss. She moves to yell at Tucker. Sitting up, I wipe the pebbles from my palms, trying desperately to hide my shook up emotions. Everyone's yelling at Tucker for being so careless and my embarrassment instantly supersedes my panic and tears.

I sense someone bend down next to me. Strong fingers brush at my palms before moving to rub the back of my head. "You okay, Liv?" Tannon's voice is full of concern as his hand moves to my knee, rubbing gently.

The warmth of his fingers on my skin lets me know my jeans ripped at the knee—*damn, I loved these jeans*. His head falls next to mine, resting his forehead on my shoulder as gentle fingers slide into the stray hairs at the back of my neck. He adjusts his leg at my side, moves even closer, and leans his hard chest on my raised knees while gently coaxing my forehead to his shoulder. I'm acutely aware of his shallow breaths and sense my fall caused him just as much panic as myself.

"I'm sorry," he whispers, nuzzling our heads together. He turns slightly, bringing the corner of his mouth to my cheek. "I should've been there to catch you."

I'm taken aback by his intensity and how affectionately he caresses the back of my neck and how warm his cheek is against mine and how safe I feel and all kinds of new and overwhelming sensations all at once.

Everyone's talking over each other, yelling at Tucker as he apologizes repeatedly, but the pandemonium around us seems to fade and all I hear is Tannon's words as his subtle yet alluring scent of musk and soap intoxicates me. "I should've been there to catch you."

Tannon has always been protective of me—almost more so than Evan and Cat—but lately his actions and comments baffle me.

"Liv." The way he utters my name, I swear it sounds like a plea of some sort. I'm trying to wrap my head around this intimate moment when suddenly he's yanked from me.

"Leave us alone," Cat spits out, before helping me up. "God, Liv, I'm so sorry." She hugs me and helps me adjust my clothes before we walk to the door. "Are you sure you're okay?"

"I don't know," I say. I can't even think. Tannon's touch has stripped my ability.

CHAPTER 3
TANNON

Watching Liv walk away sucks. Seeing her fall and not being there to catch her wrecks me. It physically pains me to see anything bad happen to her. She's the sweetest girl I've ever met. My first instinct is to protect her, like some modern day knight in shining armor.

Shitty truth is, I act more like a loser wrapped in tinfoil.

I almost forgot who I was for a minute—she smelled like sweet strawberries and I wanted to kiss her. Almost did. Now that would've freaked her out. I'm far from what she wants.

Glancing over my shoulder, I see my best friend sulking like a four-year-old. I envy Evan's ability to wear his heart on his sleeve. He's wounded and he doesn't care who knows it nor does he bother to hide his feelings as I do.

I catch him in a headlock the moment he walks past me. In no mood to play, he elbows my ribs. I loosen my hold and we walk on with my arm slung over his shoulder. "It will be okay, man. Tucker doesn't stand a chance with Cat and he knows it. She knows she had a good thing. Hell, if I was a girl, I'd want you," I tease, shaking his shoulders, but he doesn't budge from his set mood of the day. He's going for doom and gloom and he has it down pat. I hate seeing him like this. "Don't worry, she'll come crawling back by the end of the day."

"I don't think so, Tan. She said I was being too nice. Can you believe that shit? Aren't guys supposed to be nice to girls?" He sulks, his shoulders actually dropping another inch. One more inch and he'll fall on his face.

Like a typical guy, I laugh. Insensitive, yeah I know, but c'mon, he honestly was being too nice. And yes, I was raised to be a gentleman, but not a pushover, and that's exactly what Evan was becoming. They were awesome together up until these past two weeks when she suddenly started testing him for no reason, provoking fights over the most bizarre things. She made some asinine moves and he just accepted them. I told her off two days ago and she's been giving me attitude ever since. That's why she won't let me near Liv. But I'd say it all again. The girl needed to hear what a lunatic she was being. Evan worships the ground she walks on, and yet she kept testing him to see if he'd cheat or something. Who knows?

The girl is an ocean full of crazy.

"Nice to girls!" I say as if that's the most absurd thing I've ever heard. "Who told you that? Your mother?"

Now before you go jumping to conclusions, you should know I'm nice to girls; I'm just teasing Evan. I'm nice, but when I say I'm not interested in a relationship, all of a sudden I'm a prick. Whatever. Let them talk—I don't have the energy to fight them on it. But if I did, I would shed light on the fact that even with their negative opinion of me, they still seem interested. Now that's just ridiculous, isn't it? Why would they want to be with a guy they thought was a prick? What does that make them?

I won't answer that. I'm a nice guy after all.

Evan scowls at me and I quickly feel bad for teasing him. He's without a doubt the greatest guy I've ever met and I love him like a brother. He shrugs my arm off his shoulder, aggravated by my amusement. "I'm sorry, man. I really am. I know you love her, but I also know she'll come crawling back. Just trust me, all right?" He doesn't respond. "The girl has issues. Deep-seated issues. And I don't think any of this has anything to do with you. She's scared and scared people run and hide. No guy her mother ever brought around ever stayed, so she's pushing you away before you can do the same."

Evan turns to glare at me. "I'm nothing like the losers her mother brings home."

"I know that and she knows that, but you have one thing in common with them."

"I have nothing in common with them." An angry fire ignites in his eyes.

"You're male, aren't 'cha?" I point out. He lowers his head, fire extinguished.

I wrap my arm around his shoulder again and urge him to keep walking. "I'm going to tell you what I think. I know you never listen to my advice, but I'm going to waste my breath anyway." Evan huffs out a faint laugh. "I think you need to take the reins on this relationship, dude," I say, and his eyes dart in my direction. "You were being a complete pushover—she doesn't need that. Steer her in a better direction than the one she's going in. That girl needs guidance. She sure isn't getting any at home. She's on the edge, man, crying for help. You need to save her from her self-destruction. You were just going down with the ship. Be the frickin' captain."

"Wow, that's deep, TK," he mocks, but I see his wheels turning and know he's listening. Will he take my advice? Probably not. He thinks I know nothing about relationships.

I shrug. "I'm a deep kind of guy."

Evan's mood changes a bit. I notice the start of a smile playing at the corner of his mouth. "I think you're right. How come I didn't see it?"

I wave my hand in front of us. "Sometimes you need to step outside the box to see what's in it . . . or some shit like that." We laugh. And it's nice to know Cat hasn't stolen his sense of humor.

I walk into the building, watch everyone race around like rats, and groan. I can't wait to graduate. I'm not a fan of school. Bookwork doesn't come easy for me. I'm dyslexic. Reading is a slow, grueling process for me. Writing is far worse, and math . . . Well, when the problem is as simple as 96 + 85 and I see 69 + 58, it kind of takes the simple right out of it. Thankfully my math teacher started giving me verbal tests and I've been getting by. I loathe school, but I love my friends and since we became seniors, this school has been a nicer place to be. I know it's only eight days in, but the atmosphere is different, calmer.

Freshman year was hell for me. That was when my ego really kicked in and my ego didn't like sitting in the special ed classes or having a teacher's aide assist me in basic classes. It was also when I found out that good looks could be a curse as well as a blessing. Unfortunately, I learned that the hard way.

You see, the upperclassmen didn't like that their girls paid attention to me. I didn't even want their attention, but no one asked me. The seniors found out I was in special ed and, well, it didn't take long for the name-calling to start. They'd call me tart, dumbass, stupid, shit for brains, and much worse. Just thinking of it makes me heated.

My self-esteem took a nosedive, and the female attention didn't make me feel any better. I just wanted to be . . . smart. I wanted learning to be easy. It only got harder and the seniors only became more ruthless. After a while name-calling wasn't enough. They became aggressive, so Dad put me in a boxing class. I guess you can say I owe my strength to my bullies. Because of them, I worked out every day. I lifted, ran, and boxed. And I started fighting back. My fists met many faces while defending myself. I spent a great deal of time in the principal's office. Funny thing was, me and Mr. Wagner became great friends. We'd spend most of the time I was in his office talking about hockey, and then he'd call my dad and they'd talk about hockey, and then he'd send me back to class. The bullies would either get detention, be held from sports for the week, or get suspended. Even so, that didn't stop them at first. It wasn't until my teammates rallied behind me that the seniors realized I had a great right hook and a lot of tough friends, especially Teddy. That kid looked like a mean, ol', toothless, professional hockey player at age fourteen, and even though he's a gentle soul off the ice—and has all his teeth—he had no problem standing beside me when a group of seniors tried to attack me in the gym locker room. He wasn't just defending me. Teddy has a learning disability too, and when he heard the seniors calling me spesh— short for special ed—well, he took that personally and they got the beating of their lives that day. With the help of Teddy and our teammates, the senior football team got an old-fashioned whooping by the freshman hockey team and they didn't live it down until their graduation.

Thankfully that nightmare is all in the past. I'll admit a few good things came of it—I'm tougher than I would've been otherwise and my teammates and I became a family that year. I would do anything for them and I know they'd do the same.

And Evan, well, I'd take a bullet for the guy.

My fondness for him makes me squeeze his neck again. Sparks, coming out of nowhere, jumps on my back. "Get a room!" he jests.

Shaking him off like an annoying flea, I turn to grab his arm, but he jumps back and races down the crowded hall, laughing. I smirk at the fool when he spins around and jumps up to see me over the crowd. He reminds me of a court jester. All he needs is a floppy hat with bells. I simply flip him the bird and turn my focus back to Evan. The poor guy fell back into his misery. I nudge him with my elbow, but he doesn't look up from the floor.

As we walk to homeroom, a group of freshman girls standing at their lockers turn and giggle. I smile to appease them, but I'm really not interested. "It's not like you don't have your pick of the fresh fruit here, man. Any of these girls would be yours in a second. And put out too." I highlight the obvious.

"Not interested. I want Cat." Evan's not paying the least bit of attention to the girls gawking at him.

"Just throwing a few options out there. I mean, there are plenty of fish in this sea . . ." He punches me in the arm. I continue teasing him while walking backward into homeroom, "You're a horrible fisherman. Maybe you need new bait . . ." Suddenly I bounce off of what feels like firm pillows. Looking over my shoulder, I come face to face with Ms. Vine's scowl. She's a round, old woman with an enormous chest—no joke, the woman can hide small children in her cleavage.

I shake away the disturbing image and greet her with a charming smile. "Good morning, Ms. Vine." Steely eyes glare at me. I've yet to win this woman over. "You look lovely today." But I'll never stop trying. There has to be a heart beneath all that breast tissue—there has to be. I raise my brows to Evan and he laughs as he walks into the next room.

CHAPTER 4
LIV

The endless chatter of my classmates entertains me as I sit idly in homeroom. I smile shamefully at how much I enjoy eavesdropping on teenagers. "Good morning, Liv," Mr. Carlson, my homeroom teacher, says as he passes my desk.

"Morning, Mr. Carlson." I smile. He is without a doubt my favorite teacher. He teaches English and happens to be the head of the English department, and he played an important role in why I'm in this school.

When Mom and I moved in with Gary, we decided that Hardy would be the best school for me. We believed it, but the town's board of education had concerns. It took some convincing, but Mom and I were up for the challenge.

During the meeting to determine my ability to attend Hardy, Mr. Carlson was the only one who voted in my favor and helped us persuade the board. Other teachers thought it would be too difficult for me, even after I passed their tests. Technically they couldn't turn me away, but they were encouraging me to find more suitable schooling elsewhere. Mr. Carlson was the only teacher who wanted my opinion on the matter, asking, "Liv, we know you're smart enough to take our classes and we can get the technology you need to learn—that isn't what everyone is worried about. They think the social aspect may be rough with you being the only blind student in a building with hundreds of sighted ... They have concerns. What do you think?"

"I don't expect much from the other students," I told Mr. Carlson. "I'm sure they will be curious about the blind girl, but hopefully they'll see I'm just another teenager. I don't want to move away from my mom, so this is my only option besides being homeschooled and that would really make me feel like an outcast. I just want to live the life of a teenage girl. Give me a chance. I know I can do this."

They gave me a tour of the school, my final test. I counted every step I took, memorized every turn. They asked me to find the cafeteria; I led them without a glitch. With reservations, they enrolled me that day. I'm eternally grateful for Mr. Carlson's support.

Now I sit with "normal" teenagers and there is no doubt in my mind that there is really no such thing. Everyone has problems. Just sitting here listening to my fellow classmates complain about their lives makes me realize I'm not alone. Well, most of them really don't have much to complain about—not the ones who complain loudly anyway. It's the ones who whisper to their closest friend, or the ones who stay quiet most of the day, who have real issues. I feel for them but also believe our issues help us have compassion for each other. No one wants my challenges. I know that. But after hearing the struggles of others, I could say wholeheartedly that I'd pick being blind over the horrible things some of these kids are dealing with.

I love being in school. I love listening to voices. There is one voice that stands out from the rest—Trace Matthews'. He sits catty-corner to me. He has the greatest voice, smooth and deep, manly in a sea of boys. Cat says he's not her type and I'm fine with that. She doesn't like his shaggy, wild, light brown hair or his cargo shorts and T-shirts. And, she claims, he's too tall and lanky.

But I don't care about any of that. What I know about him is he's an A student and it comes easy to him. He doesn't even seem to try. He just sails through effortlessly. And he doesn't even act all high and mighty about it. In fact, just the opposite—he stays low-key and under the radar. He's not considered a nerd and he doesn't hang with a certain group, but people do call him a brain. He's in a class all his own. A class I want to be in. He's nice and witty—and did I mention his deep voice? I swoon every time he talks.

Only thing is, he's never talked to me. Ever. Hopefully that will change.

I rest my chin on my hand and eavesdrop on his conversation with the girl next to him, Rita. "Hey, Ree, can I copy your science notes from yesterday?" Trace asks, and he sounds so cute. "C'mon, I'll give 'em right back." He's flirting to get his way; I can hear it in his tone.

Wait, gosh, I hope he's not interested in her.

I don't like Rita. Not one bit. She's high and mighty and mean. Cat says Rita is a beanpole, skinny and a head taller than most in our class. Cat also calls Rita's a nerd, but the term confuses me since nerds are supposed to like to learn and always be studying, and if that's the case, then I'm a nerd too.

Jeez.

"I'm not giving you my notes. I can't wait to see what you get on this quiz," Rita says. "And don't look at me like that. It won't work." She's a bitter, jealous girl who works very hard for her grades, and she doesn't sound fazed by Trace's flirty advances.

"Jeez, give a guy a break. I was at a funeral," he says. Rita doesn't respond.

I did notice Trace wasn't in school yesterday—I missed his voice. *I wonder who died?* I quickly dismiss the thought of offering my condolences; I am eavesdropping after all.

"I don't have anyone else to ask in here," Trace adds and I twitch.

Hey, I'm in that class! Hasn't he noticed?

"You think you can just miss the lesson, not open the book, read my notes for five minutes, and pass the quiz . . . ? Of course you do," Rita groans with resentment, and I assume he nodded in response to her question. I smirk. "Ask her," she snaps.

"Who?—No." His voice changes to a whisper.

"Why not?" Rita asks.

Oh my gosh, are they talking about me?

"Because." Trace lowers his voice another octave.

"She could probably print her notes out of that laptop of hers. She'd give it to *you*—I heard she likes you," she says loudly enough to ensure I hear. She's wicked that way.

Did I mention I don't like her?

"Seriously?" Trace whispers, shocked.

I sit horrified until the bell rings. *Did that just happen? Did Rita just tell Trace that I like him? How does she even know?*

Evan calls my name from the doorway, waiting to walk with me to first period. I usually meet him in the hall. I must have been sitting here a while. "You okay, Liv?" he asks, and I slowly stand to collect my things.

Walking next to him, we make our way through the crowded hall. "You look like you saw—heard"— he corrects himself quickly—"a ghost. Okay, I know that sounded stupid. What's wrong?"

I don't mind when people say words like "saw" or "see" or "look." I say them myself. It's only when they correct themselves that I mind because it makes me think they're on guard around me. "Rita just told Trace that I like him."

"Wait. You like Trace?" Evan asks, stopping me suddenly. A throng of people rush by as he waits for my answer. I nod and he starts walking again, tapping my arm to follow. "Really?! Why didn't you tell me?"

"I told Cat in the bathroom the other day . . . Oh, no! Rita must have been in a stall and overheard. That spy! I hate her."

"You don't know how to hate." Evan laughs.

"Well, now I do. See how evil she is? She turned me into a hater?" I scowl. "But yeah, I like him. I've never talked to him before but what I've heard I like."

"He's a good guy. But you don't want to date him, right?" Evan sounds like an older brother trying to come to terms with his sister liking a boy.

"It would be nice to go on a date before I'm eighty."

"If he asks, I'll chaperone." He sounds serious.

"Are you out of your mind?" I laugh, amused. "That is never going to happen."

"Oh, it's happening." I have to laugh again. He's the brother I never had and I love him for it, but there is no way I'll let him tag along. "So . . . listen. You have to help me get Cat back. What should I do?" he asks, desperation dripping from his voice.

"I don't know. Maybe she just got scared of her feelings for you. Who knows? She's complicated. Just keep trying. She'll come around. She loves you." I rub his arm. "But she's my best friend. I can't get in the middle of this."

"Hey, I'm your best friend too," he says with over-exaggerated hurt.

"Exactly! That's why I'm not getting involved."

Hugging his arm, we walk into computer class. I sit at a large computer with a headset. I don't have to listen to Mrs. Cohen much since my computer talks me through the whole lesson. Whatever I type the computer repeats back to me. Mrs. Cohen says I type faster than the other students. Eight days in and I'm already one lesson ahead.

Only today, I'm a bit nervous to be in this class. Trace sits next to Evan, who sits diagonal to me. I don't start my computer up right away—I'm still in shock, stuck in a state of humiliation from Rita spilling my confession. The thought of Trace knowing I like him embarrasses me to the point of restlessness.

I ask Mrs. Cohen if I can go to the bathroom. Using my white cane and a hand on the wall, I walk to the third door down on the right. The pungent smell of bleach and all-purpose cleaner hits me before I even open the door. I walk inside and find an empty stall. When I exit the stall, I rest my walking stick against the wall before washing my hands. Reaching for the paper towel dispenser that is located on the wall to the left of the sink, I pull one sheet free and they just keep coming. Towels fall past my hand and onto the floor. With a groan, I bend down to pick them up.

The sound of the heavy door opening and closing echoes off the walls of the small room. When someone walks in, I ask if they can help me collect the towels. Running my hands along the floor of a public bathroom isn't something I care to do. The only response I get is the locking of a stall door.

Well isn't that just the kind of day I'm having?

I throw the towels that I find into the trash and walk to the door with an angry scowl. Reaching for the handle, I groan a "Thanks for nothing" before yanking the door open and stomping into the hall only to collide right into a hard chest.

"*Oomph.*" The boy huffs as he catches me in his strong arms. "Hey, Boo, you okay?" Tannon asks.

Thankful it's him, I say, "Sorry. Um . . . can you do me a favor and wait here with me a second to tell me who walks out of the bathroom? Just act casual." I lean against the wall and twirl the end of my braid around my finger.

He starts laughing. "Is this you acting casual? You look very suspicious to me, Boo." I slouch and grumble under my breath. "Why the act?" he asks.

"I dropped paper towels on the floor and was trying to collect them when someone came in, so I asked for help. She didn't even acknowledge me. Now I'm curious to know who it was. I just don't want it to look like that's what we're doing." It sounds ridiculous now that I've said it out loud. I sulk, feeling foolish. Maybe the girl really had to go. But still she could have said so.

"Gotcha!" He seems eager to play spy and I don't feel so foolish anymore.

A second later the door opens and Tannon unexpectedly grabs my arms and presses my back against the lockers. His hard body molds to mine as his head comes down to my neck and his lips press a kiss on my skin.

I'm completely dumbfounded, so much so that when he lets me go, I don't remember how to stand and I teeter off balance even though I'm leaning against a wall. My fingers hover over my neck where his lips just left.

What just happened?

"The name's Bond. James Bond," he says, humor in his tone. His method of having us look inconspicuous leaves me so dazed I almost forget why we're even standing here until he says, "Oh, and it was that tall girl that always looks pissed off."

Rita!

Oh, she is beyond mean. I don't feel bad hating on her at all. Although it seems she doesn't like me either.

No surprise.

I gingerly slide my fingertips over my neck, not wanting to disturb the quiver still running over my skin but unable to keep my hand away. His lips . . . I still feel them as if they seared a brand on my skin. "I . . . Thanks for the diversion," I say.

"Anytime." His fingers slide over my cheek before tucking stray hairs freed from my braid behind my ear. His touch is gentle and warm, and it does indescribable things to me. "Catch ya later, Boo," he says. His footsteps echo as he walks down the hall.

After a beat, I make my way back to computer class, puzzled by that boy's ability to leave me bewildered twice in one day.

CHAPTER 5
LIV

It's been days since Rita shared my secret and Trace still hasn't said a word to me. Not that he talked to me before this, but now that he knows I like him, I'm desperate for some kind of sign that he knows I'm alive. I sulk in Cat's room while she tweezes my eyebrows. My thick brows make this a time-consuming task, yet she seems to enjoy it. She's my God-sent angel. There's nothing but trust between us.

We were instant friends.

She was the first person to talk to me on my first day at Hardy. Tannon was the second. I was nervous—new school, no friends, the only blind girl. I sat in my assigned seat in first period and Cat turned and introduced herself, "So you're the girl everyone's whispering about." She stated the truth and I knew we would be friends in that moment. It was her honesty that lifted my spirits that day and every day after. No bull—she doesn't sugar coat anything and that is exactly the kind of friend I need. I know she wants the best for me and she'd never do anything to make me look or feel foolish.

I once asked my mom to describe Cat. She has dyed ink-black hair that she wears in an edgy bob, big blue eyes, and perfect skin. Mom says she's never seen a blemish on Cat's face. I envy that because just last month I had a crater on my cheek that lasted about three weeks and I was thankful I had no idea how horrible it really looked. Cat has an athletic physique, not curvy like me, and she likes to wear clothes that show off her toned legs. Evan loves everything about her—he loves how outgoing and energetic she is, the opposite of his reserved and calm demeanor. However, she's changed in the past few weeks. She seems almost introverted.

"What's going on, Cat?" I ask.

She gives me a long, drawn-out sigh. "I dunno. I dunno what I'm doing. Evan just has to give me time to figure it out."

"All right ... But don't you think you should explain that to him instead of telling him he's being too nice?"

"I know ... I will. I'm too confused to explain anything right now," she says, groaning.

I lift my hands in surrender. "I'm not going to push the subject." We sit quietly as she tweezes away. I breathe in the yummy scent of her pumpkin pie scented candle and wish for the real thing.

"So what's going on with Trace?" She draws out his name and nudges my knee with hers. I throw my hands in the air and shrug. "He's probably looking for his balls," she says, and I stifle a laugh. Cat has a way with words—her favorite being balls. "When he finds them, he'll ask you out. You're too sweet to resist." Her finger taps my nose. I wiggle it. "So what's with Tannon lately?" she asks, changing the subject.

"What do you mean?"

"He seems sad," she says, sounding sad herself. "I know we aren't on the best of terms since he went off on me, but he's kept that devil's grin hidden the past couple days."

"I don't know. I hope he's all right." Now I'm really depressed. All my friends are falling into a pit. Tannon's been acting different to me but I didn't notice sadness. He always seems so carefree around me.

"What does he look like in your mind?" she asks.

"Tannon? I don't know. He's really sweet to me but I don't know what to think of him. He seems so vain and that doesn't translate as beautiful to me. I can't see his cool demeanor. The way it translates is cocky."

"I don't think he's as vain or *cocky*—what a word—as he acts. I may be wrong, but there is something very deep about that boy."

The room is silent again and I assume she's thinking of Tannon. I find myself doing the same. *Tannon? A deep soul? He's not deep. He's completely superficial. Why would she think differently? Maybe I'm missing something.*

"So what about Trace ... Is he beautiful?" she asks.

My thoughts turn dreamlike at the mention of Trace. "Yes, he's smart and interesting and mature and I hope he'll consider taking me on a date because I think we have a lot in common." I can't help the grin that appears just thinking of him asking me out, but reality sets in quickly. "I wouldn't blame him if he doesn't want to get involved, though."

A loud bang causes me to jump in my seat. Cat groans peevishly. "Liv, you say vain isn't a pretty quality . . . Well, neither is insecure. You are the best person I know. He should feel pretty damn lucky that you picked him. Only a fool would think differently." She takes a calming breath, deep inhale, long exhale. "If he's a fool, then you don't want him anyway."

"You have to admit my blindness makes some people nervous."

"Well, that's just stupid and I don't care about anyone who thinks differently." Her tone is sharp, like a protective mother.

I shake my head. "You're biased."

"Damn right! You're my favorite person in the world." The mattress squeaks as she sits on the bed across from me. "You see what matters in others and you should only want to be with a guy who sees what matters in you. You have so much to offer."

"I just really like him." I drop my head and shrug.

"Then I hope he's smart enough to see how lucky he is. If not, he's going to miss his chance at being with the greatest girl on Earth." She taps my foot with hers. "Don't worry, the way you describe him, I think he's too smart to miss his chance."

"I hope so."

She sighs. "Sometimes I wish I could see people without my eyes. I've never thought twice about a guy like Trace and yet the way you describe him . . . I realize I'm missing out because I judge people on their looks." We sit quietly for a moment. Her house is still—her mom is sleeping behind a locked door, she has no pets. This is what Cat comes home to. No laughter. No "hey, sweetheart, how was your day?" No love. Just silence.

"Cat, are you all right?"

"I dunno. I'm so sad, Liv." Her emotions bubble to the surface and sniffles follow. "I never realized how heavy sadness is. I'm so tired carrying it."

I pull her hand for her to come to me but the wheels of the chair I'm sitting on roll me to her. We share a laugh as I hug her tight and she cries against my shoulder. "Please let me in."

"You are," she says pushing back. "You're all I have." Her arms wrap around my shoulders again.

"You have Evan too. Remember that, Cat." Leaning back, I take her face in my hands and add, "That one area of your life could be easily fixed. All you have to do is call him."

"I can't," she says through her sobs.

"Why? You don't have to push him away. He isn't going to hurt you." My thumbs wipe the tears from her cheeks.

"You don't understand."

'Then make me," I demand.

"I'm scared. I'm just so scared." Her sobs become uncontrollable.

"You can't live in fear all your life. I won't let you. You deserve to be happy."

"How'd I get so lucky?" she asks, squeezing me tight. I know she's trying to change the subject.

"God knew we would need each other," I reply, my heart expanding with love for her. "To simplify life, we can just live together forever like spinsters," I tease.

"That sounds like a perfect solution." She laughs over her sobs.

"I love you, Cat! I'm not going to let you fall."

"I love you more," she replies, like always. "But your simple spinster idea may change when Trace finds his balls and asks you out."

***

After dinner I walk into the living room and touch the smooth top of my baby grand piano. Mom says it's too big for the boxed room, but it's the one thing she insisted moved with us and Gary made it work in the small space.

The bench creaks a welcome as I sit and tap a few keys in response. After getting comfortable, I begin playing an exquisite score by John Barry. The beauty of the melody fills the living room as I glide my fingers over the keys. In my opinion, "Somewhere in Time" is the most beautiful piece of music ever written. I say this because it affects me like no other. When I play it, it's as if I'm transported from my living room to . . . well, another time. My mom and I rented the movie last year, and she described the beautiful dresses and the Grand Hotel. The music along with the elegant way the characters spoke and the beauty in which the story was told held me captive. The music was as significant as the lead characters and listening to it being played around a glorious love story, a love all-encompassing, was what made it sink into my soul. So when I play this piece, I actually feel the tight corset around my waist and the long dress my mom described swaying over my feet. And every once in a while, I dream of a love so vital you would risk traveling through time to live it all over again.

Maybe one day I will find a love like that.

For now, my all-encompassing love is this piano.

Our love affair started when I was nine years old when my gramps took me to a music store to buy new string for his guitar. He sat me down on a bench while he talked with the salesman. I leaned my elbow on what I thought was a table and was startled by the sharp sound that emanated. I turned on the bench and curiously tapped out dreadful sounds until the salesman sat down next to me. He explained how the keys were laid, how each key had a different sound and pitch, and how the keys were played together to create even more sounds. He took my fingers, set them in position, and asked me to press down. Then he repositioned them and I pressed again. I was in complete awe. Of course I'd heard piano music before, but never had I touched a piano until that day.

The salesman went back to helping my gramps and in his absence a simple piano score playing through the store's speakers caught my attention. I immediately tried to mimic the sounds and quickly became transfixed by getting it right. Eventually the song I was eager to teach myself ended but it restarted seconds later. I tried again and again to mimic the music. It turned out Gramps and I were in that store for two and a half hours. Someone kindly put that song on repeat and by the end I had it. It actually sounded like the music pumping through the speakers. I was surprised when suddenly the whole store filled with applause. I had acquired an audience as I taught myself how to play. Gramps said none of the shoppers that came in left until I got it. Somehow they knew I would. I was completely floored, and a tad embarrassed, but mostly I was gloriously happy. Gramps sat next to me and cried.

I hugged his arm. "Don't cry, Gramps. I just fell in love." He cried more and so did a few shoppers he told me. Although the room full of sniffles clued me in.

Then he rose and made that salesman an offer on the piano. It was way under the asking price, but the man was so inspired by what he'd just witnessed that he agreed, saying, "You have a born talent, young lady. People spend years trying to master what you just did in less than three hours. I'll sell your grandpa the piano, but you have to promise me front row tickets when you play Carnegie Hall." I made that promise with the biggest smile on my face.

I fell in love with the piano that day like I fell in love with Hank—quick and easy. My doctors say that my ability to play by ear is a born talent and has nothing to do with my blindness. It's a major misconception that blind people are gifted musicians. Not all blind people have an ear for music just like not all sighted people do, and to me that means the piano and I were destined to be together. I love that.

It's difficult for me to believe that I was born to be blind, but there is no doubt in my mind that I was born to play the piano. And the day this piano came into my life will forever be the fondest memory I share with Gramps. He passed away that next year. Now I play for him. I play for him every day. He was the father figure in my life and I miss him every day.

Every passing day.

I carefully close the lid over the piano keys and rest my hands on top.

"Still my favorite," Mom says from the couch.

I hadn't heard her come in, but I'm not surprised she's listening. I walk over, find her knee, and sit next to her. "Me too."

She hugs me to her side. I turn into her and hug her waist. Mom has been wearing the same perfume all my life—a mix of rose, lily, chamomile, and white musk—and there isn't a more comforting scent in this world. We stay like that for a moment, silent and still, and I love that we can connect without words.

A few minutes later I stand and call for Hank. "We're going for a walk," I tell Mom and walk with Hank to get his harness. Gary comes trotting down the steps as I'm securing the straps around Hank's chest.

"*The Voice* is on tonight," Gary says. It's his favorite show and one we all normally enjoy together.

"I'll be back in time," I say, opening the front door. "Hank and I are just taking a quick walk around the block."

I shut the door and Hank leads the way, knowing that whenever he's on the harness he's working—checking for cars or danger in our way, keeping a slow and steady pace, and just being a great companion. It's a warm night with a steady breeze, and I'm enjoying the sounds of the evening. A few kids play in their yards, cars drive to and from, steaks cook on grills (they smell delicious), and runners run by. Richard, a neighbor friend of Gary's, runs past me saying, "Hey there, Liv." I only smile, knowing he's already too far away to hear my response. That guy can run.

We live on a friendly road. Mom says most of the homes look the same. A few are more modern than others, but most of our neighbors seem to be in the

47

same financial bracket. Our neighbors all know me—or at least of me—and they're very friendly. I feel safe and content here, more so than I did in our old neighborhood.

Hank and I round the corner and are met with yelling. I pull Hank to a halt, recognizing the voice. It's Evan. He lives two houses down from the corner. I urge Hank to walk again as I listen intently. "This damn thing!" Evan yells. "It won't start."

"Just leave it alone," his sister, Kelly, says.

"I can't. I have to mow the damn grass before Dad comes back. I don't have the luxury of leaving the damn thing alone, Kell."

"Well, that's what you get for putting it off till the last minute."

"Thanks, Kell," he groans. "That's helpful." Their voices get closer with every step and I know I'm right in front of his house at his last response to her.

"Liv! Hi!" Evan calls, his mood changing instantly.

"Hi," I reply. "Hi, Kelly."

"Hey, Liv. Have fun with this one. He's in a great mood. I'm going inside," she says.

"Having trouble?"

Evan groans. "Yeah, my dad is on a business trip. Told me to have the grass mowed by the time he gets back. Tomorrow."

"Oh boy," I say, holding back my smirk. He's in no serious danger—Mr. Tully is as kindhearted as his son. I think what's bothering Evan is he doesn't want to disappoint his dad. Evan doesn't like disappointing anyone. He follows the rules and never crosses the line.

"Come keep me company while I create a bigger problem," he says, walking up his driveway.

I nudge Hank to follow him and get a whiff of gasoline. "Maybe you should leave it alone. You aren't much of a handy man."

"Ouch!" Evan utters with mock offense. "Sparks is coming by in a few minutes to help."

"Then you're in good hands. He'll have the thing juiced up in no time. Probably add some kind of turbo boost too." We laugh and I sit on the curb of the driveway.

Sitting next to me, Evan hangs his arm over my shoulder and rests his head against mine. "Glad you're here."

I nudge his head with mine and hang my arm over his raised knees, pulling him closer. Hank lies on the driveway at my feet. "I'd ask how you're doing but I already know."

"I just don't get it. We were so happy. It's just . . . I feel like there's something deeper going on here and I'm missing it," he says. "She still hasn't given me a real answer as to why she broke up with me."

"Me either."

"If we weren't so good together, I wouldn't be fighting to get her back." He sounds so confused and miserable about the whole thing. So am I. "I hate her damn mother. I never even met her." He lies back against the grass and I join him. "Have you?"

"Only a few times coming or going. She's never actually stopped to talk, though." Her mom is unfriendly and cold, the complete opposite of Cat.

"Well, can you believe that I've never even seen her?" he asks, flabbergasted. "All the times I've been to Cat's, I never saw her mom. If she wasn't sleeping behind a locked door, she was at work, or on a date. Cat's been on her own all her life."

"She deserves so much better."

He leans up on his side and I know his eyes are on me. I'd feel awkward around anyone else, but Evan is my *safe place*. We were friends long before he and Cat started dating. We started talking freshman year. I'd walk the block and if he was outside, he'd walk with me. We always had something to talk about, always shared our feelings easily. He's another godsend. I know someone up there is helping me through this life, surrounding me with love.

Thanks, Gramps!

I remember the first time Evan talked about asking Cat out. I was nervous that it would cause a problem between us if it didn't work out, but deep down I knew they would be good together. They balance each other out, and I knew Cat had her eyes on him for a long time, so I urged him to give it a shot. Never would I have imagined she would quit on a good thing. Now they're both hurting. And I have no answers.

He fixes the twist in my horseshoe necklace before lying back down. "She cried the first time she ate dinner here. Said we were like a perfect sitcom family and she didn't know how to fit in. She excused herself and ran off crying. Dad was nervous about me being so attached to someone so . . . wounded. He was worried for me, but Mom fell in love with her instantly. She just wanted to mother her. When Cat started testing me, Dad told me to run. I told him I wouldn't abandon her no matter how much she pushed. I wouldn't budge. But now she isn't budging either."

The distinct sound of Sparks's car engine rumbling into the driveway drowns out our conversation. We sit up to greet him. "Hey, guys," Sparks says as his car door opens. He drives a 1970

Camaro. I've run my hands over the sleek frame a time or two and it's a hot car. He takes really good care of his baby. It didn't run when he bought it, but he rebuilt the whole engine and now it's better than new. He can honestly fix anything. And building engines is all he wants to do with his life—he's known this since he was ten. I admire that.

After giving them both a quick hug, I head back home, thinking of Cat.

***

Cat's in a sullen mood as she drives us to school on Friday. This has been a long, miserable week. I sit quietly, knowing there is nothing I can say to change her mood. She seems worse since our talk, more withdrawn than usual, and I'm really worried. We walk through the halls, stopping at her locker when she finally breaks her silence. "Excuse me."

I almost ask, "For what?" when suddenly Evan says, "Cat, stop! We can't be friends?" The heat of his body moves in closer to us.

"You want to be friends?" Cat asks. "Yeah, didn't think so." She must have read the look on his face because I didn't hear him answer.

Two girls call out to him as they walk by. Cat mocks laughter. "They're calling for you. Go get 'em, stud."

It's beyond awkward standing here listening to them. Nonetheless, the chaotic morning rush holds me against the locker. I turn my back and wait.

"Is that what you want?" Evan asks.

"Only if it's what you want," she answers.

"You know I don't want anyone else," he says, anguish in his tone. I want to yell at Cat for hurting him. Hurting herself.

"That's your choice. I can't tell you what to do."

"Can you tell me one thing? Do you still love me?"

She sighs softly and closes her locker. "Evan . . . yes . . . I'll always love you."

"Then I don't get it." His tone is harsh now. "Why are you doing this?"

"Because," she says, sounding defeated.

"That's not an answer," he snaps. "I don't accept that. I love you, you say you love me, yet you break up with me 'because.' No, you don't get to walk away without an explanation. I want a real answer, Cat."

"Because my future is murky and yours is bright," she whispers. "Because I will only pull you down with me. And because you will let me."

"Cat," he utters, his voice gentle. "That's not true." His shoulder presses against mine as he moves closer to her.

Suddenly she grabs my arm and pulls me through the crowd and into homeroom. "Cat," I say as I sit in my seat, "did you hear anything I said to you the other day?"

She squeezes my hand. "He deserves better."

"He deserves to be loved by someone he loves and you deserve the same. Why do you continue to hurt yourself?" I whisper through clenched teeth.

A gust of air announces her swift exit and I sit with my sadness. She has deep-rooted daddy issues, and even worse mommy issues, and I don't know how to get through to her.

Suddenly and shockingly, a deep, velvety-smooth voice is directed my way. "Hey, Liv, it's . . ."

"Trace!" I call out gleefully and quickly regret it. *Oh my gosh, so not cool.* I blame it on the excitement of hearing him say my name for the first time. His voice—no joke—it has me melting in my seat.

"Yeah! How'd you know that?"

"I know your voice." I hope he accepts that and doesn't think of me as some stalker freak.

I hate Rita!

"Oh . . . of course . . . so . . . how are you?" he stutters.

I smile—I can't believe he's talking to me—and I've never heard him stutter before. "I'm fine. You?"

"Good. So . . ." He clears his throat and Rita laughs. Is she mocking him? I want to smack her.

"So . . . listen, I was just wondering what you were doing tonight. I mean, if you didn't already have plans . . . I know it's last minute, but . . ."

"I would love to." The words just jump out of my mouth. I want to smack my palm against my forehead. *Oh my gosh, stop talking! He hasn't even asked yet.*

"I was thinking dinner. Is that all right?" I can tell he's smiling now. Maybe he's relieved I'm so eager.

"Yes, that sounds great."

"Great. I'll pick you up at seven."

I just nod with what I'm sure looks like a crazy expression. I nervously get up when the bell rings to end the period. Evan greets me at the door.

"Why are you smiling when I'm so miserable?" he asks.

"He found his balls," I say, so pleased he has them.

"What?" Evan asks, stunned.

I start laughing when I realize I said that out loud. I tell Evan what just happened and he insists on chaperoning. I ignore him and dream of Trace.

CHAPTER 6
TANNON

Gym class sucks this week. It's track week and today's run will determine if we have to run again next week. Poor Teddy sucks at stamina exercises. His strong legs are a powerhouse on the ice and his limber moves are both shocking and impressive, but take his skates off and he's like a different creature.

Evan and I come up behind him for the second time. "You still breathing, Teddy?" I ask as we pass by. He's too winded to answer. I turn to jog backward, getting a good look at him. "Don't quit or we have to do this again next week." He waves me away, annoyed and about ready to puke.

"Love ya, Teddy Bear!" I declare, patting my chest endearingly before spinning forward. "He's about to cave," I say to Evan.

"If he does, I'll beat him with my hockey skates," he huffs.

"Did ya hear that, Teddy?" I shout over my shoulder. "If you cave, Evan's gonna beat you with his skates." I hear wheezing breaths from behind me and laugh.

"So she said her future is murky and mine is bright and she'll ruin my life or some crap like that," Evan continues to repeat Cat's excuse for breaking up with him as if doing so will cause it to miraculously make sense.

"Dude, she needs therapy," I say for the tenth time.

"What do I do?" he asks with grave desperation.

"First, you need to stop dwelling on it. It's never going to make sense to you." I offer a sympathetic pat on his shoulder. "Second, get her a therapist. And third," I take a deep breath. I've been wanting to say this for three years. "I'm gonna ask Liv out."

"What?!" He spins his whole body to me and grabs my arm, halting our run. "You're kidding, right?"

"No. I'm not kidding." I glare down at his hands on me. He releases me with a forceful shove. "What the hell, man? Don't take your anger out on me!" I snap.

"You think I'm going to let you ask Liv out, take advantage of her, and then move on to the next one?" He's pissed, which in turn makes me pissed. He starts running again. It takes me a second to accept his reason.

Wait!

What am I saying?

I don't accept his reason.

I race to catch up to him. "I have no intentions of taking advantage of her. I never took advantage of anyone," I groan, insulted. Suddenly I start sweating and it isn't from the run. I'm ticked off. "I like Liv and I think she might like—"

"No, man. She doesn't like you," he says over his shoulder. "Not like that."

Talk about twisting a knife in a guy's heart. Damn, that hurts. But of course he would react like this—he's like an overprotective brother to Liv and I've yet to tell him my real feelings for her. Or share the way I've felt about her since the first time I laid eyes on her that first day of freshman year. I remember that day like it was yesterday.

I walked into my second period health class and sat at the first available desk. Everyone was excited to see friends they hadn't seen all summer, but one girl wasn't part of the reunion and she caught my eye. I turned my whole body in my chair and just stared at her. She was a vision: the morning sun gleamed off her shiny, long brown hair, creating a halo effect around her head. I found it odd that she was wearing sunglasses in class, but she looked like the sweetest thing sitting with her hands clasped in her lap and knees squeezed together just as tight, like a timid, little bunny. I wondered why she had a laptop on her desk and looked around the room to see if maybe we all got computers in high school. I also found it odd that everyone else wasn't as enamored by her presence. Was I the only one who saw this angel? Or was I the only one who saw her as an angel? I hoped it was the latter because I wanted her all to myself.

The teacher came in, wanting our attention, but I couldn't turn from the new girl. I was completely captivated. Mr. Thompson asked me to face forward. I turned my body, but my gaze stayed glued to her. I was amazed at how still she was. She didn't look at anyone, didn't fidget in her seat. Mr. Thompson reprimanded me again and then the girl behind me whispered that the object of my affection was the new blind girl. I couldn't believe it. I turned in my seat again to stare at her. I never saw a blind person before and I never would've guessed she was. I didn't even understand what that meant. What's a blind person supposed to look like? I rubbed at my neck feeling like an idiot. Mr. Thompson called me up to his desk and whispered that since I seemed so interested in the new girl I could be the one to escort her to her next class. At first I was nervous, then I just wanted to talk to her.

Class was never-ending and during that time all I did was think of what to say. When the bell finally rang, I jumped in my seat. Slowly I made my way to her desk and just stood there like a mute moron. She was the first to speak, asking if I was waiting for her. I just stared at her perfect, olive skin and full lips. "Cat got your tongue?" she teased and thankfully it snapped me out of my stupor. I introduced myself and she did the same. Then she reached for me and, not knowing what she wanted, I awkwardly gave her my hand. Her warm, smooth skin against mine sent a tingle up my arm. I had never felt anything like it. Hers was the first hand I'd ever held that gave me chills and electric shocks at the same time. I stared at our connection as she put her backpack on her shoulder and told me she needed to get to room 103. She released my hand and held my arm instead. I walked her out of the classroom and turned left, she pulled on my arm and said, "103 is to the right." I apologized for not knowing where I was going, and she said no worries, she knew the way and that all I had to do was make sure no one knocked her over. I shrugged, figuring I could do that easy enough. I escorted her into class, but it felt more like she was escorting me. I found out quickly that she didn't need help, it was the school's policy, and she only accepted the help from students because she thought it would be a good way to meet people and didn't want an aide following her around. Later, I found her at lunch and sat with her.

That day she found a new friend in me and I found a home for my heart. She became all I cared to have, but then I found out she was super smart, and I didn't want her to know I wasn't. I became even more insecure and did all I could to hide that from her. By the second week of school the seniors started on me and then I did all I could to hide that from her too. I didn't want her to ever hear them calling me names. I didn't want her to think of me as the pathetic kid who gets bullied. I started acting cocky around her. I don't know why—I guess it was to hide my insecurities. I dealt with the seniors, but next thing I knew, I was acting boastful around everyone, and I was so convincing that they believed I was a confident, self-assured guy without a care in the world. Somehow, that became the norm. I spent three years being that guy. Three years hiding my true self and my feelings for Liv. Hiding the fact that I had nothing to boast about. Nothing at all.

I promised myself that this year I would finally stop hiding. I'd go after what I wanted. This may be the last year Liv and I have together, and I fear if I don't ask her out, I'll regret it, forever. I finally felt ready.

Not anymore.

Like a rug being pulled from under me, Evan's response easily slashed my feeling of self-worth—tenfold.

I'm his best friend and yet he doesn't think I'm good enough for her. Although, in his defense, he thinks I'm only interested in the short term with Liv, like I've been with the rest. He has no idea that the reason my relationships are all so quick is because none of them make me stop thinking about Liv. He has no idea I want her in my life forever. And I haven't a clue why I hide it from him, my best friend.

Maybe it's because I always feared Evan thought I wasn't good enough for Liv. His response just confirmed that. And the courage I had just moments ago is now gone.

Once again my fears take over.

Back into hiding.

I bump my shoulder into Evan's and continue to disappear behind a false persona—a cocky jerk I don't even like. "Damn. If she could only see how hot I am," I joke, wiggling my eyebrows, "she'd want me like all the rest."

My words make me cringe internally. I hate myself for being such a coward.

Evan finally smiles, believing I'm not serious enough to ask her out. It pains me to realize he thinks the worst of me, but why shouldn't he? Listen to me, it's what I portray. I'm not even sure why he hangs out with me anymore. Maybe it's because we've been best friends since preschool and he's just holding onto old times. The old me. I was like him until high school. I used to wear my heart on my sleeve, showing I had one.

I'm so tired of hiding. I know how it started, but I don't know how to stop it. That's the thing about living a lie—when you're good at it, people believe you and the real you becomes the lie to them. And to you.

"Just remember, bro, she only sees your insides and I guess your insides are ugly as sin." He mocks like a guy would, but the truth hurts. I'm ugly to her in every way that counts.

I'm ugly on the inside.

"Besides, she likes Trace Matthews and he just asked her out this morning," Evan says, and I stop dead on the track. He runs back, jogging in place. "What's wrong?"

"Trace asked her out?" I start walking in circles, my hands in my hair.

"Yeah."

"And she said yes because she likes him? She likes Trace Matthews? The frickin' brain of the school?" My legs stop working and my eyes stay locked on the white line painted on the track. I think I'm going to be sick. There's no hiding my reaction to this horrible news. I'm too upset to even bother trying. My racing heart pulsates in my ears, louder and louder. I bend and brace my weight on my knees. Sweaty-smelling runners weave between us as they race by, angrily shouting at me to keep running.

"Yes to all three," Evan says, jogging around me. "Tannon, wait ..." He stops jogging and grabs my arm. "You ... Wait ... Dude ... You're serious about her. You really like her?" I look up, and he sees it. The truth is out, plain as day, and his eyes widen before narrowing. "What the hell, man? How come you never told me?"

Mr. Matti, the gym teacher, starts yelling for us to keep running. Next thing I know I'm racing around the track, lapping everyone. I pass the finish line and fall to my back on the field grass, gasping for air.

Evan runs over to me after he finishes his last lap. "Jeez, TK, I'm sorry about what I said. I didn't know." He punches my arm lightly as he kneels next to me. "Is this a recent revelation?"

"Yeah," I lie. "No big deal. Trace is perfect for her." I want to bite my tongue off for saying such a thing, but, if I'm being honest, he *is* perfect for her. Wicked smart, really nice, and gutsy. He asked her out. I never did. He asked. And she said yes.

She said yes to Trace Matthews.

Pasting a smug grin on my face, I jump to my feet. "You ready to slam Dayton to the wall?" I change the subject to our upcoming hockey game and quickly mask the fact that the heart in my chest has shattered into a million pieces.

CHAPTER 7
LIV

It's six forty-five. I know because I've asked Cat the time every two minutes since she started doing my makeup ten minutes ago. My mom continues to walk in and out to see how things are going. I think she's more nervous than I am.

"Liv, I expect this boy to come in and introduce himself," she says.

"Mom, please don't embarrass me. I finally got him to ask me out. Don't scare him away now."

"I'm not going to scare him away. I just want to meet him."

Fifteen minutes later, the doorbell rings. "Mom, please," I beg.

Ignoring my plea, she leaves the room and heads to the front door. "Hello, Mrs. McKay, I'm Trace. Nice to meet you." Cat and I listen from our hiding spot in the hallway.

"Hi, Trace. It's Mrs. Sullivan." Mom and I have different last names since her marriage. "Trace, this is my husband, Mr. Sullivan."

"Nice to meet you, Trace," Gary says.

"You too, sir."

"So Trace, I expect you to act like a gentleman and return Liv the same way she went," Mom says, with a threat in her voice that only a fool wouldn't catch. "Liv took five years of self-defense classes," she adds and I quickly walk in to save him.

"Hi, Trace."

"Liv! You . . . you look . . . great," he stammers.

The A-line dress I'm wearing is one of my favorites. Cat says it's pale yellow with stitched white flowers. I can feel the raised flowers under my fingertips. I imagine I look very feminine. Cat accessorized it with a lightweight heather gray cardigan, hoop earrings, and gray Converse sneakers. Seeing as heels and I aren't a good match, I have Converse sneakers in many different colors— they're basically all I wear. And on special occasions such as this, it's Cat's job to make sure I look fabulous.

"Thank you." I turn to my mom. "Are you done, General?" I twist my mouth, hoping she'll get my point to back down.

"Love you, sweetie. Have a good time. And don't be late," she says in an innocent manner.

I just shake my head. "Love you too. And I won't."

"You can breathe now, Trace," Gary teases. I'm sure Gary's wearing an amused grin. Mom said that Gary's wide, friendly, and inviting smile was what made her, without a single hesitation, walk across the coffee shop where she first laid eyes on him to introduce herself. I smirk at Gary, being that it had more to do with Mom being scary than Trace being intimidated by her.

"We trust you, Trace," Mom adds, and that is where she gets him. No one wants to disappoint my mother when she says that.

"Thank you, Mrs. Sullivan. Mr. Sullivan."

Trace takes my hand and guides me down the front stairs, counting each step as he goes. I stifle a giggle and smile at how cute he is. I obviously know how many steps there are, but even so, I don't stop him.

Cat steps next to me and groans. "She knows how many steps her own house has, Trace. All you need to do, if anything, is watch for hazards that get in the way."

"Oh, of course. How stupid of me, I'm sorry," he says sheepishly. I want to smack Cat for interfering.

"Don't be sorry." I try to reassure him. "I appreciate the thought."

"Don't worry about it, Trace. She's virtually indestructible," Cat teases. "I don't have proof yet, but I think she's inhuman. Have fun, guys."

"Thanks, Cat!" I call out. "Love you."

"Love you more!" she shouts before her car door shuts.

Trace opens his passenger door for me and takes my hand as I sit and spin my legs in. It makes me feel like a lady. His footsteps race around the car. He's actually running. Too cute. He opens his door and slides in. The enticing smell of his spicy cologne floats past my nose and I follow it while breathing in deeply. Cat says he isn't her type—well, he's sure mine. Music blasts around me when he starts the engine. I jump and he quickly lowers the volume. We drive in silence for a few awkward moments.

"So," he says, and I'm so thankful he broke the silence that I have the urge to clap my hands. *Get a grip, Liv*, I muse. "Is it hot in here?" he asks, and I'm left stumped. He has the AC blasting due to the September heat wave we're experiencing, and it's actually quite chilly in here.

"No, I'm fine."

The silence returns. He fidgets in his seat as he plays with the AC, busying himself by pushing buttons and adjusting vents. I suppress a laugh. "I'm nervous too," I offer, hoping to ease his tension. "This is my first date."

"Am I that obvious?" He sounds self-conscious. "Wait, this is really your first date?"

"Well, yeah, I uh . . ." I stumble, ashamed to admit he's the first boy that ever asked, worried it will make me look more undesirable than I am.

"I've been on a few dates," he says unpretentiously. "Three, actually, but I've never been this nervous."

My head snaps to the side window with a sudden urge to throw myself out of the car; my blindness must make him uneasy. "I understand."

"Understand? Wait, what? No," he spits out. "I'm nervous because I never had such a pretty girl in my car. And you're smart too, so I have to up my game, and well, truth is, I have no game."

Is he serious?

I start to laugh. "Good, I don't like games. Just be you."

"That's easy enough." I sense his body relaxing into his seat as he laughs faintly. The car slows to a stop and eases into a left turn.

He's a good driver, not like Cat, and he thinks I'm smart, which is a huge compliment coming from him. He also thinks I'm pretty. I turn to the window, this time to hide the enormous grin on my face. "Can you describe me?" I ask, wishing to know how he sees me.

"Excuse me?" His nervous tone returns.

"Well, you're the artist, right? I want to know what I look like from an artist's point of view." I sit still, eager to hear his description.

"I'm not an artist, I just take the classes," he says self-effacingly, but I overheard a classmate once say that Trace was really good.

"Don't be modest. I heard you were the best in the school." Okay, I may have exaggerated that a bit.

"Me?! It's your friend Tannon who's the best. He blows everyone away."

It's shocking to hear that about Tannon. No one ever told me he was so talented. "Really? No. Tannon?"

"Yeah, he's really amazing. He submitted a painting in the state contest last year and won third place."

This news stuns me. Why doesn't he talk about his painting ability? "What was the painting of?"

"A girl sitting on a park bench. She's facing a pond and across the pond is a guy sitting on another bench. So much space between them . . . It's kind of a sad painting."

"Wow," I say, dumbfounded. Tannon paints? I can't wrap my head around this.

He rounds the car into a turn. "The girl kind of reminded me of you."

"Me?!"

He laughs at my sharp surprise. "Her long brown hair was in a braid, like you wear yours, and she had Converse sneakers on."

My mind is straining to imagine what the painting must look like. "I'm sure it's not me." Trace eases into another turn as I try to make sense of this.

"Maybe not. It's only the back of her so it could be anyone. It's a beautiful painting, though," he adds. "I only saw it because I submitted a drawing, and when I went to hand it in, the classroom was empty and the submissions were leaning against the back wall, so I took a peek at my competition. Tannon's work is nothing like his personality. He keeps his paintings low-key and nothing like the projects he does in class. I don't understand why he hides so much talent. And I honestly believe he didn't want anyone to see it but Ms. Cox and the judges."

I'm bewildered by the thought of Tannon painting. First Cat says he's deep and now Trace says he's a wonderful painter. Do I even know Tannon?

"You're right, he never talks about it. Why would he hide something so cool? Although, I did hear you are very good," I add to turn the conversation back to him. I'll let my bewilderment of Tannon return later, but right now I want to focus on Trace.

He puts his car in park and takes a deep breath. "All right. Turn to me so I can look at you."

Repositioning myself in the bucket seat to face him, he removes my glasses without warning and I look down feeling exposed. *What's my problem? I asked for this.* His finger lifts my chin gently—it's an intimate move and heat flushes my cheeks. *Great, now I'm blushing.*

Get a grip.

"You are a pretty shade of green and you have antennas on the top of your head—they're really cute."

I start to laugh. "I'm an alien. Cat was right."

He chuckles. "All right ... uh ... your hair looks really healthy, shiny. Like hair shown on shampoo commercials. You have great eyebrows, nicely arched." I smile at Cat's handy work. "Hmm ... you have high cheek bones and cupid lips."

"Cupid lips?"

"Yeah ... They kind of bow. I don't know, my mom calls that cupid lips." He laughs and moves in his seat. "Um, your skin is clear, olive toned. Your teeth are straight and white." I turn my head down again, grinning. He lifts it back up. "Not sure why you picked me," he says matter-of-factly.

"Are you kidding?" I ask, raising my brows. "You're the most appealing guy in Hardy."

"No way."

"Way," I assure, nodding.

"If you say so."

We laugh.

Our laughter runs dry and the silence that follows makes me wonder what he's thinking. Is he looking at me? Thinking he is, I slide my glasses back on. He never mentioned my eyes in his description of me and it makes me self-conscious. "I ... uh ... well, we're here," he says, his voice rises slightly. It's crazy to think he's as nervous as I am.

His door opens and closes, and seconds later mine opens too. I don't move. "You all right?" he asks. I sense his body lean against the doorframe, looking down at me. "Did I scare you away? I should be more sure of myself, shouldn't I? Ugh, let me start over."

The door shuts, a knock follows, and confused I say, "Come in?" through an embarrassed laugh.

The door opens. "Hi, I'm Trace Matthews, your date for tonight. I'm devilishly handsome with a clever mind and witty charm. I have a body most women drool over. I'm ripped—it's impressive. I lift weights just so I can carry the extreme weight of my overstuffed head. It's a lot for the average man to handle, but I'm far from average. I completely understand why you picked me. You have great taste."

Trying to stay serious, to play along, I reach my hand out and he takes it. "Hi, Trace. I'm Liv McKay. I'm overwhelmingly beautiful with a brilliant mind and captivating charm. My beauty is blinding and it should be against the law for me to leave the house. Actually, I went blind admiring myself for far too long in the mirror. FYI, don't look directly at me."

He laughs deeply. "It's lovely to meet you, Liv. I think we'll get along impeccably. You're so modest, just like me. I mean, let's be honest, we're holding back, aren't we?"

"Well, it would be unfair to throw all our superior qualities out on the table at once. Most can't handle such perfection."

"It's a shame we must hide them." He keeps cool as I struggle to hold in my laughter. "Oh, but don't you worry about me looking directly at you. I hardly ever look at others. I spend most of my time taking selfies."

"Wow, you sound too good to be true."

His deep, husky laugh follows and it's music to my ears. He takes my hand and we walk into the restaurant, teasing each other playfully. The smell of tomato sauce and garlic lets me know it's an Italian restaurant. The hostess walks us to a table and Trace pushes my chair in after I sit.

"Would you like me to read through the menu for you?" He pauses. "Jeez, I'm sorry, I didn't even tell you where we are. We're at Carmine's—have you ever been? I should have asked."

I smile; knowing he's still nervous makes me feel less so. "Don't be sorry. And yes, I love this place. I'll have the penne with vodka sauce and a Sprite."

"All right, that sounds good. I'll have the same." He shuts the menu with a snap.

"So tell me something about yourself."

"Hmm." He ponders the question for a moment. "I'm on the track team, not cool, I know. Um, I love to read classics. In fact, I read *The Adventures of Tom Sawyer* six times . . . Wow, not cool again. Don't even know why I shared that. But I read a lot. Classics mostly." He fidgets in his seat. "I do play a mean guitar, which *is* very cool," he boasts and I nod in agreement. "Your turn."

"I'm a race car driver."

"That's right! I think I saw you in the Indy 500 last year," he says. "Dale Earnhardt Jr. ate your dust."

"Yep, that was me!" I smile wide, loving how we play off each other. "I also love to read. I'm a fan of the classics too. You can find most of the classics in braille. I happen to play the piano like it's nobody's business and I love my dog completely."

"Well, it sounds like even our true selves will get along impeccably," he says. I hear his smile—I imagine he has a great smile.

"So, how long have you been playing the guitar?"

"About five years, I guess. How about the piano for you?"

"Since I was nine. And, really, *Tom Sawyer*?" I hold up a hand and a thumb. "Six times?"

He laughs. I can listen to his laugh all night long. The waitress takes our order and then I take a minute to get familiar with the table, touching the plates, the silverware, and my perspiring water glass, then finding the napkin to put on my lap.

Knowing he's watching me, I smile shyly. "What?"

"Just observing the way you move. You're very graceful. The water would be on my lap if I tried that."

"You rely on your eyes. I rely on the rest of my senses."

"It must be difficult . . . sometimes."

I fear he feels sorry for me. "Sure. I mean, there is a list of reasons why being blind sucks. Like when something is hard to do or learn or understand, I get so frustrated. And I sometimes feel like I'm missing out on the fun. And if I walk into one more thing . . . Ugh, my poor shins. But since I never relied on my eyes and I'm functioning without them, my blindness isn't something I'm always thinking about, you know?"

"Yeah, I think I do."

I smile, believing that. "Yeah, I think you do too. So where are you going to college?" I change the subject quickly. "People call you 'Harvard.' Is that where you're going?"

"No, Stanford. If I get the scholarship. I'll find out soon," he says as if Stanford is no big deal. He truly is modest.

"Wow, you are wicked smart."

"Drink's on your left, honey," the waitress says to me.

"Thank you."

"What are you going for?" he asks, stretching out his long legs under the table. His shoe nudges the side of mine and he leaves it there—maybe he thinks it's a table leg he's pressing against. A rhythmic tapping starts and I notice it's to the beat of the Italian music playing in the background. I move my foot an inch, just to see if he'll shy away. He does and I lower my head to hide my grin.

Yep, he thought he was hitting the table leg.

"Music," I say, listening to him reposition himself in his chair. "I'd like to teach one day. How 'bout you?"

"Actually, I want to be a psychiatrist. Stanford is one of the top-rated schools in the US for psychology. I'm hoping to help teens mostly."

"Why teens?"

"My cousin committed suicide when he was thirteen. No kid should ever be that alone."

"Trace, I'm so sorry." My heart expands in my chest and I wish to reach over the table to hug him.

"Me too. He lived in California, never really fit in, awkward to a fault. It took patience to be around him for a long period of time. Didn't see him much but when I did, I wasn't always patient," he admits painfully. "I wish I told him I loved him. I should've been there for him. I mean, who was I not to be tolerant? I don't exactly fit in either." His tone reveals the regret he still feels. Sorrow fills me. I lower my head and play with the napkin on my lap.

"Sorry, not the happiest of first date conversations," he says.

"No, it's not that. It's just," I pause, "I'd like to challenge something you said."

"Okay," he says, drawing out the word.

"You said you should have tolerated him. But tolerating him wouldn't have helped. No one wants to be tolerated. They want to be accepted as they are, no?"

He's quiet for a moment. "Yeah. God, you're right. To tolerate and to accept are two very different things. I should have accepted him."

I smile knowing I'm sitting across from a boy who is going to one day help others and make a difference. "Being a teenager is really hard. And I'd never wish to be a teen again."

"Me either," he agrees with a huff of a laugh. "High school is a nightmare full of demons."

"A nightmare that lasts four years."

"Exactly. So what about your dad?" he asks.

I sigh. I usually shy away from this topic with others, but there's something about Trace that makes me want to tell him everything. "He left a few weeks after I was born. I think my blindness scared him away."

I don't know much about my father. Mom doesn't like to talk about him. All she has ever told me was they were young and in love and very excited to have a child. She didn't see it coming—she thought he was the kind of guy that would never leave his wife and baby. It just goes to show that you never really know someone until you face a challenge together. Sometimes I feel sad and rejected, but mostly I feel nothing for my father. Nothing at all. And leaving his family when life got tough makes me think that maybe Gary really is a great guy. He knew exactly what he was getting and loved my mom and accepted me.

"Jeez, I'm sorry." I hear his earnestness. "Okay, topic switch. Now it's your turn to describe me," he says more upbeat, leaning hard on the table. It shifts against me.

"Well, to do that I have to touch your face so maybe we should wait," I explain, excited over the hope of touching his face. Not like I go around touching people's faces to learn what they look like, nor do I want to—that would be weird. But I really want to touch Trace. So I'm going with it.

"Liv?"

"Yeah."

"I like your name. Were you named after Liv Tyler?"

"No, Mom was going to name me Kylee but I was born with the umbilical cord around my neck and stopped breathing. She started chanting live, live, live and when I did, it kind of stuck."

There's a long silence and I start to fidget in my seat. "I like that story," he says. "I mean, how it ended."

The waitress places our food on the table. I wait until she leaves before saying, "Oh and by the way, I think being on the track team is very cool."

CHAPTER 8
LIV

Good food, great guy, easy conversation, and lots of laughter equals a perfect first date.

During the drive home, we talk about school and teachers, and that has us laughing too. Only the car comes to a full stop too soon. I don't want him to get out yet, so I reach out to find his arm. "All right, my turn." I follow up his arm and find his face, touching it playfully, pushing and poking gently. "Oh! No, I was afraid of this. Wow, this is disappointing."

"What? What's wrong?" Trace asks, worried. I smirk. "Oh, everyone's a comedian," he groans with amusement.

Stifling a laugh, I say, "Sorry. I'll be serious now." I slide my fingers along his face. He grins under my touch, which makes me smile. "You have a long nose. A slight curve to it."

"Broke it in fifth grade. Fell over the handlebars of my bike and landed on my nose."

"Ouch." I wince and move my fingers up. "Your eyebrows are thick—no unibrow. Amen to that." He laughs hard. I go on, "You have a nice big smile. Your jaw is strong. Cheekbones defined. Skin smooth, except for right here. A pimple or a mole?"

"I'm going to lie and say it's a mole," he says, embarrassed.

I giggle and move up. "And crazy hair."

"Crazy?"

"Yeah, crazy. Okay, now my favorite part is your voice. Smooth and deep." I pause before adding, "So you're a smart, sweet, good-looking, artistic guy who's also musically inclined, with a great voice and a big brain. Yeah, you're not my type at all."

"And you're a pretty, smart, sweet girl with a great sense of humor. And you think I'm good-looking, which scores you double points. Yeah, I'm not into you either."

"Damn that Rita for even wasting our time."

"Rita?" He sounds confused.

"She told you I liked you," I explain.

"You knew that?"

"I heard it."

"Oh . . . Then yes, damn her." He pauses. "I think I should walk you to your door. Your mom keeps peeking out the window."

I place my hand over my mouth, mortified. Trace walks around the car and helps me out.   "Thank you for tonight. I had a great time," I say.

"I did too." He hugs me and I melt into his embrace. He's a lot taller than me and my head rests perfectly against his chest.

"Thank you, Rita," I say teasingly. Trace laughs while walking down the stairs.

"Can I call you?" he asks. My head bobs and doesn't stop. "Okay, I'll call you."

"All right, thanks again for dinner." I lean against the railing and listen to him walk away—he has a long stride. "Oh, and Trace?" I wait until his steps stop before continuing. "I lied. Your voice is my second favorite thing. Your laugh, that's my favorite. I love your laugh."

He's smiling, I can tell. "You have a great one too."

My smile grows right along with my fondness for him. The car backs out of the driveway, he beeps twice, and then I walk in the house and proceed to do the happy dance.

***

After getting ready for bed, I lie down and call Cat. I tell her every detail before hanging up and thinking of it all over again. Trace gave me the best first date ever. And he may have just ruined any other guy's chances. He is perfect for me. I knew he would be. A bit awkward at times, but that's to be expected on a first date . . . right?

I kick my feet with excitement.

Hank jumps on the bed and licks my face. I hug him tight. Next Mom sits on my bed and brushes my hair from my face.

"So, are you going to tell me about your date?" She nudges my leg.

"I was wondering why you weren't in here earlier. Trace said you were peeking out the window." I scold her with a tight grimace, though I can't hide my excitement for long.

"Who me?" she says, faking innocence. She lies next to me and I tell her everything.

***

The next night, Cat picks me up for the hockey game after dinner. Since hockey is a winter sport at Hardy High, the guys also play for a travel league so they can play in the fall too. Tonight is the first game of the season, and luckily it's a home game.

I'm standing on the rink level against the back wall while I wait for Cat to return from the concession stand where she's grabbing us drinks before we head upstairs. The rink has two levels and most of the fans sit on the second, though some stand around the rink's glass. I fold my white cane and put it in my coat pocket.

There's so much action in the rink and I love all the sounds that echo off the walls—the cheers and boos from the fans, the swish of skates and smack of sticks on the ice, and the bang of bodies against the boards along with the roar of the crowd going wild with every body check. The fans on my side, the home side of the rink, suddenly roar and a horn blares celebrating a scored goal. The announcer calls out the names of the scoring and assisting players—Eddie Sparks and Evan Tully. I clap and give a cheer for my friends.

In front of me, I hear two boys walking by while playing with what sounds like hockey sticks slapping on the concrete floor. Suddenly, something hard hits my ankle and I shriek. Before I can process what's happening, the boys rudely start ordering me to toss their puck back to them. "Hello! Can you toss that back?"

I certainly have no intentions of sliding my hands on this floor to find the puck they hit me with. They demand again. I slide my foot around hoping to find it. No luck.

"Jeez, are you blind? It's right in front of your face," a boy scoffs.

Taken aback and utterly appalled by their manners, I bend down and swing my hand half an inch above the floor the whole time wondering why they can't come get the puck themselves, but after that remark I'm determined to find it and I finally do. "You can have it back when I hear an apology."

Standing tall, I place the puck in the pocket of my hoodie and cross my arms to show my sternness. I'm not even sure why I'm so irritated. It's not like I haven't heard that comment before, and they sound young, but there's a fire starting in my chest and I want an apology, not for being hit but for their rudeness.

"Excuse me, what did you just say to my boys?" a woman says.

"I said I want an apology," I explain with a simple shrug of my shoulders.

"Liv, what's wrong?" Cat asks, walking right into my side.

"Nothing. I found a hockey puck." I proudly hold the puck up.

"That's nice," Cat says, perplexed. "Why's that lady and her kids scowling at you?"

I shrug as if I haven't a clue.

"Mom, I want my puck," one boy says.

"Yeah, she's a thief," the other boy adds.

"I'll fix this," the mother scoffs.

"What's she doing?" I ask Cat.

"It looks like she's going to get the cop at the front door."

"No!"

"What did you do, naughty girl?" Cat's voice is full of amusement. The goal horn blares again and this time the other side of the rink cheers. "Here they come. On your left," Cat warns.

"Excuse me, miss," a gruff male voice says, obviously the police officer.

"Yes?"

"Do you have the boys' puck?" He has a sexy voice and by the way Cat is pushing against my arm, urging me to get closer to him, I can tell he has the looks to go with it.

"Yes, I do," I say.

"Please give it back."

"Not until they apologize," I say boldly, even though I'm trembling inside. This is the first time I've ever talked to a police officer and my nerves are running wild.

"Can you believe this girl?" the mother snaps.

"What did the boys do?" the officer asks.

"They hit me with the puck, which isn't really the problem, but they didn't say they were sorry and then rudely asked me to get it for them, but that's not really what I want an apology for either."

"Well then," I hear amusement in the officer's tone, "what do you want an apology for?"

"Something they said to me," I explain.

"What did they say?" the officer asks. I picture him crossing his arms over his chest, still amused.

"'Jeez, are you blind?'"

"So," the mother sneers, "give them back their puck."

I remove my glasses. "I am blind." The gasp I hear is priceless and I scowl at her before sliding my glasses back on. The fact that she had no idea pleases me in a way I can't put into words. Moments like this are when I praise my teachers for forcing me to follow voices when in a conversation, to carry myself as the sighted do.

"Then what on Earth are you doing at a hockey game?" the mother spews.

Cat steps in front of me. "You ignorant bit . . ." Cat starts but the officer halts her quickly with a clearing of his throat.

"Can I have the puck?" the officer asks. Reluctantly, I hand it over. I'm not that much of a rebel.

"Hey!" I hear the boys cry and wonder why.

"Let this be a lesson to both of you and your mother. Treat others with kindness and compassion or the law is never in your favor. And if I remember correctly, people used to sit in front of their radios and listen to shows and sports—still do in their cars—so since when do we only need our eyes to enjoy a game?"

I can't help but smile. And he's right—Gary listens to sports in the car all the time. "Thank you."

"No, thank you," he says. "Do you understand how your words hurt this young woman?" he asks the boys.

"I guess," one says.

"Can you apologize for your insensitivity?"

"I'm sorry you're blind," one says sincerely.

"No, that's not why you should be sorry," the officer corrects him.

"I'm sorry I hit you with the puck and said something that hurt your feelings," the other boy says.

"Me too," says the first.

"Thank you," I say, satisfied.

"You can have your puck back after your mother apologizes too," the officer states, and I want to hug him.

"Are you kidding me?" the mother replies, shocked.

"No, I don't find any of this funny," he says.

She groans. "I'm . . . I'm sorry for my comment. It was a stupid thing to say. I was just mad."

I nod. I'm not about to say I understand because I don't. Not at all. And I hate to think that the opinion people have of blindness will never change if kids are taught by such ill-informed parents.

"I'm here because I love my friends and I want to show my support." I don't know why I explain myself, but I continue, "As the officer said, I can enjoy the game by listening to the announcer and all the action. I can feel the energy. It's very exciting. Try it sometime—sit, close your eyes, and just listen," I say hoping the boys are listening.

The boys walk off, betting each other who can get to their seats with their eyes closed. The woman is leaving too, calling after her kids as she goes.

"Enjoy the game, ladies," the officer says before walking off.

"Thank you," we say in unison.

"Wow, I never saw you like that, Liv," Cat pokes my ribs. "It was exciting and I'm proud of you."

"I don't know why I got so annoyed, but I'm glad I stood my ground. I hope those boys learned something."

"Well, now they're walking around with their eyes closed bumping into everything." We laugh.

"Let's go sit down." We turn to go and my name is called from behind us. It's Trace's voice. I spin toward the most perfect sound in the world and almost jump with excitement. "Trace, you're here!"

"I figured you were . . . I wanted to hang with you, if that's okay?"

Cat *awws* dramatically. "That's so sweet."

I reach my hand out and when he takes it, I squeeze his tight. Surprisingly, he wraps his arms around me and I smile in his hold. He breaks the hug but doesn't remove his arm from around my shoulder. "Who's winning?"

"It's a tie. Let's go sit." Cat slips her arm into mine and the three of us walk up the stairs.

CHAPTER 9
TANNON

I look over to check on Liv. Last I saw, a cop was talking to her. It was so shocking to see such a sight that I lost my focus on the game and the player I was defending scored a goal. Coach reamed me out, and I've been sitting on the bench ever since. It looks like everything's been cleared up—the cop left—but my curiosity is killing me.

Coach calls me to get in the game just as Trace walks up to Liv. I catch him hugging her as I hop the half wall onto the ice, my mood instantly changing. I want to hurt someone . . . badly.

Skating past Evan, I say, "I guess Liv's date went well."

"Yeah, she had a good time," he says.

"That's nice," I say, skating to my position as if I really believe that.

It's not nice. It's the polar opposite of nice. It sucks.

***

The game ends 9–3 us. I basically lost it on the ice and the other team dealt with my jealous rant. Not caring to celebrate our win, I sneak away from the team and into the locker room, hide in a bathroom stall, and wait for everyone to leave before making my way to the parking lot. I'm not surprised to find my dad waiting for me at my car.

"Good game, son." He pats my back. "What caused the coach to bench you?"

"I got distracted seeing Liv." Dad's the only one in this world who knows how I feel about her and how long I've had these feelings. Hearing her name makes his expression turn sympathetic instantly.

I can't stop seeing the smile she had as Trace hugged her. She was so happy in his arms. *My* girl, happy in another guy's arms—that shouldn't even be possible. In a perfect world, it wouldn't be.

"What happened?" Dad asks.

"I think she's with someone now—this guy Trace. He's wicked smart. Nice guy, I guess." I shrug as if it doesn't matter. It doesn't take long for my jealousy to return and prove it does. I drop my huge gear bag with a thump and kick it. "I can't believe they went out. Never even knew they talked." Smacking my hands on the trunk of my junkyard car, I hang my head between my arms and sulk. "Why can't she *see* me, Dad?"

The silence that follows makes me regret I asked. I know what his answer is already and I don't want to hear it. "Have you let her?"

I groan, not interested in a lecture, but I know it's coming and there's no way to stop it.

"Please, look at me, Tannon."

I turn my head and look into his sad, gray eyes. He hasn't worn a smile that reached his eyes since my mother died three years ago and he's been in a constant state of sadness ever since.

Mom and Dad were soul mates. At a very young age, I understood their love was different than most. I could see it when they looked at each other. I could see their love even when they argued. They were best friends and did everything together. Dad worked hard at an advertising agency so Mom could be home with me, and he was home every night for dinner and always kissed her before he even put his keys down. She was a great mom, my greatest cheerleader. Helped me with school. Made me feel smart, capable. She was the most loving mom. And Dad was my best friend. I thought myself lucky—I was loved, happy, and carefree.

But my luck ran out when I was fourteen. That's when Mom started losing weight and experiencing night sweats and random fevers. She thought she had the flu and even though Dad asked her to go to a doctor, she always dismissed it, saying, "It's just a lingering flu. I'll feel better tomorrow."

When her night sweats became so bad that Dad woke up next to her soaking wet and her weight loss became too significant to ignore, he insisted she go to the doctor. After a few visits and some tests, they diagnosed her with stage IV Hodgkin's disease and things went downhill quickly after that. Her days became full of trips to the hospital or the doctor's office. Soon that became all she had the strength to do and she spent most of her time either in her bed or a hospital bed. Her frail body went through every treatment and test you can think of until the treatments stopped working. As much as I didn't want to lose her, around month eight of all this I started praying to God that if he wasn't planning on making her better, then to please take her. She was suffering and I couldn't stand seeing her like that. She denied treatment around the ninth month and came home to hospice care. Dad and I took turns sleeping with her in the hospital bed in the living room. It was my night when she died. I woke in the middle of the night, her still body next to me, and I just knew she was gone. The moment I cried out, Dad leaped off the couch and rushed to her, knowing almost instinctually that she was already gone. He pulled her into his embrace and didn't let go. He just kept rocking her, begging her to come back, begging God to take him too. As sad as I was over her death, I was choked with fear over Dad's wish to go with her. I never felt more alone.

Mom died on July 17th, ten months after being diagnosed and the summer before I started high school. Dad also died on July 17th. But it was a different kind of death.

I loved them completely and then I watched them both suffer and die. Mom left this Earth but Dad ... He suffered a breakdown after we lost her. He stayed in bed for two months and I thought he was going to die too. He did eventually get out of bed, but he's never really recovered from her death. I wasn't enough for him.

"It doesn't matter," I say, bending down to search for my keys in my smelly hockey bag.

"Why?"

"Because"—groaning loudly, completely frustrated, I rip apart my bag— "the guy has me beat. I can't compete with Trace." I continue to rip through my bag, the stink almost knocking me out. "Where the hell are my keys?"

All of a sudden I'm being lifted off my knees and my back is pressed into the door of my car. Dad's aggression leaves me in absolute shock. Anguish and misery twist his facial features. "How can you say that?" Dad asks before letting me go. Stepping back, he looks up and sighs deeply. "Compete with what? His IQ level?"

I shrug while nodding.

His hand runs over his short brown hair as he stares at me. "The kid's smart. Well, so what? So are you!" He looks exasperated. "You ask why she can't see you! Why can't *you* see you?"

I say nothing.

"What are you doing, Tan? I come to your games and watch you interact with your teammates, sometimes girls afterwards, and I don't recognize you." I nod knowingly, he groans, "So you don't either?"

"No," I admit. I don't recognize myself.

"Why do you hide the Tannon I know?"

"I don't know." Looking down at my sneakers, avoiding his eyes, I kick at the stones on the pavement.

"I think you do, so tell me why you hide the compassionate guy you are and show them this proud, conceited peacock who goes around saying things like 'it doesn't matter' when you know damn well it's all that matters to you. She's all that matters to you." His voice rises and I haven't heard this tone from him in years. "It may work on everyone else but it sure isn't going to win over a girl who can't see your handsome face."

Crossing my arms, I lean against the car, defeated. Dad leans against the car next to me, wearing his heart on his sleeve. I see his anguish; he never hides it. I don't think he could if he tried. Tonight he's holding my pain too. He sure isn't the one who taught me to hide. I learned that all on my own.

"Tell me what's really going on."

I'm suddenly defensive and it quickly turns to anger. I glance around to check that the parking lot is empty before I answer him. "What's goin' on? Why do I hide? 'Cause I don't even want to know the real me," I sneer. "The real me is pathetic. I'm sick of feeling so stupid. Five-year-olds are smarter than me. You think I want people to know that?"

"Oh my God, Tannon! This is why you hide? You think you're stupid?"

"I don't have to think. I am. But that's only part of it." I seethe through clenched teeth. "I couldn't save Mom—that I understood—cancer won. But I thought I was enough to save you. I wasn't. You wanted to leave me here alone."

"Tannon."

"No!" I shout. I have to say it. Everything. It's been bottled up for too long. "I tried everything I could to get you to snap out of it, to see I was still here, still alive, and I needed you, but I wasn't enough for you to want to live. I wasn't enough." My tears fall and I wipe them briskly with the back of my hand. Through my blurred vision I watch his eyes close. "I needed you. I needed you to tell me everything was going to be all right. I was fourteen and my mother just died. I needed you to get out of bed so I didn't have to fear losing you too. I knew she was your soul mate and you loved her so much, but ... jeez, Dad, I'm your son. And you wanted to leave me here all alone. And if I'm not enough for you ..."

"Tannon!" he shouts my name to get me to stop. His hand starts tapping at his chest. "I—I didn't want to leave you. I—I couldn't breathe. I couldn't breathe without her. I was lost in my gut-wrenching heartache and I ..." He raises his hands and drops them, like a plea for me to understand. "I just loved her so damn much and I had to watch her suffer and die. I couldn't protect her. That was my job. I promised to always protect her and I couldn't. The cancer ate her from the inside out and there was nothing I could do to stop it. And I thought ... what good am I?" He looks to the left, at a dark area of trees, as he falls into his painful memories.

"Yeah, and what good am I?" I counter. Not wanting him to answer, I go on, still heated, "I hide behind this face because it's enough ... for most." I huff a humorless laugh. "Not for Liv. But there's nothing about me that will be enough for her. I'm far from her type. So I hide behind this face and hope no one can see past it. No one will see I really have nothing to offer."

"Tannon. God, son, you are so wrong. Do you know why I finally snapped out of it?" I shake my head. He goes on, "I got up from my bed because *somehow* my bedroom window was open. When I went to close it, I heard you praying on the front stoop. You had your hockey bag at your feet waiting for Evan's dad to pick you up. I heard you begging Mom to help me. To give me part of my heart back so

I could survive without her. You told her you needed me and you were scared for me. You begged her to save me and if she couldn't, then to please take you too when I go." He wipes his face; I don't even bother to wipe mine, my tears just keep coming.

"I stayed up all night sobbing over what you must have gone through as I tried to sleep my grief away. I thought of how disappointed Mom must've been with me for neglecting to see you needed me." He looks up at the stars and I watch his shoulders lower as he exhales deeply. "I promised to always protect her and I couldn't. I also promised to always protect you and I didn't. I felt so selfish and guilty. I was so ashamed. I knew I had to find some strength. I took a shower, shaved for the first time in two months, and swore that I'd never fail her, or you, again."

He smiles faintly, sorrow behind it. "The next morning I was in the kitchen making breakfast when you woke up. You stumbled back from shock when you saw me—showered, shaved, cooking. You remember what you asked me?"

"I asked if you were back."

"Yeah, and I said . . ."

"'Mom gave me half of my heart back,'" I finish for him, remembering that morning as if it were this morning. "I kind of thought it was true."

"I think it was. She did answer your prayer, Tannon. I didn't have that window or any window in my room open for two months; Mom opened it. She opened it so I would hear how much you needed me, hear how much I was hurting you." His eyes are full of regret and disappointment. "I'm so sorry, Tannon. I failed you and I'm sorry."

I fall into his chest and cry on his shoulder. "You are more than enough, son. Do you hear me?" His arms squeeze my back. "You did save me. You shouldn't have had to, but you did."

"Why didn't you ever tell me this?" I ask, stepping back.

"I guess the same reason many things are left unsaid ... fear. I was scared to bring it up and I didn't know you were carrying it around like this. If I had, I would've brought it up." He grabs my shoulder, pulling me to him again. "I'll forever regret not talking about those two months with you now that I know it caused you to hide who you really are."

He pushes me back to look into my eyes. A few moments pass in silence when he looks up at the stars, then he locks eyes with mine again. "You've had to grow up so fast, but I'm proud of the man you've become, the one I know, the one you hide from everyone else. You are so much more than you allow yourself to see. Liv can't see it because you don't see it."

"I lost my chance."

He shakes his head. "No, but I think it's easier for you to believe that than to put yourself out there. Don't you see that you've been hiding behind exactly what she doesn't want? I think you know she would love the real you and that scares you. If she did, you'd have to fear one day losing her like you lost Mom." He takes a long breath. "You can't lose what you don't have, right?"

Yeah, he's right.

"What if I expose the real me and she still doesn't like me?"

His gray eyes widen. "Tannon, if she knew the real you and didn't fall completely in love with you, well then she's completely insane."

I laugh and he pulls me back into his embrace. His chest shakes as he laughs and I laugh harder. We haven't hugged since Mom died. It's funny how much bigger I've gotten. We now stand at the same height, five foot eleven, but I'm fitter than him. He's not overweight but he did lose a great deal of muscle over the years. His brown hair is starting to get some salt in it and his skin is starting to show the stress he went through. He was so young and vibrant until Mom got sick. The cancer took Mom's life, Dad's vitality, and my courage. We lost each other since she passed, but here, now, in his arms, after what he told me, there is no awkwardness in this embrace. I'm his son and he's my dad, and I just need to lean on him. He takes my weight, my sorrow, and holds it firmly.

I finally move back to wipe my face with my shirt and he taps my arm again. "Damn, you're bigger than your old man now. That isn't right," he frowns. "I'm going to have to start lifting weights or something."

"Nah, you look good, Dad. You should maybe start . . . dating," I say nervously, not sure how he'll react. "I'll be leaving the nest soon . . ."

"Hey, don't you worry about me. You live your life. And live it well." I look down at the pavement because I am worried. He asks, "I just need to know, do you really think Liv is the kind of girl who cares how well you read?"

"No," I say. "But I care. I want to be what she wants. She's attracted to smart . . ."

"Maybe if you stopped hiding you'd find out you are what she wants," he snaps. "Tannon, you are smart. And you're talented—you're an amazing artist—don't you ever forget that." He pokes my chest then grabs my neck and pulls my forehead to his. "I'm sorry I let you down. I never meant to hurt you." I hear his emotions bubbling up his throat.

"I know, Dad. I miss Mom every day, and I understand you died that day too, but you just didn't get the luxury of going with her." I nudge my forehead into his. Hoping the sting will keep my tears from falling again. "You're here. You need to live again. You need to find someone to make some new memories with."

He stays silent for a long time, but this time I don't care if I said something he doesn't want to hear. He looks at the stars again before looking back at me. "I'm going to help you win this girl over." He thinks for a moment. "You need a grand gesture to get her attention. Get her to realize you aren't who she thought you were . . . or who you pretended to be. I'm going to have to think on this one for a while."

I'm thinking myself when out of nowhere he starts to laugh. "What?" I ask, thrown.

"Grand gestures! Listen to me, I sound like Mom."

I start laughing too. I haven't heard him laugh like this in years. It sounds like heaven to me. Suddenly he stops and grabs my shoulder. "I got it!"

"What?"

"The grand gesture!" he exclaims. "Paint her a picture."

"What? How's she going to see it?" I say, baffled.

"She doesn't have to see it; she has to feel it." He holds his chin as he thinks.

"Like braille?" I ask.

"Yes!" he exclaims, his eyes widen. "She needs to know the real you and your heart and soul are in your paintings. That's where the real you is, Tan, in your art, and she has to be able to experience it."

"I don't know if I can execute . . ."

"Yes, you can," he says, cutting off my doubt. His enthusiasm is contagious and I suddenly become excited. I have no idea how I'm going to do it, but I'm excited nonetheless.

"I'll try."

"You can do it." He pulls his keys out of his pocket and plays with the hockey stick keychain I got him when I was eight. "I love ya, kiddo. Please know that."

"I do. I love you too."

"You heading home?"

"Yeah, I have to shower then head on over to Tucker's house. Victory party," I explain, holding my fist up.

"All right, I'm going to pick up some Chinese so I may miss you at home. Be safe." He pulls me in for another hug and turns, heading to his car.

"Dad," I call, he spins around. "Thanks."

"No, Tannon. Thank you." His eyes tear up again. "Damn, who thought going to a hockey game could be so emotional?" he teases. I laugh while opening my door.

"Remember, grand gesture!" he shouts, hand raised triumphantly as he gets in his car.

***

I shower and make my way to Tucker's house. This night knocked me out but Evan texted twenty times and Sparks thirty, both saying if I don't get my ass to Tucker's they'll hunt me down and drag me there. They would do just that, so I came at my own will. It should be fun—Tucker's known for great after parties. He never played hockey in his life, but he sure loves celebrating the game, and since his parents go to Atlantic City every other weekend, he celebrates a lot.

I walk inside and see Tucker's sister pulling Evan up the stairs. Teddy gives me a bear hug, saying, "It looks like someone's over Cat."

"No, he isn't," I say as I watch Evan disappear up the stairs, wondering what on Earth he's doing.

"Tucker isn't going to like Evan with Ana." Teddy seems worried, but everything worries him.

"Who's thinking of Tucker right now?" All my concern is for Evan when suddenly the front door opens behind me and Cat and Liv walk in laughing over something the other said. I clamp my mouth shut.

"Oh man, I didn't know they were coming," Teddy whispers.

"Stall them . . . I have to get Evan," I whisper and run up the stairs, ramming right into Evan at the top.

"What the hell, man?" he reprimands me, rubbing his stomach.

"Oh thank God, I thought you were with Ana," I huff. Relief over not having to interrupt him flashes over me.

"Gross, dude. She's like a sister," he says, disgusted by the thought. "I had to piss. Why?"

"Cat's here."

His face lights up like a Christmas tree. "She is?!" I nod and he races down the stairs. I walk down and see him tap her shoulder. She turns, her big blue eyes look him over. Running his hand over his messy hair, he says, "I didn't know you were coming."

"I dragged Liv along. I wanted to talk to you." She looks down shyly. "If that's okay?"

He grabs her hand. "It's fine. Let's go talk." Evan pulls Cat upstairs and Teddy walks toward the kitchen, leaving me alone with Liv in the small foyer. She has on a pale blue T-shirt with a peace sign that says "Live to Love . . . Love to Live" around the circle, a pair of faded blue jeans, and gray Converse.

She looks adorable.

"So I heard you went on a date last night." I try to sound unaffected.

"I did," Liv says, and I frown at the smile that crosses her face. "I had a good time." I can't see her eyes through the dark lenses of her glasses. I hate when she wears them, mostly because I love her face.

"What happened at the game?" I ask. "I saw a cop talking to you."

As she explains what happened, I find myself gazing at her lips—she has full lips, the bottom bigger than the top, and I long to kiss them.

Always.

In fact, her lips have been the star of many of my fantasies through the years.

"Sounds like you taught them a lesson," I say when her lips stop moving. Her shoulders rise and fall sweetly. "You want to go for a walk?"

Her head pops back with a flummoxed expression on her face. "I . . . uh . . . I should probably stay. . ."

"No worries," I say, not wanting to hear the reason she doesn't want to be alone with me. I asked since I know she's not really into these parties. Wrong move I guess. "I'm going to get a drink," I say, suddenly wishing I had stayed home.

There's loud music coming from the kitchen down the hall to the right and the sounds of an intense pool table game going on through the archway on my left. I want nothing to do with any of it.

I want my bed.

"You are?" she asks, tilting her head with a grimace.

"Yes, Liv, I am," I say after realizing she's talking about me getting a drink.

"Will you take me on that walk instead?"

I stare, perplexed, suddenly realizing she must think I meant alcohol. I can't drink—no one on the hockey team can. If we get caught or someone tells, we can't play. The only people drinking at these parties are either not on the team or are willing to take the chance. I love playing too much to risk it. Though I do wonder why she's so worried about me drinking. She never was before.

"Why?"

"Because I ... I don't want you to drink," she whispers.

"Why?" I don't tell her I'm not going to. I want to hear her reason.

"Tannon." Her delicate hand reaches out and lands on my chest, then recoils quickly, only to return again. The warmth from her palm melts through my shirt and every layer of my skin and seeps into my heart, leaving me aching to hold her. Slowly her hand moves up to my shoulder and slides down my arm in search of my hand. She laces her fingers with mine and turns to the door, pulling me.

"No, Liv."

I pull her back by the hand, her side hits into my chest and I hold her still, my forehead resting at her temple. Her hair is like silk against my skin and smells like flowers. Fingers squeeze mine as her other hand moves to my shoulder. Is she touching me to feel me or is she setting herself to push me away? I don't know and right now I don't care. I tilt my head until my lips touch her ear. Sliding my other hand around her back to find her hip bone, I squeeze her closer to me. "Why don't you want me to drink, Liv?" I whisper, letting my lips slide over her ear. She quivers in my hold.

My touch has an effect on her. That's a good sign, right?

Who knows? Maybe it means nothing at all.

"Because," she says, using her hand at my shoulder to push me back. "You're my friend and I care about you. You love playing hockey."

She actually thinks I'm the kind of guy that would risk losing what I love for a good time.

I hate that she thinks that.

I also hate the word "friend" that keeps repeating in my mind. My gut aches. I quickly deflate and turn to leave her. This has been an emotional night and I don't want to hear about being her friend. I have enough friends. I want more than friendship. As I walk down the hall, she calls my name. I try to ignore it and will my feet to keep moving, but I can't. I feel like I'm abandoning her, so I turn back, grab her hand, and pull her into the kitchen with me.

Tucker shouts our names as we enter. "Come sit by me, sweets," he calls out to Liv.

As I walk with her around the table to get to the drinks, he grabs her hand and pulls her to his lap. I want to pull her back but don't have the energy. I'm so far in the friend zone with her I don't think it will matter what kind of grand gesture I make.

Utterly depressed, I gaze at the plethora of alcoholic beverages to choose from and contemplate how important playing hockey really is to me. Then I hear Liv's voice in my head. With the devil on one shoulder and Liv on the other, the devil doesn't have a chance. I grab a grape soda, wanting to hurl it through the window.

Groaning miserably, I take a seat across from her at the table. "Deal me in, Tuck," I say.

Tucker wraps his long arms around Liv's body so he can deal the cards. His cheek rests against the side of her bare arm and he teasingly bites at her skin as he deals the cards. She giggles and I wince. He's in the friend zone too. I guess that's all right for friends to do.

Hey, maybe I'll start nibbling on her too.

Teddy and Samantha sit with us at the small, round table. Sam's a nice girl. She dated Tucker for a while last year and they've stayed friends. She's a wicked poker player, whipped our butts many times.

Sparks picks up his cards and frowns—he's yet to learn the meaning of poker face. I swig my grape soda and pick up my cards. "What's with the girly drink, TK?" Sparks mocks. "Do you at least have vodka in that can?"

"No," I reply flatly, and he leaves it alone.

A content smile shows on Liv's pretty face. Sparks lifts his water bottle in a cheers gesture and winks. Smiling knowingly, I cheer him back. He's a player who chances getting caught; there's no water in that bottle, just straight vodka. He's a very mellow drunk so he can stay under the radar. I, on the other hand, get very loud and *friendly*—I'm sure I'd get ratted out. I'm center defense and I know more than a few JV players want my position. With camera phones anyone can tape me being an ass and show it to the coach, so I take my chances off-season, not during, or when I'm alone with my trusted friends.

Tucker isn't on the team. He has no responsibilities, can host parties and be wild all he wants, and that's just how he likes it. He leans back and yells, "Learn the words!" to a group of girls singing a rap song in the living room. They yell for him to shut up.

Another group of girls is standing around the kitchen island making nachos and a few guys are eating them before the cheese is melted. "Save me some!" I say.

"Sure thing, TK!" the girls say in unison.

I pull my cell from my pocket and call for pizza. "Who wants pizza?" I shout.

"Me!" is called out from all directions.

"Good! Put money in a pot," I yell back. Everyone groans and Marco, a junior varsity player, grabs a pot and starts collecting money. I throw mine in as I'm placing the order. Liv stands to reach into her pocket. "I got you, Boo."

"No, that's okay."

"Don't worry about it," I insist.

"Okay. Thanks," she says, smiling.

"Can we play already?" Sam groans with impatience. "If I win this hand, you're all writing "Sam rules" on your chests with permanent marker."

Sparks lifts his water bottle and tilts it toward Sam. "If I win this hand, my name is going on your boobs, Sammy, and I get to write it. My full name. I have three," Sparks says to her, wiggling his brows. "And I'm a very slow writer."

We all stare at him, knowing he'll never win. Never has. Never will.

I laugh while shaking my head. "You are so delusional, man."

My comment doesn't faze him, and he sits back all proud and self-assured. I laugh harder.

We drop and draw for a few minutes and then it's my turn to wiggle my brows. "Well looky, looky. Four kings," I boast, laying my cards out on the table. "It looks like Tannon is the name to write, suckers."

Sam offers a phony frown before laying her cards on the table. "Sorry there, TK, but you boys are writing my name tonight," she says as she reveals four aces and jumps gleefully in her seat.

"Daammnn!" I rub the back of my neck while staring at her cards. "How do you do that . . . Every. Effin'. Time?"

"I have skills," she declares. "Now find a marker!"

"Do you really want Teddy to take off his shirt?" Sparks asks, and at first Teddy smiles, thinking he's off the hook, but he quickly realizes it's an insult when he catches Sparks gesturing to his large midsection. Cursing at Sparks, Teddy throws his cards at him.

"Actually, the only guy I care to see shirtless is Tannon," Sam states, causing my head to snap her way in surprise and Tucker to scowl at her. She shrugs at him and gestures to Liv on his lap, as if saying, "Two can play that game."

I have a feeling there's still something going on between them.

Tucker lifts Liv off his lap and grabs Sam's hand, pulling her out of the room. "Wow," Sparks says, "someone's jealous."

Liv stays standing, so I lean over the table and take her hand to guide her around the scattered chairs. I pull Sam's abandoned chair next to me so Liv can sit. "You deal, Teddy."

CHAPTER 10
LIV

The party is starting to wind down and I'm tired, but Cat has yet to return since she walked off with Evan. The comfort of Teddy's big belly keeps me cozy as I wait. We're sharing the loveseat in the family room. His arm stays on the back of the couch behind me like a perfect gentleman and I think that's why I feel so relaxed resting against him. He truly is a big, cuddly teddy bear and an all-around nice guy.

I'd probably fall asleep if not for the annoying flirtation coming from across the room where Frankie and Tannon play a game of pool. I don't know Frankie very well, but from what I heard from her tonight, I'd say she's a tad brazen. She slurs sexual innuendos every time Tannon's up. I assume she's trying to make him miss the pocket but, as a bystander, she sounds desperate and her flirting with him leaves me agitated, which surprises me. He gives her a few jests back, but for the most part it sounds like he's just playing pool.

Why am I so bothered by her flirting?

"I need a ride home tonight, TK," Frankie says, and I stiffen against Teddy's side.

"What's wrong, doll?" Teddy asks sweetly. "You all right?"

"Yeah, sorry, I have a kink in my neck." I rub at my neck to cover up my lie. The truth is, the thought of Tannon alone with Frankie makes me . . . jealous? I'm trying to figure out what I'm really feeling when suddenly quick footsteps are heading my way and the next thing I know hands are on my knees.

"Liv, you ready?" Cat asks.

"Yeah, are you all right?" It sounds like she's been crying.

"I dunno. We have to drop Evan off because he shouldn't be driving," she says. My heart aches for Evan. "He's upset and pissed. I took his keys. He's waiting in my car."

"I—Maybe I should leave you two alone." It would be awkward getting in the way of their time together. Maybe they can still work it out? But who else would I go home with?

"I'll drive you home, Liv," Tannon says from across the room.

"Are you sure?" Cat and I ask in unison.

"It's not a problem," he says.

"Did you drink tonight?" Cat asks, full of concern.

"No," Tannon answers.

"He didn't," Teddy offers to ease her worry.

"Is that all right, Liv?"

"Yeah, go. I'll be fine." She kisses my cheek and rushes out. Sitting in a car during a lovers' spat is nothing I'd volunteer for, but suddenly I realize what I traded that for. Sitting in a car with Tannon . . . oh my gosh, I'm suddenly nauseous.

He's been acting so different around me—his touch is different, his responses are different—and I don't think being alone with him for ten minutes is something I want to do either. A loud bang makes me jump against Teddy's side. "What was that?"

"Frankie threw the pool stick on the table," Teddy explains.

"Why?"

He shrugs. "She looked mad, threw the stick, and walked out. I think she was hoping to get a ride home from Tannon."

"Oh." *Jeez, what kind of "ride" was she hoping for?* After giving Teddy a quick kiss on his soft cheek, I sit forward and reach for the coffee table before standing.

"You want help, doll?" he asks, touching my elbow.

"No, thanks, I know my way." Tucker's house isn't too complicated to maneuver around in. Knowing I'm in the family room, I just have to watch out for the coffee table, a chair to my left, and a pool table straight ahead and then I have a clear walk to the hallway and the bathroom is on the right. I open my walking stick and make my way to the bathroom. The only glitch I encounter is someone coming out of the door as I'm reaching for the handle. "Oh, excuse me."

"Whatever," Frankie says. She has a scratchy voice, so she's easily recognized.

"Oh . . . kay," I say as she storms past me.

"Liv!" Tannon calls from down the hall. "You ready?"

"I just have to use the bathroom."

"All right, meet you at the front door." He starts a conversation with someone else as I'm shutting the door. When I come out, I hear him still talking and Frankie's voice responding, "You could've had a good night if you didn't offer to take Miss Needy home."

The thought of hitting her with my cane like some angry old woman offers me a moment of pleasure, but wanting to hear Tannon's reply, I step back into the bathroom. "First off, I had no intentions of bringing you home. And second, the only needy girl I see in this house is you," he reprimands her. From his tone, I'll bet he's right in her face. "That girl can run circles around you in a china shop."

"Yeah, I'm sure," she scoffs.

"Why you being ugly, Frankie?" Tannon asks.

"Whatever," she retorts, as if he's supposed to believe she doesn't care what he thinks of her. She's been trying way too hard tonight for anyone to believe that. "What's your problem lately? You used to be fun," she challenges.

"Yeah, and you used to be cool," Tannon counters. "Jeez, just let me breathe."

"You'll be calling," she says matter-of-factly.

"Please hold your breath for that," he says.

Whoa!

"Why are you letting her get to you?" Teddy asks. I guess Frankie left.

"She called Liv needy." Tannon sounds hurt and outraged. "How could anyone think that of her?"

"You're talking about Frankie, so what do you expect?" Sparks points out with humor in his voice.

Tannon huffs out a laugh. "Too much, I guess. Way too much." The three guys laugh and smacks follow—the kind that come when guys are patting each other's backs or egging each other on. I step out and walk toward them.

"There's our girl," Sparks greets me warmly, hugs me tight.

"Good night, Sparky," I tease.

He wobbles me to and fro. "Good night, Livy Livy."

Shaking my head, I laugh and turn to Teddy. "Thanks for the pillow, Teddy."

"Anytime, doll." His soft lips peck at my cheek.

"Tell Tucker I said thanks."

"Will do," Teddy replies, and I know he's smiling. He must have the sweetest-looking smile, I muse.

I head toward the door on my own and Tannon nudges his arm at my side for me to take it; I do. I know doing so doesn't make me needy. It makes me smart—he has great arms.

The door to his car squeaks open, sounding like it sticks halfway. Tannon groans. "My uh . . . My car is a piece of crap, Liv. Sorry but you have to squeeze in 'cause the door won't open all the way."

He sounds embarrassed so I place my hand on his arm. "Looks good to me," I tease.

He laughs and his forehead falls to my shoulder. "Thanks."

The tension from earlier keeps him rigid and I'm suddenly concerned. He does seem off lately. I'm not sure if I should, but I slide my hands up his arms and wrap my arms around his neck. There's no response on his end, leading me to think I shouldn't have hugged him.

Just as I'm pulling away, his arms wrap around my back and he lifts me to his height in a snug embrace. My breasts crush against his hard chest, his shoulders flex under my arms, and his face turns into my neck. Warm lips press at my skin, unmoving, and yet they still cause goose bumps all over.

He simply holds me off the ground with his lips on my neck, silent and still, except for his exhales against my skin and inhales that squeeze me in his embrace.

His muscles surpass any guy's I've ever touched and I'll admit it feels good to be in his arms. I feel safe and comfortable and . . . desirable?

Or do I mean desirous?

It must be the latter because he's so still I'm the one with the racing heart. It is my body that is yearning for things I don't quite understand.

God, I wish I knew what he was thinking.

These unfamiliar sensations make me feel anxious and uncomfortable, and I wish to cut this hug short. "Tannon," I whisper, "I should really be getting home."

I push back in his hold, my feet dangling off the ground, our faces inches apart, and I bite my lip as something happens to the air around us—it heats up, thickens. I can't breathe. *What is happening here? Why isn't he saying anything?*

"Tannon?" His name comes out like a plea.

Without warning, he lowers me to my feet and helps me into the passenger seat. The door squeaks shut and he hits against it a couple times until it clicks. The driver's door opens easily enough and he starts the rumbling engine. Unexpectedly, his hands reach around me and pull at something over my shoulder—the seatbelt. He yanks and tugs and finally draws it over my chest, grazing past my right boob and as he does, I hear his breath hitch.

Or was that mine?

"Sorry, the belt sticks too." The click echoes through the car. He shifts the car into drive. A moment later, loud noise jolts me in the seat. He adjusts the volume level and flips through the stations. Settling on Keane's "Somewhere Only We Know," I listen to the verse singing about simple things. I turn a bit in the seat to face Tannon.

"Tan?"

"Yeah?"

"Are you all right?" He stays quiet. I don't give up. "It's just you seem like something may be bothering you and, well, if you need to talk, I'm here."

"I'm all right, Boo." His hand finds mine in my lap and he squeezes. I place my other hand over his. He started calling me "Boo" freshman year. He'd walk up behind me and say, "Boo." Shortly after, it became his nickname for me. I like it; it's cute. "Really. I've just been thinking a lot lately."

"About your mom?" I ask, believing that may be it.

"Yeah, well, I always think of her, but yeah, and other things."

The conversation pauses and I listen to the song again as it talks about needing somewhere to begin.

"You don't want to tell me?" I feel sad and alone. It's as if he's lost in his thoughts, a million miles away, and I want to hug him again just to bring him back. His fingers twist under my tight hold until he gets them to lace with mine. Holding his hand was always the most natural thing to me and yet now, my heart is racing at an uncomfortably foreign pace.

"It's not that. I . . ." He stops and I fidget with anticipation. "I don't think it's something I should share at this time."

"Oh . . ." Turning my head down, disappointed and curious, I trace the lines of taunt muscles up his forearm and back down absentmindedly.

"So, you going out with Trace again?" he asks, sounding upbeat all of a sudden as he pulls my hand playfully.

"I uh . . . I don't know." I adjust my sunglasses on my nose and sit perplexed by his quick change of mood. "If he asks."

"Do you hope he does?" Still sounding cheerful, he squeezes my fingers.

"Yes, I do," I say and notice his fingers loosen.

"He will."

"He will?"

"Yeah."

"Would you?" I don't know why I ask. I want to take it back so badly but I also want to know his answer.

"What do you mean?" he asks, confused.

Instant embarrassment prickles at my cheeks. Why'd I ask that? He isn't interested in me like that. He probably hugs every girl the way he just hugged me.

"Nothing. I'm just excited for him to ask again. We had a great time together," I ramble and turn to face the window. His hand releases mine as he turns the car and shifts it into park. We sit in silence.

CHAPTER 11
TANNON

"You're home," I say, wishing I had driven around the block again.

"Thanks for the ride." Liv's voice is soft. I swear she sounds sad. *Why would she ask if I'd ask her out?* I desperately want to ask if she'd say yes, but she's waiting on Trace and I have no grand gesture to offer her that will make me a better catch than Harvard Boy.

"I'll walk you to the door." I get out and walk around my car. The door squeals as I pry it open.

Embarrassing piece of crap!

I take her hand and remember I forgot to unbuckle the seatbelt. She'll never get the trick button—no one does. Squeezing into the door, I lean over her and start fighting the seatbelt free. Cursing under my breath, I hear her giggle. I try my best not

111

to curse in front of her. I know they aren't words she uses, yet this she finds amusing. "Oh you think this embarrassing moment is funny?"

"Yes. I'm sorry." She covers her mouth to hide her laughter. I kneel on the ground and lean my upper body over her legs as I push my thumb into the button. The darn thing won't give. I start to laugh and she laughs harder and I rest my forehead on her knee.

"I hate this damn car," I say through a groan.

"I think it's great," she offers seriously. I lift my head, stunned. "I do. I love it. And that's good since I'm stuck in it." She laughs again and I look up at her mouth. Her sweet lips I long to kiss. *What if I just do it? What would she do if I just leaned up and kissed her?*

I shift and the door squeaks loudly. No girl has ever been in this car—I take my dad's on dates—and yet this unexpected need to drive her home landed her in this piece of crap and she says she loves it. I'm not a fan of my scrap heap, but after all the medical bills my father had to pay for Mom, I wasn't about to ask Dad for help with a car payment, so I went to the junkyard with the money I made landscaping in the summers and bought the least disgusting car there. With the help of Sparks—the guy is clueless about most things but a genius when it comes to cars—we got this 1998 Toyota Corolla to purr like a kitten. The frame resembles a mangled rat but the engine is a feisty cat. It gets me from A to B and that's good enough—for now. But again, I've never subjected a girl to it and here this perfect angel, the one and only girl I want to impress, loves this rust bucket. I want to kiss her even more for loving it. I want to kiss her for keeping my broken heart pumping for three years . . . and just when I lean up to do just that . . .

"Liv, honey?" I hear called from the house and pull back quickly, bumping my head on the top of the doorframe. "Is that you?"

"Yes, Mom!" Liv calls out. I stand and wave over the car. "Hi, Mrs. Sullivan."

"Oh, hi, Tannon," she replies with a big grin. "How are you?"

"Good. Just trying to free your daughter loose from my junkyard car," I explain with an embarrassed smile.

She laughs. "All right, I'll leave ya to it then." She waves and shuts the door.

"She likes you," Liv offers.

"Good, 'cause I like her too."

Leaning back in, squishing my body in the narrow opening of the broken door and stretching over her legs to start fighting the button again, I think about how I was just about to kiss her. Hopefully the button will put up a good fight and give me time to find the courage again.

"Tannon," she says, and I look over at her. "I . . . I'm glad we're friends." She smiles, reaching out her hand to find my face. "You've been a really good friend. Always make me feel like I fit in."

"Because you do." I sigh. Kneeling down on one knee again, my ass pushing at the door causes a loud squeal as my chest and arm rest over her legs. "I can't imagine hanging out with the crew or being in school without you. You make everything better," I admit. *Friends say that, right?*

Her thumb rubs over my cheek, so I smile. "Wow, you do have deep dimples," she says, placing her other hand on my opposite cheek. Her fingers glide over my face to my forehead, then across my eyebrows, down my nose, and along my lips. I'm no angel but this is the most intimate way a girl has ever touched me. And I'm scared to death of how she'll see me. Her fingers play along my ears and move along my jaw to my chin. "You have very handsome features, Tannon."

I breathe out my relief, but this is just my shell—I want the part that matters to her to be attractive. And it never will be.

I lean the back of my right shoulder against the dashboard and stare at her lips illuminated by the light post next to the driveway. They shine from her strawberry flavored lip gloss. The scent is faint in the air and yet completely intoxicating. I want to kiss her and taste it off her lips. I run my right hand through my hair and rub my neck. While looking down, I notice my other hand is resting on her jean-covered thigh. I wasn't aware of how close my fingers were to her inner thigh, and now that I do, my body responds.

Gazing up, my eyes freeze on the seat belt pressed over her beyond-perfect breasts and I bite my lip. Liv has curves—she's not a frickin' twig. Some guys like that, I guess, but not me. I don't fantasize about stick figures—I fantasize about Liv. Even her imperfections are perfections to me. I stretch my left leg out along the car and stifle a moan. What this girl does to me.

Nonetheless, she just thanked me for being a good friend.

Suddenly her hand reaches up to find my hair and the tips of her fingers comb through my short, messy 'do. "And no premature balding!" she exclaims with amusement.

I grin. "You're beautiful, Liv," I say earnestly. I catch her eyebrows rising over her sunglasses and know she's taken aback. "The very first time I saw you, I couldn't stop staring."

"I stood out?" she says, frowning.

What? How could she have possibly heard anything negative in my compliment?

"Yeah, you stood out, like an angel stands out in hell. Liv," I grab the sides of her face before continuing, "stop thinking like that. Ugh," I say frustrated, "I know you do because of the hurtful things people say, but I can't stand that you let those jerks get to you. You can't control what people think or say. 'Blind girl shouldn't go to a hockey game,' 'blind girl shouldn't go to a sighted school,'—that's bullshit! What they think doesn't matter. Some people are ignorant and self-absorbed. They can't see past themselves or what little they know. We all deserve to go to a hockey game, to cheer for our friends, or get a good education no matter what we look like, wear, or see. No matter our circumstances." My fingers spread over her ears and I hold her head firmly. "Don't you ever think differently."

"Tannon," she whispers.

"Liv, I—" I catch myself. "*We* love you and *we* want you everywhere we are." I long to plant my lips on her quivering mouth and make both our sorrows go away, but she pulls me in for a hug, as a friend would.

Damn, this sucks!

"So when someone gives you a compliment, you just say 'thank you,'" I state, my stern tone causing her to hug me even tighter. "You don't think the worst and question everything."

"Thank you, Tannon," she whispers.

"You're welcome!" I pull back and jam my thumb on the seatbelt button and the metal clip finally releases. *Thank the good Lord.* I have to get away from this girl before I do something that may scare her away forever.

"You're free!"

"Yay!" she cheers.

Man, she's so sweet. Trace is a lucky guy.

Harvard jackass.

I hate him.

I take her hand and pull her out of the scrap heap. "You going to the beach tomorrow?" I ask. A bunch of us are going. It's supposed to be a nice day, weather-wise, and I know Evan asked her and Cat to come.

"If Cat's still in."

"Okay, well, good night, Liv," I say at her door. "Sweet dreams." Turning, I hop down the stairs before I take her in my arms and never let go. Running away like a coward . . . I seem to do coward well.

"Tannon," she calls out and I look over my shoulder. "I . . . uh . . . Sweet dreams."

"Thanks." I walk to my car, wondering what she really wanted to say.

CHAPTER 12
LIV

The endless back and forth of male banter entertains me while sitting in the backseat of Tucker's Jeep. We're heading south to the beach. It's a beautiful Sunday morning and this wild crew is set on enjoying this crazy heat wave. I'm so glad they asked me to join them.

Sparks is sitting shotgun and I'm in the back, in between Teddy and Cat. The top is off, the warm wind is whipping stray hairs freed from my ponytail at my face, and Teddy's round belly is cushioning every left turn Tucker makes.

Evan is in his own Jeep with Tannon, Evan's sister Kelly, and her best friend, Tami. Sparks was yelling to them a minute ago, so they must be driving close.

The fact that I'm included in this group of guys makes me so happy. They started asking Cat and me to tag along when Evan and Cat started dating. There's nothing I enjoy more than sitting back and listening to guys talk. I don't understand it half the time, and they can get very crude, but it sure is entertaining.

Sparks and Tucker are having an argument about which movie is the funniest of all time. Sparks is stuck on *Dumb and Dumber*, Tucker demands it's *Spaceballs*, and Teddy is all for *Anchorman*. Cat argues that they are all wrong and the funniest movie of all time is *Airplane*. They all stop arguing and start quoting scenes from that movie. We laugh the rest of the drive until Tucker parks.

He announces we're here with a long honk of the horn and a "woo-hoo!" out his window. We file out of the Jeeps and start collecting our things from the trunks. Sparks hands me my chair and bag, spins me, and directs me to walk straight and be careful of raised boardwalk boards. I pull my white cane out of my bag, snap it open, and make it to the sand without a glitch as everyone else fights over who's carrying what. The sand is hot and the sun is blazing, though, thankfully, a steady ocean breeze makes everything a little more bearable. I love being here. The smell of sunscreen and the taste of the salty sea breeze lifts my spirits.

I love everything about the beach.

Cat walks up next to me and finds a perfect place for us to set up our stuff. It takes a while for the guys to get to our spot. They have wave boards and coolers and a football and volleyball—I know all this from them arguing about it when they packed the cars.

Cat tells me that the guys covered Teddy with as much as he could hold and now he's leaping from one bare foot to the other, dropping stuff as he walks on the hot sand. "Where are his flip-flops?" I ask Cat.

"He took them off," she says, amused. "Guess he thought it would be easier to walk through the sand without them. Boys."

Poor guy. I call out words of encouragement. "You can do it, Teddy!"

"No, he can't," the guys chant.

Tannon breezes past me calling Teddy a big baby. Stuff clanks and crashes to the sand before he breezes back, sand kicking up on my legs. My guess is Tannon dropped all his stuff in a pile to chase after the trail of stuff Teddy has left behind. Cat and I set up our gear. The guys drop their stuff like Tannon did and then I listen to them race each other into the water. Cat sits and asks me to join her. I pull my sundress over my head and sit in the sand in front of her so she can coat my back with sunscreen.

"Let me help you with that, ladies," Tucker says out of breath, dripping water all over me. He must have raced out of the water just to offer his help. Cat scolds him, sending him away, and he runs off groaning with disappointment.

Kelly and Tami set their chairs up next to ours and start mocking the guys when waves knock them over in the surf. I raise my face to the sun and smile as my fingers play with the sand at my sides. Cat asks me to turn and playfully slides sunscreen over my nose and then hands me the tube so I can coat my chest and legs. I have a one-piece on—it's easier that way. The thought of going into the ocean in a bikini makes me cringe. Who wants to deal with that nonsense? A one-piece stays where it's supposed to and, even though it might not be as young and flirty

119

as a bikini, there's a lot of voluptuousness going on up top for me—maybe too much—and I never feel properly supported in a bikini top.

Easing into my chair, I listen to everyone playing a game of volleyball. They spend most of the time arguing over what's in and out of bounds. The whole game is very entertaining.

Someone huffs toward me, kicking sand at my shins. "Would you mind getting my back?" Tannon asks me, plopping down at my feet.

I hold my hands out and wait for him to find lotion to squirt in them. The scent of coconut invades my nasal passages and I breathe in deeply. "Yum, I like the smell of this one."

"I found it in Evan's bag. Don't tell him. He failed sharing in kindergarten."

Tannon sits back between my legs and I start at his neck, working down. His skin is hot and smooth. Thick muscles define his traps and lats and then taper to a narrow waist. I won't lie, his back is nice to touch and I actually frown when I run out of skin to coat. I take the remainder of lotion on my hands and rub it on his ears, taking them between my fingers and thumbs and rubbing in small circles on the lobes.

"Keep doing that," Tannon says. I go around his ears once more, stopping at the lobes again, rubbing them between my fingers. "I can sit here all day with you doing that."

He eases back against my legs and I circle my arms around his neck to hug him, my head resting next to his. Thinking of all he said last night makes me want to hug him. His head turns and the tip of his nose runs over my cheek before warm lips press against my skin.

The mood, or energy, seems to change, leaving me confused. I lean up, smack his shoulders, and ask if he's up for a walk. Tannon's hand takes mine and he pulls me to my feet. I take my white cane with me. He nudges his elbow in front of me; I take that too.

We walk quietly along the surf's edge. The waves slide over my feet and it feels so good. Kids race noisily up and down the beach as we walk in silence.

"Watch your step," Tannon warns before my white cane hits something and slides right over it. "It's about to get squishy. A bunch of jellyfish washed on shore. They're dead though."

A cushy goo squishes under my feet and I squeal. "Can I touch one?"

"Yeah." We crouch down and I slide my hand over one.

"They're so smooth."

"They're clear, transparent, red in the middle and nasty when alive," he explains, and then moves my hand over a seashell. I run my finger over the jagged surface and flip it to feel the inside. I take it with me as we continue our walk.

"It's a beautiful day." I lift my face to the sun.

"That it is," he replies.

"I had a good time in your car last night," I say. Tannon laughs; I cringe. "That sounded wrong, didn't it?"

"Yep, and I'm sorry I missed the good time it sounded like we had," he teases. "Watch it!" he warns again, pulling me to his side just as a strong wave rushes up my legs. I laugh and wipe the salty spray from my face. My hand moves to his bare chest, solid and smooth. His muscles bulge under my palm as his arm moves to brush my ponytail behind my back. He releases me and starts walking again.

We don't talk, we just enjoy each other's company, at least I'm enjoying his . . . *Wait, is he enjoying mine?*

"So when are you expecting to hear from Trace?" Tannon asks nonchalantly.

Not sure why he's thinking of Trace, I turn my head toward the surf. "He called this morning actually."

"Oh," he says, his tone different, humorless. "When are you seeing him?"

"I asked him to come to Tucker's party with me on Friday."

"Oh, that's nice," he says. "He's never come to a party before."

"I know, but I want everyone to get to know him better." I sure hope Trace doesn't feel out of place at Tucker's. He knows everyone, but he just doesn't hang out with them. "I'm hoping it works out with him," I say. Tannon doesn't respond. "You like him, right?"

"We've never really talked much, but he seems like a nice guy."

"He is," I say smiling. "He's really sweet."

"That's good. Smart too."

"Yes, so smart." I nod. "He's ideal." I hear a faint huff of a laugh. "What?"

"Nothing," Tannon says. "I'm happy for you."

We walk in silence again, but now he seems to give me more space than before. We're past the jellyfish hazard and I walk next to him with the aid of my cane. It's as if he's a million miles away, deep in thought.

"You okay?"

"Me? Yeah, sure," he says quickly.

"Will you take me into the water, Tannon?" I ask, as sweat drips down my back.

"Sure. Let's head back and go in by the others."

We walk back, dodging jellyfish, and by the time we get to the chairs, I have jellyfish slime between my toes. I'm obviously very bad at dodging. I put my cane and sunglasses in my bag and turn to the sea.

"You going in?" Cat asks.

"Yep!" I say. The thought of swimming in the ocean has me feeling giddy.

"I'll come," Evan says. I hear the sadness in his voice. He and Cat are talking civilly, and are willingly hanging out with each other even though they broke up, but it's awkward. Last night's talk didn't change much—it only seemed to make them sadder. Evan still wants her back, but he's not pushing the matter today. He takes my hand and Tannon takes the other, and we walk into the cool surf. The waves come quickly, one after another, though they're not very high.

"The tide is changing, the waves are calming down," Evan says. Sparks and Tucker call our names from deeper in.

We walk knee deep and take a moment to get used to the chill of the water before we go even deeper. The waves crash against my stomach and as they get higher Evan and Tannon lift my hands up to raise me over the tops. A thrill rushes through me. It's like marching into the unknown. It's exhilarating.

CHAPTER 13
TANNON

I watch Liv smile as we lift her over each wave. She asks to go under and releases our hands, disappearing under the surf. I worry over her, never wanting to see her get hurt, but I know my worry is just that . . . mine, and I don't want my love for her to get in the way of her independence. That would be a sure way of losing her.

And I can't lose her.

Ever.

When she surfaces, she pushes her hair from her face and I shamefully watch the water slide over her olive skin—she looks beautiful. The V-neck of her black one-piece taunts me and I can't even explain what seeing her in a swimsuit—one-piece or not— does to my seventeen-year-old mind and body.

Evan pulls her to his side as a wave comes and lifts her over the water. She wraps her arm around his shoulder, laughing every time he leaps them over a wave.

A football lands in front of me and I turn to see Teddy walking into the water with his hands up ready to play catch. We throw it back and forth a few times and then it lands in front of Liv, splashing water in her face, and she giggles.

Damn, she's cute.

Evan lets her go and grabs the ball, throwing it to Sparks. I watch Liv bob in the water; dark hair slicked back off her beautiful face, the sun's rays glistening off her wet skin. I swallow hard. Sparks throws the ball at me—knowing I'm not paying attention to their game—and it lands next to Liv. She wipes the water from her face and reaches out to me, finding my shoulder and hopping on my back as my arm is in a throwing motion. The shock of her legs wrapping around my waist and her breasts pressing against my back causes me to fumble the ball. I retrieve it quickly and look up to find Sparks laughing at me knowingly. I chuck the ball at him and take hold of Liv's thighs as a wave comes.

Heaven help me.

We rise and fall with the waves. Her head rests on her arm over my shoulder, she relaxes against me, and I know she trusts me. I love that she does.

"Can we go under a few times?" I hear the excitement in her voice.

"Sure." Holding her thighs tighter, I call out the dive before plunging us under the white cap.

We surface and she says, "I want to go myself," before popping off my back and moving next to me.

"Be sure to go down deep enough so the white cap—the top of the wave—doesn't grab you." Liv waves off my warning. I shake my head, amused, and let her have her fun.

She dives under two waves perfectly, but the third is much stronger and the white cap catches her, flipping her over and over, all legs and arms. I swim after her like a mad man, my heart in my throat, luckily catching her by the waist before the next wave has its fun with her too. She spits and chokes, her hair plastered to her face. I sweep it back to get a good look at her.

"Jeez, you all right?" The fear of losing her trust courses through me.

A loud laugh erupts out of her. "That was awesome!" Pushing back from my chest, Liv grabs my face and kisses me right on the lips, quickly, just a peck, but I can't even explain the joy that washes over me.

She pushes from my hold and asks me to teach her to body surf the waves. "All right, what do I do?" she asks, pumping her shoulders up and down.

The water is just under our chests where we stand, and she can jump over each wave with no problem. A few roll over her head when she doesn't time them right, but she loves it.

"You should use a board." I yell for Sparks on the beach and shout, "Wave board!"

He signals a thumbs-up and brings one in. "Liv wants to surf," I say.

Sparks's whole face lights up. "Well, all right then!" He's eager to teach her. He's patient when it comes to teaching skills he knows well. The guy's an awesome wave boarder; he can do all the fancy tricks. He takes her and positions the board against her stomach. "First, just listen to the waves. Here comes one. Let it go past you. I just want you to get familiar with the sound you need to listen for."

Another wave follows. "All right, listen, when I say 'go,' listen to the sound of the wave. That sound at 'go' is what you want to listen for and then you start paddling toward shore, okay?"

Liv nods. The wave comes and he announces the perfect time while holding her on the board next to him. We rise and fall as it goes by.

"All right, Liv, now you listen and when you think it's time, I want you to start paddling. This is your ride, baby." He steps back. His teaching technique suddenly makes me like the guy even more. He's treating her as he would anyone wanting to learn how to wave board and the look on her face lets me know she appreciates it.

"Oh my gosh!" she yells at the sound of the wave and starts paddling. The white cap dies suddenly and the wave slides under her, taking her only a few feet.

Dud wave.

Sparks swims after her and grabs her ankle, pulling her back into place. Her mouth twists with disappointment. "That was it?"

"No. That was a dud wave," I say.

"Oh good, because that one really sucked," she says, scrunching her nose.

Grinning at her comment, Sparks glances at me and lifts his brows. "Sorry, Livy, sometimes they die before the shore. They look and sound all impressive and then they leave the party early," he says, and repositions her on the board. "This one is all in," he says, psyching her up.

The rumble gets louder the closer it comes and Liv starts paddling exactly when she's supposed to. She catches the wave and it takes her to the shore. Evan catches her before she hits the sand. She jumps up with her arms over her head. "I did it! Did I do it? I did, right?"

"Yes, you did it!" I yell. Sparks and I share a high five.

Cat cheers from the blanket. "That's my girl!"

"You did great!" Sparks shouts. "Now come back and do it again."

We guide her back to us with our voices and she makes it back without a problem. I honestly believe there is nothing this girl can't do. She jumps into Sparks's arms the second she reaches him. "Thank you! That was scary and thrilling and wild and I want to do it again."

His eyes are wide. Liv's taller and thicker than him, and he gets lost in her embrace—it's a comical sight.

"Okay, ready?" Sparks sets her up on the board and holds the side close to him. She nods her readiness.

The wave approaches and Liv starts paddling. It takes her and she goes zipping to the shore. Cat's taking pictures with her phone—I want copies of those. Evan catches her right before the sand again. She leaps up and Cat drops her phone on the towel and races to hug her. Liv wraps her arms around her and they jump up and down like little girls—or seventeen-year-olds with great bodies. Really. Really. Great bodies!

Again, heaven help me!

Two lifeguards walk up to the girls and, next thing I know, they're having a conversation that looks a lot like flirting. Liv has her head down but Cat is talking and the guys are gawking and moving closer to her. Evan looks at me at the same time I look at him, an angry scowl on his face. I start walking out of the water. Evan looks about ready to pounce. Teddy, who hates confrontation, sees Evan coming and takes matters into his own gentle hands. He walks up behind the girls and throws his arms over their shoulders. His height and weight are intimidating to most and even these in shape lifeguards back away with "we get it" expressions. I give Teddy a thumbs-up and Cat frowns at him. Evan scowls at that too. *Was she really going to continue to flirt with them right in front of Evan?*

Kelly and Tami move in on the lifeguards like hungry mice to cheese. Liv doesn't seem to care what's happening and turns to the water holding her hand out. "Sparks," she calls. "Can I go again?"

Evan calls Liv back to the water, glaring at Cat the whole time. Cat lifts her arms innocently. "C'mon, Livy, I'm waiting for you!" Sparks calls out.

Since I'm already out of the water, I sit on the sand off to the side where the waves stop and watch Sparks get her ready again. Liv starts paddling and I can see her expression from here. She has the widest smile and her eyes are closed with a look of anticipation as she squeals with glee. The sight causes my heart to expand. I've never been so happy. Seeing her like this, complete elation on her face, I don't think I'll ever forget it.

She leans daringly to the left and glides over the wave before going straight again, laughing and grinning joyfully. I do the same as I live this moment through her, trying to reach her level of excitement. I've never seen her look more beautiful. I can't even handle how much love pours into my heart for her. I'm shocked it's even possible for my love for her to grow. It heats me up. It's overwhelming.

It actually hurts.

I'm startled out of my thoughts when Teddy sits next to me. "She's free," he says, gesturing to Liv. I turn and watch her ride the wave. And I smile.

That's the perfect way to describe her—she's free. She doesn't need assistance, from anyone or anything. The wave takes her and she's free to just enjoy the ride. We all search for moments like this, where we don't have to think, where we can just let go. She's experiencing one of those moments.

"She is, man. She's beautiful," I reply.

"So are you ever going to tell her?" he asks, and my head snaps to him, eyes narrowing in confusion.

I look around to assure no one is around us, and ask, "Tell her what?"

"That you've loved her for years?" He stares at me in a way that says, "Don't bother pretending, I know, man."

My jaw drops. "How did you know and not Evan?" I ask, shocked.

"Because I sit back and watch? I know more than you think," he says shrugging. "And Evan is too caught up in his own crap to notice anything else."

I laugh, shaking my head. "I love ya, man!"

"Brotherhood." Teddy holds his fist up. I bump it with mine, grinning. We haven't said that to each other since freshman year. When I was being bullied we made up the brotherhood.

Cat walks up. "What are you two talking about over here?" she asks, hugging Teddy's back.

"C'mere, Kitty Cat." Pulling her over his shoulder, he flips her into his lap, then stands easily with her in his arms and starts marching into the water. She yells and fights, yet can't break free from his hold.

I look at Evan standing by the water's edge waiting for Liv to ride in again. He catches the commotion and then looks at me. We laugh hard as Teddy tosses Cat into the air. She lands in the water with a splash. She has a completely different body type than Liv. Athletic, toned, sick six-pack stomach—Evan's ideal. Tucker's too. He drools from afar whenever Cat's in a bikini. Or whenever she's in anything really.

Cat emerges quickly, ready to scold the big bear. "Teddy! That wasn't very nice."

"Aww ... Kitty Cat," he says, feigning remorse. "I'm sorry."

She jumps on his back and he carries her deeper into the water. Looking over, I watch Sparks get Liv set on the board again. She starts paddling just as two girls about my age walk right in front of me to stand in the water. I rise, frowning that they're blocking my view of Liv, and walk toward Evan. The wave brings Liv zipping to the shore and I grab her under the arms, lifting her off the board. She wraps her legs around my waist and leans back. I have to hold her ass to balance her properly.

Poor me!

Her hands clap rapidly in front of my face. "Did you see me?"

"You're like an expert out there!" I say.

The water drips down her face and over her closed eyes, making spikes out of her long lashes. She pushes her hair back without a care of how it falls. "It's awesome! This is the best day! Thank you!" She turns her head toward the water and shouts, "Thanks, Sparky!"

"Anytime!" Sparks calls out.

Evan walks up next to us and pulls her face down to kiss her cheek. "Forget Jersey waves, you're ready for Hawaii," he praises.

She's riding on adrenaline so I don't think she realizes her position in my hands. Evan notices, though, and shakes his head. I shrug innocently, even though not a single thought in my mind is pure right now. He rolls his eyes and walks away. My attention turns back to Liv as she goes on and on about her surfing moves. I listen intently with a great, big smile on my very happy face.

All of a sudden her expression changes to one of awareness. She places her hands on my shoulders and unhooks her feet from behind my back. Lowering her legs, her body slides down mine, and I suck in a breath as she frees herself from my hold.

She pats my shoulder, almost as if to say "nice try." I can't help but laugh. "You're fresh, Mr. Keaton. Very, very, fresh."

"Yes, I am, Ms. McKay. Indeed, I am."

Without warning, her leg slips behind mine and she pushes me back. I fall to my ass, but not before grabbing her and taking her with me. She lands on my chest. I wrap my arms around her back and lock her on top of me.

"Pulling out the karate moves, little ninja? I bet you can't get away now." She squirms over me, all breasts and curves. "That's a bad move right there," I state.

Getting my meaning, Liv freezes instantly. "Tannon, that's not fair," she says.

"You want me to let you go?" I ask.

"Yes," she says quickly, seriously. I let go. She leans up to leave me and then leans back down. "Sucker!" she calls in my face. "Ha. I won!"

I laugh and pull her back down, spinning until her back is in the sand, and look down at her. "You cheated."

"I did not," Liv says, appalled. "The bet was I couldn't get away and I did. Now let me go. This is a completely inappropriate position to be in on a public beach."

"Tell me, where is this position appropriate so I can take us there?"

"Tannon, let me go. I'm in a bathing suit."

"Believe me, I know."

She pinches my chest. I laugh and let her go, never wanting to push too far. We sit next to each other, settling into a comfortable silence, and I watch her make circles in the sand with her finger.

Looking up, I see Evan swim over to Cat. She shakes her head for him to stop, looking completely wounded. *If she's so miserable without him, then why the hell isn't she with him?*

No wonder Evan's so confused. He ignores her weak protest and pulls her off of Teddy's back, quickly trapping her in his arms. She pushes in objection, fights ineffectually for a moment, then gives in quickly and hugs him back. He rests his chin on her toned shoulder and closes his eyes. They float like that, without talking, and let the current take them.

"What's everyone doing?" Liv asks.

"Evan had enough of that platonic thing and now they're floating away hugging each other as if their lives depended on it."

"I'm so confused by them." Hanging her head solemnly, Liv's finger makes little hearts in the sand. I write "I love you" above her hearts and frown as the waves slide up the shore and erase everything.

"Yeah, they're all kinds of dysfunctional," I add. "Then we have the other defectives: Teddy and Sparks are playing football in the water. Tucker looks like he's tanning with Tami and Kelly, but he's really watching every *hot babe* that walks by." Liv grins, amused. "And I'm thinking of where I can get you in more inappropriate positions," I finish.

Liv smirks while nudging my leg. Gradually her hand slides down my leg, following along my swim shorts that stop below my knee. Her finger runs over the hem. She seems sadder and sighs, hanging her head again. "What's wrong?"

"I wish I could see everyone. See the ocean."

I throw my arm around her back and pull her to my side. "Hey, this is a good day, Boo."

"Yeah."

My knees are up and her hands hang over them. Her face turns against my chest and I feel her soft cheek against my skin. Pulling her in tight, I kiss the top of her head. "It's a good day!" I repeat, watching a wave slide over her blue painted toenails. This is it, I have to tell her what she means to me. I have to tell her.

"Liv . . ."

"I'm sorry," she cuts in, pushing up a bit but still leaning into my side.

"For what?"

"Feeling sorry for myself," she says, moving her hands together and playing with the hem of my shorts at my knee once more. "It's such a good day and I don't want to ruin it."

"Liv, you think I don't feel sorry for myself on a daily basis? Besides, we are allowed to wallow sometimes. In fact, I think it's unhealthy not to. And we are especially allowed to wallow in front of our friends. If not, then what the hell are they for? Only good times? Screw that."

"You don't wallow. You're always so carefree."

"Uh . . . yes, I do, and no, I'm not."

"Yes, you are!" Liv protests. "Today's a great day. My friends are all here having fun. I got to wave board. A sweet, smart guy wants to date me. That's all that should matter right now, but sometimes I feel like I'm missing out."

The "smart guy" comment is ripping me raw. How could she still be thinking of Trace? "Liv, today you haven't missed anything."

"That can't be true?" She pushes off me with a tight grimace.

"I just witnessed you wave boarding and I've never seen any other person in my whole life look as blissful as you did." I sigh, desperately wanting to tell her I love her.

"Really?"

"Really! The expression on your face, riding that wave, is burned into my memory and I will recall it every time I'm having a bad day or when I just want to smile. That moment—your moment—was the happiest moment of *my* life. I'll never forget the feeling that rushed through me." I breathe. "I felt really alive for the first time since my mom died. And yet I know that your joy exceeded mine by a mile and I wish I could experience that kind of euphoria, but I don't have the ability like you do. You live in the moment. Experience everything to the fullest. I don't know how to live like that. I wish I did."

"Are you just saying this?"

"No. I'd give anything to experience that moment as you did," I say, meaning every word. "I swear on my mother's grave—and I'd never lie on that—from what I see, you experience everything and miss nothing. Then there's Tucker," I add, looking to change the mood. "He's only experienced gawking at girls and missed everything that has made this day great."

The force she uses when she pulls me to her is shocking. Her arms circle around my neck and she squeezes me so tight. "Thank you, Tannon." She spins her lower body and sits sideways in my lap not letting go of my neck. "I had two favorite days in my life—the day I got Hank and the day my gramps bought me my piano—and now I have three. This is a favorite day. Wave boarding, being here, you. This is a favorite day."

"Mine too! This is my favorite day too!"

Tell her, you idiot!

"I don't know what I'd do without you. You, Cat, and Evan are my best friends."

Best Friends!

The smile on my face flips instantly. I just put myself in the best friend zone. I think I'm going to puke. After squeezing her one more time, so as not to reveal my need to hightail it out of here, I move her off of me and stand. Holding in my need to run away just a bit longer, I help her to the blanket by Tucker before telling her I have to go to find the bathroom.

What the hell!

The more I open up to her, the more I'm growing a friendship instead of a relationship.

No, dammit!

I race down the beach until I'm out of the group's sight and sit in the sand. I'm stuck here with no way to escape. I didn't even drive. Why is this happening? Not only does Liv not see my truth, but she doesn't hear it either. It doesn't matter what I do or say. She doesn't understand me. My best day is going to morph into my worst—the day I became a best friend. Next she'll see me as a brother, like how she sees Evan.

Life sucks!

* * *

The hot lunch line is out the door and moving slowly. Evan and I stand in line. This is the first time I've gotten him alone to talk. We couldn't with Kelly and Tami in his backseat on the way home from the beach and I'm dying to know what happened between him and Cat this weekend.

"We fought and kissed and fought and kissed," he says, looking more confused than ever. "It was like she was battling her feelings right in front of me. Finally I said, 'That's enough! I can't handle this ping-pong match. Either you want me or you don't.'"

"What did she say?" I ask when he leaves me hanging.

"She said she can't want me. It's for my own good." His shoulders drop from the weight of his heavy heart.

"Damn, man, I'm sorry." Squeezing his shoulder, I pull him against me as discretely as I can in a room full of many immature teenagers.

"I'm being punished for her mother's choices," Evan groans.

"It's a vicious cycle," I state. "Cat has to break it or she'll end up just like her mom."

"This sucks." He looks me in the eyes and I see just how much. *I feel you.* I muse, *I'm a best friend now. Next Liv will think of me as a brother, like you.*

Being in love sucks!

CHAPTER 14
LIV

The week flew by and Trace called me every night. We talked and did homework together.

He's picking me up for Tucker's party at seven tonight and I can't wait. If it wasn't for him, this week would've been horrible. Cat's been in a funk and for some reason Tannon's keeping his distance. I can't understand why. I thought we had a great time at the beach. After all the stuff he said, I don't get it. I guess he just focuses his attention on the one he's with. I heard a rumor that his attention is now focused on Nicole Walker, which is fine, but I still don't know why it feels like he's avoiding me.

While waiting for Trace, Hank and I took a walk to the local Mini Mart. I bought a pack of gum and a box of bones.

"Who's a good boy?" I ask while removing his harness.

Hank barks. I offer him a bone and then sit to play the piano. The doorbell rings a few minutes after I start playing and I open the door with a smile. "Hey, Liv." That great voice of his fills my ears. "Was that you playing?" I nod. "You're so good!"

"Thank you." I grab my hoodie off the hook next to the door and walk out to his car. We chat about music and art on the way to Tucker's. Trace is so easy to talk with that I almost wish we weren't going to a party so I could talk with him with no interruptions. I decide this is just what I want to do and ask if he wouldn't mind skipping the party.

"Are you sure?" he asks. I nod vigorously. "Great! I wasn't really interested in going anyway."

"Trace. You should've said something." I feel bad thinking he was just going for me. "Can we just go for pizza or something? My treat."

"That sounds perfect, but my treat," he says.

We end up at a little pizza place in the heart of town. We eat and talk and laugh. Then we walk down the street to the ice cream store where Trace buys me a vanilla cone and we cross the street to eat our cones by the lake. I listen to the crickets as he skips stones. It's a beautiful night—the weather has changed in a matter of days and now the crisp air of fall feels refreshing as it fills my lungs.

"Just so you know, my stone skipping skills are world-renowned."

I giggle. "Oh, I know. I read about you in the paper last month."

"What, that six-page spread? That was nothing. *Sports Illustrated* placed me on their cover," he jokes and sits next to me. I turn to face him on the grass, sitting cross-legged. Trace takes my hands in his. "So we never really put a label on us. I know it's only been a week, and I'm probably jumping the gun, but I'd like to call you my girlfriend, if that's okay with you?"

"Really?"

"Nah, just kidding," he says. "Yes, silly, really!"

"Yes. Yes!" I exclaim happily, reaching to hug him. "I'd love to be your girlfriend."

"Awesome," he says, and I can tell he's smiling. "Can I kiss you?"

My eyes widen with nervousness. I want to kiss him—it will be my first real kiss—but I'm so nervous. I finally nod and his long fingers slide slowly along my cheeks, gently pulling my head to his. I feel the tender press of his lips on mine and sigh against their warmth. Our first kiss. It's so exciting, but aren't we supposed to be doing something?

Should I move my lips? Should I touch his face? Oh my gosh, what do I do?

"Liv," Trace utters against my lips.

"Yes?" I utter back, embarrassment rushing through me.

He leans back. "I froze. I need a do-over."

I grin at how adorable he is. "Okay. We've got this, rookie," I assure him, and he laughs. That wonderful laugh.

"We do! We've got this! Scratch that—whatever that was. This next kiss is our first kiss." He pulls my face to his again. "Breathe," he says gently, and we do together.

I relax in his hands and he tilts my head and eases against my lips, slow and soft, and I follow his lead. Leaning in, I rest my hands on his legs before me and surrender to the moment. My lips feel super sensitive to his touch as his lips move softly over mine. I want to start jumping up and down with glee, but I know that would be humiliating for the both of us, so I just kiss him back. And it's good. I'm good at it. He's good at it. We're good at it!

Woo-hoo!

This is the most perfect first kiss from an unbelievably amazing guy who genuinely likes me and just asked me to be his girlfriend and I'm so happy and ... I have to stop this internal dialogue or I'll never remember the details of this kiss. And I want to remember every single detail.

Warm lips slide over mine and suck slightly at my bottom lip before he pulls back. Leaning in for one more peck, Trace says, "We do got this."

His thumbs graze over my cheekbones. I take hold of his wrists and smile with my forehead pressed to his. "I never doubted it. You gave me the best first date and now the best first kiss. You are awesome at this."

"I've read a few of my mom's romance novels."

"You haven't!" I exclaim with mock horror.

"Nah, just kidding," he says laughing. "Well, maybe one or two."

We laugh and kiss again.

And it's even better than the first.

CHAPTER 15
TANNON

On Friday night, I shut off my phone and hunkered down on the couch to watch a *Deadliest Catch* marathon. I had no intentions of going to Tucker's party, not with Liv taking Trace. That would be like volunteering to have pins shoved in my eyes. No thank you!

I found out at the game on Saturday that they never even went to Tucker's. I thought that was weird, but since I was trying to be all cool about it, I didn't ask for details. It wasn't until Evan called me Sunday night while I was cleaning out the shed for Dad that I found out the two lovebirds decided to skip the party and have pizza and ice cream by the lake instead.

Cute, right?
No, it's not cute!

Whose side are you on?

Evan also spilled the beans on the fact that they shared their first kiss and ... I guess you can say I didn't take that very well. I punched the back wall of the shed multiple times until my hand was a bloody mess.

I just can't believe it.

That kiss was supposed to be mine. I wanted to be her first. But I waited too long. Now that ship has sailed. Without me. And I'm left wondering if I was ever meant to be on that ship at all. Heck, I don't think it had anything to do with me wasting time. I don't think I was even standing on the right pier, or the right continent, or speaking the right language. She is everything to me and to her I am just a guy standing on the wrong pier, watching her sail by.

It's not fair. Life is hard enough, and loving someone shouldn't hurt this much. There should be some universal law that ensures you won't love someone with every inch of your being unless they're meant to love you back.

Yet why am I surprised?

Life has taught me that love equals pain. I loved my mother completely and she's gone—pain. I love Liv with all my heart and she's with Trace—pain.

Trace sucks.

I hate that guy.

Now I have to suffer through a miserable day of school. I slam my locker shut and turn to see Liv walking by herself through the crowded hall. And I'm surprised to see her walking alone. She has a joyful smile on her face as she swings her white cane back and forth on the floor. People usually get out of her way if they see her, but as she swings the stick, she hits the leg of a freshman boy with his back to her. He turns with a scowl.

"Hey, watch it! What the hell?" he snaps. My back stiffens. Did he seriously just tell her to watch it?

"I'm sorry," she says, embarrassed.

"Jeez," he sneers. He looks like the kind of kid who thinks he's tough and hasn't been taught differently yet.

I see Trace's head over the crowd. He's a tall, lanky guy. He sees Liv and beams, not knowing what's going on. Her head is down, self-conscious and worried, but when Trace slides his arm around her shoulder and whispers in her ear, her head pops up with a wide smile. She apologizes to the freshman again before walking off with Trace. The boys start laughing and mocking her. Swinging an invisible stick back and forth while bumping into each other. I drop my backpack next to the wall before heading over to introduce myself to the new freshman badasses.

Mr. Carlson, head of the English department, is standing outside his door and we make eye contact, his eyes widening. I just shake my head and turn my attention to the little twerps. "Hey guys," I say upbeat and friendly-like. They turn, see me, and glance at each other perplexed before returning my greeting. My forearms are wider than their thighs so I keep my cool. Mr. Carlson keeps watch of my every move. "I'm Tannon."

"We . . . uh . . . know," the kid says, staring up at me nervously. Not so tough after all. He was probably the big fish in eighth grade. Well, now he's at the bottom of the food chain.

"So since you're new here, I'm going to explain the rules. There are two major rules here at Hardy

High. One"—I hold my pointer finger up—"no bullying, and two"—next finger—"show respect. If you can't follow rule two, I won't follow rule one." I smack my hand down on the little twerp's skinny shoulder. "Got it?"

"Yy . . . yes," he stammers.

"Great! Nice meeting you all. Enjoy your day." I smile and walk away. Mr. Carlson nods with a grin and walks into his English class, pulling his right leg behind him. Rumor is he got in a bad car accident when he was younger. High school is full of rumors—everyone seems to want to direct attention to anyone but themselves.

Rumors suck!

Shit, I think I'm stuck on suck.

That really sucks.

***

The rest of the week goes by and, again, the only highlight is hockey. Now here we are, another Monday, and I walk into my basic skills English class and lay my head on the desk.

Teddy plops down in the chair next to me and groans. "I hate Mondays." He squeezes his tree trunk legs under the desk and I laugh when it rises off the floor. It looks like a kiddy tray table on his lap. He shakes his head, annoyed.

When I was a freshman, the seniors used to call this classroom the "spesh class." They would stick their heads in and yell, "Hey, spesh!" when Ms. Harper wasn't looking. I would beg her to shut the door and leave it shut, but the room was small and stuffy with no windows so she refused.

I was never scared of what the seniors could do to me physically. I was always on the big side for my age. Even though that still didn't put me in the same league as guys three years older than me, I wasn't scared of fighting. I didn't care what they did to my face. The reason I started working out was to be able to shut them up before they could even open their mouths and call me names. That's what I was scared of—their verbal taunts and others hearing them. That's how they hurt me. Calling me exactly what I believed I was but tried so hard to hide. I'd take the sticks and stones over names any day. The names always hurt me.

Billy Jones was the first to start with me. He was a big guy, a football player, with a huge ego and a hot temper, and he was obsessed with Monica D'Marco, a sophomore who had a crush on me. She broke up with him, hoping something would start up with me. I wasn't the slightest bit attracted to her and don't know why she thought I was, but that's how I got a target on my back. It started with name calling—names that I could handle—then moved on to pushes and shoves, and then graduated to elbow pops to the side of the head and thrashes against the lockers. The day Billy saw me walk into this classroom was when he found my weakness. He would mock me, saying, "Figures the male model would be dumb," or "What's two plus two?" or "I don't know my ABCs because I'm a stupid ass. I'll earn no degree."

Ridiculous and so unoriginal, but damn did it sting when others heard him.

One day he called me "spesh" in a crowded hall and I punched him in the face. He beat the crap out of me—I had a swollen eye for two weeks. After that,

Dad took me to a boxing class three nights a week and Tommy, my instructor, taught me how to defend myself against someone bigger.

Two months before school was over, I felt pretty confident in my ability to defend myself. I was stronger and faster.

The day I got my life back was the day I found myself in the gym locker room with Teddy and Evan and six other hockey teammates. Billy walked in with ten of his varsity football friends. Long story short, he started and we finished.

Oh, and I must give credit where credit is due. Teddy was what made a difference. They made the fatal mistake of going for him first. He stood his ground as if he was in goal and anyone who came at him got the worst of it. The rest of us just had to hold our own and we beat the seniors.

That's when it ended, but the names left scars on my self-esteem that have yet to fade. Billy Jones made me hate being in this classroom. He made me ashamed of who I was.

Seems my classmates feel the same about this room. I watch the five other students walk in with resentment on their drawn faces. Penny, a sweet girl who's been in this class with me since 9th grade, sits in the corner and lowers her head. David, who joined the class in 10th grade, sits down the same way. And Cathy, another veteran, is smiling big until she walks through the door. It's as if this room sucks the self-worth right out of us.

Two new students joined our class this year. Jack is a loud freshman who hides his insecurities behind humor. He's always cracking jokes about himself, as if he's trying to make light of what he believes others are thinking of him. I don't laugh at many of his jokes, even though they are kind of funny, because I know the reason behind them. And Laura is a quiet, new sophomore who walks with her head down and hardly talks. When Ms. Harper introduced them on their first day, Laura turned and Teddy and I gawked at each other after she turned back—she's beautiful. No one would know it since all she shows is the top of her head, but she is, with her big brown doe eyes and long blond hair. She has toned arms and nice legs. She's a gorgeous girl who's too insecure about her so-called lack of intelligence to look anyone in the eye. She also races out of the room before the hall gets crowded, hoping not to be seen.

Teddy has tried to get her to talk to him since the first day, but she only responds with one-word answers. Ms. Harper had her read something last week and she stumbled and stammered through the whole thing. It sounded all too familiar. I wanted to hug her.

It's not Ms. Harper that has us all hanging our heads. She's great—actually, we have a good time together once the bell rings and the halls empty—so it's not her. It's what this room represents to us. It shines a spotlight on our imperfections.

Fortunately, there's another class across the hall that has sixteen students with behavioral problems, and most of the students walking down this hall keep their eyes on that room. They are a wild group, always up to something that's gossip-worthy. Mr. Benton, their teacher, looks like he needs a drink at the end of every day—or maybe the whole bottle. The only difference between this class and that one is no one ever makes fun of the kids in that class—at least not anymore. Sophomore year, a senior stuck his head in their classroom and yelled, "Freaks!" The next day, that senior was found stuffed in his locker. Rumor was a freshman from that class did it.

Sometimes my insecurities make me feel so self-absorbed. I mean, it really could be worse. I have my health. Isn't that what I'm supposed to say? But honestly, why does my class level affect me so negatively? Why can't I let this part of me roll off my back?

"Tannon," Ms. Harper calls my name. She's a young teacher. I didn't find her attractive in the beginning, but her looks have grown on me since her personality is a ten. Now I see her as a pretty woman who will make anyone very happy. "Mr. Carlson would like to see you in his classroom. Now."

I shrug, lift my backpack, and walk to his classroom. He must want to talk about the incident in the hallway last Monday, but I don't know why. He seemed all right with how I handled it.

"Mr. Carlson?" I say, finding him sitting at his desk in the empty classroom. "You wanted to see me?"

"Hi, Tannon, come in." He gestures to the empty desk in front of his and I sit. "I had a few meetings with Ms. Harper and your child study team last week."

"Okay." I shrug, not knowing where he's going with this.

His smile reaches his dark eyes and salt and pepper hair by his temples. "The thing is, we don't believe you're working to your full potential."

"What?" I sit up, ready to argue. "I'm working my ass—butt off."

"No, we don't believe that." He shakes his head looking down at an open folder in front of him. "We don't think you're being challenged enough in your English class."

"Mr. Carlson, I—Does Ms. Harper agree?" How could she? She knows how hard I work.

"Yes, Tannon, she agrees. And so does your study team."

I shake my head in disbelief. "I can't believe this! Like I don't feel stupid enough. Now you want to challenge me more?"

"First off, Tannon, you are far from stupid. Your IQ score proves it. And second, we believe you are hiding behind your learning disability, using it as an excuse not to push yourself out of the basic level classes. Or challenging yourself to read more." I try to interject; he waves his hand. "You keep yourself at a safe, comfortable level. We believe you can do so much more and we decided to prove it to you."

Heat rushes to my face. I want to scream. Do they not understand how much English sucks for me already . . . at the basic level?

"I'm putting you in my Honors English Lit class." My eyes bug out of my head, but he goes on, "and believe me, you will be challenged in that class. Those kids are a competitive group."

I stagger. "Are you out of your mind? Are you trying to push me to an early grave or something?" I look around the room. "This is a joke, right? I'm being punked, right? Where's the camera?"

He actually laughs; I frown. "Don't be so dramatic, Tannon. You have all it takes to compete with those students. You were just never given the chance to see that. I saw something in you last week, and I pulled your team together to see if they saw it too, and they do. We believe in you." His expression is serious, sincere. "You aren't who you think you are or who you settle on being. You are smart and creative and you're a good person."

151

"No, I'm not. I'm none of those things." I look out the window. "Thanks but no thanks."

"Oh, that's funny," he says with little amusement. I scowl out the window. "You think I was asking. I'm not asking. You are going into this class and getting at least a B, and if you fail, you're not graduating."

I jump out of my seat. "You can't do that!"

"Yes, I can." He challenges me to argue more. I just stare at him while wondering if he really can do this. His expression reveals nothing. He points to the seat and I sit. "Tannon, I'm getting older. I've been a teacher for thirty-two years. I've seen kids come and go and sadly I've only had fourteen students, in all those years, who have inspired me. This year, I have two. One is in the class I'm placing you in. She has inspired me like no other, and the other is you."

I stare at him like he must be mistaking me for someone else. He goes on, "You are a passionate young man with a great deal of potential but you got stuck in the system. Sadly, it happens. Kids get a label and that label stays with them. Some need that label to help them through, get them the help they need, but others ... sometimes it hurts more than helps."

I don't say anything. He shrugs his broad shoulders. "Those students take on the label and let it define them. They give up. I see it happening to you. You need the help for math. I see it in your scores, so I'm not going to push you there, but in English I'm going to push. You're judging your IQ by how fast or well you can read. Judge it on your ability to understand the material. You do understand it."

"You can't use me as an experiment or whatever. This is my life," I say, crossing my arms and sagging into the seat.

He's silent for a moment. "Describe yourself to me in four words." He gestures for me to start. I stare, speechless. "Four words." He urges me again. I continue to stare. "You have nothing? Really?"

I shrug. "What do you want me to say?" He folds his arms over his chest. He's not exactly fit but he has the frame that shows he once was.

"Tannon, you're just a kid who took on a label." He looks down at my folder. "'Dyslexic. Slow reader. Needs modified lessons and tests. Needs verbal math tests. Needs more time given during tests. Needs test questions read to him to ease anxiety. Suffers from classroom anxiety when under pressure.'" He looks up again. "That's you?"

I shrug, embarrassed about the anxiety part. "Guess so."

"So, do you need to have your art lessons modified?"

"No."

"How 'bout . . ." He thinks a moment. "Does your hockey coach modify your drills so you can understand them?"

"No!" I roll my eyes, insulted.

He shrugs. "But it says here you need lessons modified?"

"That stuff comes easy to me." I groan, sitting back in the chair.

"Really, why?"

"Because," I bite out, and then think of my answer. Looking down, I say, "It just does."

"They interest you?"

"Yeah."

"Exactly." He shakes his head with a big grin.

I stare, confused. "What are you getting at?"

"Basic English doesn't interest you. You don't put your heart into things that don't interest you. You've had no lower than a 97% average in every level of Art History all three years of high school, Tannon. Art History is no easy subject, but it interests you." He looks back at my folder. "You like Greek mythology?"

"I guess."

"You got a B in Social Studies that marking period. Also last year when they were teaching the Trojan War you got a B. Though, you didn't seem to like American History." He raises a brow, looking up again. I got a D that marking period. He goes on, "This is not the folder of a student incapable of learning. This is a folder of a student who succeeds in areas of interest. I understand it doesn't come easy for you. You have to apply yourself and you seem to only do so when you are challenged with interesting subject matter. Basic English is boring. I'd rather listen to nails on a chalkboard myself."

I laugh. "I guess my D proves I feel the same."

His eyebrows furrow. "Why don't you let me teach you?" he offers. "I bet you will find my lessons interesting. I bet my *job* you will succeed."

My eyes widen. "Don't put that on me."

"Oh, it's on you," he states firmly. "If you don't pass my class fair and square, no favors, I will retire."

"You are crazy, aren't you?" I shake my head with disbelief.

"I don't think so. I think this is one of the sanest things I've ever done."

"Then you've done some seriously insane things," I retort.

"If I let you graduate without even trying to show you what you are capable of, then what kind of teacher am I?"

"A good one," I mutter.

"I'm going to pretend I didn't hear that," he says.

"Why can't you just give Ms. Harper your book and I can do the lessons in her class?" I ask, wanting to stay where I feel comfortable. No matter how much I hate that classroom, I am comfortable there. I belong there.

He shakes his head, denying my request. "Ms. Harper is a great teacher, but the students won't challenge you. You need to be around peers that pull you to another level."

"I know what you ask that class to do. Read frickin' Shakespeare and poetry out loud. There is no way. Do you know what happens to me when I have to read out loud?"

"Tannon"—he holds up my folder—"it's all here . . ."

"No, it's here," I point at my chest. "You don't get it. I study for hours but when a test is placed in front of me, my mind goes blank. Anxiety takes over. All the words mush together. I forget how to spell words as little as 'had' or 'has.' And reading out loud. Forget it. I have actual panic attacks in classrooms with kids that read like me or worse. I heat up and shake. It's not pretty," I stress. "You want me to be in a class full of students that zip through *War and Peace* like they're reading 'See Jane Hop?' I'm having anxiety just thinking about it." I grab my head, shocked we are even talking about this crazy idea.

"I understand your fears—"

"They aren't fears. It's my reality. Everything on a page looks ten times worse when I'm under pressure. Tests. Reading out loud. I stumble on words like 'the' when I read out loud. I'm seventeen years old and still have to stop and think which way is left or right. I see 'b' as 'd' and 'P' as '9'. Everything's a mess in my head. I appreciate your confidence in me, but I can't do it."

"Tannon, you won't have to read out loud. Just, on occasion, stuff you have written yourself. Besides that, I promise I will never call on you to read from a book. This is about helping you, not hurting you," he stresses. "You owe it to yourself to try."

"No, I don't. This is my last year and then I'm done and I'll never look back."

"You will always look back. You will always regret the time you had a chance to show you can do it and you didn't." He stands and hobbles to the window. "Tannon, we are given moments to love ourselves and if we don't take them, they will haunt us forever. You struggle academically. I struggle physically. My leg ..." He pauses, looking unsure if he should confide in me. "I got into a car accident with friends when I was eighteen. I was a swimmer, had a promising future, coach saw Olympics potential in me—I was that good. After the accident, I fell into self-pity. I avoided the water even though my doctors told me it was the best thing for my leg, told me I would be able to compete again if I worked hard. I never got back in the water."

"I'm sorry."

"Me too. That's what I'm trying to tell you. I had a chance to show myself I was worth the hard work, the effort, but I didn't take it. I foolishly thought if I couldn't get back to the Olympics level in time, what was the point? My ego got in the way, my fears took over, and they kept me from my passion. To this day, I have yet to swim. Your ego is getting in the way of this moment, Tannon." He stares down at the parking lot below the building. "The ego is a funny thing. It believes it's protecting you, keeping you safe, but really it's hurting you. Safe is no way to live."

I sit back and ponder all he's said. "Mr. Carlson," I say, and he turns at the window to look at me. "Why honors?"

He grins. "Because it's the highest level there is to put you in. Because it scares the—the you-know-what out of you. Because you wouldn't realize how much we all believe in you if we just raised you up one level." He leans against the sill. "And because I'm not going to let a young man who sticks up for my favorite student in all my years of teaching, and makes up school rules about bullying and respect, graduate from this school thinking he was anything but capable. That guy deserves to leave here knowing he can pass Honors English."

"What if I don't? What will I think of myself then?" I ask.

His head turns to the side and he frowns. "You will know you tried. You took a chance on you. And that's more than I can say for myself."

I look down at the desk and think of what this all means. I can fail miserably, I can completely embarrass myself, but I can also maybe, actually pass. Wouldn't that be something? If my mom were here, she would tell me to take this challenge on. "Okay. I'll try." The words come out before I realize I even made a decision. He smiles and I shrug. "But your job is off the table. I have something else you can offer."

"Ohh-kaay," he says suspiciously and waits for my proposal.

"If I get a B, then you are getting into the water with me. And we don't get out until we swim ten laps. That is the only way I will face this fear. You have to promise to face yours."

He looks back out the window. And then he starts to laugh. "You are a crafty young man."

"I think it's only fair," I counter.

"Okay." He moves to me. "You have yourself a deal. You give me a hundred percent effort and I'll get in the water."

"Ten laps," I challenge. "Not all at once, but before we quit."

He shakes his head with a grin. "I'm an old man now, TK."

"They say it's like riding a bike."

"All right. You're on! But let's compromise with five laps." We shake on it, although I already know, if this happens, I'm pushing those other laps out of him. He hands me my new schedule. I study it as I walk out.

Never in my life would I ever have thought I'd see "Honors" written in the subject column on *my* class schedule. I look up and smile. I can't help it. I smile so damn wide I feel it hit my ears. And then I start laughing.

This is insane! He is insane!

I wish I could show Mom. She'd do backflips over this.

I look down at the schedule again. The rest of my classes are the same. Some of the times moved, but my eyes can't stop looking at "Honors" fourth period. The joy over that beats the fear—for now. The bell rings and I find Evan in the hall. I show him the schedule and he stares, perplexed, until spotting the change. His eyes dart up to mine and his mouth opens wide.

"Dude, that's my class!"

"I know."

"Dude, is this for real?" he asks. I nod.

"Dude, this is awesome!"

"I know," I repeat, grinning.

"Dude, I'm so happy for you." He smacks my back hard then shakes his head. "How many times did I call you 'dude'?"

"I think it was four, dude."

He laughs and smacks my shoulder. "How did this happen?" he asks as we walk through the crowded hall.

"Mr. Carlson doesn't think I'm being challenged enough."

"I love that guy," he says, meaning it.

"Yeah, now I do too," I admit.

No teacher has ever believed in me like this. He even put his job on the table. I hope I can deliver. I really want to see him get in the water.

PART 2: WINTER

CHAPTER 16
TANNON

The first marking period in Mr. Carlson's honors class ended and I got a D. He wasn't too upset about it, but I was. He said I still had time to show my B. I hold onto hope. His lessons are interesting; he's a really good teacher. I enjoy listening to him talk. He teaches with such passion, it's hard not to get swept up into it.

There were a few times he asked me to stay after class and read him my test answers because my writing was unreadable. I would have to translate my mixed up letters and flip-flopped words, but he always said the content of my writing was smart.

There's no denying his class is hard. The other students don't seem to think it, so I keep my struggles to myself.

Liv is in my class, along with Trace, and it's hard to see the happy couple together every day. They sit next to each other, and unfortunately, I sit a few rows behind them. Every now and then Trace reaches over to tuck a hair behind Liv's ear or whisper something that makes her laugh. For some cruel reason, I always catch their shared moments. Besides the torture show, I enjoy being in the class. It's done a great deal for my self-esteem, although it is demanding work. Long hours of homework. Evan says it doesn't take *him* long—funny, *I* seem to stare at the book for at least two hours a night. Thank the good Lord Mr. Carlson doesn't believe in weekend homework. Between hockey practices, games, chores around the house, and homework for other classes, I hardly have time to breathe.

Electives just changed for the new marking period and now I'm taking cooking. The bell rings just as I walk into class. The room is divided into stations with cooktops and two stools at each. All the stools are taken except for one and its right next to Liv. I sit next to her and say hi. Mrs. Wilson shuts the door and announces that the seat we're in will be our seat for the quarter. I hear classmates groan and complain about being stuck with the person sitting next to them. I'm not too happy about my partner either, but not for the same reasons as my classmates. I actually like my partner. Love. I love my partner. And there's the reason for my unhappiness. I don't have the strength to be this close to Liv. I've been surviving her relationship with Trace by staying away and now I can't avoid her. How am I going to make it through this class having to talk to her every day and be next to her in this really close space, smelling her sweet smell and hearing her sweet voice?

Shoot me now.

"All right, settle down," Mrs. Wilson demands. She's one grumpy woman. "Your grade will reflect three things: food prepared in class, a final for which you and your partner will cook a meal for the whole class, and there will also be a written test. The test is the only part you will be graded separately on. You need to pick a theme for the final meal. Whether it be Italian, American, German, Mexican, and so on—it's entirely up to you. But it must be a healthy, well-balanced, four-course meal, enough to feed everyone, and if the class can't stomach it, then you get a zero. You better learn how to work well together quickly. You have to plan out your meal and create your grocery list for your first meal and also your final meal before the bell rings."

She passes out a sheet with check boxes next to what looks like a menu. "Read through this menu. Select a soup, salad, main course, and dessert from the list provided for your first meal. You can make your own menu for your final. No lobster or filet mignon, please. Think it through because once you hand this in, you don't get to change it. And don't copy each other. I don't want fourteen kids making the same thing. Now get picking," she says, then sits at her desk and turns on her computer.

The room fills with chatter as the partners start arguing over what they want to make. I turn my stool to face Liv. She has on a navy blue sweater and a pair of amazingly fitted jeans with her cute blue Converse sneakers. Her hair is down today—I love it down—parted in the middle, long and shiny, reaching the middle of her back. Her lips shine with

163

her strawberry lip gloss and I grimace—that damn lip gloss is going to be the death of me. Of course, she has her sunglasses on.

A sweet smile grows on her face. "Well, partner," she says with a bad Texan accent. "What are our choices?"

I look down at the paper and all the words start to blend together. Then my skin heats and the paper starts to shake from my trembling hands.

Oh my God, not now. Please.

I look up and she's facing me, patiently waiting for me to start reading off the list. I look back down. My anxiety triples. It's just food. A long food list. I put the paper down on the counter and place my fingers to my temples.

Breathe, you idiot. You can do this. Breathe and focus. You got this.

I pick up the paper and stare until the words start to come into focus. This is what happens when I'm put under pressure to read out loud. It doesn't matter if I see the words right or not, my anxiety creeps in and then all the words blur together. My fear of embarrassment takes hold and makes everything worse.

The rest of the class is already in heated arguments with their partners and I haven't even read the first item. I breathe deeply and cover the page with my hand, exposing one word at a time, and I start to read off the list slowly. It's a list, so I can get away with slow. I stumble a few times, skip some of the words I can't spit out, and we make our decisions with no argument. Chicken noodle soup, arugula salad, flank steak with grilled asparagus, and oatmeal cookies. Simple as that. Everyone else is still arguing over appetizers while Liv and I start discussing our final test meal.

"I can make chicken piccata," she offers, her voice timid as if she's worried I won't believe her. One thing I know for sure is Liv can do a helluva lot more than most give her credit for. "I can ask my mom for her recipe. I just need you to help me measure things. And maybe we can make tortellini soup."

"Yeah, that sounds good," I say. "My mom used to make an unbelievable tiramisu. So simple, but so frickin' good."

"That sounds amazing!" She sighs. She's so darn sweet. "And maybe we can do a tomato and mozzarella salad."

"Sounds good to me."

"Now we just need a side for the main course."

I pick up my phone and search Italian side dishes. I drool over the first picture that comes up. "What about parmesan roasted potatoes?"

"Yum!" She claps. "Awesome. So we're set, now what?"

"We sleep." I lay my arm on the counter and rest my head on it, positioning myself to stare at her profile. She leans forward and rests her chin on her stacked hands. Her hair lies over her shoulders like a velvet curtain. Her chest presses against the counter's edge.

Damn, there is no way I'll survive this class.

A frown appears on her sweet face and I watch it deepen. She pivots her chin to face me. "Tannon, do you regret sitting next to me? I'll pull my weight. I do pretty well in the kitchen."

"What? Of course not," I say.

"It's just you seemed so hesitant to get started."

I almost laugh. She thinks my fighting back an anxiety attack was just me contemplating if I want her as a partner? *Wow, I dodged that bullet.* "I have no regrets, Liv. I consider myself lucky."

"Oh my God!" Michelle bellows from behind us. "Are you frickin' kidding me? Mrs. Wilson!" she cries out. "Can you please tell Nick that German potato salad has no business being on a Mexican menu?"

"See?" I whisper. "I'm lucky. We make a great pair."

Liv smiles, resting her cheek on her hand. Her glasses tilt and I slowly pull them off. Her eyes are closed and I admire how her long dark lashes lie on the top of her cheeks. There isn't a stitch of makeup on her face. Her complexion is so even, except for a little red pimple on the side of her forehead. I used to get pimples from my hockey helmet—sweating in that darn thing did a number on my skin—but I learned to take the time to wipe the inside down after every use and I've been clean and clear for a year now. I've seen Liv with one or two pimples every now and then, but she seems to just leave them alone and they go away quickly. So many girls cake a pound of makeup over a pimple and it just makes it even more noticeable than before. They should take a cue from Liv and just leave it alone.

"Tannon?" she whispers.

"Yeah?"

"Are your eyes open?"

I grin. "Yes."

"What are you looking at?" she asks. We are inches from each other and I know she senses my eyes on her.

"You."

One hand slides from under her cheek to cover her face. I pull it away, laughing. "Don't stare," she says, fighting to get her hand back.

"Why?"

"It makes me self-conscious," she utters.

I'm suddenly melancholy. She has no idea how beautiful she is to me. "You have nothing to be self-conscious about."

She reaches over and places her hand on my cheek. The room buzzes with voices talking over one another yet it feels like we're all alone. "Did you just get a buzz?" she asks, running her fingers along the side of my head.

I buzzed around my head with a one clip yesterday, leaving the top a mess so I can faux hawk it when I want. I wasn't in the mood today.

"Did it myself."

"I like it."

Good.

Her fingers get lost in the mess up top just as the bell rings, I curse under my breath. Slowly, she slides her hand out of my hair and reaches down to grab her backpack. I watch her move so effortlessly, so gracefully, so aware. She walks around the counter and turns to say goodbye. Cat calls her from the door and she's gone.

This is going to be a rough marking period, English Lit and now this. There's no avoiding her.

***

Two periods go by and I finally have art class. My favorite class with my favorite teacher, Ms. Cox.

She's young and kind of hot, but mostly she's really cool.

She stands by the door with an eager smile. "Mr. Tenley, Mr. Nichols, and I are joining forces for one marking period," she starts while everyone takes out their sketch pads. "We are asking our advanced classes to be a part of this."

She talks as I burn a hole in the back of Trace's head. He sits three rows in front of me. Why is he always in front of me? Does he do it on purpose to ensure I'm always reminded of him and what he has?

Nah. He doesn't even know I like her. Does he?

Either way, he's still with Liv. Still gets to hold her, kiss her, and I can't even fathom what else. I wish I really did hate him. Truth is, I don't. I don't hate him. He's actually a really good guy. I watch him with his friends—yes, I've turned into a stalker—and they all seem to laugh when he's near. Liv does too, so I'm guessing he's funny.

Isn't that great?

Funny and smart.

So perfect!

Okay, I hate him.

"It's for a good cause," Ms. Cox continues. "A charity fundraiser that I've been working on and I really need your help. Mr. Tenley's music class has volunteered, as well as Mr. Nichols's performing arts class. So if you would please rise and walk across the hall into music, we will all explain the charity and how you'll be graded."

I follow the class into the music room across the hall and, what do you know, there's Liv front and center.

Seriously?

Why is the universe being so cruel?

Trace takes a seat next to her. There are a few open seats in the large room, but I choose to stand in the back. "All right, now this is the plan," Ms. Cox says, and I have to smile at how excited she is about this plan of hers. "We are going to have a charity dinner before the end of the semester. I'm asking my students to donate one piece to be auctioned off at the dinner, whether it be a painting, sculpture, or drawing, and Mr. Tenley is asking his students to play at the dinner, and Mr. Nichols's students will be performing. You will be graded on your—well, really all you have to do is show up with a smile on your faces and your art piece or musical instrument or lines prepared and you get an A."

"That simple," Mr. Tenley adds.

He's young like Ms. Cox and I don't see a wedding ring on his finger. He looks like a classic rock lover, even though he wears a shirt and tie every day. I have a feeling he hates it. I picture him in jeans and rock band T-shirts. He seems like a cool guy. His eyes light up whenever he looks at Ms. Cox so I'm assuming it didn't take much convincing on her part to get him to help her cause.

"You all get to come to the dinner and eat for free. The rest of the tables will be filled with some very influential people in the art world, so donate your best work and perform your best. Of course, you can opt out. We are asking you to help—volunteer—but if you decide not to, then you will be graded on the work you do in class. It's entirely up to you."

Liv raises her hand. "Yes, Liv," Mr. Tenley says. He looks at her warmly, affectionately. She's been with him since freshman year and I can see in his smile he cares a great deal about her.

"Sorry, what was the charity again?" she asks.

Ms. Cox throws her hands in the air. "Oh, I can't believe I forgot to say! It's called New Jersey Arts for All and the money raised will go to help keep the arts in underprivileged schools. This is a statewide benefit. Art departments in 308 schools are participating. Everyone's district is having their own banquets. I think we're going to raise a great deal of money and help a lot of schools in the state to keep their art departments."

"There is one more way you can help," Mr. Nichols says, stepping forward. He's a short guy with an awful comb over, but he's always smiling—he has good teeth. "The talent show will be in a few weeks and the money for the tickets will be donated to NJAFA. The only thing is, not many students go to the talent show, so we are asking if you would come. It would help even more if you would enter the show and persuade your friends to either do it with you or come watch. If you say yes to performing, then we will help in any way we can."

I watch the faces of most of my art classmates grimace and frown. We aren't performers. We hide behind canvases and sketch pads. We don't stand on a stage and act talented. Many of my fellow classmates wear black and haven't said more than two words to me in three years. I can't wait to see how many volunteer for this.

I won't be. I don't have a talent. Well, I guess maybe checking my opponents against the boards in hockey is a talent. I start to smile at the thought.

"Mr. Keaton," Ms. Cox calls my name. "You look very eager. I knew I could count on you."

I stand still, stunned. I'm not eager; I'm amused. There's a difference. I stare at her wide-eyed and shake my head vigorously.

She smiles that great smile of hers and says, "Thank you." I'm left speechless.

Oh my God, are you kidding me? Is this really happening? When did I lose total control of every aspect of my life?

Donating a painting I can do. Hell, I'll donate twenty, but get on a stage in the talent show?

No frickin' way!

The bell rings and I'm too stunned to move. I watch Trace walk out with his arm around Liv's shoulder. He's whispering in her ear and she's laughing loudly. Yeah, I hate him. I do. I. Hate. Him. He has my girl and he's making her laugh while I sit in hell.

Hate.

Hate.

Hate.

Ms. Cox appears in my line of vision with a gigantic grin. "Oh, Tannon, I'm so glad you're on board with this. With you in the talent show the whole school is sure to show." Suddenly she's grabbing both my arms firmly. I don't even know what's happening. "What are you going to do?"

"I ... uh ..." *What? Nothing. I'm going to do nothing.*

"Sing? Do you sing?" she asks.

Huh? No! I don't sing!

She squeezes my arms. "Oh, I can't wait to hear you."

Hear me what?

What the hell is happening here?

"Maybe someone from the music department can accompany you by playing a guitar or piano. It sounds nicer than using a recording." She lets go of my arms and steps back. I watch tears form in her eyes. "I can't thank you enough, Tannon. You have such a huge heart."

Really? Well that heart is pounding abnormally in my chest. I think that heart is having an attack. I need medical assistance. I think I'm going to hyperventilate. *What the hell is going on this year?* I'm a senior and Mr. Carlson and now Ms. Cox want to challenge me. Why? I don't need challenging, I just want out!

I can't find the words to ask for help. I'm just standing here with a terrified expression on my face. I feel it. I know I look terrified and yet she looks at me as if I'm delighted to stand in front of the whole school and sing.

Me.

Sing.

I don't sing. I even stop myself in the shower, it's that bad. But how do I disappoint her now? She's worked so hard on this and she's always been there for me. Though she will regret wanting to hear me sing when she hears the screeches-of-the-dead come out of my mouth. I guess it won't matter to her then since the money will already have been donated.

Wait, that's all that matters, right?

I just have to get the people there and then maybe I can fake laryngitis or actually have a real heart attack and no one will have to suffer—but me.

Yeah, this sucks!

CHAPTER 17
LIV

I wake up to a snow day. School is canceled and I'm stuck home. I'm not a big fan of snow. I enjoyed it when I was younger. I have fond memories of playing in the cold, crunchy, sometimes fluffy blanket covering the ground, making snow angels, and letting the flakes fall on my face and tongue. I would sit on the front of the sled as Mom sat behind me, legs wrapped around my waist, shrieking as we raced down a hill, the cold wind at my face and the sharp sting of snow on my skin. I remember the exhilaration, the joy, the freedom, the wonder, and the sheer bliss of it all.

But I haven't done that in a long time. Maybe that's why I'm not a fan of snow. I don't play in it anymore.

I decide right here and now that I want to go sledding. I call Trace and ask if he'll take me. He laughs out a very quick, very enthusiastic "yes," and picks me up twenty minutes later. We drive to the big hill behind the middle school where kids are shouting and yelping with delight as they slide down the hill. Trace takes my hand and we trek up the slope.

We position ourselves on the sled and he kisses my cheek. "You ready?"

"Yes!" I squeal. And he gives us a big push.

We flash down the hill, adrenaline racing through me. I smile and laugh as we hit a bump and bounce against the sled. He steers us, yelling for kids to get out of the way. And he doesn't go slowly; he's not being overly cautious. We're just two kids on a sled being wild.

I love him for it.

The wind at my face threatens to take my hat, but I don't dare let go of the sled. Using his legs against my sides, he angles me to the right. I'm gleeful as we hit another bump and catch some air. We bounce down on the sled and then he curses and suddenly we are tumbling off the sled and sliding to a stop. He lands on top of me. "Whoa! Are you okay?"

I pull my hat down on my head and laugh. "Yes. Yes. I'm great!"

Suddenly his cold lips are on mine. And they feel so good. The kiss feels different—his lips are usually warm—but I do like this cool, almost hard kiss given by frozen lips. "You wanna go again?"

"Yes! At least ten more times."

He pulls me to my feet and we trek back up the hill. Kids congratulate us on our awesome jump as we walk by. We make twelve more trips up and down the hill. I haven't smiled this much in months, and I'm utterly exhausted and completely elated. After, he takes me to Millie's Coffee House in town and we drink hot chocolate and share a warm cookie.

"That was a good time. I haven't done that in years," he says, sitting across from me at the small square table. Adele plays in the background and the smell of coffee and chocolate fills my nose. Content and blissful, I thank him with a huge smile on my face. He thanks me in return.

"Liv?"

"Yeah?"

"You look adorable with your red nose."

I rub my cold nose, giggling giddily. The big pom-pom at the top of my knit hat wobbles as I do. I feel like a little kid, youthful and alive. "I feel good."

His finger slides down the slope of my nose. "You look beautiful."

Truth is, I feel beautiful. I truly do, and I think it's because I'm so happy. "You wanna go to my house, maybe listen to music?" he asks.

"Yes," I answer quickly. "I do." I want to go to his house and lie next to him on his bed and listen to music and take a nap in his arms. Only first, I want to kiss him again and when he returns from throwing out our cups, I reach out to find his coat and pull him down to kiss his chocolaty lips.

I sigh.

Does it get any better?

He smiles against my mouth. "God, I love snow days," he says, taking my hand.

***

175

We walk into his empty house—his parents are at work—and up to his room. We're alone and this is the first time that's ever happened. I take off all my snow gear and walk to the bathroom. The layout of his house is similar to mine. I return and sit on his bed, and my heart begins to race. The mattress pops me up and down as he gets comfortable. I turn and lie next to him, facing the ceiling like a stiff board.

Oh my gosh, this is awkward.

He turns to face me, his fingers comb through my hair. "You can breathe. I'm not going to try anything."

I'm suddenly disenchanted. "Why?" The word just slips out and he huffs a laugh.

"Do you want me to?" His voice rises a few octaves and he swallows loudly.

"I . . . I don't know. I just hope you want to," I admit and cringe.

"Liv," he turns my head to him. "You don't know how bad I want to, but you just seem nervous. What if we just take it slow? Draw a line." His hand cuts across my midsection.

"All right." Above the belt. I can handle that. My lips find his and we melt into a kiss.

We kiss for a long time and his hands stay at my face. Eventually, he moves to lay his chest on top of mine, his legs long against my side. His lips move down along my jaw. I tilt my head back and he moves to my neck, causing me goose bumps. A daring hand slides down my sweater and slowly under. I suck in a sharp breath. The next thing I feel is his smooth hand sliding up my stomach. His hand cups over my bra and I gasp, pushing it down.

"I'm sorry," he says.

"I just need a minute," I explain, and he thoughtfully fixes my sweater back into place, kisses my cheek, and lies beside me again.

I feel him adjust his position and I turn to my side, facing him. A daring hand slides over his tapered waist and I find the hem of his shirt. Sliding underneath, I follow his narrow waist up to his chest. His skin is so smooth. He's slimmer than me, which is a bit disconcerting, but his body is tight and toned. He's on the track team so he stays active. He just doesn't have the build that will ever have bulky muscles. Which is fine.

He turns his head to kiss my lips. I kiss back and take over. Maybe if I lead I won't be so nervous. My lips trail down his jaw and over his taunt neck. Kissing him like this feels natural. And I think I'm good at it. His hands get lost in my hair and I slide on top of him. A loud moan escapes him and he swiftly pushes me off his lower half. At first I worry I did something wrong, but then quickly figure out what he's trying to hide from me. And I'll admit, his body's reaction to our kiss scares me, but it also leaves me curious. Very curious. Only, I know I'm not ready for that yet and I go back to kissing him.

I love kissing him.

We make out like the horny teenagers we are and then lie wrapped in each other's arms, legs tangled. I listen to his shallow breaths and feel the beat of his heart return to normal, and the next thing I know we're waking up. I'm not sure how long we slept. He kisses the top of my head and gets up to get us water and peanut butter and jelly sandwiches. We eat and drink and I lie against his chest as he reads *Macbeth*, our assigned reading in English. He's a fast reader, emphasizes the right words, and even changes his voice for different characters. He doesn't stumble on the Shakespearian language as I do. His reading makes the story come to life in my mind.

Besides lying on his chest, we don't do anything physical the rest of the time we're together. I fear things may have changed between us—I thought I was ready to take another step but I wasn't—but to my relief, we talk easily as he drives me home, he gives me a sweet kiss goodbye, and just like that we fall back into our comfortable relationship. No awkwardness. Nothing has changed. I go to sleep with a huge smile on my face as thoughts of our day dance dreamily through my mind.

***

Mom wakes me in the morning. The snow subsides and the streets are clear enough for school to be open. One day off and I can't seem to get back into the swing of things. I walk the empty hallway during third period. My white cane leads me back to class from the bathroom. I didn't even have to go. I was just looking to get out of class. I had so much fun yesterday and wish to live the whole day over again.

The murmurs of students and teachers drift from under closed classroom doors, reminding me where I am. There's an echo of footsteps coming my way and I shift to the side of the hall so as not to be in anyone's path. I smile and say hello as they walk by, receiving a quick hello back.

My cane slides across the smooth floor in front of me. It's all clear until, out of nowhere, my head hits against a hard, pointy surface. I stumble back, disoriented and dizzy, and reach my hand up, feeling the door of a top locker swinging. I groan with pain and disappointment. I usually never walk so close to the lockers for this reason. Touching the top of my head, right at the hairline, I feel wetness. The bell rings and students start to crowd the hall.

Great...

"Liv." I hear Mr. Tenley's voice. "Are you all right?" He takes my shoulders, turning me to face him, and when I lift my head up, he gasps. Warm blood drips down over my left eyelid.

"The locker was open."

"Oh, Liv, I'm sorry," he says, then hastily ushers me through the hall, snapping at students to make way, until a door creaks open and I smell the sterile scent of the nurse's office. "Helen," Mr. Tenley says. "Liv hit her head and she's bleeding."

Chair legs squeaking across the floor echo off the walls and Nurse Helen's cold hands are on me in seconds. "Sit, Liv. What happened?"

"A top locker was open."

She gently moves my hair to reveal my wound and then I can actually sense her glance back at Mr. Tenley. It must be bad. Suddenly, a wet pad pushes against the cut. "You're going to need a few stitches, sweetheart."

"Really?" I ask. It doesn't feel that bad; I'm just really dizzy. "Is it bleeding badly?"

She lifts the gauze off and instructs Mr. Tenley to get more. "Yes. It looks like you walked right into the metal corner."

It felt like that too. All of a sudden the pain is excruciating; my head starts to throb. I lie back on the hard plastic-covered cot and groan. Funny how pain affects you most after you are told how bad the wound is.

"Liv, are you all right? Do you need water?" Mr. Tenley asks, full of concern.

"I just need to lie here."

"Please call her mother. Number's in the computer under contacts," Nurse Helen asks of Mr. Tenley.

"My backpack?" I say. I must've dropped it when dealing with my head. "My computer's in it."

"I'll have someone bring it down." Mr. Tenley dials a number and he asks for someone to find my bag in the hall and bring it to the nurse's office. He pushes a few more buttons and his deep voice becomes soft and calm as he talks to my mom.

A few minutes later the door swings open and someone races to the cot and sits next to my side. The cot shifts from the new weight and my body rolls with it. Nurse Helen snaps in appall as the cot wobbles on weak legs. A wide palm brushes up my arm. "What happened, Liv?" Tannon asks.

"I walked into an open top locker," I say.

He curses under his breath and Nurse Helen reprimands him again. For some reason, the sound of his voice causes my emotions to get the better of me and I start to cry. I don't even know why. The pain has subsided since the initial shock. Maybe I'm embarrassed. Maybe the stitches scare me. Not sure why, I've gotten them before.

His hands slide under my shoulders and he pulls me up into a tight hug. Nurse Helen protests, barking about my wound and how inappropriate his handling me is, as if I was naked and he was groping me.

Wow, she's old fashioned.

Mr. Tenley steps in, thanks Tannon for bringing my bag, and instructs him to go back to class.

Tannon ignores them both. Laying me back down, with his head next to my ear, he whispers, "Don't cry. You're okay, Boo."

Nurse Helen pushes him; we rock and the cot squeaks in protest. "Mr. Keaton! Get your hands off of her."

"Okay, jeez, I'm just comforting her."

"You don't manhandle a young lady. Now get out!"

"Let's go, Tannon," Mr. Tenley orders.

He brushes a tear from my cheek before standing. "I'll call you later to see how you're doing. Your bag is by your feet." He walks out slowly. I wish he'd come back and hold me again. I felt safe in his arms and now I feel alone.

Mom races in fifteen minutes later. Her cold hands grab mine. Nurse Helen lifts the gauze to show her my cut. Mr. Tenley went back to class a few minutes ago and Nurse Helen has changed the gauze three times since. "It's not clotting so you should get her to the hospital for stitches."

"C'mon, sweetheart," Mom says, helping me to my feet. "Thank you," she offers to Nurse Helen and we walk into the hall. "We'll get you stitched up, honey," Mom says, squeezing my arm.

"Liv, wait up!" Tannon calls from my left. I turn. His sneakers screech against the floor as he rushes to me. "How you doin'?" his hand grazes mine, "Hi, Mrs. Sullivan."

"Hi, Tannon."

"Tan, why aren't you in class?" I ask, surprised he's waiting for me.

He taps my arm. "I needed to make sure you were okay. Nurse Ratched in there was ready to chop my head off," he says, huffing.

I laugh. "She was a tad ridiculous. But I'm okay."

"Okay. Good. I'll call you later."

"Okay."

"Thanks, Tannon," Mom says as he's walking away.

Mom and I walk out of the school and she helps me into the car. After getting in herself, she blasts the heat. I hold the gauze at my head and turn to face the window, hating that this happened, hating what's to come.

Hating . . .

Just hating.

CHAPTER 18
TANNON

The day dragged on forever. I couldn't wait to get home and call Liv. I had to get through hockey practice first, though, and that was a long, grueling experience. I normally enjoy practice, but not tonight. I couldn't stop seeing Liv's tears roll down her soft cheeks. She looked worried and it shocked me. She's too tough to cry over stitches.

I jump in and out of the shower as quickly as possible. Standing in a towel, I grab my cell and finally make the call.

"Hi, Tannon," Liv answers.

"Hey, how you doin'?" I ask, sitting at my desk chair. A large canvas painting of her hangs over my desk and I stare at her lips—lips I painted—as we talk. "I was thinking of you all day."

"I'm fine. Just six stitches up at my hair line," she says with a lighthearted laugh. "No biggie."

I rub my hand over my wet head and mess up the top before it dries flat. "Battle wounds to tell the grandkids," I tease.

"Exactly," she says. "Listen, thanks for calling, Tannon. Trace is here and he's just leaving. Can I talk to you tomorrow?"

My heart sinks in my chest. "Yeah, sure. No problem. Tell him I say hi." I hit end and chuck the phone on my bed. "'Tell him I say hi,'" I mock. "How 'bout tell him to jump off an effin' cliff."

The thought of him being there comforting her guts me completely. I spin to find something else to throw. My reflection in the hutch mirror catches my eye and I turn to stare at myself. How can I possibly win against Harvard Boy? She likes how he thinks. He isn't jaded. And for as smart as he is, he's easy to be around. It's almost like he hides his genius and tries to act average, but we all know he has never had to study a day in his life. He was offered the opportunity to skip sophomore year but for some reason he declined. Maybe he didn't want to rush life. Maybe it was to avoid social awkwardness. He seems to have a few good friends—maybe he didn't want to leave them? Who knows?

All I do know is that I can't compete.

He has me beat in every way. Every way that matters to her anyway.

He wins.

I turn from the face of disgust that looks back at me and see the blank canvas on my easel. It's for my grand gesture to Liv but I haven't even started it yet. I'm not sure if I ever will. I pull on sweatpants and lower the canvas to replace it with a larger one. I have to start my donation painting for Ms. Cox. I have no idea what I'm going to paint. With the mood I'm in, it might not be salable. My foot hooks the leg of my chair and I pull it behind me as I pick a thin paintbrush. Sitting, I squeeze black paint onto my palette.

Let's see what gutted creates.

***

I'm sitting in English class with my head on the desk. Mr. Carlson recently changed our seats. Now Liv is next to me on the right and Trace is in front of me, so I keep my head to the left and stare out the window. Mr. Carlson calls my name and I turn my head slowly. "You're up," he says.

"For what?" I ask, puzzled.

"We're reading our poems today and you're first," he explains, moving in front of his desk and leaning against it, holding out my paper with a pleased grin.

"I don't want to read it," I state. What the hell? I thought we had a deal. I glare at him and he shakes his head.

"Your words." He rustles the paper.

Crap, he did say I'd have to read things I wrote.

"C'mon, don't be shy. It's one of my favorites in the class."

"I—you read it," I basically beg in front of everyone.

"No, let's go." His happy-go-lucky demeanor is running dry.

I stand and reluctantly walk to take my paper from him. I don't know how I missed the great big detail that these poems must be read aloud in class. I

185

would've written something entirely different if I had known. Something that was three words or less. I roll my head on my shoulders and huff out a breath. *These are your words,* I tell myself. *You read them a million times after writing them to ensure they were poem-worthy. You're going to do fine.*

I start out in a whisper and he stops me. "Louder please."

"'Highway of Regret.'" I read the title and glance at Evan. He's sleeping on his desk. I wish Liv was too. I don't look, but I know she's wide awake. I continue.

I stand on a highway of regret.
Behind me lurks my past mistakes,
before me, my future wrongs.
So I turn left and run.

I take a long breath and glance at Mr. Carlson, begging him with my eyes to let me stop. My hands are shaking, my cheeks heated, my voice cracking—I'm about to pass out. He shakes his head and gestures with his hand to keep it rolling. I rub my neck and see Evan staring at me, awake now. I shrug, take a calming breath, and look back down.

I stop hiding behind all the wrong moves of my past
and all the awaiting mistakes of my future
and I run. I run to her.
She is all that makes sense, all I desire.
And I hope that when she sees me with my guard down,
she will wipe away my past and clear my future.
She will love me.

So I drop my armor.

I stood on a highway of regret and
now . . . Now, I stand before her, real and bare.
I stand before my soul's mate,
before my healer, before my peace.
I stood on a highway of regret
and now . . . Now, I hold her.
I hold her in my arms.
I feel her melt into my thick skin,
filling my gutted heart.
Dancing with my soul.

I stood on a highway of regret,
but wait . . . wait.
I'm still here, with empty arms.
She's gone. It was all just a dream.
No more than a dream . . .

I stand on a highway of regret
and I walk into my inevitable future.
Alone.

All is silent. I focus on my inhale and exhale, not believing I got through it. I stumbled a few times, paused longer than needed as I concentrated on words, corrected myself a time or two, but I didn't pass out like I imagined I would. Maybe they'll just assume I'm not good at public speaking.

Yeah, that's what I'll say if anyone makes a rude comment.

I don't look at anyone. I don't want to know how they thought I did. After shoving the paper back into Mr. Carlson's hand, I walk to my desk with my head down. "It's a great poem, Tannon," Mr. Carlson states and calls off the next victim. Cat.

She stands and takes her paper. Short jet-black hair frames her pale face, a fragile girl hiding behind a tough persona. "'A Mother's Love.'" She reads the title and continues without looking up.

> *If I was loved by my mother,*
> *I would be whole.*
> *If I was loved by my mother,*
> *I'd have a soul.*
> *If I was loved by my mother,*
> *I'd be free to love others.*
> *If I was loved by my lousy,*
> *good-for-nothing,*
> *piece of crap mother,*
> *I wouldn't be turning into a lousy,*
> *good-for-nothing,*
> *piece of crap myself.*
> *If I was loved by my mother . . .*
> *oh, who am I kidding?*
> *I never needed her anyway.*

She shoves the paper in Mr. Carlson's hand just as I had. He looks down at it sadly as he smooths out the wrinkles. Cat walks past Evan's desk and he grabs her hand. She pulls it back and keeps walking. Her pale face is now as red as can be. "Catherine, please see me after class," Mr. Carlson says, full of concern.

"Great!" she barks, falling to her seat.

He calls on Rita Mills. She's a tall, awkward overachiever, and I don't think I've ever seen her smile. Mousy brown hair lays flat on her head and her green eyes look as if they are analyzing and dissecting everything they see. This is the only class I have with her and the only time I ever notice her honestly. Last week she was arguing with Trace over a test score. She's another brain and she seemed jealous he scored higher than her. Trace told her Liv beat both their scores on that test and her head nearly burst into flames.

Rita stands next to Mr. Carlson and holds herself in a way that makes me believe she thinks she's better than all of us, like being here is a waste of her time. "'You're a Flea to Me,'" she says the title loudly.

My dog had a flea and if it wasn't for me,
that flea would've stole his glee.
So I picked that flea right off his knee
and tossed it into the sea.
Now that flea doesn't bother me.

But my dog still does.

Her eyes glare around the room as if we are all fleas. Wow, she's a strange one. I sometimes wonder who in this school would be the one to snap—well, it may very well be her.

"Thank you, Rita," Mr. Carlson says.

"What did I get?" she asks sharply.

"I'll be grading them after everyone's presentation." He seems to have little patience for her tone. She scowls, which is her normal expression, and stomps to her seat.

Evan is called next. He walks up and takes his paper and holds it down at his side. "'Cat,'" he says the title, staring right at her.

I'm getting off your crazy ride.
I'm taking you with me,
don't even bother to hide.

You don't get to decide anymore.
I won't just comply anymore.

My heart is in it too.
I won't just sit while you turn it blue.
So stop fighting, baby, just stop.
We deserve to be happy too.
Just me and you.

He didn't look down at the paper once. His eyes are frozen on her. I look back and see he's staring at the top of her head. Her arms are crossed on the desk and her head is laying on them, hiding.

Like we all do.

"Thank you, Evan. We seem to have a theme here," Mr. Carlson says, taking the paper back. "See me after class too." Evan rolls his eyes and takes his seat.

Trace is next. He stands tall and confident. "'A Wise Man,'" he reads the title.

A wise man has no worries.
A wise man knows no pain.
A wise man has no regrets.
A wise man knows no shame.
A wise man has no sorrow.
A wise man never cries over yesterday
nor does he fear tomorrow.
A wise man only carries

what he can fit in his heart.
For a wise man knows
we are just passing through.
And a wise man knows
he has nothing to prove.

Oh, I wish I were a wise man.

"Excellent," Mr. Carlson states. Rita groans loudly. Trace doesn't hold a smug smile or righteous grin. He just hands Mr. Carlson his paper and sits quietly. "All right, we have time for one more. How about it, Liv?"

She stands and walks to where she knows his desk to be. He touches her elbow and she turns. "'My Eyes,'" she says, speaking from memory. Her head is pointed in my direction, glasses on, like always.

I ask for comfort,
they offer pain.
I ask for dignity,
they offer shame.
I ask for light to guide me home,
they offer darkness,
and so I roam.
Why won't they just let me be?
Why won't they just let me see?

"Heartfelt, Liv," Mr. Carlson says with a sympathetic smile.

Rita throws her hands up in the air with disbelief, as if her poem about a frickin' flea was better—the girl is insane. I wonder if Liv wrote that after her accident with the locker. It sounds like she was in a despairing mood when she wrote it. She makes her way back to her desk and I want to reach out, pull her into my lap, hug her, and never let go.

CHAPTER 19
LIV

What a melancholy day. Everyone is miserable, completely depressed. I can't even begin to understand what's happening between Cat and Evan. Cat's poem revealed so much and Evan's ... Well, he sounded like a different person—an assertive one—which surprised me. And Tannon's was full of longing and sorrow. I guess Cat was right—he's deeper than I realized. *I wonder who the poem was about and why he had armor?*

I walk into cooking class and sit at my assigned station with Tannon. Except, he never shows up and I have to make the grilled asparagus by myself. I search the cabinets for the grill pan and lightly grease it with olive oil. I find the asparagus in the refrigerator, wash it, and snap the ends off. Mrs. Wilson helps me line the spears up in the hot pan and I count to twenty before turning them with a fork. I repeat this until the fork tip pushes into them easily. I place the cooked asparagus on the plate and dress them with the vinaigrette Tannon made yesterday. Mrs. Wilson tries a taste, and I take one too.

"Not bad," I boast.

"Very good, Liv," she says, patting my shoulder.

I sit at the counter, sorrow weighing my shoulders down. Michelle chats with me about how much she wishes she sat next to me instead of Nick. The bell rings and I make my way to lunch, place my bag down at the third table in, and receive no welcome. No one's at our table. I sit and pull my lunch bag out of my backpack. My head is sore from the stitches but for the most part it only hurts when I mistakenly touch it.

My shoulders slouch and I frown from loneliness. Cat isn't here and I'm wondering if maybe Mr. Carlson asked her to go to guidance or something. Her poem was kind of unsettling. But I guess mine wasn't a ray of sunshine either. I came up with it in the hospital waiting room, so that explains that. I take a few bites of my sandwich before pushing it away.

A moment later, Mr. Tenley asks if he can join me and I welcome the company. We talk about my stitches and about music and the upcoming charity banquet. He's a really nice guy, easy to talk to. "Are you seeing, Tannon?" he asks.

"No, Trace Matthews," I correct.

"Oh, I just saw how concerned Tannon was for you yesterday and you two seemed close."

"We're friends," I say, thinking it's nice he saw a connection between us.

"That's nice." The sudden pop and fizz of a soda can being opened causes me to jump. "Ms. Cox said he's going to sing at the talent show."

"Tannon sings?" I ask, stunned by this new revelation. I don't know Tannon at all.

"I guess so," he laughs. "Well, I better go. See you in class."

"Thanks for the company."

I take my bag and walk into the hall. Students rush in and out of the lunchroom as I make my way to the exit door. I push it open, sit on the brick ledge, and let a few tears fall. I don't know why I'm crying, but I can't help it. This was supposed to be a great year and, aside from Trace coming into my life, it seems like everything is falling apart. Cat is a mess, Evan is close behind, Tannon is beyond strange. I especially can't keep up with his behavior. One day he's my best friend and then I don't hear from him for days. He's in English yet he doesn't show up to cooking.

Where is everyone?

The bell rings and I walk back into school. The clock seems to slow for the rest of the day. At final bell, I go to the music room and sit at the piano. The room is empty so I play, hoping the music pulls me from my worries.

"I love listening to you play." Tannon's voice pulls me from my trance.

I turn on the bench toward the door. "Where have you been?"

"I'm sorry. I was in Ms. Cox's room all day." Art is across the way so he must have heard me playing this whole time.

"Why? I made the asparagus and . . . you weren't there." I feel foolish saying that. I didn't need him, though I sure sound needy now. "They came out great," I add, trying to make myself sound less pathetic.

"I don't doubt it. I'm sorry I ditched on you." His voice gets closer and he sits next to me on the bench. "Play something else."

I turn to the piano and start "The Rose." I sense him rest his arm on the top of the piano and hang his head. "'The Rose.' This was my mom's favorite," he whispers. I stop, feeling badly. "No, please don't stop."

"This is one of my favorites too," I say, starting again. I start singing the words softly, albeit poorly. The end is what always gets me.

There's such hope in the ending. My fingers stop moving; neither one of us speaks. The song is so sad, you need time to let your emotions settle. He gets that and I love that he does.

"Have you ever been in love?" I ask, although I'm sure he has after hearing his poem.

The bench squeaks with his movement. "Yes, and I agree with everything this song says about it. '. . . it is a razor, . . . a hunger, an endless aching need.'" He taps a few keys, trying to play chopsticks.

"Is it really that painful?"

"In my experience," he says, still hitting the wrong keys. "You in love with Trace?"

"I'm open to it."

I care deeply for Trace, and I'm open to falling in love, but that all-encompassing feeling hasn't hit me yet. Or maybe it has and I just never experienced it to recognize it. *I would recognize it, right?* I recognize my jealousy over whoever Tannon loves, which is all-encompassing at the moment and also leaves me swimming in guilt and confusion. I'll never understand the feelings he stirs in me.

I push those confusing feelings down deep and play the right keys for chopsticks. He follows. The smell of paint hits me as I'm leaning against him. "So you paint?"

"Yeah."

"You never told me."

"I don't talk about it much," Tannon says, brushing it off.

I'm not about to let it go. "Why?"

Silence.

He gives me nothing.

I wait him out. The silence is broken by his occasional, drawn-out breaths. "It's my thing and I like keeping it that way."

"I understand that," I say. "It's your special thing and you're protecting it."

"Yeah."

"You protect a lot about yourself. Your poem said you wear armor. What are you protecting yourself from?"

"It was just a poem." He turns on the bench and leans back against the keys, creating an unpleasant sound until it fades out.

I don't believe that, but even so, I let it slide for now. "I hear you're a singer," I say, poking him. I get his ribs.

He laughs, and it sounds like a cheerless one. "A singer I am not. Ms. Cox asked me to be in the talent show and next thing I know . . . I'm a singer."

My mouth forms an "O" and I stifle a laugh. "Well, let me hear you in action. What are you planning to humiliate yourself with?"

"Thanks. That makes me feel much better."

I laugh again. "C'mon, I'll play and you sing. You have a nice speaking voice so it can't be all that bad."

"It's bad," Tannon states. "And I'm not singing here."

"C'mon, I'm the perfect audience. I can't see a thing."

"You can hear just fine and my singing is something you should only have to deal with once. But can you do me a favor?"

"Sure."

"Do you know 'Make you feel my love'? The way Garth Brooks sings it?"

I swat him off the keys. He sits up and turns on the bench, and I start playing. "Is this what you want to sing?"

"I think so. But it doesn't really matter what song I pick—it will be bad either way," he says. There is fear in his voice. He's terrified just thinking about the talent show. I never heard him sound so nervous.

"Stick with this one," I say, still playing. "It's a beautiful song."

"One of my favorites." I sense his eyes on me and smile bashfully. "Well, I better get back to painting. I have hockey practice tonight, and this donation piece isn't going to paint itself."

Footsteps, laid in a long stride, walk to the door. "Hey!" I call out. "Will you be in class tomorrow?"

"Yeah, I'll be there." And with that the room is silent again. I play his song, whispering the words as I do. It really is beautiful. Sad. Though I'm beginning to think that's what Tannon is—sad. I always thought he was so happy-go-lucky. I was so wrong.

CHAPTER 20
TANNON

The weeks creep by. It's been a miserable winter. I wish I could blame my mood on the winter blues, but I don't think this mood will leave me in the spring. The talent show is tonight and there is no doubt I'm going to make a complete fool of myself. Half of the school bought tickets just to watch me fall on my face. I keep reminding myself it's for charity. I thought of taking a comedic angle, laugh at myself so I'm part of the joke, but I don't want to hurt Ms. Cox's feelings, so I figure I'll just be me and deal with the heckling afterward.

What the hell do I care anyway? How much worse could this year get?

Talent shows suck.

I step out of the shower and wipe the fog from the mirror. Tired eyes look back at me. I was once so good at hiding my feelings, but now it's written all over my face. Now I'm like my dad and Evan. "Help her see me, Mom," I say looking up. "Please, help me stop being so scared of showing her the real me."

I brush my teeth, gel my hair into a faux hawk, and walk to my room.

"Hey, Tannon," Dad says, walking past me in the hall. "What are you up to tonight?"

"Talent show."

He stops short outside his bedroom door. "Anyone you know in it?"

"Yeah, me!" I huff through a laugh. He spins on his heels to face me, big grin on his face. "Don't ask. It's for charity."

"You didn't tell me about this," he says. "What's the act?"

"I'm singing." His eyes widen, first with confusion and then amusement. "I told you not to ask."

He grins. "I wish I could see that. Well, knock 'em dead."

"Yeah, that's what I'm afraid of." I sulk and walk into my room. After throwing on jeans and a blue long sleeve shirt, I grab my winter jacket and hop into my junkyard car. It sucks in the snow. There's a light dusting on the road, so I have to drive slowly.

Stopping in front of Evan's, I beep the horn and he comes out, wearing the same gloomy expression as me. We've been great company for each other lately—misery loves company. He yanks my broken door open. "I can't believe you're doing this," he says, fighting the door shut.

"Me either."

"Have you practiced?" he asks, holding in his laughter.

"Maybe," I say, recalling my singathon in the shower. He gives me a curious side-glance. "I'm not kidding when I tell you I suck."

"I believe you," he says, grinning ear to ear.

"Thanks," I groan miserably. He offers a sympathetic pat on my shoulder while still laughing.

We talk about nothing of importance for the rest of the ride. It seems to be all we can handle lately. I park in the crowded parking lot and groan.

"Well, it looks like you attracted an audience. Ms. Cox will be pleased." His eyes are wide as he scopes out all the cars. I nod. "Hey, breathe, man. It'll be over soon."

We walk through the backstage door of the auditorium and gasp at all the commotion. People are racing around in every direction. Evan pulls his ticket from his back pocket, wishes me luck, and makes his way to the seats. My blood heats from the inevitable embarrassment that awaits me.

Spotting Liv sitting in the far corner of the room, I walk to her. She has a sweet blue dress on, tight in the waist then flairs out, covering her knees. Her phenomenal body makes her look sexy in something that is little-girl cute. She could be covered head to toe in garbage bags and still look sexy. She's leaning forward in the chair, hands under her knees, as her Converse-covered feet swing back and forth, sweet as honey. A tight ponytail shows off her beautiful face and awesome cheekbones, and pink lipstick draws attention to her full lips. Need I say she has on sunglasses?

She's sitting all alone and yet she has the biggest smile on her face. I wish I could lift her into my arms and just breathe her in. "Hey."

201

Turning her smile up at me, she pats the seat next to her. Her hand grabs my knee when I sit. "How's the rock star tonight?"

"I'm still upright," I state, causing her to laugh. "You playing tonight?" I realize she must be if she's back here. I've been dreading this night so long, I haven't even asked who else is performing.

"I already went." She shrugs as if it's no big deal.

"Oh shit, Liv, I'm sorry I missed it," I say and mean it. I love hearing her play.

"No, I'm not a contestant. I just played piano for Melissa Gordan as she sang. Mr. Tenley set it up." She waves it off again.

"How'd she do?"

"Not bad," she says, and then one side of her mouth tilts up. "Is Tannon Keaton actually nervous?"

"Yes, he is," I admit. "How many have gone?"

"The second act is up now. I think you're number six so there's still time to fake a heart attack or something," she teases.

"I don't think I'll have to fake it."

"Hey, don't say that." Her hand finds mine on my knee and she squeezes my fingers. "You got this, Tannon. Just remember it's for charity. It sounds like a good crowd out there and I'm sure most are here to see you. You raised a lot of money doing this."

I say nothing. "It's a slow song," she goes on, "so just put feeling into it. People will respond if you sing from the heart."

The song, to me, is about her, so I know there will be feeling behind it when I sing the words, but I'm not sure it will be in tune. I'm certain it won't be.

"Do you think . . ." I start but think better of it. "Never mind."

"What?" she asks. I stay silent. "Spill it, TK."

"I just thought that maybe ..." I pause, and she coaxes me on by tugging my hand. I breathe deeply and go for it. "You want to maybe play the song on piano for me? I mean, I know we didn't rehearse, but you know the song." I talk fast and unevenly. Damn I'm nervous. "If you play it slow, even slower than the recording, it may help me—Okay, truth is, only an apocalypse will help me, but maybe your playing will keep them from booing me off the stage." Then I think of them possibly booing her off with me and I smack my palm against my forehead. I can't do that to her. "No, forget it. I don't want to embarrass you too."

"Tannon, breathe," she says, squeezing my hand. "I've never heard you so frazzled." She pulls my hand to her chest and kind of hugs it. "Relax. I'll go out there with you. I'll play."

I finally exhale. "Really? You sure?"

"I'm really sure," she says, nudging my shoulder with hers. "If they boo, we'll skip off the stage together."

Damn she's cute.

I love you, I want to say. *I frickin' love you so much.*

Trace walks up to us. "Hey, guys," he says, glancing at our joined hands pressed against her soft breasts. I want to say, "Don't worry, dude, I'm too stressed to enjoy this."

She drops my hand and stands to greet him. He kisses her cheek and holds her at his side, comfortably. They are relaxed and content in each other's arms, like an old married couple. The awkwardness is gone; they are set in a groove. I'm a third wheel so I stand to leave them alone.

Did I mention how much I hate him?
Yes.

Well, tough, I'm saying it again.

I hate Trace Matthews.

"Hey, good luck, Tannon!" Trace calls out. I turn and wave. Why does he have to be such a nice guy? If he were a jerk I could beat the crap out of him and throw her over my shoulder like a hero, but no. He has to be her *ideal*.

Damn, I hate that word.

CHAPTER 21

LIV

Next act up is Tannon. Though I'm not sure where he is, so Trace helps me to the side of the stage to wait. "I won't be able to watch, but I'll hear you as I work," he says at my ear and presses his lips to the sensitive skin underneath.

I find his arm and pull him in for a quick peck on the lips. "Find me after," I say. Trace is on stage duty tonight. He has to set up and clear off the stage between each act and has had little time to hang with me. He promises to find me when I'm done and races off to help get the drum set ready to push out onto the stage for the solo after Tannon.

Mr. Nichols calls Tannon's name. I decide to take my seat at the piano and walk onto the stage with the help of my white cane. I'm told the piano is positioned in the middle of the stage and find it easily enough. The audience is strangely silent and I suddenly wish I had waited for Tannon. Mr. Nichols calls his name again and I frown with concern.

Where is he?

Suddenly the crowd cheers and I know he's walking out. I wait for him to tell me to start. He breathes into the microphone and the loud, high-pitched screeches coming out of the speakers cause everyone to shriek. He apologizes and finally asks me to start.

He sings in a whisper and stops. "Sorry," he says. His movements on stage are amplified through the microphone before he is suddenly sitting next to me on the piano bench. "I can't do this, Liv."

"Yes. You. Can. It's just you and me," I urge him on with a nudge of my elbow. "Just us."

After exhaling loudly, he clears his throat. "Start again," he says, sounding unsure. I start playing and his arm moves next to mine as he lifts the microphone.

He starts singing and my body heats from the outside in, as if his words provide warmth. He doesn't hold the right key, but the words coming out of his mouth are heartfelt and gut-wrenching. I don't know if it's because he's right next to me, but it really does feel like it's just the two of us. Everything else disappears in my darkness—the crowd, the stage—it's just me and him and a piano. It's just us and it feels so comfortable and comforting. His words feel like a warm blanket over my heart, and I feel . . . lucky. Lucky I get to experience this moment with him. I have to will my fingers to keep moving and control my emotions from taking over.

When he sings the last verse, I swear he's facing me. Looking right at me. Singing right to me. Tears well in my eyes. The last note is played and his head falls to my shoulder. I turn and take him into my arms. We hold each other as if we are all alone and then suddenly the crowd goes wild. They scream and cheer his name and I hear Evan yell, "That's my boy!"

"You did it!" I whisper. "You can breathe now."

"Don't let me go," he says back. I hold him tighter. His back is to the crowd and I wonder if he's trying to hide. His lips find my neck. "Thank you for being here."

"You didn't need me. You were . . . Wow, it was beautiful."

"I needed you. I need you," he repeats, and a droplet of water slides down my shoulder. *Is he crying?* The buildup of anticipation must finally be letting go.

"Tannon," I whisper. "It's over."

"I know. I know it is. It's over. It is," he says and gets up, leaving me. The crowd cheers after him. He never returns so I sneak off the stage and ask everyone I bump into if they saw where he went. Someone tells me he went out the back door. I follow after him with my white cane until Trace calls my name, stopping me in my tracks.

"Hey," he says, touching my arm. "Sounded like the crowd loved you guys. I have to run. Will you wait here for me?"

I so desperately want to follow Tannon, but that's not my business; this is my business. I smile and nod. Trace kisses my cheek and races off. After a pause, I sit in a chair at the back corner away from all the action and think of Tannon. I swear he was crying. I worry about where he went and what he's thinking and if he's all right.

CHAPTER 22
TANNON

The heat in my car sucks. Makes sense—it matches the rest of this piece of crap. I turn it off and let the chill of the air bring my body temperature down. I feel guilty for leaving Evan there, but he can hitch a ride. The air in that building was too thick to handle, so I ran.

Who am I kidding? Holding her was too much to handle, so I ran.

I don't know what happened. Somehow I got through the song. Somehow it sounded like a melody and not a bunch of words. I stayed calm and low-key. I stayed next to Liv and sang every word to her, hoping to God she heard me. Hoping to God she knew it was for her, about her.

I realize I'm not paying attention to my driving when I pull into the parking lot at the park instead of my driveway. Getting out, I pull my hat on, zip my jacket high, and walk through the snow to the park bench that overlooks Hardy. I can see the school, the full parking lot. She's in there, probably wondering why a tear ran down her shoulder. I couldn't help it—it couldn't be controlled. Just one tear and of course it had to hit her skin. I felt her flinch and knew she felt it. Her arms tightened around me and I had to get the heck out of there before I lifted her in my arms and took her with me.

It wasn't until I was racing off that I noticed the crowd cheering. Now I can't help my grin. They actually thought I was good. I didn't make a total fool of myself. Go figure. "Thanks, Mom," I whisper, looking up.

A car pulls up behind me, a door shuts, and then the car drives off. It sounds like the growl of Sparks's engine, but I don't look back. "Hey man," Evan says, sitting next to me.

"Hey."

"I saw your car. Sparks dropped me off, so you can't leave me here."

"Yeah, sorry about that."

"Tan, you were really good." He hits me with his shoulder. "It almost brought a tear to my eye. I mean, I wouldn't try out for *American Idol* but, man, it was good." My eyes widen, his expression sincere. "So why do you think the universe hates us?"

I shrug, sliding my hands into my jacket pockets. "It definitely doesn't want us to have the girls we want."

"I don't get it. Total cavemen get the girls they want and somehow keep them, and us, two good guys, can't get or keep a girl." He stands and walks to the hill's edge. "It's hard to breathe."

I know he's not talking about the cold air. "Yeah."

He sighs deeply. "Maybe I *was* being a pushover with Cat."

"You were."

"Okay, I was. Shit, I was." Pulling his hat off, he runs his fingers through his hair before sliding it back on. "But I'm not now. I know what she needs and I can give it to her."

"I know you can," I say, trying to offer him some hope. "You'll get her back. She needs you. She needs to be loved by you."

"And you," he gestures to me and drops his hand. "Damn, Tannon. Why don't you just tell her? I never knew you to be a chicken shit."

"She picked Trace."

"Because she doesn't know how you feel."

I glare at him. "Oh, so you think if I go and tell her I love her, she's going to just dump him? Don't you see them together? They're perfect."

"Yeah, I would have agreed with you before—"

"Before what?" I interrupt.

"I thought I was your best friend." He looks wounded.

"You are, Ev, c'mon," I say, not wanting to get all deep with him over this.

"No, I *was*," he snaps. "Before high school I was, but then your mom died and freshman year sucked and you put this guard up and you've been hiding everything from me. When did you start loving her?" I open my mouth. "The truth," he adds, pointing a finger at me.

"The first time I laid eyes on her."

He huffs a humorless laugh. "Since freshman year?" I nod and look away. "You bastard." My head snaps back, stunned. He goes on, "And the other girls, how you acted all blasé about relationships—that was all an act?" I shrug. "Jeez, TK. What the hell, man? Why didn't you tell me?"

"You love her like a sister," I say. "I'm not good enough."

"Yeah, then—the way you were acting—I wouldn't have wanted you with her. Like I said, before—with your macho guard up. I would agree that Trace is perfect for her. But the way I've seen you with her lately ... The real you is surfacing and this guy, my real best friend since preschool, is more than perfect for her. Dude, no one is better for her. You have to be with her."

"It's too late," I say, finally accepting the truth. *It's over.*

"Why did you wait? Why didn't you tell her freshman year?"

"My mom just died. I was scared." I don't mention that I felt inadequate, stupid, and pathetic. I don't want to get into that, not now.

"But you're still hurting now, so you didn't exactly protect yourself from getting hurt, did you?" He shakes his head in disappointment. I shrug knowing he knows he's right. "So you're sitting here gutted and bleeding. How much worse could it be if you tell her? What do you have to lose now?"

"If I actually come out and ask her to be with me and she says no ..." I pause, the thought alone causes me pain. "It would kill me."

"But, dude, look at you. You're dying already. You think it matters who sticks the knife in?"

"Yes. It matters."

He sits next to me again. "You and Cat stay all armored up, thinking it's protecting you, but you don't realize the armor is what's causing you the most pain. If you'd just shed that heavy weight, you would breathe easier." He nudges my knee. "You said to me once that sometimes you need to step outside the box to see what's in it. Well, you need to get out of this box and look inside. Like now!"

"Stealing my lines?" I tease.

"Yeah, if you won't take my advice, take your own." His arm goes around my shoulder and he pulls me to his side. "I know what you're going through, man. I'm going through it too. But at least I'm not hiding."

"You always were stronger than me mentally." I hit the side of his head with mine.

"Physically too," he adds, punching my arm. I just laugh, knowing he knows that's not true. "Whatever you decide to do, just do me a favor. Don't shut me out."

"Okay."

CHAPTER 23
LIV

The routine of my days cause the weeks to merge together. I can't tell one from the next. All I know is Cat is drifting, Evan is on the verge of a breakdown, Tannon is . . . well, he's acting normal, like nothing is bothering him. Happy-go-lucky Tannon, flirting with girls, flirting with me, acting like a duck, everything rolling off his back. I think he wants me to believe that anyway, but I don't, not anymore.

I might not know who he really is, but I know he isn't this guy.

Besides all that, Trace and I have been good. We still have a line that neither of us has tried to cross, but we are getting more comfortable touching each other. We spent Christmas Day together and New Year's Eve. It was nice not being single over the holidays. But for the most part, life has been uneventful. And now it's the last week in January. I can't believe it.

I walk into cooking class. Our final is Thursday, so we have to start preparing the food. Tannon walks up behind me in the station and smacks my butt. "Hey honey, I'm home!" he bellows. I laugh at his joke and ignore his inappropriate touch.

"Time to get to work, mister. I want to get an A in this class," I say.

"Yes, ma'am."

See, he's being normal and I don't get it. All that heartache he was carrying around just disappeared after the talent show. He came to school the next day like big man on campus. Everyone cheered for him and he seemed so upbeat and wild again. It makes no sense. This is why I don't understand him and why my feelings for him are always confused.

We get right to preparing. Working well together in the kitchen, taking on tasks without being asked, moving around each other comfortably, feeding each other like an old married couple—it's weird how easy it is.

"Tomorrow's the charity dinner," I say, cutting carrots. "Is your painting ready?"

"Yeah, it's been ready for a while now." He's standing at the sink washing something. The classroom is noisy: pots banging, knifes chopping, students laughing, and arguing—especially Michelle and Nick, with Mrs. Wilson trying to calm them down.

"What is it of?" I ask.

"Um . . ." Tannon stops and I turn to him, holding the knife out. He laughs. "Hey, easy there, Boo, no need to get violent," he teases. I lower the knife with a smirk.

"Well?" I wait.

"Uh . . . you," he says, and I hear the sink go on again. I'm frozen in space and time. I can't move.

"Me?" I finally have a voice to ask. "The painting's of me?"

"Yeah," he says, his words hit off the wall in front of him while he's facing the sink. "No big deal. So are you playing tomorrow?"

"Yes," I answer, though I can't get past the painting. "Me?" I ask again.

"It's you, Liv." He sounds cross, annoyed. "You're playing the piano on a stage, the lighting is dim, like candlelight. That's it! Now keep chopping."

Still in a daze, I turn and continue to chop the carrots. I feel myself starting to cry and find the onion to hide the reason for my tears. I wish I could see his work, but I can't. I wish I could know him, but I don't.

Suddenly, Tannon's finger rubs across my cheek to catch my tear. "Want me to cut those?" he asks. I shake my head firmly. "Why not? You have water works pouring into our food," he jokes.

I stop cutting. Releasing the knife, I turn to the sink to wash my hands and wipe my face. He takes over and I start cleaning the spinach. Everything has to be ready for the final, so I focus on that. We finish our tasks without another word.

The bell rings and I grab my bag and unfold my cane. I make my way to the nurse's office and tell her I'm not feeling well, which is the truth. I feel sorry for myself and want to go home and wallow in my pity. Mom picks me up and I go right to my room.

***

215

There's a knock at my door after eight p.m. and it opens before I even respond. "What's going on, Liv?" Cat asks, sitting on my bed. "You haven't answered your phone."

"Me? What's going on with you?" I sit up, taking my pillow to hug at my chest. "Where have you been? You hardly answer my calls. You don't come for dinner anymore. What the heck's up, Cat?"

She lies on my bed, pulling me to face her. "I'm sorry. I just don't want to bring you down with me. I was sparing you my misery."

"That's why I'm here. You think I can't handle it?" I say defensively.

"You can handle it. I just don't think you should have to."

"Cat, if you are in pain, then I'm in pain no matter if you're here or across the world. I'm going through it too and I'm losing you in the meantime."

A heavy sigh escapes her. "I got in a huge fight with my mom before school started and she's kicking me out after graduation. Once I'm eighteen, I'm out."

Without a second's hesitation, I have her in my arms and I'm hugging her tight. "Oh my gosh, Cat! Why didn't you tell me?"

"I just told you why. I didn't want you carrying my problems. You're so happy with Trace and I don't want to bring you down."

"Stop saying that. Shutting me out is the only thing that will bring me down. Everything else we can handle together. You've been holding this in since September?" She nods her head against my shoulder. "Cat, you should've told me."

216

"I was hoping she'd change her mind and no one would have to know how horrible she is."

"Come live with us," I say, drawing back. "Gary will let you stay in here with me."

"Liv, she's not helping with college. My future is . . . I have no future," she cries uncontrollably.

"That wicked, evil witch." I'm not big on cursing so that's about as wild as I get and Cat actually starts laughing over her sobs. "Is that why you broke up with Evan?"

She squeezes my hands. "Yes, I can't pull him into my pit of sweaty balls. He has a great life ahead of him. I don't want to ruin it."

I pull our joined hands to my chest. "He thinks you're pushing him away because of your trust issues. If he knew why . . ."

"I'm no good for him."

"Uh . . . yes, you are. And that's his decision," I point out.

"I'm stuck here, Liv. I have no money. Not only does she not love me, now she's ruining my life. I know she thinks having me ruined hers." Her tears pour and she can hardly catch her breath. I hug her tight and cry with her.

"We can figure out financial aid. There has to be something we can do." Cat dreams of being an interior designer and she'd be great at it if she gets a chance. We just have to get her that chance. "I'm going to figure something out. You're sleeping over because I'm not letting you go."

"I brought a bag," she says. "I already invited myself."

"We'll figure this out," I pledge. "You're going to have a great life, Cat."

217

CHAPTER 24
TANNON

Tonight's the banquet dinner and, here we go again, another fun night watching Trace hold my girl. I've been playing it cool around Liv—silently praying that they break up—but it's exhausting, and ineffective. My phone rings as I'm buttoning my dress shirt—I hate wearing a suit. "Yeah?" I answer, not looking at the screen.

"Hey, Tannon." It's Liv's sweet voice on the other end. I sit on my bed and feel a smile grow. "I uh . . . I know it's last minute, but I was wondering if you can maybe—I mean, you don't have to—"

"Spit it out, Boo," I coax.

She sighs. "Okay. Trace just called. He thinks he has the stomach bug or food poisoning. Cat left to go to a movie with Evan right before Trace called and

Mom and Gary are out. I can ask Cat to come back and drop me off, but I thought since—"

"Liv, I'll be there in ten minutes."

"Great. Thank you so much!"

"No problem."

The call is ended, the phone goes sailing, and I spin in a haphazard circle not knowing what to do first. I suddenly care about what I look like tonight, which makes no sense since I'm picking up a girl who could care less. I'm picking up a girl who has a boyfriend. I'm picking up a friend. I go back to not caring about how I look. My tie is tied without concern and I drag myself into the bathroom to brush my teeth.

My dimples are deep while I brush. Mom used to call them "the deal closer." Funny how they've done nothing to help me land my girl.

"Dad!" I call out into the hall before spitting the toothpaste out.

He's standing in the doorway a second later. "What's up?" he asks and looks me over. "Hey, you look good."

"Thanks. Can I borrow your car? I have to drive Liv to the banquet."

His gray eyes light up. "Sure. Let me fix your tie." He undoes my bad knot and easily makes a perfect one. He was always a stickler for a perfectly tied tie. I check out his skill in the mirror and smile. "Is this a date?"

"I wish. She's still with Trace. She just needs a ride."

"Just be yourself. Leave the other guy home," he teases. I nod and walk to the kitchen to grab his keys. "You have your painting?"

"Ms. Cox already has it."

"Have a good time, Tan."

"Thanks." The cold air hits me the second I step outside. What a brutal winter; I can't wait for it to be over. I scrape the ice off the windshield of Dad's Ford Escape. The doors open without a fight and the seat belt works properly. No embarrassments tonight.

I pull into Liv's driveway a few minutes later and notice every light in the house is off. The sight causes me to sit back and reflect on her normal. She's home alone. Her mom probably left before it got dark. What does Liv need lights for?

She doesn't, but I do. I leave the car's headlights on to light the path to the door. I knock and she yells to come in. I do, annoyed she left the door unlocked. I can hardly see into the room it's so dark. I flip the porch light on for her mom when she comes home and it illuminates part of the front room with what looks like yellow, glowing candlelight.

A moment later, Liv walks around the corner and my breath hitches in my throat. She's stunning. I've never seen her in anything so form fitting before. The black dress has long, fitted sleeves and a neckline that curves close around her neck and scoops down low in the back, revealing her shoulder blades. Her breasts . . . I can't even go there. And her hips—heaven help me. The dress reaches just below her knees and, surprisingly, she has on silver flats, not her usual Converse. She grabs a small silver purse off the piano, slides her sunglasses on, and turns to me.

Her body is like a beautiful hourglass and I just want to lay her down horizontally to stop time.

Her long dark hair is in a pretty side braid and she has very little makeup on, just pink lipstick. "Liv, you look beautiful!" I say, after catching my breath.

"I do?" she asks, running her hands over the front of her dress. "I love this dress. It feels really good on. Like a comfortable T-shirt."

I love it too!

"I just have to let Hank in from the back." She disappears into the dark kitchen and I flick the lights on. I've never been in her house. The room is small and the piano takes up most of the limited space. It feels like a happy home, cozy and warm. There are a few pictures on a hutch next to the door and I look at every one. One is of Liv as a little girl. She has a puffy, pink winter coat on and a knit hat and she's walking on a sidewalk with her white cane and smiling proudly. I do the same. She was adorable. There are a few photos of her and her mom. One of her and an older man. Her and Hank. Her with an owl on her arm. Her with her mom and Gary—it looks like at their wedding. Another is her sitting on a swing. She's not swinging, though, just sitting with her hands holding the ropes and her head facing up with closed eyes, the sunlight hitting her skin. She's just taking in the moment, smiling. In another she's a little older, sitting on a pier with her head down and bare feet skimming the water. She looks to be deep in thought. No smile, but still she looks beautiful. The last photo shocks me because I'm in it, along with the rest of our gang. It looks like Evan's birthday at his house this past summer. I don't remember the picture being taken, but I have my arm around Liv, and it looks like Cat is tickling her. Liv's laughing with an open mouth, her arms wrapped around my waist as if looking for protection, and everyone else is huddled around us. I lift it to get a better look. We all seem so happy. She looks so good in my arms. *How can't this be the way it should be?*

Hank comes trotting in seconds after I set the frame down. I turn to greet him. "Hey, buddy." He sits before me and offers his paw, like a handshake, and I laugh while kneeling down to take it.

"Is he doing the paw shake?" she asks, amused.

"Yep. He's very polite."

"He's a charmer. Aren't you, boy?" She kneels down next to him, he instantly leans toward her, and she hugs him around the neck. "I love you. I'll be home later. You watch the house. No parties, you hear me?"

His ears go back and his eyes droop. He honestly looks upset about that last order. "I think he had one planned," I joke.

"Oh, I'm sure he did. He thinks he's the mayor of the block." She gets up and reaches her hand out to feel my suit. Touching my tie, she grins. "Good job."

No way am I telling her my dad fixed it. Her fingers touch the shoulders of my jacket and then move to my neck and hair. I hold my head down to her. "Love the hair," she says, about my faux hawk. "You look really handsome, Tannon."

"Thank you. Ready?"

"Yep." She reaches for her jacket. I help her slide it on, fixing the collar and buttoning the buttons. I want to kiss her so badly. She thanks me and walks around me to the door. I offer my arm after she shuts and locks it, and she holds my elbow. The stairs are clear of ice, but I go slowly.

"I have Dad's car so there should be no glitches tonight." I open the passenger door for her. "Did you hear that? No, you didn't. This door works," I say.

She turns her head to show me her pout. "I have to say, I'm disappointed. I love your car." She sits and I shake my head as I shut the door and mouth the words, "And I love you."

Van Morrison's "Into the Mystic" is playing when I start the car. I never changed the station Dad had on. Actually, I don't even think I realized the radio was on the whole way here.

"I love this song. My mom always played it when I was younger," Liv says, pulling her seat belt on. I watch the lucky belt cross over her amazing body.

I hate you, Trace Matthews.

She sits back and listens to the song as I drive, slender fingers tapping her leg, as the sweet smile on her face lets me know Van Morrison has her spirits "flying into the mystic." I sit back, wishing I could "rock her gypsy soul."

"Do you get nervous when you play for big groups?" I ask when the song ends.

"No. I can't see them so I just pretend I'm all alone." She giggles. "It works better than pretending they're naked or something."

I laugh with her and stare at her profile while waiting at a red light. She has a great slope to her nose and I have the urge to let my finger ski down it. Her head turns to me. "You're staring," she says.

"Yes. Yes, I am."

"What do you see?"

The light turns and I start driving again. "I see an angel sitting next to me. I see a kind heart and a compassionate soul," I say. And I think, *I see my favorite person in the world. I see the girl I love.*

223

"You see that looking at me?"

"Yep."

"You must have great vision," she teases. "X-ray vision, since you saw right through my skin."

"Oh, you want to know what you look like to me," I say. "I thought you wanted to know what I see. I don't think you want to know what you look like to me. Tonight, in that dress, the details would be X-rated."

Liv shakes her head. "Tannon. You're crazy." We stay quiet for a few blocks. The music fills the silence, only I can't tell you what song is playing. The charged energy in the car is making it difficult for me to think. And the energy is all coming from me. I so desperately want to touch her. "Thanks for picking me up."

"You don't have to thank me." My hand moves to her shoulder of its own accord and brushes her long braid behind her back and then somehow ends up rubbing her neck before traveling to her ear and gently pulling her lobe. She shivers but my hand doesn't stop. It moves to her cheek and slides down her jaw bone, halting at her chin as I stop at another light. My naughty hand pinches her chin and turns her head to face me as I face her. I'm so proud of my brave hand. "Did I tell you how beautiful you look tonight?"

She nods and turns from my hold, but I catch her smirk before she can hide it. "Is that a smile, Ms. McKay?"

"Nope." She keeps her back to me for a moment, before turning to me. "What were you like as a little boy?"

"I don't know," I say, laughing. *Where'd that come from?*

"C'mon," she urges. "I want to know."

"I guess I was a typical boy. And I was happy," I say. "I was really happy. My dad was my best friend. Mom was ... my everything. I thought I was a superhero. I'd race around in my Underoos and cape thinking I could save the world, be a hero. I was a happy kid."

"Underoos?" she questions with a silly giggle.

"Yeah, underwear with superhero cartoons on them." We laugh.

"You must have been so cute running around in your Underoos." Glancing over, I catch her smile turn to a frown. She asks, "You're not happy now?"

"My world changed. It's not that I'm not happy. I mean, I have good things in my life and all that stuff, but I wasn't a hero. Everything changed." I shift in my seat. "Anyway, what about you?"

"No," Liv says. "No redirecting the question yet. What was she like?"

I rest my arm on the door and hold my head while staring at the road. "Mom was fun and funny, but sometimes stern. Whenever I got into trouble, she made me talk it out, realize the different endings my choices could have led to. She wanted me to understand every action has a reaction. Even the most innocent of mistakes may never be changed or fixed, so think before acting." I switch hands on the steering wheel and lower the heat. "She wanted me to be kind. She said that her job as a mother of a son was to raise me to be a strong man with a compassionate heart."

"You are," she says. "You couldn't fight her cancer, but you are growing into the man she hoped you'd be. She's proud of you, Tannon."

"Yeah. Liv, I don't really want to talk about this now," I say, hoping she'll let it go. "It's hard to talk about her."

"Okay." She leaves it be and sits quietly.

"I saw your baby pictures on the hutch. You were adorable."

"I was?" she asks, her face scrunched up in disbelief.

"Mm-hmm, always smiling."

"I was happy too. My world changed when I started hearing the opinions of others. They started telling me there were things I couldn't or shouldn't do and I was left confused and scared." She plays with a button on her coat. "Sometimes I think that all people see is my blindness. They get hung up on it. I guess I get it. But I was born blind—it's my normal—and to me, it's the least interesting thing about me."

"You're not happy now?" I ask the same question she asked me.

"I am." Shrugging, Liv turns toward the window again. "I like who I am."

I smile and I take her hand. "I like who you are too. And you are a very interesting person, Liv, and there are a million reasons why."

"Thank you," she says, patting my hand.

I pull into the parking lot of the hall and stop at the valet sign. "We're here, Boo. A valet is going to open your door."

A young guy helps her out of the car. "Good evening, miss," he says.

"Good evening, and thank you," she replies. He smiles. I come around and take her by the waist, not being able to resist touching her, wishing her wool coat wasn't in the way.

"Can I have your arm?" she asks, moving from my hold.

"But you already have two."

I think I heard that line in a movie, but I can't recall which one. Or maybe it goes, "But that would only leave me with one." *Damn, how does it go? It's going to drive me crazy all night.*

Liv smacks my back, giggling. I offer my arm, knowing she likes to have control of where she goes and that's why she holds everyone's arm, so she can let go whenever she wants. Though, she doesn't seem to mind when Trace hugs her as they walk. I remind myself of my place here—I'm just a friend.

Yippity friggin' do da!

"What does the place look like? It feels grand," she whispers.

"It's very nice. High ceilings, huge crystal chandeliers, grand staircase, which we can take unless you want to take the elevator?"

"Oh, let's take the grand staircase. I want to experience the full effect of this night," she says.

"You got it!" I let her know the stairs are starting right before her cane hits them. "I feel like I'm going to a wedding."

"Me too!" Liv giggles, taking one stair at a time. Slowing my pace, I patiently let her lead and slide my right hand over hers on my left arm just to be sure she doesn't fall back. The stairs whirl up and we can hear the music playing before we reach the top.

"This place even smells fancy," she says. "Like expensive perfume and polished wood."

We walk in the banquet room and are met by a throng of well-dressed people mingling. Mr. Tenley said some very influential people would be here tonight and these people sure look well-to-do.

"There are a lot of wealthy people here," I whisper. "Wearing very expensive perfume."

"Well, well," Liv replies, lifting her brows high on her forehead, making them visible over her glasses. "My nose never fails."

Mr. Tenley sees us and walks over. "Liv. Tannon. I'm glad you're here."

"Hi, Mr. Tenley," Liv says.

"I have a few people I'd like to introduce you to, Liv," he says, holding his arm out for her. "Take my arm. Mr. Swords is here. He's the director of Carnegie Hall."

"I'll go find Ms. Cox," I say to Liv and watch Mr. Tenley lead her away. Craning my neck, I see Ms. Cox by the donated artwork. As I get closer, I realize there are many people standing around my painting with her. She's talking about me. Calling me "the artist." Telling them about my other pieces.

A dapper man—the description suits him—with gray hair walks up close to the painting. "I love the dark colors," he says. "And the females are so elegant."

"Yes, the pianist. I believe she's his muse. He's painted a few of her. He painted one of her in a park that is heartfelt as well. He received third place in the state for that one. Her name is Liv McKay. She will be here tonight playing piano. Every time I hear her play I stop whatever I'm doing and close my eyes. It's so captivating."

The man turns with interest. "I can't wait to hear her play."

"And the other woman in the painting?" Another man asks. "Who is she?"

Ms. Cox smiles sympathetically. "That's the artist's mother. She died a few years back."

After I heard Liv play "The Rose," I wanted my mom to hear it too, so I gave her that moment. I positioned her in the painting leaning against the baby grand, listening to Liv play.

"There must be a story behind that," a woman with a large diamond necklace wonders.

"The artist told me that Liv is playing his mother's favorite song," Ms. Cox explains.

"Which was?" the first man asks.

"'The Rose,'" Ms. Cox says. "And so the title of the work is *The Rose*."

"Oh, I just adore that song," the woman says. "Is he in love with the pianist?"

"He never said." Ms. Cox leaves it at that. I never did tell her, but then again, she never asked. She's a smart woman, though. Liv's in most of my paintings, so I'm sure she's figured it out by now.

"I want to believe he is," the woman says. "And he wanted his deceased mother to meet the girl he loves. They meet in one of his paintings. It's beautiful." I grin at her assumption. She's half right. Most of it had to do with the song.

"What will you start the auction off with for this one?" another man asks, gesturing at my painting.

"This one is starting at one thousand dollars," Ms. Cox says and my jaw drops. "It's our highest start for the night." Wow. I'm completely blown away. I had no idea my work could go for that much. Ms. Cox turns and notices me; I quickly act like I'm walking to her.

"Oh here's the artist," she says, glowing. "Tannon Keaton, this is Mr. Franklin and Mr. Stoltz. They are from the Metropolitan Museum of Art. They are both avid collectors personally as well as for the museum.

And this is Mr. and Mrs. Michaels, also avid collectors."

"It is nice to meet you all," I say, shaking their hands. Perspiration starts under my collar. I'm suddenly very nervous.

"You as well," Mr. Michaels says. "Is this the first piece you've ever sold?"

"Yes."

"Ms. Cox says you have others just as exquisite," he goes on. "Are they for sale?"

"Some. But a few are too meaningful."

"Understood. I love your texture and color selection. There's a great deal of emotion in this piece. I would say you're too young to understand such emotion, but we have heard you did lose your mother."

I nod and say, "I'm glad you like it."

"You're very talented," he says.

"Thank you so much!" I can't keep the silly grin off my face.

CHAPTER 25
LIV

Mr. Tenley introduces me to a number of people. A few make me feel like a science project, asking all kinds of questions about my blindness, but most are just interested in my playing. In particular, Mr. Swords is lovely, asking if we can talk again after my performance, and I have to hold back my glee. The director of Carnegie Hall is actually here. I feel so blessed to have this opportunity.

Mr. Tenley guides me to the art section. I'm hoping I can at least hear what others have to say about Tannon's painting. "Oh my, this must be her," a man's voice calls out.

"Yes. This is Liv McKay," Ms. Cox says, and I smile, confused by the attention.

"I must say you captured her likeness accurately, Mr. Keaton," a man says.

Wow. They recognized me from his painting. He must be really good. "How's it look?" I ask, scrunching my shoulders up shyly.

"It's lovely," a woman says. "This young man has a great future ahead of him."

A warmth pours over me, I want to squeeze Tannon's hand and tell him how proud I am of him. Only I don't know where he's standing. "What am I wearing?" I wish I could see it, but I refuse to let my sadness show.

"You're wearing a long, flowing, burgundy gown and his mother is wearing a long navy gown."

"His mother?" I ask, shocked.

"You're playing for her," the woman says and goes on to describe the painting in great detail.

"Tannon?" I utter, feeling touched and wishing to know where he is.

"The painting's called *The Rose*," Tannon whispers, now standing behind me.

"Her favorite song," I say, feeling overwhelmed with emotion. "It sounds like a tender painting, Tannon." I feel honored to be in a painting with his mother, although I wonder why he put us together.

"I added her after you played the song for me."

I'm blown away and don't know what else to say. Feeling everyone's eyes on me, wishing to divert their attention, I ask Ms. Cox about Trace's drawing.

"It's this way," she answers.

The group asks to see it as well and I follow closely to hear what they say. We walk a short way and then the man in front of me asks, "Is this it? Wow. It comes right at you, doesn't it?"

"What is it?" I whisper.

"Hands cupping a beautiful orchid. They seem to be coming out of the paper," the woman says.

"Trace Matthews can bring life to everything he draws," Ms. Cox boasts.

"You have some talented students this year," a man says. "It's almost as if the hands are offering us the flower."

"Actually, the flower is for Liv," Ms. Cox says. I wish I could see it. "And this real orchid is for you, Liv. From Trace."

Reaching my hand out, she places the delicate flower in my palm. I pull it close to my chest and caress the delicate petals. I'm so touched by his thoughtfulness.

"Well, it seems you are admired by your peers, young lady," the man says. "Is the artist here?"

"Sadly, no, he's under the weather," Ms. Cox explains.

"It's time to take our seats now. Dinner will be served shortly," Mr. Tenley announces.

Tannon walks with me to our table and we sit with our classmates. The performance from the drama department starts, so I sit quietly and listen to the show, holding Trace's flower in my hand and wishing he was here to thank.

CHAPTER 26
TANNON

How do I compete with a guy who's ten steps ahead of me? I can't believe he sent her a flower. I wanted to throw it on the floor and stomp on it like a jealous child. We were doing so good, having a great time. I kept forgetting about him, but he's smart enough to know he has to remind me. And maybe her. I can only hope she forgot about him as we were driving here ... but I doubt it. She was the one who asked about his drawing.

If Dad were here, he'd say the flower was a grand gesture on Trace's part. They say sometimes wicked smart people have no street smarts. Well unfortunately, Trace has all kinds of smarts. He planted himself here, right now, in that flower, in her hand. He's here and I may as well not be. His drawing is fantastic. The hands really do look like they are coming off the page to offer the flower.

A loud screech catches my attention. Someone's squawking on stage. *What the heck are we watching?*

This performance is bizarre to say the least. Everyone's in black and they're moving really slow and talking really weird.

I glance at Liv. Her head is down and her finger is sliding over the flower's petals. The strange bird calls on stage can't even pull her away from thoughts of perfect Trace. Her ideal.

Hate.

Hate.

Hate.

The show ends and the food comes and I welcome this next distraction—and feel thankful the eccentric show is over. Zack, a sophomore in my art class, sits next to me and talks about sports and cars. He has a sculpture—a horse head—in the auction and it's really cool. The guy has talent. We get into a long conversation about engines. I share all I know from Sparks while Liv talks with Remi, from her music class, across the table. He plays the violin and seems nice. Things start to look up again. The flower is placed at the center of the table while Liv eats, and we talk to each other every now and then.

While dessert is being served, Mr. Tenley comes to the table to escort Liv backstage. It's time for her solo. A few minutes later I see her walk on stage with her white cane. She sits at a lone piano in the middle of the stage and starts.

The music is sad, slow, as if every note is a cry for help. Every press of a key hits me right in the heart. My chest tightens. My vision blurs. Without uttering one word, she reaches into my soul and releases a floodgate of emotions. I want her to stop and yet, at the same time, I never want the music to end. I drop my head, straining to breathe, willing myself to get a grip.

Hearing a whimper behind me, I realize it isn't just me. Liv affects everyone. The melody changes, becoming louder, faster, and then as if mimicking a sudden death . . . it's over.

Zack nudges my arm. "Damn, she's good. I felt that in my bones."

Pulled from my turmoil, I look up at Liv. Sitting in her element, looking stunningly beautiful, I find myself smiling proudly. "Yeah, she's amazing."

Next she plays a classical piece that I don't know the name of but I've heard playing through the hall of the art department many times. It must be one of her favorites. I like it. It's haunting and almost tragic, but fitting for how I feel. There's complicated finger positioning in this one and watching her hands move so fast it's impressive. She does another classical piece after that. Her whole body gets into this one. Her fingers move faster and faster as her foot stomps on the pedals. It looks like she's having a dramatic argument with the piano and she's winning.

Last she plays an upbeat tune that gets people moving in their chairs. She ends, stands, and bows. The room explodes in applause.

A few minutes later she's sitting next to me again. I lean over and wrap my arms around her shoulders, pressing my lips to her ears. "Liv, you are gifted."

Her body freezes in my hold and she turns her head. Now my lips are at her cheek. "Thank you, Tannon," she whispers.

I press my lips to her cheek. She kisses mine too.

Suddenly a man crouches down next to Liv's seat. Calling her name, he pulls her attention from me. I'm annoyed by the interruption. The man compliments Liv. He says he's impressed and would like to talk to her more about playing at a young artist's night at Carnegie Hall. She's beyond ecstatic. And I'm happy for her too, but then I notice his proximity to her. He's way too close and he's touching her knee. He starts with a fingertip, adds another, soon they're all resting on her skin right below the hem of her dress. I shake my head and look again, hoping I'm mistaken.

I'm not. He's close and he's touching her. And now I'm about to clothesline him to the ground. I shift in my seat, moving closer to Liv. He doesn't notice.

"Maybe we can talk a bit more privately later," he says, and she nods enthusiastically. His fingers slowly slide over her skin and she moves slightly, pulling her knee back, but he only follows.

I snap.

"Remove your hand from her leg. Now," I demand through clenched teeth. "And anything you need to say to her you can say right here or with Mr. Tenley present. There will be no private time."

The man stands but doesn't leave. "I don't know what you're implying, young man," he says with his nose up like he's better than me.

I stand and step into his space. His potbelly stops me from getting any closer. "Tannon!" Liv exclaims. Reaching for me, she finds my shirt and tugs. "What are you doing?"

The guy crosses his arms and cocks his head, all high and mighty. I stare, unblinking. My adrenaline is pumping through my body and it takes all my strength not to hit him. I don't want to fight at a charity dinner, but the way he's looking at me is making it hard to care where I am.

"Be careful, young man," he says, warning in his eyes.

I get a glimpse of a wedding ring on his finger as he jabs at the air between us. "Maybe you should be taking your own advice. Is your wife here tonight? I'd love to tell her how her husband was pawing a seventeen-year-old girl."

The guy turns bright red, boiling with anger, before he storms off. I sit and take Liv's hands. "Are you okay? God, what a sleazebag."

"Okay? No, I'm not okay," she snaps.

"I know, I'm sorry. Jeez, I should have reacted the second he touched you."

"Him? It's you, Tannon!" she sneers in my face. "I'm not okay because of you! How could you do that to me?"

"Me?" I throw back, confused by how she can possibly be mad at me.

"Just leave me alone." She lowers her head. "I can't believe you."

"Liv, I—"

"Go away," she says, giving me her shoulder.

I turn and gawk at Zack, wide-eyed, and send him a look to silently ask if I was way off base. Maybe I was being a jealous hothead, but I seriously doubt it. Zack shakes his head, confirming I saw what I saw. I huff out a humorless laugh, get up, and walk out of the room. My mind totally blown.

Turning the corner, I walk down a narrow hall to be alone. Pacing isn't helping so I sit against the wall. I hear quick footsteps rushing toward the hallway, and then Ms. Cox and Mr. Tenley turn the corner.

"Tannon." Ms. Cox kneels next to me in her dress. "What happened?"

"Mr. Swords said you accused him of some pretty awful things," Mr. Tenley says, cross.

"Yeah, I did."

"What did he do, Tannon?" Ms. Cox grabs my arm.

"The guy's sick! I saw it! I saw how he was looking at Liv. She's only seventeen. She—"

"Tannon, you can't accuse everyone that looks at her of—"

"Are you serious?" I snap, not caring to hear anymore. "If you saw the way he was looking at her. If you saw his hand on her knee and the desire in his eyes as he stared at her body. If you heard how he invited her to talk privately later and how she accepted. If you were there, hopefully, you would have called him out too."

"No, Tannon. We are adults and adults don't—"

"Yeah, adults don't when others do. That's the problem with this world, isn't it?" I throw back at Mr. Tenley and jump to my feet. I'm so pissed right now. He's talking to me like I'm six.

"I understand that you . . . like Liv and—"

"That's enough, John," Ms. Cox stops him with a raised hand and he shuts up. "Tannon's not overreacting." She tilts her head up to look at him. "That same man made me very uncomfortable earlier. And then he asked me to spend some time with him someplace more private so we could talk about some contacts he has in the art world. He was handsy. The guy gave me the creeps."

Mr. Tenley grabs her arms and spins her to face him. "CeCe, why didn't you tell me?"

"I said I wasn't interested and he moved on. But to think of him moving on to Liv . . . That pig!"

239

After hearing that, I wish I had hit him. I turn to stomp down the hall to do just that, but Mr. Tenley grabs my arm, halting my steps. His bottom lip starts twitching. He's seething.

"I'm sorry I didn't believe you, Tannon." There is fire in his eyes and I suddenly like this guy again. "Excuse me, I have to take out the trash." He storms down the hall. Ms. Cox races behind and I follow.

"John, don't do anything you'll regret," she warns, rushing behind him in her heels. "Remember where we are."

He doesn't respond. We find the guy standing outside the banquet doors.

He sees us coming and steps forward. "I hope you dealt with the matter," he says, glaring at me. Since I know what's coming, I offer a tight smile.

"I'm about to," Mr. Tenley says coolly.

"Excuse me?" Mr. Swords bites back.

"You need to leave now." Mr. Tenley grabs him by the arm and ushers him down the staircase. Ms. Cox chases after him, telling him to stay calm, and I follow hoping he doesn't.

The man is trying to get out of Mr. Tenley's tight hold, yelling about who he is and who he knows, and stumbles down the last three steps. Mr. Tenley catches him by the neck, not caring who he is or who he knows, and opens the exit door with the guy's body. The valets stare in shock when the man is pushed forward and stumbles into the middle of the blacktop.

"This is a private party and you aren't welcome anymore," Mr. Tenley informs him.

The guy stumbles back, scowling, and turns to get his car from the valet. The wuss gave up so easily. In my eyes, it only proves his guilt.

"John!" Ms. Cox exclaims, searching the entrance for witnesses. Thankfully, only the valets saw. When she sees there were no spectators, she grabs Mr. Tenley's face and kisses him. He must've just become even more attractive to her after seeing him all fired up. I can't help but smirk. He pulls her against him then quickly remembers I'm standing here and breaks their embrace.

"I'm sorry," he says, holding his hand out.

We shake hands. "It's all right."

"Please keep my relationship with Ms. Cox between us," he says. I nod and work my way back to the table and sit. I catch the grimace on Liv's face out of the corner of my eye. She doesn't say a word and neither do I.

***

The night is finally coming to an end. Ms. Cox comes to the table and tells me that my painting sold for nineteen hundred dollars in the silent auction. I'm beyond floored. I know this is a charity dinner and people are willing to spend more for charity. My starting prices won't be that high, not at first, but maybe I can really make a living out of this after all. Liv asks how much Trace's sold for. Ms. Cox says two hundred, which is a great price for a drawing. Liv smiles proudly. We say good night to everyone and I turn to grab my jacket off my chair.

"Ready?" I ask, sliding my arms through the sleeves.

Stubbornly, she sits back in her chair and pulls her cell from her purse. "I'll call my mom to pick me up."

Here we go . . .

"No!" I snatch the phone from her hand.

She turns, shocked by my action. "Give that back!"

"No! I drove you here and I'll drive you home. Now let's go, I'm tired." I stand.

Can this night get any worse?

"I can take care of myself, you know," Liv grumbles, then turns her head, sinking back against the chair, making sure I understand she isn't going anywhere with me.

"In most areas," I retort.

"Most areas! Oh, why's that, Tannon?"

I know she's challenging me to say because she's blind. As if that was why. Jeez, I'm beyond peeved right now. I feel my lips curl. "Get over yourself, Liv," I snap. I can't believe I'm yelling at her. "You think I wouldn't have said something to that douchebag if you weren't blind? He was out of line with a seventeen-year-old girl—that's why I reacted. I saw you move from his touch, but he kept his hand on you anyway. It shouldn't have been there in the first place."

I drop into the chair and place my elbows on my knees, rubbing my hand over the back of my neck. The crowd is dying down; most stand by the door as they file out. Just a few waiters are cleaning around us.

"Liv," I say calmer, "his eyes were all over you." I can't believe she's mad at me for defending her. Mr. Tenley got a kiss for defending Ms. Cox and here I am getting yelled at.

"You had no right interfering. I can handle myself."

"Oh, so I should have let him take you to a private room to *talk*?"

242

"You don't have a right to decide where I go or who I go with," she bites back. Her face is red and blotchy. I never saw her so angry.

"He was no good," I say, defeated. I have no energy to defend myself. And she's right—I have no right to her.

"You should have left that up to me to decide. Having one big brother is enough." She drops her head into her hands.

Big brother?

Oh, Evan.

She thinks I'm acting like an irrational big brother. Wow. Now I'm a brother. Another nail in the coffin. Yep, this is definitely over. All hope is gone.

"Well since you're so upset that I called him out, I guess it's good I didn't beat the piss out of him like I wanted to." She lifts her head, appalled by my confession. "I'm going. Are you coming?" I sneer, completely pissed off.

"I'm not some defenseless bird who can't protect herself. If he tried anything, I would have removed his testicles with my bare hands." Her face scrunches, as she squeezes her fists. My eyes widen. Seeing how angry she is, I believe she would've succeeded. "You think I'm pathetic and helpless, don't you?"

I stare, shocked. "No, I do not. Are you ready to go?" There's so much I want to say but don't. Not here.

"Yeah, I want to go home," she says. Standing, she slides her hand around the table to find Trace's flower, and then starts making her way to the door, using her cane. Finding the railing, she guides herself down the stairs. I know better than to go anywhere near her. And I hate the distance.

We stand on either side of the atrium as the valet gets Dad's car. I slap a tip in his extended hand and drop back into the seat. I'm pissed and annoyed I have to sit in a car with Liv for twenty minutes. I'm mad I even came at all.

We ride in silence. She faces the side window and I stare straight at the road. About two blocks from her house I turn the wrong way and pull into the park.

Lowering the music, I turn in the seat to face her. "Thanks for the ride," she says with a groan and reaches for the door.

"You aren't home yet."

She turns swiftly in the seat and grabs my arm, scowling at me. "Take me home, dream killer!"

"Dream killer?!" I screech, utterly wounded. "Wow! You think so little of me."

"You were completely out of line with the guy who might have made my dreams come true, Tan. You think he's going to let me be part of that event now? Take me home!"

"I will after you listen to what I have to say."

She turns forward and crosses her arms, guarded. Shaking my head, I say, "Sit how you want, but you're going to listen. I don't think you're pathetic or incapable or needy or weak. I don't think you're defenseless either. I think you're incredible and talented and smart and sweet and beautiful and giving and capable and independent and strong and inspiring. Jeez, Liv," I groan and grab my head, frustrated. She still won't turn to me, sitting like a statue, wordless. "There is nothing negative about the way I think of you, so stop believing there is. I just know some guys are sick and I know I don't want you to ever get hurt. So be mad at me. I don't

244

regret what I did. If you are in danger or in a bad situation, I will always protect you. Always."

She exhales and turns her head to her side window. I continue, "Not because I think you can't handle yourself. But because I . . ." I catch the word "love" before it hits my tongue. "I'm your friend."

Jeez, I hate what a coward I am.

"How could you think so little of me?" I ask, my sadness heard in my own ears.

"Exactly!" Liv spits, and I stare back, puzzled. "I don't know you at all. Who are you? The cocky teen on a mission or the sad artist?"

"Cocky teen on a mission? Are you serious?" I actually feel maimed.

"Yes, I'm serious. Who's the girl this month?"

"What?" I'm completely stumped.

"Where's Nicole?" she sneers.

"Nicole who?" I groan back—we have five in our senior class alone.

"Whatever, Tannon." She folds her arms again.

"First off, I haven't had a girlfriend since last year. And second, what do you care?"

"I don't. But I don't believe you either," she says, turning her head down and lifting Trace's flower to her chest. The frickin' guy is sitting in this car with us. I can't get away from him. Or the false rumors people start about me. Who said I was dating a Nicole? I turn and put the car in drive. Not talking again until I pull into her driveway.

"Think what you want, Liv, but I would never do anything to hurt you. And your dream is going to come true," I say, looking out my window. "Everyone was so in awe of your playing tonight. Some people just do things for the wrong reasons. That guy is on a power high, using his position to take advantage of anyone who wants to play at Carnegie Hall. I'm sure you're not the first musician he was hoping to take advantage of—or has, for that matter."

"You were out of line. Like some stupid, immature teen."

"You think I'm stupid?" Hearing *her* direct *that* word at me cuts me deep. The silence that follows sticks the knife in deeper.

"I don't think I can ever forgive you for this," she says and her anger turns to sorrow. After opening the door, she sits for a minute. "Bye, Tannon," she says and gets out, slamming the door. I watch her make her way easily to her front door and go inside. The second the door closes, I punch the steering wheel and drive home, sick to my stomach.

***

It's three a.m. and I'm lying in bed still devastated by our fight. *Does she think I'm stupid?* Hearing that word always hurts, but hearing it from her . . . I want to rip my heart out so I don't have to feel anymore. I wish I could talk to Mom right now. A memory of her pops into my mind.

It was the night of the sixth grade dance. Evan and I raced out of the school laughing about something and found Mom leaning against her car. She smiled wide—Mom had a great smile. Her light brown hair was up in a short ponytail. She always looked younger than her years. She was wearing jeans and a T-shirt with a light blue hoodie. I still remember the writing on her shirt. It said, "He's my other half," with an arrow pointing right. Dad had the corresponding shirt that said, "She's my better half," but Dad wasn't there, so her shirt pointed to no one and for some reason it made me laugh.

Our classmates Jerry and Shawn were waiting for their rides and as we walked by Jerry asked, "Tannon, is that your mom?"

"Yeah."

"Wow, she's hot!" Jerry said, wiggling his eyebrows.

"I'll let her know you think so."

"No, dude, don't tell her that." He grabbed my arm and glared at me to stress how much he didn't want me to tell her.

"Mrs. Keaton!" Evan yelled out across the parking lot. Mom smiled and waved. "Jerry thinks you're hot!" he said. I laughed and Jerry punched Evan's arm before spinning to hide his face. Mom's eyes widened and she quickly got in the car. She was probably easing Jerry's embarrassment.

Evan and I raced to the car. "Hey guys! How was the dance?" she asked as we climbed into the backseat. I was old enough to sit in the front but Mom thought it was polite to always sit in the back when a friend was in the car.

"It sucked," I said.

"Never volunteering for that drama again," Evan groaned.

"It was that bad?" she asked, amused.

"Yeah, we got in trouble for break dancing and all the girls were crying. It was horrible." I told her and she giggled as she drove out of the school parking lot.

"Wait! Why were the girls crying?"

"Oh, you don't even understand the drama of sixth grade," Evan started.

I cut in, "Yeah, girls want the boys to ask them out and when they do, the girls say 'no' and then the boys get mad and storm off and the girls cry. Total drama."

247

"No!"

"Yeah, it's crazy." Evan started laughing hard and then said, "Frankie—that's a girl—told Carrie to tell Tommy to ask her out and he did—he doesn't even like her, but he felt bad so he did. She said no and ran away crying. It made no sense."

"That doesn't make any sense at all." Mom giggled again.

"Why is this so amusing, Mom?"

"It's just, I remember sixth grade and, believe me, nothing has changed. Do kids still date for two weeks, never talk to each other that whole time, and then break up?"

Evan and I gawked at each other. "Yes!" we said in unison.

"Yep! Hasn't changed. Did anyone want either of you to ask them out?"

"Well, Janice Vine was chasing Evan all night but he wouldn't let her catch him."

"Good for you, Evan," she said. "You don't need that drama."

"Exactly!" Evan bellowed. "Other guys are catching the bug, though. We don't even hang out with Nick anymore."

"Oh no, why?"

"Because he sits at the girls' table at lunch," I answered.

"Oh boy, he wants a girlfriend?" Mom asked, sounding worried.

"Ha, don't worry," Evan and I said at the same time. "There is no chance he'll get one anytime soon." We started laughing hysterically.

"Why? He's a nice boy."

"Mom, all he talks about is video games and his action figure collection. I don't think any sixth grade *girl is going to be tripping over her feet for that kind of excitement."*

She laughed really loud and then scolded me. "Tannon, that's awful."

"Yeah, for everyone who has to listen to Nick talk about his action figures," Evan chimed in and we cracked up again.

"Well, just remember to be nice to everyone," she said seriously.

"Mom, we're always nice. We're the two nicest kids in the whole stinkin' school."

"Yeah, we really are. You should hear how middle school kids talk," Evan added. "Every other word is a curse. The boy with the worst mouth came from a Catholic school."

"Yeah, go figure," I said, thoughts of how wrong that was danced through my head.

"No! That's horrible," she exclaimed. We laughed at her reaction again. "Well, it's nice to hear you boys are being nice. And I'm glad you're steering clear of the drama. You should wait on the girlfriend talk at least until high school."

"No way," I protested. "No girlfriend for me until after college. I just want to play hockey and hang with my friends. All that crying and misery . . . my mama didn't raise no fool," I said in a southern accent and Mom and Evan laughed.

"No, she didn't," Mom boasted.

"Yeah, I'm not getting involved with girls until after college too. Dad says I should be young and free for as long as possible and just enjoy my youth," Evan said.

"He's so right," Mom agreed. "There's plenty of time to fall in love when you get older."

We dropped Evan off and then stopped for ice cream, just Mom and me. "Mrs. Perkins talked to me at the dance, said my painting in class is the best she's seen from a sixth grader. She thinks I have great potential."

Mom's eyes lit up. "Well, I agree. My son, the artist."

"It was nice of her to say that," I added.

"I'm sure she wasn't just saying it, honey." I shrugged. She tilted her head, studying me for a moment. "You're a very talented young man, Tannon." Then she pushed my cone into my nose and I laughed while wiping cookies and cream off my face with my sleeve.

"Yeah well, I got a 54 on my science test. I couldn't remember anything we studied."

She frowned, not in disappointment but empathy. "You knew it so well. I'll call and see if maybe they'll let you take a verbal test. You do so well with them."

I shrugged again. "Am I stupid, Mom?"

"Tannon, no!" She turned me to face her. "You are smart and talented and kind and loving and athletic. You are so many things, but stupid isn't one of them. And I don't like that word."

"But . . ."

"No!" She shook her head firmly. "Tannon, what would you do if coach said you didn't skate fast enough? Would you quit?"

"No way! I'd get faster."

She nodded. "Yeah, I know you would. Well, that's how you have to take on school. Think of it as a challenge, like a new drill in hockey. Keep practicing. You'll get it." I nodded. "I know how your struggles in school make you feel. You have to work harder and longer and that's tough, but you always get it in the end. Remember that."

She sat back as if pondering a memory. "Remember when you first started to skate?" I nodded while *licking my cone clean. "You got it so quickly, but Evan had a hard time, right?"*

"Yeah. He was a mess on skates."

"Yeah, but it was so easy for you. Thankfully he didn't quit and now it's easy for him too. Some things come easy to us and some things we have to work at. Evan had to work twice as hard as you on the ice and you have to work twice as hard as him in school. Everyone has areas in life they have to work harder at." She hugged me. Mom gave the best hugs. "I'm not going to lie. Growing up is hard. Just do your best. Never give up. Ever."

"I won't. Evan and I are going to college together to play hockey."

"That sounds great!" She smiled proudly. "You just be yourself, Tannon. They say happiness is found by those who stay true to themselves. Never give up on you."

"I won't."

God, I miss her.

Funny how all my plans changed. I believed I wouldn't want a girlfriend until after college, and that I'd actually go to college, and that I'd never give up on myself. Well, I fell into the drama of young love, gave up on the college dream, and stopped being myself freshman year. I gave up the second I lost Mom.

I can't believe I turned my back on that little boy. How could I do that to him? Hide who he was, feel ashamed of him and all his struggles—how could I do that?

Now I feel him wanting to surface, looking for love and acceptance, and I keep pushing him back.

That poor kid. The one person in this world who's supposed to love him hides him in shame.

I'm a horrible person.

I suck.

CHAPTER 27
LIV

Trace isn't in school today, and I so wish he were. He said the bug got him bad and he's still not feeling well. Tannon's here, although, sadly, I wish he weren't. I'm still mad at him.

I walk to Mr. Tenley's class with Cat, hoping he can help me clear things up with Mr. Swords.

"He's in there," Cat says, and I walk in.

"Mr. Tenley?"

"Hey, Liv, how are you?"

I suddenly feel nervous. "I wanted to talk to you about last night. It's just that Mr. Swords was going to arrange for me to play at the Young Artist Night and Tannon ... Well, he thought Mr. Swords was hitting on me and he kind of ... accused him of wanting more from me than to play." My cheeks heat from embarrassment. "I'm just worried that now the offer is gone. I always dreamed of playing at Carnegie Hall and—"

"Liv," he interrupts. "I'm sorry about Mr. Swords ... He wasn't who I thought he was. He was inappropriate with Ms. Cox as well. I made him leave the banquet."

"You did?" I ask, stunned. "He hit on Ms. Cox?"

"Yes. Asked her to go into a private room with him. He had a hand problem, as in he didn't know how to keep them to himself," he explains, annoyance in his tone.

"He never had any intention of letting me play there, did he?" I cover my face, feeling like such a fool.

"Liv, don't you dare think this had anything to do with you. You have extraordinary talent. Mr. Swords isn't the professional I thought he was."

"Oh my gosh, Tannon!" I exclaim, feeling horrible. "He was right about the guy?"

"Unfortunately, yes, Tannon was right. I didn't believe him at first either, but then Ms. Cox shared her experience. I felt horrible for not believing Tannon right away," he says, sounding sincere.

"I have to go." I turn and walk toward the door with my cane and tell Cat everything as we walk to next period.

I have cooking with Tannon.
Oh my God, I don't know how to face him.

At the beginning of the day I was all, "He was out of line, let him be the uncomfortable one in class." And now I know I was the one out of line ... I feel really uncomfortable now.

"I have to apologize. I feel so horrible," I whisper to Cat.

She rubs my shoulder supportively. "It sounds like he was just protecting you from that sleazeball."

I'm so disappointed with the way I treated him. He was just looking out for me. Cat says goodbye to me at the door and I make my way to our station. Tannon doesn't greet me—not that I expected him to today—and I don't know if he's here until I hear him respond to a question Nick asks.

I drop my bag and walk to the sink to wash my hands. "Tannon?" He doesn't respond. He only opens the drawer next to the sink and noisily pushes utensils around before shutting the drawer loudly. "Tannon, I ..." My throat tightens and I take a calming breath. "I talked with Mr. Tenley. He told me about Mr. Swords. I'm so sorry. I was awful and— Please forgive me."

Pots are clanked down from the cabinet. He's ignoring me. Someone in the room is burning something. I smell the charring scent before Mrs. Wilson starts shouting at Nick to remove the pan from the burner. Nick and Michelle start arguing over whose responsibility the pan was. The rest of the students are busy with their own tasks and are either laughing or talking while doing them.

I turn to find something to do. It's just, since Tannon isn't communicating with me, I'm not sure what job to take on. I sigh deeply. "Tannon, I was so excited about being invited to be part of that event and then I thought you were just overreacting so then I overreacted and I'm just so sorry," I say in a desperate ramble. "I was so wrong. Please forgive me?"

He laughs faintly but he doesn't say anything. "You have to say you forgive me, Tannon. I feel awful." Still no response. "Tannon, please say something," I whisper my plea.

"What do you want me to say?"

I turn to his voice. "That you forgive me."

"I don't know if I do," he states, and I lower my head, hopeless. "You thought the worst of me. You actually believed I would do something that would destroy your dream. You called me a dream killer. And you said you'd never forgive me … so why should I forgive you?"

I turn, wanting to cry, and find myself washing my hands again. Not being able to hold it in any longer, my tears fall and I do my best to cry silently. He reaches around me for something and then stops mid-stretch. "Are you crying?" he asks softly.

"I'm so sorry. I didn't mean what I said. I know you would never hurt anyone's dreams. I was upset about losing the chance to play and also about you thinking I was a naïve girl. I regret how I treated you. I regret everything I said."

"Liv, don't cry," he whispers but he doesn't touch me, which isn't like him. He's always touchy-feely. "Don't worry about it. I was just being a stupid, immature teen, right?"

"Tannon. God." I start to cry harder and stay facing the sink so hopefully no one except Tannon can see. Thankfully Michelle and Nick are dominating the room with their argument. "I didn't mean that. I don't think that. I was the one being stupid. I—"

"It doesn't matter," he interrupts. "Bygones."

"What?" I say, snapping my head toward him. "Of course it matters."

"Why?"

I stand, puzzled. "Because you're my friend. Or at least I hope we're still friends."

"Sure. Well, we better get this food ready for tomorrow." He turns from me and starts chopping something on the cutting board.

"I can't believe this class is basically over," I say, hoping to clear the tension between us.

"Thank God!" he retorts, and I turn to fight back how badly his response makes me feel. He can't wait to get away from me. I say nothing the rest of the class. And neither does he.

And after class he just disappears without a word.

***

The last bell rings and I make my way through the gym and out to the student pick-up area. I hear Gary calling my name and then I feel his hand on my elbow. It surprises me that he's the one here.

"Hey, Liv," he greets warmly. "Mom had to work late and asked that I pick you up."

"Okay, thanks." I get situated in the passenger seat as he gets in and starts to drive.

"So . . . how was school?"

I think on this a minute. The two of us never really have in-depth conversations but I need to talk with someone and being a guy, he may have a different perspective to offer. I sure have no answers. I decide to tell him what happened with Tannon. He listens quietly and doesn't interrupt or speak until I'm done.

"So the music guy . . ."

"Mr. Swords," I remind him.

"Yeah, this Mr. Swords was looking to take advantage of you and your friend Tannon called him on it?"

"Yes."

He sits in silence for a moment. "You're a good person, Liv, and you believe most people are. Sadly, there are many that aren't and sometimes it's something seen in their eyes. Tannon saw what you couldn't. You have good instincts—I don't think Tannon or anyone else could say differently—but there are times you are going to have to trust and believe in the people around you to tell you when you're missing something. You aren't helpless because you need help every now and then. We all need help."

"I just—I wish I didn't need so much of it."

"I know," Gary sighs. "That's why I try to stay out of your way. But I . . . I love you, Liv."

I sit, stunned. He's never said that before.

"I just don't know my place. I don't know what role you want me to have in your life. I don't know what I'm allowed to say or do, so, foolishly, instead of asking you, I've stayed on the sidelines."

Tears pool in my eyes. "What role do you want?"

I hear him breathe deeply. "Well, I think of you as a daughter. *My* daughter."

"Really?" I ask, shocked.

"Yes, I guess I haven't done my best to show you that—again, I'm a fool—but I do. And I've had to catch myself from interfering in your life. And stop from adding my two cents when I don't agree with what your mom does or doesn't let you do." He laughs. "Mom's like a scary mama bear when it comes to you and since I never knew if you even wanted me to get involved, I've steered clear of the bear."

I laugh. "Well, if you're on my side, then please, by all means, step in," I say, making him chuckle. "I guess we both didn't know our place, because I've felt the same. I mean, you picked my mom and had to take me in the deal."

"No . . . no . . ." he corrects. "I picked you both. And it was the easiest decision I've ever had to make. When I met your mom, I was instantly attracted to her. I was falling for her before I even met you but when I did meet you, that was it." He pauses. "Meeting you and seeing your mom as a mother sealed the deal. She's the greatest mother I've ever met. Not because she raised a blind girl, but because she didn't . . . Do you understand what I'm saying?"

"Yes," I say, nodding with a smile.

"I've been watching and taking notes from her all these years, staying back even when I wanted to interfere and help or just do it for you. That would be my first instinct, but I had to remind myself that your mom would never interfere unless it was completely necessary." He sighs. "Remember when you moved here and you asked to walk around the block for the first time with Hank?"

"Yeah, I think so."

"I followed you."

My mouth makes a big dramatic "O." "You did?"

"Yeah, and when you made it home, I went inside and Mom scolded me. I said, 'You think I followed Liv because I don't trust she could do it?' and she said, 'Yes.' I told her that I really followed you because I don't trust anyone else."

"What did she say?" I ask.

"She kissed me," he says, amused. "I've wanted to be a dad to you from the beginning. I just didn't know what kind of dad you needed. Or if you even wanted me to be one."

He parks the car and turns the engine off. "We're home." He sits for a moment and then opens his door.

I reach out and grab his arm. "Gary"—he leans back in the seat—"I do need a dad. I need a dad who trusts me and no one else." My tears finally fall.

"Really?" he asks, sounding choked up.

"Really!"

He pulls me into a tight hug. "I can be that kind of dad."

"Thanks for picking me up today," I say, because if he hadn't, it could've been another four years before these things were said.

"Oh and about Tannon," he says, drawing back. "He did exactly what I hope anyone with you would do. Just remember, you are a strong, independent woman, like your mom. Know that. Know who you are and then when someone's trying to help you, you'll take it for what it is and not think the worst."

I nod feeling so sad about Tannon.

"It sounds like he cares about you. And if he does, he'll come around," he reassures me.

CHAPTER 28
TANNON

The marking period's over, thankfully, and now the only class I attend with Liv is English. Somehow I survived the last day of cooking—grinned and bore it—and we made our last meal together. I got a B and Liv got an A; the written test brought my grade down. Friday and Saturday went by in a blur. Evan and I spent a lot of time playing hockey on the frozen lake a few blocks from my house. We both seemed to know not to talk about girls.

Sparks, Tucker, and Teddy showed up to the lake at five o'clock Saturday night with hot dogs and a case of beer. We made a fire in the pit, cooked hot dogs on sticks, and drank without worrying who would tell the coach. Sparks entertained us with stories of his date the night before. He took Robin Porter out and things got pretty hot and heavy in his car. He was boasting about his conquest until the fire died down.

* * *

I stayed clear of Liv all week. I raced in and out of English at the bell and avoided Evan whenever he was walking with her. Now it's Friday, thank God. I can't take one more day of this miserable week. I make my way to math class. The halls start to quiet as everyone scurries into their classrooms like rabbits into their holes. Just as I'm about to enter my little box of a room, I catch Cat walking up to Jimmy Gorjanski, the frickin' biggest druggie in school. He's a big guy who wears black all the time, dyes his hair black, and walks around with a smirk on his face and half-closed eyes.

Never have I seen Cat so much as look in Jimmy's direction before. No one does; he's a loose cannon, set to go off at any second. He's in the classroom for the behavior problem students and out of everyone in there, he definitely belongs. If there was a section in the yearbook labeled "most likely to end up in jail," his picture would be there. So what is Cat doing approaching him?

They haven't said anything to each other yet. She looks nervous and he looks like he's enjoying it. She suddenly shakes her head, as if she changed her mind, and tries to turn from him. Jimmy grabs Cat by the arm and spins her, leaning into her personal space. She looks worried. I call her name from down the hall, and she notices me and cringes. Jimmy lets go of her as he glances over his shoulder, and Cat turns and runs through the stairway doors. I chase

262

her, stopping long enough to tell Jimmy to stay away from her.

"Oh yeah," he sneers. "What are you gonna do about it?"

I turn before pushing the doors open. "Stay the hell away from her, Jimmy. I'm not kidding."

He laughs. "She came to me, man." I shake my head. There's no talking to him; he's probably high as a kite. I'm more interested in talking to Cat anyway.

I push through the doors and find her cowering behind the empty stairwell. "Cat, what are you doing?"

"Nothing, Tannon. It's none of your business," she snaps. Despite her angry front, I can see the shame in her eyes.

"Why were you with Gorjanski? Tell me! I'm not leaving you alone until you do." I step into her space and stare down at her to show my seriousness.

"Please . . ."

"No, start explaining or I'm telling Evan."

"I . . ." She starts to cry. "I thought"—her hands rise and fall—"I thought maybe I could just see if something he had would make life easier to bear," she admits. "But the second his empty eyes looked into mine, I realized that anything he had would only make my life worse."

"Jeez, Cat. Why are you falling down this hole? You've always been so strong. What's going on?" I grab her chin and tilt it for her to look me in the eye. "Tell me!"

"My mom's kicking me out when I turn eighteen. I was the mistake she had to live with for eighteen years. She's never loved me and now she's doing all she can to ruin my future. I have nothing." Her blue eyes are brimming with tears. She turns from me as they pour down her cheeks. My heart breaks for her. "I have nowhere to go. I'll have to get some crummy minimum wage job just to pay for an apartment. Forget college."

"Jeez, Cat, I'm so sorry." Damn, I had no idea her mother was this horrible. "When did she tell you this?"

"The end of August," she says.

That was exactly when she changed with Evan. "So this is why you broke up with Evan?" She nods. "He loves you—"

"Tannon, I know. And I love him. Too much to bring him down with me." She presses her body against the wall and turns her head to look at me, her cheek against the cold concrete. I've never seen Cat look so vulnerable. She loves him that much that she would let him go because she thinks she'll be a burden. Here I thought she was testing him and comparing him to the men her mother brings home, and yet she was just protecting him from her bleak future. I've always liked Cat, despite her craziness, but my fondness just turned to love.

She was always so tough, such a fighter, but there, in those moments before she approached Jimmy, she was ready to give up. She thought she wasn't strong enough to deal with her sorrow on her own. Does she not see how strong she is to put herself through this misery for all those months—wrong or not— just to protect Evan's future? Does she not realize that her strength is what got her to turn down the temporary escape Jimmy could have given her? Grabbing her arm, I pull her into my chest and hug her tight.

"Cat, he deserves to know the truth. He deserves to know why you deny him. I don't think he'll care if you go to college or not."

Pushing against my chest, she looks up at me in a panic. "Tannon, I care. He deserves better than me." She fists my shirt in her hand. "I don't want to be some loser girlfriend he comes home to on holidays."

I pull her against my chest again, amazed how this girl who never grew up with love around her can love so deeply. But sadly, because of the lack of love shown to her, she doesn't believe she's worthy of being loved back. I figured her all wrong; she's nothing like her mother. She's been holding onto this dream of escaping, racing off to college, and starting a new life. And her callous mother now has Cat convinced her dream is dead. She has no one besides her friends. Evan and Liv are completely in love with her, and now I totally get it. She is the kind of person you give your heart to and she protects it with her life. She puts those she loves before herself. She has their love and now I want to give her mine too.

"Cat, I love you," I say, and her knees give out. I hold her up and kiss her head as she sobs against my chest. I can't believe how easy it is for me to say those words to her and yet I can't say them to Liv. Maybe it's because it's not life or death if Cat doesn't love me back. I just want her to know she's loved, she has a place in my heart, and she has a friend in me. I wish she'd tell Evan so he can know how much love she has for him. The girl she's revealing to me today is the girl he's been fighting for. I totally get it now.

"Please promise me you will never turn to Gorjanski. Come to me, talk to me when you feel that low. You have to promise me that or I'm telling Evan."

"Tannon, I swear, the second I walked up to Jimmy I wanted to cry. I knew that second that I couldn't do it. I don't want to end up like him. My future sucks but I don't want to make it any worse." She lowers her forehead to my chest. "Please don't tell Liv or Evan about Jimmy. I feel so ashamed."

We hear the door swing open and turn our heads to see Sparks stop short and Evan crash into him. "Dude!" Evan says, laughing. Sparks stands motionless, as if he's staring at a car crash.

Evan follows Sparks's gaze and sees Cat and me. Staring at us through the open stairway, Evan's face turns white and he steps back as if we just punched him in the gut. We realize we're still holding each other and push away. Our position definitely looked compromising and Evan looks dumbfounded.

"What the hell's going on?" he shouts in a whisper after blinking hard. His eyes narrow and they turn to me, glaring as if he's trying to shoot fire from them.

I hold my hands up. My expression must look guilty. And I do feel guilty—I know Cat's secret and I feel uncomfortable keeping it from him. "Dude, it's not what it looks like."

"I hope not," Evan says, his tone reveals doubt and it guts me. Sparks steps back as if he doesn't want to be involved. I wish I could do the same.

"Cat, please!" I beg for her to explain what's happening here. I'm pissed by Evan's blatant mistrust, but maybe he isn't thinking straight due to the shock. He just walked in on his best friend holding his ex-girlfriend under the stairwell.

Yeah, it looks shady.

Cat's eyes widen, silently pleading with me, as if she expects me to come up with some lie to explain this. I can't. I have nothing. She has to tell him. Not about Jimmy, but she has to tell him about her mom or else I will. Evan sees how she's looking at me and I can tell that he's still taking this the wrong way.

"Cat, you can't let his imagination go wild here," I say, gesturing to his pained expression. "Please tell him. He needs to know."

"Know what?" Evan asks. Now he looks as if we're about to tell him we're together or something. I cringe at how quickly this is going south.

She lifts her hands to me, looking so miserable, and I shrug, feeling horrible for her. I have no idea how to help her out of this. I feel for her and I feel for him too. I understand she still wants to protect him, but I also know this isn't only about her. He has a right to decide what's best for him. "You need him, Cat."

She starts crying again and Evan peers at her, confused. "Evan, sneak her out of here. Take her home and talk to her," I say, and he stands motionless while trying to figure out what's going on. "It's gonna be okay," I say, turning back to Cat.

Shaking her head, she walks past me, past Evan, and through the door. "What's going on, TK?" he asks, pleading for answers.

"You need to talk to her. It's not what you think. She loves you, man. Go!" He turns and races after her. Sparks just looks at his feet. He doesn't want to know what's going on and I don't tell him. I walk past him and back to math class.

CHAPTER 29
LIV

Cat walks into my room cheering my name. I hold my hand out for her to hold her thought until I get off the phone. "Hey, Trace, can I call you back? Cat just walked in all singsongy. Okay. I will." I hang up and smile at Cat. "What has you all cheery?" I ask, pleased to hear the joy in her voice.

"I reached my lowest low today, but somehow I ended up at my highest high," she says. I sit, waiting for her to continue. "I told Evan everything and he was so pissed at me for hiding it, but in the end he said he wanted me back and we would make the long distance thing work when he goes to Virginia. We talked with his dad, and Mr. Tully's going to look into state schools for me and financial aid. He said if all else fails, he'd cosign a student loan for me for the first year. Can you believe it? I didn't think that guy even liked me!"

"Oh my gosh, that's awesome!" I jump up. She races into my arms and we start jumping up and down. "I can't explain how happy I am for you!" I pull her to sit on the bed with me.

"Evan brought me home to get some stuff. Is it all right if I stay here a while? I can't be in that house just waiting for the day she kicks me out."

"Of course. I kind of already hinted about it to Mom. We'll talk to Gary tonight," I say, and I think of Evan. "Evan must be smiling again."

"Yeah, he is," she says, and I detect a hint of naughtiness in her tone.

"Spill it, missy."

"He was so mad and scolded me good. He was pacing and yelling, pissed I ruined our senior year." Cat groans and then giggles. "Funny thing was, I've never seen him like that. It was kind of hot."

I start to laugh. "You're nuts!"

"Yeah, well, we knew that already," she says. "After that, we kind of had a hard time keeping our hands off each other." I can hear her smile.

"Keep talking!"

"Letting him touch me finally felt right. I guess in the past, I wanted so much not to be like my mother that I couldn't even let a guy I love touch me without feeling like a whore, like her. Today, I didn't think of her at all, which is huge, and it was so nice. We didn't do the deed, but we got pretty darn close. God, do I love that boy!"

Her mother's easy reputation was what created the line Cat refused to cross. I'm glad she sees the difference between her and her mother now. "You

269

can't compare your relationship with Evan to any of hers."

"I know," she says with resolve. "I denied myself so much because of her. But when your own mother can't wait to kick you out of her life, it makes it hard to believe anyone else would want you. I'm tired of crying over her. I'm done."

"I want you in my life. Always and forever." I hug her tight then draw back. "Wait, what was your lowest low?"

"I was feeling hopeless. Tannon found me in a desperate state. He pulled it out of me. I told him about my mom, and then Evan walked in on us hugging under the stairwell . . ."

"Tannon?" I draw back even more. "Hugging?"

"Yeah, he was comforting me and . . ." She pauses. "He was so different today. I can't figure that guy out. He actually told me he loved me."

I move back more, pressing my back to my headboard, feeling envious and confused. "He did . . . ?"

She doesn't respond for a moment and I feel her eyes on me. "Yeah, it shocked me too. I always thought there was more to that boy and how he was today makes me believe I'm right. He really cares."

I don't know why I feel completely jealous over Tannon telling Cat he loves her, as a friend or not. It leaves me blue. He hasn't even talked to me since cooking class ended. I miss him and he's avoiding me.

Listen to me. God, this isn't about me.

I reach for Cat's hand and squeeze it. "I'm so happy for you."

CHAPTER 30
TANNON

The guys and I decide to make another weekend of it at the lake. The ice is perfect today, so we shovel the snow off to make a big skate area and use branches to create goal posts before lacing up our skates and grabbing our sticks. We're in the middle of an intense game of two on two—Teddy and me versus Evan and Sparks—when Tucker's Jeep pulls through the snow-covered dirt road and parks. I see Cat in the passenger seat, which doesn't surprise me since she and Evan are together again, but seeing Liv in the backseat certainly does.

I glare at Evan. "Why'd Cat bring her?"

"Why does that surprise you?"

He's right—they go everywhere together—but I can't handle being around Liv right now. Especially today, my birthday. Liv is all I want, all I wish for, and it's a wasted wish. It seems the guys forgot about my day, but I'm not about to remind them. I'd rather just pretend it's any other day anyway. Dad remembered. He gave me two gift cards for the art supply store and a hockey store, and we're going to my grandma's tomorrow for dinner.

Tucker races to Liv's door to help her out. As he walks with her to the stump next to the fire pit, her laughter echoes over the ice. We are in the middle of the woods, and it's kind of our own private spot, just for us guys. I may sound like a baby, but I don't want Liv here. It's impossible to get over her when she's always around.

Tucker comes running onto the ice in his boots. "I brought beer and dogs."

Evan skates off to greet the girls and help Liv lace up her white skates. She has skated with us before at the rink so she knows how. Evan skates her onto the ice as I'm taking slap shots at Teddy. While Teddy retrieves the pucks, I glance at Liv. She's so cute in her hat with the big yarn pom-pom on top and her oversized mittens, and she's smiling so big. *So damn sweet.* I curse myself for taking a peek. Teddy shouts his hello to her and she waves. Sparks skates circles around her and she holds her hands over her face while squealing. He takes her mitten-covered hands and guides her around while skating backward.

I'm the only one who hasn't said hello and I don't especially care. Rather, I don't want to care.

All right, I care.

Ugh, I'm such a jerk! But why does she have to be here?

Cat skates over to me and gives me a big hug. "Thanks for yesterday."

"You don't have to thank me," I say. "You two good now?"

"Better than good," she says, wiggling her brows suggestively and skating away backward.

Shaking my head, I say, "Thanks for the visual."

"Anytime, TK." Cat spins in a circle and finds Evan charging across the ice at her. Turning with a squeal, she skates away, but he grabs her around the waist before she even knows what's happened. Cat laughs as Evan spins her and then pulls her against his chest. Tilting her chin up, he leans down and kisses her before lifting her off her skates and skating her off the ice. Wobbling over to the fire pit, Evan sits her in his lap to continue kissing. With their lips locked, Cat lifts her hands to his hat and pulls it down over his eyes. They laugh. It's a welcome sight. I'm glad to see them happy again.

Tucker races behind Liv and grabs her hips. Sparks lets go and Tucker pushes her on her skates. "Faster!" Liv cheers and Tucker picks up speed, making her face light up with excitement. Teddy calls for him to slow down, but Liv yells back not to listen. She loves it.

Tucker, not owning a pair of skates, slips from the bad traction his boots provide as he's running behind her. He nearly does a split and then falls to his knees, sending her skating forward on her own. She's heading straight for a snow mound. Sparks yells a warning, and panicking, Liv tries to turn except she's going too fast. With my heart in my throat, I skate as fast as I can in hopes of reaching her in time. Seconds short, her skates hit the mound, sending her sailing over the snow bank and landing in the snow inches from a tree. I leap through the mound, skates burying deep in the snow with every jump, and fall to my knees at her side.

"Liv!" I exclaim in a panic. Face down, she lifts her head out of the snow. Her glasses are broken and they fall off her face as she spits out a mouth full of snow. With a panicked expression, she lifts her upper body out of the snow and then freezes. I'm about to reach for her when her frown turns and she starts laughing hysterically.

Tucker races to kneel at her other side. "Liv, shit, I'm sorry," he says, feeling horrible. He must think she's crying. She turns to him and he sees her wide smile. Glancing at me, stunned, I shrug before smiling and he starts laughing. "You're okay?"

"Yes, I'm fine," she says, nodding her head. "But where are my glasses?"

"They broke," he says. "I owe you new ones."

"Yes, you do," she says lightheartedly.

"You're a wild woman, Liv!" Teddy shouts.

"You got air, girl," Sparks praises. "I'd score that a nine point five."

I take the bottom of my sweatshirt and wipe the snow from her face. Seeing a cut on the bridge of her nose from the glasses, I hold my sweatshirt on it to stop the bleeding.

"I'm all right, Tannon." She pushes my sweatshirt away, waving me off as if not to fuss. Helping her up, I lift her over the mound, pat the snow off her coat and jeans, and skate away backward, creating distance.

"You still hate me?" she asks, with a dramatic pout.

"I don't hate you, Liv." *I could never hate you.* Reaching down to pick up my stick, I lean on it, looking for anything to hold besides her. The guys skate away, leaving us alone and I wish they'd come back.

She keeps her head down, fixing her hat. "I can't handle you being mad at me, Tannon. I want to make this right."

"Why?"

She lifts her head, with both bewilderment and disappointment written on her face. Even with closed eyes her face is so expressive. "How could you ask *why*? I care about you and I miss you and I . . ." Her arms rise and fall and she starts slipping and sliding as she loses her balance on her skates. I grab her and almost fall myself. She's in my arms, pressed against my chest, and I close my eyes. Holding her is excruciating. She isn't mine and I have to let her go—both emotionally and physically.

"You have to forgive me, Tannon." Her skates slip over the ice and I have to balance us both. Lifting her higher, to support her more easily, she wraps her arms around my waist tighter, as if she's worried I'm going to step back again.

The urge to hold her wins and I bury my face into her hair at her shoulder and just breathe her in. "You have to promise you'll never believe the worst of me again."

"I promise," Liv says, squeezing my waist. Her head nods vigorously next to mine.

I lift my head and look down at her. "Then I forgive you."

A wide smile grows on her face. "Really?"

I smile at how happy she looks. "Yeah, don't worry about it anymore."

"Yay!" she cheers and jumps up to wrap her arms around my neck. I lose my balance on the skates and fall back onto the snow mound. She falls on top of me. We laugh and I flip us to lie on top of her.

Her big wool mittens grab my face and she smiles. "I'm happy again," she says joyfully.

I lean down and give her a peck on the lips. Hell, I deserve a birthday kiss, don't I? She laughs and bats me away.

A gust of wind sweeps through the valley and lifts the powdered snow off the ice and onto us. Her body shivers under me. I pull her up and place my hockey stick in her hands. "Here, use this as your guide."

She skates away beaming, swinging the stick back and forth and getting acquainted with her surroundings. The uneven ice on the lake takes some getting used to, and yet Liv seems to get the feel for it quickly. The expression on her sweet face shows how happy she is to do it on her own. She swings the stick and glides around freely, stumbling every now and then, finding the edge of the mounds and turning to skate on.

She's beautiful.

So frickin' beautiful.

We decide to play another game, this time with the girls. I stand behind Liv and hold the stick in her hands, slapping the puck whenever it comes our way. We get a goal on Teddy and she cheers with delight when he groans. "We did it!" she says.

"Yep!"

"Hah, one nothing, Evan!" Liv calls out.

"Damn, I should've picked you instead of Cat," Evan says and skates away when Cat tries to hit him with her stick.

Liv laughs at his reply. "Are we up?"

"Yep, I'm moving back. Puck is at the stick. Goal straight ahead. Take a shot." I skate back and watch her wiggle her butt. "Hey, that's not fair."

"You're on my team," she reminds me.

"Oh yeah. Okay, keep wiggling," I encourage. She does and Teddy grumbles that she's cheating. Taking the shot, the puck goes straight to the goal; however, she didn't hit it hard enough so it stops a few feet shy. Sparks skates up and takes the shot, scoring.

"Eat that, suckers!" Sparks yells victoriously. Evan, Cat, and Teddy boo him.

Liv turns and skates toward me. I grab her when she almost passes me and I pull her in for a victory hug. Sparks joins in. Tucker calls us from the fire, letting us know the hot dogs are ready. He's like our camp counselor—well, a counselor who doesn't live by any camp rules and offers beer to the underage campers. We sit around the fire eating dogs and drinking beer. Liv passes on the beer but doesn't say anything about anyone else drinking it. She's sitting on a blanket in front of me and I'm sitting on a stump. She leans back between my legs and I squeeze her torso between my thighs, since she's shivering. I figure it's the gentlemanly thing to do.

At least that's what I tell myself.

Sparks starts telling us a story about his latest date with Robin Porter. This time he almost went all the way with her, but unfortunately, her parents came home and he had to jump out her second story window. He lifts his jacket and shirt to show the scratches from the bush that cushioned his fall.

Cat laughs so hard beer pours out her nose. She turns and wipes her nose on Evan's sweatshirt. He pulls it from her tight hold with disgust. "Gross! Use your own shirt." She grabs his face, kisses him hard, and all is forgiven.

"Hey, Sparky," Liv says. "You shouldn't kiss and tell. Robin really likes you."

"Are you kidding me?" he exclaims. "She gave it up to Dillon Mitchell in ninth grade. And many after him. She doesn't like me. She's that kind of girl, Livy."

"But," Liv pouts, "she told me she liked you . . . a lot."

"She can like all she wants," he bellows. "I don't like her back."

"But you were going to—"

"Livy, you're a good girl," Sparks says. "You wouldn't understand." She drops her head against my thigh, looking embarrassed.

Leaning over, I cover her head with my upper body and look at her upside down. "What's wrong?"

She shrugs. "I feel bad for her."

Sparks grabs her hand that's resting on my knee. "Liv, Robin isn't the kind of girl guys have relationships with."

"But she likes you, Sparks," she protests. "No matter who she was with before or how easily she gave it up, she likes you. Maybe you should find someone else to *not care about* because you're going to hurt her."

He releases her hand and sits back with his beer. His gaze locks on the fire and I assume he's thinking of Robin. Maybe he didn't know she actually liked him. It's not his fault. She does have a reputation, and there is truth behind it. Nonetheless, he looks remorseful now.

"You can't blame him, Liv," Tucker says after considering Sparks' somber mood.

She sits up quickly. "I'm not judging him. No, Sparky, I didn't mean it like that." She holds out her hand and moves to hug him when he takes it. "You were just being a . . . guy. I get that. I'm not the goody-goody you guys think I am."

Evan and I exchange a look. "You better be!" Evan states firmly.

Her shoulders drop. "I don't mean like that. I just mean I get how you guys think—sometimes. And girls too—sometimes. I am one if you haven't noticed."

"Oh, I've noticed," I say, and Teddy laughs uncontrollably.

"Me too!" Tucker bellows. "It'd be hard not to, sweets."

She blushes.

"You were blessed with boobs, girlfriend," Cat states.

"Oh my gosh, Cat!" Liv scolds, red-faced. Cat shrugs, knowing she only spoke the truth. "All I was saying, Sparky," Liv draws out his name, turning the conversation back to him, "is now that you know she likes you, I think you should move on if you don't like her back. You guys sure are judging her on her past decisions. Who knows why she was with those guys? Maybe she thought that's how you get guys to like you or maybe she just likes sex." Our jaws drop again. "All I know is those guys didn't matter to her. You do, and if you use her, it will hurt. You're the one that will hurt her. That's all I meant." She takes his shoulders in her hands. "I don't think badly of you. I love you."

A wide smile grows on his face. "I love you too, Livy Baby."

She cracks up laughing, and he kisses her cheek before sitting back with his beer. She moves back between my legs. I pull her hat over her face and she giggles. "You're too cute, Liv," I say, hugging her with my legs.

"I forgot something in the car," Evan announces and hobbles away on his skates. We start talking about hockey again and then out of nowhere everyone starts singing happy birthday. Liv sits up and turns to sing to me. I look over my shoulder and see Evan carrying a cake with lit candles toward me.

I grin, shaking my head. "I thought you guys forgot."

"No way, bro!" Evan says. "Happy eighteenth."

Liv holds my knee and I grab her hand. "Make a wish," she says.

God, please give me this one. I wish for Liv to be my girl and blow out all the candles. I pull her to me and hug her tight. Cat jumps on top of my back and everyone piles on me. Teddy waits until everyone moves before lifting me off the stump to bear hug me.

Evan hands me a big bag and gestures for me to open it. "It's from all of us."

I sit back down with the bag between my legs. "You didn't have to get me anything. The cake was enough."

"Open it!" Sparks demands.

I open the bag and pull a heavy, wrapped package out and tear it open. A brand new hockey helmet is revealed. The whole helmet is custom painted and a snarling face with wicked eyes stares back at me. "Are you serious? This is sick!"

"You like it?" Evan asks and turns it to show me the back. It says "Crusher," my nickname on the ice.

"Oh my God! I love it!" I say, amazed and touched. Deeply touched. "I think I'm gonna cry."

Evan bear hugs my head. "Happy birthday!"

"I ... Wow, thank you," my voice trembles. "Really, everyone, thank you!"

"We love ya, TK!" Tucker shouts. "Happy birthday, dude!"

Cat grabs my face and kisses the side of my lips. "Happy eighteenth!"

"Thanks, Kitty Cat," I purr.

I pull Liv into my arms. "You really thought we forgot?" she asks.

"Yeah. This is a huge surprise."

"We love you, Tannon. Don't you know that?" she says, hugging me tight.

"Yeah." I know Liv loves me as the others do, but I wished for her to love me as I love her. *Please God, let it come true.*

Cat cuts the cake and passes it out on paper plates to everyone. We go back to laughing and teasing each other. I glance at the awesome helmet every now and then. "Who painted it?"

"A guy my dad knows," Tucker says. "Sick right? Just picture that on the ice."

"Yeah, it's awesome." I can't stop smiling. "Thank you, guys. Really. I feel really lucky."

Liv's sitting between my legs again. I bend down and shake my legs back and forth, wiggling her between them. "I love you, guys," I say next to her ear.

I hear someone clear their throat behind me and look up to see everyone's eyes widen as they look over my head. I turn and see Trace standing outside the fire pit area, staring at us with a wounded expression on his face.

I grimace, annoyed he's here. How did no one hear him pull up? Probably all the singing and joking. Why is he here anyway? Turning to Liv, still leaning back between my legs, I say, "Trace is here." She sits up straight as a pin.

"Trace!" she calls out. "Hi! Hi!"

"Happy birthday, Tannon," he offers. I nod back. "Should I come back?" he asks, staring at me. "Or leave altogether?"

I vote for the latter!

"What? No. Why?" Liv rushes up and almost spins her leg into the fire. I pull her back to me to save her from getting burned, but for some reason she starts batting me away. "Stop it!" she snaps. "Let me go."

Realizing she must think I'm trying to get her into trouble, I grimace. "Wow!" I exaggerate the word. "Back to thinking the worst, are we? That didn't take long." I stand and walk back to the ice, wobbling on my skates through the snow.

"He was just saving you from the fire, doll," Teddy says in my defense.

"Tannon!" she calls out sounding apologetic. I ignore her. Trace turns to walk back to his car.

"Trace is leaving, Liv," Cat whispers.

"Wait, Trace!" she cries out. "Where are you going?" I see her trip over the log framing the circle and land on her knees. Cat helps her through the snow to Trace. He leans against his car with his head down and she looks like she's trying to explain why she was cuddled between my legs.

Every time I find some sort of hope, he shows up. Whether it be in a phone call, a flower, or crashing my birthday party, he's always there just when I'm feeling special to her. I guess that's the point—I'm not. I'm not that special to her—he is. She was just in the position to make a decision, go to him or me, and she chose him.

It cuts me deep. But what have I been holding onto anyway? False hope? I skate to my stick and see them get in his car as I'm picking it up. So much for birthday wishes.

Teddy comes out onto the ice. "You okay, TK?"

"I'm done, man. I've said it a million times, but this has to be it. I can't keep grabbing at nothing. I keep thinking maybe I have a chance, maybe she . . ." I groan. "It doesn't matter. I'm done."

Birthdays suck!

CHAPTER 31
LIV

We sit in silence as Trace drives down the bumpy road. "He seems to be an active part of our relationship." Trace finally speaks and I can sense his head in his hand against the window.

"Who? Tannon?"

"Yes, Tannon!" he says.

"We're friends, Trace. It's not like that." I turn to face him. "You're acting like you just walked in on us or something."

"I feel like I did interrupt something, Liv," he says. "You all looked pretty comfortable there and I was the party crasher."

"Trace, I asked you to come. You weren't crashing anything. They're my friends. We are comfortable around each other. We were just talking and laughing. It's his birthday. He was emotional about his gift." I sigh. "He was just happy. I'm with you, Trace."

"Well, you looked like you were with Tannon a minute ago."

I sit back and lower my head, feeling horrible he's so upset. "I'm sorry it looked bad."

He stops the car and I hear him turning in the seat. "Tell me right now, do you have feelings for Tannon?"

"He's my friend and I care about him. I have feelings for you," I say.

"Does Tannon have feelings for you?"

I huff out a laugh. "No, Trace! He flirts, but he always has. And he flirts with everyone, doesn't he?" I ask, sure he's noticed.

"Not lately, no," he says.

"Really?" I sit bewildered. "Well, I assure you he thinks of me as a friend. Everyone was hugging him. He was hugging everyone. We were happy that we surprised him—Trace, I'm with you."

"Fine, let's not talk about it anymore."

"Sounds good to me," I say. And I feel out of sorts, because I'm saying all these things to Trace with Tannon still on my mind.

Ugh . . .

PART 3: SPRING

CHAPTER 32
LIV

With the help of April showers, our relationships grow. Trace and I are happy. Evan and Cat are going strong. And Tannon, well . . . We haven't talked much since his birthday, but I heard he went on a few dates with Eva Marco, a junior. I miss him desperately, but he doesn't seem to want to be my friend, not after I thought the worst of him twice. I don't know why I reacted as if he was trying to get me in trouble with Trace. I think my reaction stemmed from my own guilt. I guess deep down I knew I enjoyed cuddling next to him and I felt guilty about that. I took it out on Tannon only to find out, yet again, he was just looking out for me, protecting me from getting burned . . . *Ugh, why'd I have to react like that?* And why can't I hang out with him as we used to without feeling guilty and confused? I guess it doesn't matter—he won't talk to me anyway.

All I know is it doesn't feel right without Tannon in my life. His absence leaves a big hole, and I don't believe I have the right to say so. I'm left to accept his choice and hope he changes his mind soon.

Things have changed at home. Mom and I talked to Gary about Cat staying with us and he was cool with it. He teased, "What's one more strong-willed female?" Cat told her mother who simply said "fine" with no emotion, and Cat moved in with us that same night. She's been here a month and I've loved having her as a constant fixture in my life. She walks to Evan's or he comes here. He and Gary have become buddies and Trace comes to hang out with them a lot too. Dinner has become a loud, crowded table full of entertainment. Mom loves it because it reminds her of the loud, Italian table she grew up eating at.

Cat and I lie in bed at night talking about anything and everything. We talk about the future. Our plans have changed since the beginning of the school year but we are still excited for what's ahead. Mr. Tully helped Cat enroll at New Jersey Institute of Technology (NJIT) in Newark. It's a great school, and it's not so far away so she'll be commuting. He helped her figure out financial aid and was also willing to loan her money for whatever the aid won't cover during her first year. She already has a job lined up at a design firm as their front desk receptionist starting right after high school graduation. She says it's a great way for her to meet all the big shot designers and maybe get her foot in the door.

Things were never as bad as she believed. Not getting the scholarships she applied for and her mom denying help scared Cat into thinking life was over and college was a dream that would never come true. She may have had to change her dream a bit but she's going to become an interior designer and that's all that matters.

As for me, I applied to a few schools out of state but when I got accepted into the music department at Drew University in New Jersey, I decided I'd stay close to home as well. My dream was to go away with Cat and the thought of going alone scares the heck out of me. I'm super excited I got in to Drew. Mr. Tenley asked a few of the influential people I met at the banquet to write letters of recommendation for me and those seemed to help seeing as the director of the music department called me directly to welcome me into the school. I'm not sure if that is a common occurrence, but it made me feel pretty special.

Trace is going to Stanford like he wanted. However, we still haven't discussed that it's across the country. California isn't exactly a hop, skip, and a jump away. I wonder what will happen to us when the time comes. Will our relationship have what it takes to make it long distance? Is he even interested in long distance?

Ugh . . . I wish I had the guts to ask.

I can't believe this year is almost over. Everyone's talking about prom and graduation and the after parties for both. Trace asked me to the prom by writing out "prom" in large braille letters with Skittles that he glued to a large rock behind my house. I laughed at this and of course said yes.

Evan asked Cat on the loud speaker at school during the morning announcements. He got in trouble for grabbing the microphone right out of the announcer's hands. He said it was worth it though. Tucker asked Samantha by spelling out "prom" with playing cards he taped to her garage door—using only aces. He bought many packs. And I heard Tannon, Sparks, and Teddy have yet to ask anyone. They still have three weeks, but us girls like having time to pick out the perfect dress.

I wish I could talk to Tannon. The only thing is, I never know when he's nearby. Well, I know he's in English, but he races in and out as the bell rings so I've yet to get my hands on him. Besides, Trace is there and that would be awkward. Tannon stays quiet in class, only getting involved if he's called on, and seems distant when he does speak. I've thought of calling him a few times but don't know how to start the conversation. Cat says Evan doesn't really answer any of her questions about Tannon and she's not sure why he's so tight-lipped. I guess I really ruined a special friendship with a great guy.

**

Cat and I meet Evan by his car after school and he drives us to Tucker's house to hang out while the guys ride dirt bikes. Trace had to go to his grandmother's for her birthday, so he's meeting me here after he visits with her. We walk through the woods behind Tuckers' house to the clearing.

I've never been back here before. I can sense the clearing the second we enter it; everything feels open to me and the sun is on my face again. The rumbling of an engine races by, leaving behind the smell of dirt and gasoline.

"Wow, Tucker's crazy on that thing," Cat says.

Tucker's been riding dirt bikes since he could walk. His father is a huge motocross fan and lives vicariously through his son. He even bought three new dirt bikes with his Atlantic City winnings last year. Rumor was Mr. Jenson won big—he's a professional gambler—and spent most of it on extravagant things, like the bikes and an inground pool, and then gambled the rest. He built the track back here in the woods and this is a huge pastime for all the guys when the weather is right. Another bike races by me and I realize there are two riding at the same time.

"Who else is here?" I ask Evan.

"Tannon!" he shouts over the bike flying by. I tense up instantly.

"Are you riding?" Cat asks and Evan answers yes. "Okay, Liv and I will go sit in the chairs."

She waits for the bike to go by again before guiding me across the dirt mounds. She sits and places my hand on the lounge chair next to her. I feel it and take a seat.

A bike skids to a stop in front of us, dirt trickles against my skin, and the dust makes me cough. "Hey, Liv, you want a ride?" Tucker asks.

"Really?" I sit up eagerly.

"Sure. I won't go too fast over the jumps."

"I'd love to!" I stand and walk toward the rumble and heat of his bike. He takes my hand and stands me in front of him while strapping a helmet on my head before guiding me onto the back of the bike. The seat is hot and I can feel the engine vibrating against my legs.

"You be careful, Tucker," Cat demands. I hear two bikes zip past. Evan must be on one already.

"Of course." Tucker wraps my arms around his trim waist. I smell a mixture of sweat and men's body spray. "Hold on tight, sweets. Ready?"

"Yes!"

The bike lurches forward and dirt kicks up, hitting my bare shins. I can't help but smile. He picks up speed and starts hitting jumps, my body rising off the seat and slamming back down as I squeal with delight each time. "Faster?" he asks.

"Yes!"

Tucker pops us into a gear and we suddenly flash forward. He hits a jump and it feels like we're in the air forever before we land with a thump and my butt bounces against the seat. I hold on so tight my arms hurt, and I love every exhilarating minute of it. He hits four jumps in a row before we turn into a tight bend and then hit five more. It goes on like that for ten laps and it never gets old.

He slows down. "You want to drive?"

"Me?" I ask, shocked. "Really?"

"Yeah, I'll help you," he says, sounding excited to let me try.

"Oh, Tuck, I'd love to try." I squeeze his waist. He stops the bike completely and slips off. Seconds later I feel him behind me. It's a tad awkward. More so than when I was holding him. He's close. Really close.

A bike stops next to us. "What are you doing?" Evan asks.

"Get Tannon off the track. I'm going to let Liv drive for a while," Tucker orders, and I've never heard him talk so sternly before. Maybe he doesn't want anyone to ruin this for me.

I love Tucker!

Long fingers wrap around mine on the handlebars and he pops something down by my left foot. He lifts both of my feet one at a time and rests them down on a part of the bike. "Keep your feet up on the pegs. I'll shift. You turn this"—he twists my hand down while squeezing the right handlebar grip—"to give it gas. And this"—he pulls my fingers to touch a metal bar in front of the handle—"is the brake."

"Okay."

He pulls my left fingers to touch another metal bar. "This is the clutch. I'll ask you to squeeze it when I need to shift gears. And this is how you release it." He eases his pressure over my fingers and we release the bar, slow and steady. "Now squeeze it again and I'll pop us into first." I do and he does something that makes the bike lean to the left for a second.

"Tucker!" I hear Tannon shout. "You're two for two—you really want to hurt her on a bike too?"

I cringe. I guess Tucker doesn't have the greatest track record with me. It is true—every time Tucker tries to have fun I end up getting hurt. Even so, I really want to do this. "We'll be fine," I say.

"Fine," Tannon snaps back.

"Yeah, hi to you too," I retort. Tannon doesn't respond. I twist my wrist down to give the bike gas while releasing the clutch too fast. We shoot forward, Tucker grabs control of the bike as it stalls.

"Easy, sweets," Tucker says, his tone gentle.

"Sorry."

"Get off," Tannon barks. Thinking he's ordering me, I turn and scowl at him. "I was talking to Tucker," he says, calmer. "I'll take you."

293

"We're fine," I say. Who does he think he is? He hasn't talked to me in a month and now he's trying to control what I do and who I do it with? No way.

There's some kind of silent exchange between them. I can tell something's going on, and sadly, Tucker caves, lifting off the back of the bike with a grunt of disappointment. I beg him to stay; he doesn't respond. Then I feel Tannon's larger frame sit behind me and the bike lowers dramatically.

"Hey," I sulk, "let Tucker take me."

"No!" Tannon squeezes my fingers around the clutch and pops the bike into gear. "Go." He holds my waist with his right hand while his left hand covers mine over the clutch bar.

For some reason I can't move—his touch leaves me motionless. I just sit there rendered powerless by his closeness, the intense heat of his body. His hard chest flexes against my back as his right arm reaches forward and his hand wraps around mine on the handlebar. He squeezes my hand down to give it gas. We start to move. He lets go and holds my waist again.

"I'll tell you when to turn or brake. And when a jump is coming," he says matter-of-factly. "Four jumps on this side and a right bend and then five on the other with another right bend. The track's an oval. Stay on the left side of the track. There's a lot of mud on the other side."

The track is already in my memory from when Tucker was driving. I'm just not sure how fast to go or if I can handle the bike, but I know Tannon will help. Every now and then his left hand covers mine to squeeze the clutch bar. He calls out the jumps and I ride over them slowly, then he calls a right bend and helps me with the steering. I gun it a little too fast at the next jump, and he grabs my waist with one hand and the handlebar with the other. "Easy, tiger," he says.

A flat palm presses on my stomach as his fingers spread wide. I can't think—he's making it difficult to concentrate. I hit another jump too fast and my head pops back, hitting his. Tannon groans and I realize he doesn't have a helmet on. "You should have on a helmet, especially when driving with a blind girl."

"Blind girl. Where?" he retorts, but I hear no amusement in his tone. He's still mad at me.

We ride up and down the jumps and he gives me full control. It's thrilling to have power over such a machine. The vibration of the engine, the loud noise, the wind and dirt—all of it makes me feel mighty. He shifts the gears when called for and holds on as I ride like the wind—well, more like a steady breeze, but still, it's exciting.

Tannon's thick thighs squeeze against mine as his chest presses against my back and his chin rests on my shoulder. Awareness of every part of him makes me forget what I'm doing and we start slowing down when I neglect to squeeze the throttle. A large hand wraps around mine and gets us going again.

"Where is everyone?" I ask.

"On the other side. There's a huge dirt pile in the middle of the track."

I squeeze the brake to stop us and pull the helmet off before speaking. "Tannon, why are you on this bike with me?"

His body tenses before he answers. "Because I don't trust Tucker with this."

"Why? What do you care?" His feet hold the bike level on the ground. I felt him place them there, so I lift my leg over the seat and stand next to him. "You haven't talked to me in a month."

"Because you broke a promise the day you made it," he says, his hurt evident. I lower my head, shamed. "But that doesn't mean I want to see you get hurt."

"I've been wanting to apologize for that, but you've been avoiding me," I say.

"Not like you don't know my number."

My shoulders slouch, feeling miserable. "I'm deeply sorry about how I reacted ... yet again." Tannon doesn't respond. "I think maybe I should ride with Evan."

"Why?"

"Because I can't think with you ..." I stop before the truth slips out. His touch is too much for me and I don't understand it. Mostly I don't understand why I like his touch so much.

"With me what?"

I lift my hands and groan. "Stop, Tannon."

"Stop what? I don't even know what I'm doing."

I drop my head. Unsure of what to say, I can't exactly tell him that I crave his touch.

"Do you smell that?" he asks suddenly, sniffing deeply. "That sweetness? Do you smell it? I think its honeysuckle."

I turn my head, left and right, and breathe in deeply, catching the scent of something sweet now that the dust has settled. The bike creaks and suddenly Tannon is standing before me. He takes my hand and pulls me off the track. My feet tangle with tall grass or weeds before he stops. "Yep, here it is. Wow, there's tons of it."

The sweet scent of honey fills my nose. "Honeysuckle's a plant, right?"

"Yeah, c'mere." He pulls me to sit down on the ground. "We had this plant in my backyard when I was little. Mom and I used to sit together and pull the flower apart to get the little drop of nectar on our tongues."

"You can eat them?" I reach my hand out to find the plant. The soft petals tickle my palm.

"You take the flower and then pull the skinny stem thing out of the middle very slowly, and then you can taste a tiny drop of the plant's nectar." I hear a snap. "Here, stick your tongue out."

I do, trusting him without question, and that makes me smile. I didn't think twice before offering my tongue so he can feed me a plant. *That says something, doesn't it?* He slides a thin, almost string-like stem across my tongue. I taste the faint sweetness and smile. "Yum!" Laughing faintly, he offers more. "You have some." I gently push his hand back toward him.

"No, I can't, not without her," Tannon says, and I feel his sorrow. "I ripped the plant out of my yard after she died. I couldn't stand it being there without her."

Taking his hand, I follow his arm up to his face and hold my palm against his cheek. "Tannon, you should embrace all those wonderful memories you have of her. Those are the ones she'd want you to hold onto." His hand lies over mine on his cheek and he presses it tightly against his hot skin. "I'm so sorry I hurt your feelings again. I've missed you so much."

His other hand slips behind my neck and into my hair. Goose bumps prickle down my spine. "I missed you too," he says. Fingers spread wide at the base of my skull and he pulls my head to his shoulder. "It's been ...," he starts but the sound of a motorcycle coming our way stops him.

Without warning, a wave of water hits me. Soaking the whole right side of my body. "What the ..."

"Son of a ..." Tannon groans. "Sparks, you jackass!"

The bike stops and Sparks yells, "Whoa, man, I'm sorry. I just got here and Evan asked me to see if you guys were okay." And then he starts laughing. "Really, I'm sorry, I didn't see you there," he says, trying to stop his laughter and failing miserably.

"This is mud, right?" I ask Tannon, holding my hands out as it drips off my hair and plops into my lap.

All of a sudden, Tannon starts laughing. "Yes, I got it too."

"Seriously, Sparks?!" I whine.

"I didn't mean it, I swear," Sparks says, not laughing as hard. "I'm sorry, Livy. I'll go get you a towel." The bike starts up again and he races off.

Tannon continues to laugh uncontrollably. I sigh and pout. "How is this funny? I have mud in my ear."

"Me too!" he says through his hysteria. I shake my hands and mud flies all over me. Then a slop of mud slides down my nose and onto my chest. I lift my hands and gesture to what just happened. "Really?" I say, feeling it slip between my boobs. "Did that just happen?"

"I'd be happy to scoop it out for you," Tannon offers.

So kind of him.

My mouth twists. Tannon falls to the side with a thump. A bubble of laughter works up my throat and breaks through my annoyance. I fall to my side and join in the comedy of this scene. He pulls me to him, pressing his forehead against mine, and we laugh. And it feels so good to be this happy with him after being away from him for so long.

His hand brushes the heaviness of my hair away from my face and he slides his thumb along my cheek bone, smearing mud across it. Suddenly we stop laughing. And a bizarre energy radiates between us and I know instantly that this isn't a friendly energy and I shouldn't be feeling this with someone other than Trace. But the thing is, I never felt anything like this with Trace. I suddenly feel sad and guilty and start to stand up, but Tannon tries to pull me back down.

"Here, Livy," Sparks calls, huffing as he runs toward us. Tannon lets me go as a towel is dropped on my head.

"Thanks. Can you bring me to Cat?" I ask Sparks. He takes my hand and I stand. "Thanks for the ride, Tannon. I'm going to get cleaned up."

"Yeah, no problem," he says.

"Hey, Liv!" Trace calls out.

Shocked, I spin to his voice. "Trace, hi!"

"Wow," he says, suddenly beside me. "What happened?"

"Sparks rode past us and covered us with mud."

"Oh, uh . . ." he pauses, probably assessing the situation. Ugh, I'm sure it looks bad, again, with Tannon and I being the only ones over here covered in mud.

"My bad," Sparks says.

Trace huffs out a dead laugh. "Well, you ready to go?"

"Uh . . . you want to go?"

"Yeah," he says.

Confused and sad, I say, "Sure." Trace was actually looking forward to coming. He and Evan were talking about riding the other day and Trace seemed eager to try. Now it sounds as though he can't leave fast enough.

We say goodbye to the others and head to my house. The whole way home I think of that crazy energy between Tannon and me. And feel guilty for it.

Again.

CHAPTER 33
TANNON

Eva walks up to me as I'm pulling my English book from my locker. She's a pretty girl—great face, perfect skin, big brown eyes, thick dark hair. And when she's pissed, she curses in Spanish—it's kind of hot. But she's not Liv. We've been on two dates. I thought someone so vibrant could distract me from my gloom, but unfortunately, dating anyone that isn't Liv only makes it more apparent that I don't have the girl I want. And yesterday just put Liv right back into the forefront of my mind. No matter how hard I try to erase her image, she always reappears. This past month of not talking to Liv was hell to say the least.

Sparks's damn timing sucked yesterday. But it's good he showed up because I was about to kiss Liv and then she'd feel guilty. If Trace got there a few minutes earlier, he'd have seen Liv in another compromising position with me. The way he looked at me before walking away made me wonder how much he really did see. If he did, he didn't say, although he did hightail it out of there. Who knows?

And who cares?

Not me.

"It's Friday," Eva cheers, snapping me out of my daze.

"Yep," I say, shrugging at the obvious.

"Well"—she taps my chest—"where are you taking me tonight?"

I stare at her pretty doe eyes and frown. "You're great, Eva." I shift from one foot to another, not sure of what to say next. I should've never put myself in this situation. Or her for that matter. She's a cool girl. Maybe if things were different . . . who knows? "I just don't want a steady thing with anyone. I thought that was clear."

All I want is a forever thing with Liv. That's all I want. And I'm not going to get that so I should just stay clear of all girls until I graduate from this place.

"But," Eva starts and looks around before moving in closer. "I thought maybe we would go to prom together."

What?

Why would she think that after two dates?

"No. I don't even know if I'm going."

Truth.

"Seriously? You're such a jerk!" Here we go . . . She switches to Spanish and goes wild. I lean against the locker and try to figure out what curse words she's calling me.

I stare, shocked by all the times she calls me a *pinga.*

"Oh, I'm so done with you!" There are no tears in her eyes, just flames—she's pissed. After two uneventful dates, go figure.

"I'm sorry you thought we'd go to prom. Not sure why you thought that, but I'm sorry just the same." I look her in the eyes so she can see my sincerity. "I'm sure you'll have no problem finding someone to take you."

Eva glares at me. "You don't even seem fazed by this."

"It was two dates." I stare at her, perplexed by what she might possibly want from me. Does she want me to cry over two dates? I shrug not knowing what else to do. "I'm sorry."

Shaking her head, she turns and storms off down the hall.

Wow, is it me?
Who knows?

***

I walk into English class telling Evan all about Eva. He laughs through the whole story. "Is it me?"

"No, dude," he says, smacking my shoulder. "Not this time. How does two dates equal prom?"

"Exactly. Thank you."

Taking our seats, we notice Liv's seat is empty along with Cat's. Evan shrugs. Mr. Carlson gets right to asking questions about the new Shakespeare play we've been reading, *The Two Gentlemen of Verona.* I had a hard time with it so I sat with Mr. Carlson a few times after class to go over the basics.

"Trace, tell us what you got from *The Two Gentlemen of Verona.*"

"Well, Proteus loves Julia until he goes to Milan to meet up with Valentine. Then he falls for Valentine's girl, Silvia. He forgets all about Julia the second he sees Silvia. He's so damn selfish. Valentine was his best friend. He had no right pursuing her. There are rules and he's too greedy to follow them. You don't go after another guy's girl." Trace glances over his shoulder at that last part.

I roll my eyes. He obviously saw more than I thought yesterday. Good, maybe he got a chance to walk in my shoes for a minute. I'm sick of seeing her near him too.

"That part didn't affect me as much as Julia's." Beth, who sits in the front row, pops into the discussion. "When Julia dresses like a boy and finds Proteus in love with Silvia, she stays, still wanting him. I don't get it."

"Yes, but she, unlike Proteus, remembers what they had," Mr. Carlson explains.

"Proteus is a player. The only good guy in this story is Valentine," Trace says.

"Proteus isn't a player," I jump in. "Maybe Proteus feels that Silvia should be with him."

"Silvia isn't his girl. He doesn't care about her, he just wants to conquer and move on," Trace snaps.

"That's so far from the truth," I retort.

He turns in his chair. "Whatever. Proteus just walks around thinking his looks win all. Well, they won't win her."

My blood boils. "If Valentine was right for her, then no one would be able to get between them."

"Proteus is playing her. He wants to take advantage of her—"

"No, he doesn't!" I snap, moving forward in my seat. "He never would. You don't know him, so don't assume you do."

"TK," Evan says as a warning to calm down.

"Oh, I know him." Trace stares me right in the eye. He's tougher than I thought; I'll give him that. "He just wants one thing—"

"You don't know him, Trace," Evan jumps in, defending me. "You have no idea, so leave it alone."

"Yeah, he wants one thing," I say, continuing this staring contest Trace started, "but it's not what you think."

"Are you forgetting about her father, the Duke? He has her marriage arranged with that other idiot, Thurio," Beth says, totally clueless to what's really going on here. "I don't understand what they're talking about, Mr. Carlson."

"They're not talking about the play anymore," Mr. Carlson states, knowing exactly what's going on.

"Yeah, these two idiots are turning a Shakespearian classic into a high school love triangle," Rita barks. Trace and I both glare at her.

"That's enough, Rita," Mr. Carlson says, and she throws her hands up and points at us. "What about them?"

"You two better figure this out before the test because—and I do feel your pain boys—I will fail you if you give me these answers," Mr. Carlson states.

"Thirty or so pounds," Trace mumbles. I raise a brow, confused by what that means. "That's all you have over me. And it means nothing to her. Looks didn't win this one. Brains did." He taps his head. I want to rip it off his shoulders.

"That's enough guys," Mr. Carlson orders.

Trace turns his back to me. I edge up closer and lean forward over my desk. "Tell me one thing, Trace. If you *won*, then why are you even talking about this?"

"Because you don't seem to get that she's with me," he says, not turning.

"Oh, I know she's with you. Believe me, I know. I'm reminded of it every damn day," I say, moving even closer, inches from the back of his head. "And I thought that you were right for her, but now I'm starting to wonder . . ."

Suddenly Liv and Cat walk in. "Sorry, Mr. C.," Cat says, "Liv couldn't find her computer."

"Did you find it?" he asks, concerned.

"Yes." Liv lifts her backpack. "I forgot it in science. I'm sorry we're late."

"It's fine," he says and gives me and Trace a stern look. "We are going to move on now. Right guys?" No one responds. "Beth, why don't you read your poem?" he says.

Beth moves to the front of the class. I pay little attention to her. I can't even think. I'm fuming over the crap Trace said. Believing I'm only after one thing—he has no clue how I feel about Liv.

"Tannon, why don't you go next?" Mr. Carlson says. I roll my eyes at him. "C'mon, shift your focus."

I stand and walk to him in a fog. I have no paper in my hand; I memorized this one. "'Nothing More,'" I say.

If I could feel her love for just one day,
I would accept my death the next and say,
"I have lived a blessed life.

I was loved by the girl I adore.
She was all I wanted . . . nothing more."

The room is quiet as I sit back down. Trace turns in his seat and glares at me. "You don't know me at all," I whisper. "And more like forty pounds."

The bell rings and Liv turns in her seat. "That was beautiful, Tannon."

"Thanks." I grab my bag and walk out.

***

Either the lunchroom is overly loud today or I'm especially sensitive to it, seeing as I'm still boiling and wishing I'd hit Trace right in that smart mouth of his, I'd say it's the latter. Teddy sits across from me with a thump, his narrow eyes glaring over my shoulder, distracting me from my own problems. "What's up?"

"That little twerp is messing with Laura again." Teddy's chin points across the room and I turn to see Laura, the sophomore from Ms. Harper's class, sitting with her head bowed down and that little runt who messed with Liv in the hall leaning over her. His friends are laughing at whatever he's saying to her. Why is she letting a freshman bully her?

"He's getting under my skin," Teddy grumbles. Looking back at Teddy, I see how heated he is and it shocks me. He never gets this worked up. "Twerp asked her out on Tuesday, she said no. Now he won't leave her alone. Calls her names every time she walks by."

"She bruised his fragile ego and now he's trying to act like he doesn't like her," I guess, although I'm sure I'm right.

"Yeah, well, I'm about to bruise more than his ego." Teddy stands and walks to the edge of our table. I grab his arm. "I'm with you, man, but answer this," I say, smiling. "Does the big guy like her?"

He looks down his nose at me. "What does it matter? Girls that look like that don't go for guys that look like me."

"Oh, I think she's too smart to not see a good thing." I stand, patting his back. "C'mon, stud, time to show her what a catch you are."

We walk up to Laura's table and stand with our arms crossed over our chests. The little squirt has yet to notice us. His head's down by hers and he's rambling off insult after insult. My least favorite is, "Laura, Laura is a stupid whore'a."

Seriously?

It takes every ounce of control for us not to jump the kid and pull on his limbs like a wishbone. We rein it in . . . tight.

"Wow, Teddy, did you hear that?" I ask. The kid looks up and steps back quickly. His friends slide down the table, taking their food trays with them. Laura glances up only to drop her gaze again immediately after seeing us.

"Sure did," Teddy replies, his lip twitching from anger. "I heard a helluva lot of name calling and a few threats. Even saw some inappropriate hand gestures. What about you, TK?"

I turn my even gaze to the freshman. "Yeah, I heard the same. Would you call that bullying?"

Teddy nods. "Yeah, but maybe we heard wrong. I mean, he has a smart look about him. Doesn't he?"

"He sure does. And a smart guy would never bully a girl with crazy friends."

Teddy tilts his head to the side with a shrug. "Definitely not, but looks can be deceiving."

"You're right," I agree. "Weird because I also remember having a nice chat with this young man not so long ago. What was it we talked about . . . ?" I pretend to rake through my memory, pulling my mouth to one side while squinting my eyes. "I remember now. It was about Hardy rules. If he can't follow them, then I won't either."

"Really, TK?" Teddy asks. "He was already warned?"

"Yeah, and if we heard him correctly, he broke the rules." I cringe. "Oh boy, I don't know what to do. Maybe his looks are misleading and he didn't understand my warning."

"This is a tough one," Teddy says. "If the young man is smart, then he is in the wrong here, but if he isn't, then we would have to let him go. I mean, we're crazy but we can't blame a kid for not knowing any better."

"You are so right." I gesture for Teddy to step forward. "Please, you ask."

"Why thank you, TK." Teddy takes a step closer to the kid. He's over one hundred pounds heavier and a great deal taller. The kid is clearly shitting himself right now. "So, little man, which is it?"

The kid glances at his friends before following Teddy's every move. "I didn't know any better," he's smart enough to say through a nervous stutter.

For a brief second part of me feels bad for him, but then I think of how he was talking to Laura a minute ago, putting her down, getting the whole table to laugh at her, and I also recall how he treated Liv, and all that feeling bad for him disappears.

"Yeah, we thought so. I think you should apologize to Laura for not knowing any better." Teddy gestures him toward her.

"I'm sorry, Laura," he says, his hands are shaking at his side. She nods her head, still looking down. Teddy frowns. It's breaking his heart to see her so timid. He gestures for the kid to sit next to her and then leans between them.

"She's a very pretty girl, little man," Teddy says. "You asked her out, she said no, it bruised your ego, I get that. It hurts. But the names you called her, not one of them fit. You better say something really nice to her right now, and make sure all your friends can hear it."

"You're not a whore, Laura. I know you're not. I'm sorry I said that," he said it loudly but with his head down.

Teddy's big mitt grips the kid's shoulder. "FYI, if you ever so much as look at her cross-eyed, high school won't be much fun for you. I'll have eyes on you even after I graduate. Do you understand me?"

"Yes."

"Good. Remember, when you make fun of her, you're making fun of me," Teddy leans in closer. "Do you really want to make fun of me?" The kid shakes his head. "Tannon gave you yet another chance, but you'll only get one strike with me." He turns his head to Laura. "Come sit with your crazy friends, sweetheart." He reaches his mitt out and she slips her delicate hand into it. I catch a smile on her face before her chin falls to her chest again.

He holds her hand the whole way back to our table. I follow with a happy grin and notice he takes the long way. *Look at the big guy in love*, I muse. God, I hope she'll accept him. He looks like he can use her as a toothpick but they also look cute together. She's only a sophomore but Teddy would never push her in any way, that's for sure. Even if she just held his hand until he graduates, he'd leave here a happier guy.

How could anyone not love him?

I feel like a proud papa.

CHAPTER 34

LIV

"Five more days until prom!" the female student announces on the loud speakers as Cat and I walk to fourth period. "I hope you guys have your tuxes ready. And be a gentleman and pick up a corsage," she urges. "Remember this is a school event so drinking is not permitted. Limos will be searched if staff suspect any funny business. Let's try to make it a great night. This is it, seniors! I can't even believe it's almost over."

We walk into English a little sadder. It's almost over.

Cat whispers to me that we have a substitute teacher today. I sit down and the bell rings seconds later. The sub introduces himself as Mr. Berman and asks us to open our books to page eighty-nine. I open my braille textbook and wait.

"I know it's Monday, but let's wake up people," he says. "Mr. Matthews?"

"Trace is in a meeting with guidance," I say.

"Okay, take off your sunglasses please," he demands.

"I . . . I'm allowed to wear them."

"Oh, you're the blind one," he says, and I hear Tannon shift in his seat next to me, grumbling under his breath.

"Yes. The one and only in Hardy," I retort, and hear Cat call him a nasty name behind me.

"Can you read, Ms. . . . ?"

"McKay. And yes, I can read." *Jeez, this guy is so brass.* I start sliding my fingers over the braille and read the first paragraph.

"Okay," he says after I finish. "Mr. . . ." He pauses and I realize he's reading over the class list. "Keaton."

Tannon doesn't respond. "Is Mr. Keaton here?" the sub asks.

"Yes," Tannon finally replies.

"Then please read the next paragraph," the sub says, irritably.

"I'll read," Evan calls out quickly. And I wonder why he's jumping in.

"No, Mr. Keaton is here. He can read it."

"I'd rather not," Tannon says. "Let Evan read."

"No, I called on you. Now read." His voice rises to a stern level. "Read the paragraph please."

Tannon clears his throat and shifts in his seat. "When we na—I mean, an—ana . . . lysis—analysis— and para . . ." He stumbles and curses under his breath.

"Any day now," Rita says, faking a yawn. Tannon says nothing and what sounds like a leg bumping the bottom of a desk starts from his direction.

"Shut up, Rita," Evan snaps. "Paraphrase," Evan whispers to Tannon. I don't understand why Tannon's stumbling over the words, and I sit confused as I follow along.

"Para . . . phrase," Tannon continues, but his voice is cracking, "Shakespeare's son—sonn . . ."

"The word is 'sonnets,'" the sub sneers.

Evan groans heatedly. *What is going on?*

"Why don't you read it?" Tannon mumbles.

"Obviously someone else has to. This is an honors class isn't it?" the sub asks. "What is your real name? And where is Mr. Keaton? I'm writing you both up."

Tannon slams his book shut, cursing again. "Yeah, you're definitely in the wrong class," the sub says. "Get out!"

"You got a problem with me?" Tannon sneers.

"Sure do. This isn't my first day on the job. Had this prank done a million times," he says. "But never in an honors class. Fun is over. Get out."

"What's your problem?" Evan asks. "He is Tannon Keaton. This is his class."

"Sure," the sub draws out. "What's the story this time? Are you covering for Mr. Keaton? Well, he should've picked someone who could read if he didn't want to get caught."

Suddenly there's a loud crash. A desk? Tannon's desk? I jump up and swing my arms, feeling for him. Finding his arm, I step in front of him. "Tan," I plead. "What are you doing?"

"Liv, be careful!" Cat shouts.

Tannon's hands wrap around my arms and he pushes me aside. I try to hold him back but fail. He keeps walking despite my protest.

"TK!" Evan shouts, and more desks slide and crash. "He's not worth it!"

With my arms wrapped around Tannon's waist and my cheek pressed to his spine, he walks effortlessly and purposefully forward. My sneakers skid across the smooth floor trying so desperately to stop his progress. I know I've done little to hold him back when I feel his arms thrust forward and hear what sounds like a body hitting the wall. Desks screech and scrape across the floor. Students yell, followed by adult voices. Firm hands are on my shoulders and Evan shouts for Tannon to calm down as he sandwiches me between them, holding Tannon from behind me. The adults are all shouting for Tannon to let go of the sub. I hold onto his waist for dear life. I think he's holding the sub against the wall.

All goes silent when Principal Wagner's distinct and demanding voice yells for Tannon to stop.

CHAPTER 35
TANNON

The sub's shirt is in my left fist and my right is aimed at his face. I feel someone wrapped around my waist but haven't a clue who. Evan is shouting in my ear, my adrenaline is racing, and heat is radiating out of every pore. I'm about to slam my fist down into this douchebag's face when the person around my waist is pulled off and someone big grabs me from behind, locking my arms at my side. The sub takes a shot at my face as I'm being pulled back. I'm swung to the left by whoever's holding me and the sub misses.

"That's enough!" Mr. Wagner, the principal, shouts by my ear, pulling me back. He's the one holding me. "Calm down, Tannon," he warns.

Evan moves in front of me, holding Liv in front of him by the arms. "Mr. Wagner, the sub started it."

Evan tries to defend me, but as I watch the sub fixing his shirt, I know I'm in deep. I just rammed a sub into a wall, although he did try to hit me after.

"Call the police!" the sub shouts. "I'm pressing charges."

I groan in Mr. Wagner's hold, disappointed in myself for losing my cool. The douchebag was so not worth it and I didn't even get in a good shot. Suddenly Liv rushes out of Evan's grip and reaches for me. Catching my shirt, she steps forward and wraps her arms around my waist. I quickly realize it was Liv who was attached to me before.

Mr. Wagner turns us and walks us toward the door. "I'll deal with you in a minute," he says to the sub and asks Liv to let go of me, but she doesn't.

"I'm scared," she cries. "I don't know what's going on." Mr. Wagner lets go of my arms in the hallway and I wrap them around Liv. "You're shaking," she cries against my chest.

Evan holds her shoulder, consoling her for a moment before turning to Mr. Wagner. "Please believe us, the guy was being a jerk. He had a problem with TK or something. He was completely out of line."

Cat takes a step into the hall only for Mr. Wagner to halt her in her tracks with a raised hand and a pointed finger. She stomps back into class. Our principal looks like a badass biker in a suit. He totally doesn't fit the look of principal but he takes his job seriously and he's good at it. However, due to his intense appearance, no one messes with him.

"Evan, go back into class and please take Liv with you," he says. Evan tries to pull her from me, but she still won't let go. I see Trace walking down the hall, his eyes fixed on Liv's refusal to release me.

"Please, I'm scared, Tannon," she cries. "Don't let me go."

I squeeze her tighter. My eyes lock on Trace's as he gets closer. Mine full of pain, his . . . the same. He stops and we just stare at each other. I feel as if he is looking right into my soul. He glances at Liv and his gaze drops to the floor. Mr. Wagner moves close to us and lays his hand on her head. "Liv, I promise Tannon will be all right."

"You're going to call the police on him. But it wasn't Tannon—it was the sub. You should have heard him. Please believe us," she says through her sobs. "I can't let Tannon go. I need to know he's all right."

Mr. Wagner looks for me to step in. I don't want to let her go either. Her tears are wetting the front of my shirt and she's trembling . . . or is that me? We're both trembling I guess, but for different reasons. I didn't mean to frighten her. Trace is standing behind Mr. Wagner now. He has no idea what got us here, but he can see how distraught she is.

"Liv," Trace says, and I feel her tense in my arms. "What's wrong? What happened?"

I'm waiting for her to rush from me to him, but she doesn't. She doesn't even answer him. All she does is tighten her arms around my waist. "Trace and Evan, will you please take your seats in class," Mr. Wagner says.

Evan walks back in with his head hanging low. Trace is hesitant but follows in the same manner. "Liv, I understand you're scared, so I'm going to make you a promise. I promise I will make sure nothing happens to Tannon. You can trust my word," Mr. Wagner whispers.

He glances at me again, urging me to help out with a stern look. "Liv," I say, "I'm all right. Don't be scared. I'm okay. You can let go."

"I didn't know what was happening. The yelling and crashing and banging. I didn't know what to do. I was so scared." She finally lifts her head from my chest. Her face is wet with tears, glasses gone. I wipe her tears with my thumbs. And press my lips to her forehead.

"I'm sorry, Boo. I'm sorry I scared you."

Mr. Wagner waves Cat out of the class and asks her to take Liv to the girl's room to splash cold water on her face. Cat wraps her arms around Liv and pulls her from me. The separation is grueling and I want her back.

They walk down the hall and Mr. Wagner rubs at his neck, his expression pinched as he watches them go.

I look down at my shaking hands. My adrenaline is at an all-time high. To think of how scary that chaos must have been for her ... desks crashing, chairs flying, me fighting.

He sighs deeply. "Tannon, how am I supposed to help you out of this one? This isn't a bunch of seniors bullying a freshman. This is a substitute. What happened?"

"Mr. Carlson said I'd never have to read out loud in class. But that guy forced me to read in front of all those brainiacs and when I stumbled, he made some rude comments. He thought I wasn't the real Mr. Keaton. Then he said something about how Mr. Keaton should've asked someone who could read to cover for him. I was already having an anxiety attack and then he accused me of playing a prank because clearly I didn't belong in this class ... I snapped."

319

I grab my head. "I felt stupid. That Rita girl was pushing me to hurry up. The sub was being an asshole—a jerk. I told Mr. Carlson I didn't belong in this class. I told him." I feel my anxiety and adrenaline burn hot in my veins and fight for composure. "He was completely rude to Liv too. Saying, 'Oh you're the blind one.' Where'd you find this guy?"

"Tannon, I get that buttons were pushed and I understand your anxiety is real, but you can't attack teachers." Leaning against a locker, I lower my head and cross my arms. "I'm going to have to suspend you. I should expel you, but I won't."

"And the cops?" I ask, looking up.

"Hopefully I can talk Mr. Berman out of pressing charges. He was out of line too. Teachers should never insult students like that. Not that that made your reaction acceptable." He points a stern finger at me. "I will attest to the fact that he did take a swing at you as I was holding you. He can't exactly call that self-defense. Go home and I'll call your father when I figure this out."

He walks to the classroom door. "Mr. Berman, please come with me."

The sub walks out glaring at me. "I'm calling the police. That punk is out of control," he says, following Mr. Wagner down the hall, his eyes on me the whole time.

"First, we will talk about your conduct as well as Tannon's, and then we can decide if you also crossed a line in there," Mr. Wagner replies over his shoulder. The sub groans with irritation, but, again, no one messes with Mr. Wagner.

I walk back into class. All eyes are on me. The cat's out of the bag now. I'm the class idiot. Anyone who didn't know knows it now.

"You okay, TK?" Evan asks. I nod. He comes up to me and wraps his arm around my shoulder. "Sorry, man. I tried . . ."

"I know." I collect my things and walk out.

CHAPTER 36

LIV

Cat walks with me back to class and everyone is all fired up about what just happened. My nerves are too shot to get involved.

"Why is that moron even in this class?" Rita asks someone, and the volume and ease in which she talks lets me know that Tannon isn't here.

"Beats me," Keith says. "He was in that spesh class every other year. All of a sudden he's in here? He can't even read."

"Shut the hell up!" Evan shouts. I feel him standing next to me and grab for his hand. Finding it, I hold on tight. I can't handle any more fighting.

"You shut up!" Keith snaps back. "He doesn't belong in this class. His stupidity lowers our level."

Evan tries to pull away from my hold and I grab him with both hands. I hear Cat calming him down and feel her next to us. She's standing in front of him. "He's not stupid, you are!" Evan says. "He's dyslexic. The words are backwards in his head."

"He is?" I whisper, completely shocked. Though, I don't know why this surprises me; I don't seem to know anything about Tannon. Never have.

"Yeah." Evan bends down to whisper in my ear. "He didn't want you to know."

"Why?"

"He . . . ," he pauses. "It embarrasses him. He tries to keep it hidden."

"Like everything else about him," I groan. I'm so mad right now I want to scream. Why doesn't he trust me enough to let me in? He sounded so sad and embarrassed as he was reading.

Something in me snaps. I turn to Keith and Rita. "Who are you to say who belongs where? He's a smart guy. He gets the work done. His poems are awesome—yours suck. Frickin' 'flea on my dog's knee.' Give me a break, Rita!" I shout.

"Whatever," Rita retorts. "You don't even belong in this school. If they let you in, then I guess they'll let a total moron in an honors class. This school sucks."

I'm on my feet in seconds and start pushing desks out of my way to get to where I believe her to be. I want to hit her and I'm usually never violent, so this reaction surprises me but I still want to do it. My fists are screaming to meet her face. I have to remember she's tall and aim high.

Evan shouts my name and grabs my arms. Just then I hear a loud crash, and Evan yells for Cat to stop. He lets me go and pushes past me. I hear Cat fighting out of his hold. "Let me go. I'm gonna kick her flat ass!" she yells, and without delay another adult voice is yelling over her.

"What has gotten into this class today?" The teacher scolds us as the bell rings.

Everyone clears out and I wonder where Trace is. He hasn't said a word. I call out his name.

"I'm here."

I turn to the sound of his voice and lean against a desk. "Are we alone?"

"Yes."

It finally hits me. He saw me attached to Tannon and I didn't even let go when he said my name. I'm scared again. "What are you thinking?"

"I'm here thinking that everything has an end."

My heart drops. "I was so scared, Trace. There was so much noise and I didn't know what was happening. Tannon was having such a hard time reading and I didn't—I didn't know what to do." I'm rambling and take a deep breath. "I'm sorry."

His hands touch my arms unexpectedly and I flinch before reaching to grab hold of his waist. He pulls me into his arms and hugs me. Nothing is said, we just hold each other. I start to cry.

Is this our end?

"I'm holding you, you're in my arms, but he's on your mind. Let's be honest, he always ends up on your mind."

"You're on my mind. I'm worried about us. I'm thinking of you."

"Liv, it's okay." Trace rests his chin on the top of my head. "Today, I saw something I never saw before. I was wrong about him."

"What do you mean? Stop being so cryptic."

"Liv, I'm going to Stanford. I'm going away."

I lean back. "You're breaking up with me?"

"No, I'm just letting you go figure things out," he says.

"I don't want to go. I want to stay right here." I fist his shirt in my hands. "I'm sorry I keep putting myself in positions that make you second guess us . . ."

"Liv, let me be your eyes today." His hands move up to hold my face. "Go talk to Tannon."

My tears pour. "Why?"

"Tannon has that answer, not me."

"You're being cryptic again." He kisses my forehead before letting me go. "Go talk to Tannon."

With that he walks out and I fall into the seat behind me and cry. Light footsteps walk toward me and Cat takes my hand. We walk out.

"Is Tannon's car in the parking lot?" I ask as we walk down the stairs. I know there's a window overlooking the parking lot in this stairwell. Cat has stopped us here before looking for people's cars, mainly Evan's. We stop on the landing as Cat searches the parking lot and I rest my forehead on the warm glass.

"It's not there. He was parked right next to me and now the space is empty."

"Can you sneak me out of here and take me to Tannon's?" I beg. I have to get out of here.

"What about Trace?"

I cringe. "He asked me to talk to Tannon. I don't know what's going on."

We get in her car and she quickly drives out of the parking lot. "Did you know he had a learning disability?" I ask.

"No, I knew he was in lower level classes but I didn't know he had a real problem. I thought he just didn't care. But remember freshman year, when the seniors used to bully him?"

"Only from rumors. The guys never talked about it."

"Yeah, I guess they were protecting his secret. But I remember one time I was standing in the lunch line and Billy Jones—remember him?"

I grimace. "That guy was a hothead."

"Yeah, well Billy was obsessed with Monica D'Marco, but Monica wanted Tannon bad. She was constantly in his face, hugging him and trying to get his attention. Anyway, I was in the lunch line and heard Bill yell across the room, 'Look, spesh is here! Hey, spesh! Do you need help reading the lunch menu?' I had no idea who he was talking about and then suddenly I saw Tannon leaping and jumping from one lunch table to the next and when he landed on Billy's table, he kicked him right in the face with his booted foot."

"No way!"

"Yeah, it was impressive. Especially since he was a freshman charging up to a senior. Billy's friends at the table jumped on Tannon and beat him good, but he got his glory shot in. It was before he was even big. He had the courage to charge a football player before he even had muscle on his body."

"I think he's always been fearless in that way." I sit back and think of Tannon before he started working out. He had to be fearless to race right into the line of fire with little to defend himself with. He was always on the bigger side, but he definitely tips the scale now.

"I never knew it was Tannon that Billy was talking about. I thought Tannon was just being

Tannon, defending the world. Now I know. Now I want to cry for him," Cat adds, sounding so confused.

"Me too!" I say, feeling the same way.

"I'm shocked at how well the guys hid all this. I mean, I knew he was bullied, but the names the seniors called him didn't make any sense. I figured they were just jealous of his looks and were looking for anything to piss him off," Cat continues, trying to make sense of today.

I nod in agreement. "I don't know Tannon at all." I sigh and she squeezes my hand.

"I don't think he even knows himself anymore." Cat huffs out a humorless laugh. "We are a messed up bunch."

"God, we really are," I agree.

She stops the car, helps me to Tannon's front door, and then goes back to wait for me in the car. I ring the bell, my stomach in knots. The door swings open and then . . . nothing.

"Tannon?"

"Hey . . . Uh . . . What are you doing here?" He sounds mad or embarrassed. I think it's the latter and my sorrow doubles.

"Can I come in?" I ask. His hand takes mine and he leads me inside. The smell of tomato sauce fills the air. "Cooking?"

"I started making sauce for my dad." He sounds jumpy. "Uh . . . sit down."

He guides me to the couch and I sit. I've never been in Tannon's house before and wonder how it's decorated—does it still have his mother's touch or does it look like a bachelor pad now? He's making sauce, so I guess they don't eat takeout every night.

He sits next to me and I smell soap. "You smell clean." I don't even know why I just said that. I'm so nervous.

"I guess it's the dish detergent. Why are you here, Liv?"

"I was worried about you."

"I'm fine." His tone is sharp.

Feeling like I'm not welcome, I wish I had just called instead of stopping by uninvited. My hands drop to my side and I sink back into the couch, speechless. We sit in silence for a long minute.

"Tell me a truth, Tannon?"

"What do you mean?"

"Just tell me a truth about you." I shrug. He doesn't respond. "Do you know how to tell the truth?"

He huffs. "Jeez, Liv, that's nice."

"I want to know one true thing about you. About Tannon Keaton. Because I can't keep up. I don't get you. You paint, but you don't talk about it. You do selfless things, like the talent show and donating paintings, but then you act as if you don't care about anything. You enter our Honors English class and recite poetry that's heartfelt and deep. You say things to me, the most amazing things, that make me feel so special, and then the next day you ignore me and I don't feel special at all. And then today, Evan tells me you have a learning disability and you didn't want me to know and I don't understand why you felt you needed to hide that from me. Knowing hasn't changed what I think of you. I still think you're just as smart and talented as I did yesterday."

He stays silent. I exhale my held breath. "Just tell me why you hide everything about you that makes you you."

"It doesn't matter."

"Yes, it does." Why do we keep running around in this circle? "I'm so sick of returning to this spot with you. Move us in a different direction."

"Why?"

"Because—"

"We're friends," he mumbles.

"Yes! What's so wrong with being my friend? Am I that bad?" I grab the sides of my head and then drop my hands again.

"No. That's not it."

"Then what?" I plead. "Just tell me."

"Fine. I'll tell you," he says sounding annoyed. I lift my hands again, gesturing for him to get to it. "I've always struggled in school. As I got older, it took a toll on my self-esteem. I felt stupid and pathetic. I hated feeling that way. It got worse freshman year because the seniors started bullying me, called me names. The names hurt, mostly because I believed them, and having others say out loud what I was always thinking made it real and made me ashamed of who I was. I hid the real me. I started working out. By sophomore year I was a new person. Acted confident and carefree. People bought it because my exterior had what it took to pull it off. I hid my learning problems behind an excuse that I didn't care enough to work hard and made everyone believe that was why I was in those classes, and ta-da! Just like that I'm this guy that looks like he's got everything going for him and no one ever brought up freshman year again." His words are backed with pain and I know he's telling me the truth.

"So you've been a fake this whole time?" I ask, feeling betrayed even though I kind of understand why he did it.

"Not all the time. In my car after Tucker's party, on the beach, singing on stage, my poems, my paintings, at the banquet, today—that was all the real me." Tannon pauses and gets up. "Now you know." He moves to the far side of the room. "The real me is just an insecure, gutless loser. I don't want to be that guy, but I'm tired of pretending I'm not."

I stand, fighting between my desire to leave or to hug him. I opt to hug him now and be mad at his lies later. I bend a bit to find the coffee table with my hands—I forgot my white cane in my backpack— and then swing my hands to find other obstructions between me and him. I'm worried I may break something and stand tall. "It would be easier if you came to me."

He stays silent for a moment. "I can't."

"Why?" I ask and feel my shoulders lower with my disappointment.

"Because if I hold you . . ." He stops.

"What? You're still hiding. Just be real with me." I raise my hands, palms up in surrender, hoping he'll do the same.

"You have your ideal guy."

"What does that mean? Do you want to be with me?" He doesn't respond. "I don't understand, Tannon? Please help me understand."

"There's nothing to understand." I hear his voice crack and then a horn beeps outside.

Oh my gosh, I forgot about Cat.

"Go, Liv."

"Tannon," I utter his name, trying so desperately to read between the lines. I slouch and raise my hands again. "This is why I never know what's going on with you. One minute I think you're touching me or hugging me or saying things to me like someone

330

who may have feelings for me and then you turn on a dime and I'm left thinking you just touch or hug or say those things to everyone."

"I only touch and hug and say those things to you." He sounds sincere again. I don't even know what to think.

"See, what are you saying, Tannon? Say it! Just say it!"

"I—I have nothing to say."

A sob escapes my lips in an odd-sounding whimper and I shake my head. "Please tell me what I'm not seeing."

"You're with Trace."

I don't even know if I am anymore, but I don't tell Tannon that. "Because he tells me what he thinks and feels and he holds no secrets and I don't have to guess and then feel like a fool for guessing wrong. He is open and honest. He isn't living a lie."

"He's perfect. Your ideal," he says, and I hear how much it hurts him to say those words.

"He doesn't hide behind my blindness."

Cat's car horn beeps again. She has to get back to school. If she misses sixth period again, she's in trouble.

"Go, Liv. It's been a really shitty day. I . . . can't do this."

I make my way to the door and freeze with my hand on the knob. "Tannon," I say, turning my head to him, "I was so scared today and I believed everything would be all right if you were holding me and I was holding you."

"Liv . . ." My name is followed by a long pause. "You have Trace to hold you."

"Yeah," I say. Nodding solemnly, I open the door. "I don't even know what you're telling me or not telling me, but I guess it doesn't matter, right?" I ask. Again, no response. "You're right. You are gutless, Tannon."

And with that I walk out.

CHAPTER 37
TANNON

I can't breathe. I can't think. I can't move. All I can do is lie on my living room floor and stare at the dust collecting under the hutch. I wish my problems were as easy to clean as the dust. Wipe and go. Problem solved. Clean slate. New beginning.

But no, life is as cruel as love. The dust just keeps collecting and eventually you don't even remember the beauty it covers.

I wish I told her I loved her. I wish I said the words, but they were stuck in my throat and I couldn't free them. She's with Trace and she would reject me. I had about all I could handle for one day. I wasn't up for hearing her say she's staying with him.

Mr. Carlson said we are given moments in life to show self-love. Well, I just wasted another one. I didn't fight for her or me. I just let more dust fall.

What a chicken shit.

Dad comes in the front door, sees me laying on the floor, and races to my side. "Tannon! Are you all right? Are you hurt?"

I don't answer. I only grab his arms and pull myself into his chest. I don't cry or say a thing. I just need him to hold my weight for a while. And he does, without asking questions or probing for answers. He just holds my heavy sadness so I can feel lighter.

Eventually I say, "I wasted another chance and now I can't breathe."

"God, I understand that," he says. "I wish I could say you are putting too much life or death in this love, but I did it myself. I loved a woman that deeply. And now I have to live without her love. I get what you're going through."

Funny how I don't even have to explain anything for him to know I was talking about Liv. "I got suspended today." I figure why not add to the bad news. Throw a suspension on top of it all. "Rammed a sub into the wall."

"I heard. Mr. Wagner called me at work. I'm not happy about it, Tan." He sits back. "I got you boxing lessons to defend yourself, not to start fights."

"I was so overwhelmed with anxiety I don't even remember going after the guy." Which is the truth. "He made me feel stupid and I acted . . . stupidly."

"Yeah well, he isn't pressing charges. Mr. Wagner kind of threatened his career. Said he'd spend all week calling every school in New Jersey letting them know how unprofessional he was as a sub."

I lean against the wall and raise my knees. "I love that guy."

"Yeah, he always has your back." Hitting my leg, he adds, "That's because he believes you're worth fighting for. You remember that."

I nod and tell him what happen between Liv and me.

"It's not over," he states, after listening quietly. "You both have a day to think things over. Then go to school on Wednesday and find a way to tell her how you feel. You need an answer from her, because you got it all wrong. Unspoken love is far worse than rejected love. At least you know the answer when you're rejected."

CHAPTER 38

LIV

Cat drives me home and heads back to school after I assure her I'm fine. The moment she's gone, I wish I had told the truth—I'm not fine. I head out back with Hank and lay on the grass while trying to wrap my head around everything Tannon *didn't* tell me. He was acting as if he had feelings for me. He sounded emotional—every other comment made me think he cared for me—but then he acted guarded or sidestepped the conversation only to leave me guessing, believing I was wrong about everything.

He's making me feel really blind.

Hank stands up next to me with a whimper and then a shadow blocks the sun. "Hi, Liv," Trace says and sits down.

"Hi." Sitting up, I wipe my eyes under my glasses. "School over already?"

"No, Cat said you were home. I left. I'm a rebel like that," he teases and I smile. "So are you all right?"

I shrug. "I don't know why you thought I should go to Tannon. He didn't exactly explain anything to me." I nervously pull a strand of grass and twirl it around my finger. It's true Trace told me to go, but now that my head is clear, I know I can never change the fact that I went. I went to Tannon. "I shouldn't have gone. This is it between us, isn't it?"

"I've been dreading our end since the beginning. It's just happening sooner then I figured it would," Trace says. My head snaps in his direction, taken aback. *What does that mean?* "Even if it wasn't for Tannon, I think we both knew this would end when college started."

"I didn't," I say, turning my head from him. "You knew you never wanted to try long distance?"

"I just . . . ," he pauses. I cry. Not out loud. It's silent, completely silent. Tears fall from the heart, not my eyes. "College will be intense, long hours of studying, and I will be so far away."

My heart releases its sorrow, weeping I lie back down, turning my head from him. He always saw our end. Always knew it was coming. It hurts to imagine that. "Liv, I'll be home three times a year, if that." He puts his head close to mine and I can feel his breath on my neck, smell his minty gum. I don't turn. "How would we survive that?"

"I don't know," I admit, "but I was always willing to try."

"How do you feel about him?" he asks. I offer no response. I don't even know what to say. That's really what this all comes down to. The fact that he always saw our end isn't as bad as me having confusing feelings for someone else. "Liv, he's been a constant in our relationship. Maybe you saw him as a friend, but I think something changed, especially today. So how do you feel about him today?"

"I'm confused. I don't know how I feel." Hank lays his head on my lap and I play with his soft ears. "I don't get him. And I have no idea if I ever will. I don't want to lose you, but I know that's selfish of me. I made a thoughtless decision. I shouldn't have gone to him."

Trace pets Hank's head next to my hand and then takes my hand, pulling me to him and entwining our fingers affectionately. "I'm sorry if you think he was a constant in our relationship," I say. "I thought he was my friend. I thought I was his. Whenever I thought he wanted more, I figured I was mistaken. Then today, I was scared and worried for him."

I wanted to hold him and never let go—and there's the truth. And because of that truth I can't stay with Trace even if he wasn't going to Stanford. "I never meant to hurt you," I say, praying he believes me.

"I know that. That's why I'm able to have a mature conversation about this."

"I was always attracted to your maturity," I say. He laughs.

"I'm just trying to see the truth past my own ego. I think your feelings for Tannon, even if you don't understand them, are deep." Hank licks our joined hands and we both sit in silence for a moment. A breeze rushes by, blowing my hair into my face. Trace gently tucks the strands behind my ear.

God, I'm going to miss him.

"You're going to be a really good psychiatrist."

"Maybe," he says. "But I also want to kick his ass, so maybe not."

We laugh.

"This hurts," I say. "You're my first boyfriend. My first kiss."

"It hurts me too. You gave me the best school year of my life. I loved calling you mine."

"So did I. I love you, Trace." *Wow, I don't know why I never said that before.*

Pulling me in for a hug, he says, "I love you too. I always will."

CHAPTER 39
TANNON

The best parking spots are already taken by the time I pull into the school lot. I end up pretty far back and have to make a run for the entrance in the pouring rain. I pull my hood over my head, grab my bag, and run. Water splashes over my sneakers, soaking my jeans as I go. I sprint under the entrance awning and notice Liv and Trace standing outside the building. He's leaning against the brick wall, one knee up, and she's standing in front of him with her hand on that knee. It's an intimate picture. She falls against his chest, his arms slowly encircle her, and his chin rests on the top of her head, eyes closed. The first bell rings and he holds her at the shoulder to guide her into school, her head resting on his shoulder as they walk.

I follow behind, the crowd filling in between us. He kisses the top of her head as they walk into homeroom. I was gone just a day, and it looks like nothing's changed. He still has her.

***

I'm spent by fourth period and walk into English with my head down, feeling embarrassed and foolish to even return to this class. Everyone knows I don't belong. Mr. Carlson calls me to his desk just as I'm sitting.

"Sorry about the sub. I should've left a note about you being excused from reading," he whispers with a pinched expression.

"I don't think it would've mattered with that guy."

"You're probably right. He sounds like a real . . ." He catches himself.

"Winner," I say.

"Yeah. Anyway, I'm sorry."

"It's not your fault." I turn and take my seat next to Liv. Trace is in front of me, leaning back in his seat, legs stretched into the aisle. Must be nice being so at ease with life.

"All right, class. I'm excited to discuss *Romeo and Juliet*," Mr. Carlson says, moving to lean against the front of his desk. "Two rival families, the Montagues and the Capulets. The Montague's son, Romeo, falls desperately in love with the Capulet's daughter, Juliet, who falls just as hard in return. From the first scene Shakespeare wanted us to see how privileged these two families are. What shows us this, Keith?"

"The young men in both families use their status in the community as a free pass to disregard the laws," Keith says.

Mr. Carlson smiles with approval. "Yes, the young men, out of anyone in the two families, enjoy the rivalry. We see that by how the play starts. How is that, Evan?"

"With two men fighting," Evan says.

Mr. Carlson lifts a yardstick and points it at Evan. "Yes, and there is no real reason for the fight, so, to me, it shows their privilege also offers them too much free time on their hands."

"Boys," Cat says, rolling her eyes.

"Exactly," Mr. Carlson replies, pointing to her with the stick as if she's got it. "Boys will be boys, right? And bored boys with no regard for rules get into trouble. Okay. Now what do we learn about Romeo right away?"

"He wants to get lucky," Evan says. Everyone laughs.

"How do you know that, Evan?"

"By how the guys tease him," Evan says.

Mr. Carlson nods. "Yes. They tease him, but I think Romeo is after love as well. Shakespeare lets us know right away that Romeo is a passionate young man, ready to love and be loved. We believe he's in love with Rosaline in the beginning. He's then invited to the Capulet's masquerade ball by Peter, who doesn't know Romeo is a Montague, and Romeo goes because he wants to see Rosaline. When he enters the hall and sees Juliet, all feelings for Rosaline fly out the door. What does everyone think of that?"

"He cares about looks?" Liv questions.

"Maybe," Mr. Carlson says. "Some may argue that it was love at first sight."

"I wouldn't understand that," Liv says with an easy-going shrug. "But I do understand feelings and in their first conversation he slyly convinces her to kiss him. And she does and falls for him in that kiss. I understand their connection, but even so, is it love? I mean, he's attracted to her beauty and she's attracted to his touch—is that love? Aren't they just charmed?"

"Point taken," Mr. Carlson says. "But in their first exchange they are both also drawn to each other's playful wit."

Beth raises her hand and he gestures for her to get involved. "Romeo convinces her that a single kiss from her will erase his sins," Beth says. "After that, I took him for a player. It was like he was trying to steal her innocence or con her."

"Wow, that's deep, Beth," Evan teases. She glares at him.

"No, let's talk about that," Mr. Carlson says. He seems to love this. "In the first kiss he is the aggressor. Juliet doesn't even move, but in their second kiss, moments later, she's the aggressor."

"I like that she did that," Cat steps in. "With the first kiss he says she's taking his sins. But she asks him to take them back. I thought that showed she wasn't going to let him control her or the moment."

Mr. Carlson smiles and nods. "Yes, I believe that was a smart move on Shakespeare's part. It showed us that Juliet wasn't as naïve as we so quickly assumed." He thinks a moment before continuing. "Whatever it is between them, attraction or desire, Romeo believes he loves her in an all-encompassing way." He walks to Trace's desk and taps his finger on it. "Trace, when Romeo finds Juliet on her balcony, she asks how he got there. What was his answer?"

A few seconds go by before Trace replies. "I think he said, 'Love led me.'"

"Oh, what a line," Cat mocks.

"Romeo's the man," Evan boasts. Everyone laughs. Mr. Carlson smirks.

"I know it's a play and things have to move quickly, but they state their undying love less than an hour after they met," Cat says and rolls her eyes.

"Yeah, not only did they fall deeply in love in act one, scene five, but Romeo went there to see Rosaline," Beth adds, amused. "What happened to her?"

"It seems you girls find this play more amusing than romantic," Mr. Carlson says, grinning.

"I did find romance in their exchange, but, for the most part, I didn't understand how their love was felt so deeply in one meeting," Liv says. "How could they call it love?"

"You don't believe true love can be that overwhelming, that instantaneous?" Mr. Carlson asks.

"I don't know how to relate to them. I mean, I did fall in love with my dog instantly," Liv says, beaming.

Cat lifts and tucks her leg under her butt to sit higher, looking as excited by this conversation as Mr. Carlson. She says, "Everyone falls in love with Hank instantly."

Liv smiles. "Yeah, but with people, I have to know someone in order to fall in love. I obviously never experienced love at first sight." She shakes her head with a shrug. "Does it even exist?"

"Does it?" Mr. Carlson asks the class.

"Yes," I say, shocking even myself.

"Go on," he urges.

I doodle on the back of my notebook, keeping my focus on the pen, not wanting to look at anyone as I talk. "There is such a thing as love at first sight. It's real and extreme. I believe you can see someone across a room and know instantly that your heart will never beat the same again. I believe Romeo fell in love with Juliet that quickly."

"Well, okay," Mr. Carlson says, rubbing his hands together as if things are finally getting warmed up. "Now I have someone on my side. I thought it would be the girls, but I'm happy to have someone agree this is a tragic romance."

"Tannon, you only believe in love at first sight because every girl in this stupid school fell in love with your ridiculous face at first sight," Rita sneers.

I ignore her, which is a challenge, but I do, and respond to Mr. Carlson. "I don't think this play is tragic at all. Sad, but not tragic." He stares, puzzled and gestures for me to explain. "Romeo loves Juliet and she loves him. Quick or not, they feel love for each other. They try to fool their families so they can be together, but everything goes wrong. Even still, he loves her and she loves him," I repeat, stressing the fact. "They die knowing they loved each other."

"They *die*, Tannon!" Cat emphasizes.

"That's not tragic?" Beth asks.

"They die together, having had each other's love," I say. "They die believing there was nothing else they needed. To me, tragic would be if they died before feeling that kind of love. Tragic would be if Romeo was killed the moment his eyes landed on Juliet, the moment he realized he just found his true love, and then never got to feel her love in return, never got to know she felt the same. That would be tragic. This is sad, very sad, I'll admit, but not tragic."

"Wow," Evan says. "I agree with Tannon."

"We have a few romantics amongst us, ladies," Mr. Carlson says, smacking my shoulder as he walks by. Cat laughs. Rita groans that we're stupid. And Liv lowers her head.

"Well, we skipped a lot but I enjoyed this conversation. We will talk more about it tomorrow. We have time for one poem before the bell. Who's up for it?"

"I'll go," Liv says and stands next to her desk. "'Coward,'" she says the title.

There is agony in your voice and need in your touch,
But you tell me nothing,
Fearing you'll reveal too much?
So I sit in my darkness, alone and crushed.

Is this it?
Is this how it will be?
Is this it?

All right . . .
You play the coward and I'll play
the girl who can't see.

All right???
Are you frickin' kidding me?
Is she mocking me?
I play the coward, as if this is all just a game to me? And how could she be alone and crushed when

346

she has Trace? Does she want me to open my wounds so she can pour salt on them as she denies me?

Standing next to her, my temper flaring, I get in her face and say through tight lips, "'Play?' Yeah, you're right, this is just a game to me. You still think the worst of me. Yeah, this is it, Liv. This is all of it! And it's over."

She grabs my shirt and Trace stands, turning to us, just as the bell rings. I pull from her hold and push past Trace before he says something stupid and I do something stupider. Evan calls my name, but I don't stop. He calls me again in the hall, and I still ignore him. I skip next period and head to my car.

***

My hands are red and throbbing from hitting the steering wheel repeatedly, but I don't care and hit it again. A knock at my passenger window startles me as I'm wailing on the wheel. Glancing over, I see Trace looking in.

Are you frickin' kidding me?

I ignore him, looking forward, yet he knocks again. And again. I knew I should've left the school parking lot.

"Open the door, Tannon," he says, annoyed.

Leaning over, I unlock it. I don't know why. I should leave him out in the rain. "You have to yank hard. It's broken!" I yell. He fights the door open and gets in. "What the hell do you want?"

"The truth," he says, wiping a hand through his wet hair before he turns to face me. "Why don't you tell her?"

I huff out a laugh. "What do you care?"

"I'm what stands between you and her, so you better hope I care," he says.

What the hell is that? A threat?

"She's all you want, isn't she?"

I shrug and he shakes his head. "Look at you." He points at me with indignation. "You really are a coward."

"Screw you, Trace!" I groan, about ready to elbow him in the face, until I remember her poem. "Why'd she say she's alone? Did you guys break up?"

"No."

"Then what do you want?" I sneer. "Get out! I'm not kidding!" He tries to open the door but puts little effort into it. "Get out!"

"I'm leaving," he says, turning to me again. I stare, confused—he's still sitting here. Raising my hand, I point to the door. "No. I mean I'm leaving for Stanford. Starting summer classes soon."

"That's nice." What, now we're gonna be buddy-buddy? Share? No thanks. "Get out!"

"I'm leaving," he repeats. "Would you?"

Suddenly realizing what he's asking, I answer, "No. If I had her, I'd never leave her."

"So you love her." He sits quietly for a moment. "You've been a constant in my relationship with her. I've been trying to figure out what you really wanted the whole time. Now I know. You love her. If I could kick your ass, I would."

I laugh. "Too bad you can't. I wouldn't mind a good fight right now. It'd feel better than this misery."

"Maybe I can use a bat." He smirks, enjoying the thought. I shrug, not caring either way. "I saw how much you love her in the hall the other day." Leaning his back against the door, he sighs deeply. "I love her too. She's the sweetest girl I ever met. She's easy to love."

"I'm sure you will make the long distance thing work," I say, looking away. "You're her ideal."

"Crazy, right?" he laughs loudly. "I'm better looking than you in her head." He sounds so pleased.

I roll my eyes. "You have the brains she's attracted to. Again, you're her ideal, so . . . good for you," I congratulate him, wondering why we're even having this conversation. Is everyone looking to torture me today?

"Yeah, I was when you were acting like a conceited ass. But now she's confused. Now she wants to know who you really are." He pauses. "She wouldn't if she didn't think there could be something between you two."

"Friendship. That's what's between us," I say with a toothy grin.

"I guess you both see things differently than me." Trace shrugs. "You're not even going to try?"

"Why do you want me to tell your girlfriend that I love her?"

"We both have a right to know who she really wants."

"Yeah, you!" I fling my hands at him. "You want to see me get rejected. Would that make you feel good?"

"Probably," he says. "But I wonder who she'd pick if I wasn't the only one being honest."

"Still you, I'm sure."

"It might be you."

"If you think that, then why would you take this chance?"

"You may have bigger muscles, but I have bigger balls," he says, raising one eyebrow. I laugh at that and he joins in. "I just want to know the truth. If we try the long-distance thing, I want to know she's as committed as I am."

Shaking my head, I say, "You want to use me and my fragile heart to find out if she really likes you?"

"Yep," he says, nodding.

"I always wanted to hate you but didn't . . . until now."

"Well, I've hated you the whole time," he says, and I can't help but laugh again. "You seem to think she belongs in your arms even though she's with me. So yeah, I hate you."

"I like her in my arms. Hate her in yours," I say, shrugging. "You always show up at the worst time. The frickin' flower at the banquet was priceless."

"I always show up? You're always there," he counters.

I raise a brow, knowing he's right. "I love her. I tried to stay away. I couldn't."

"That's why I think you should let her know," he says and offers his hand. "May the best man get the girl."

"And may it be me," I say, taking his hand.

"It might be, but if she doesn't pick you, then you have to swear to stay the hell away."

"Fair enough," I say. We shake and get out of the car as the bell rings.

Again, I can't help thinking this frickin' guy is perfect. He handled this so cool, so smart. I'm still trying to figure out what just happened. He is, without a doubt, the toughest competition imaginable.

***

Trace and I go our separate ways when we walk into school. An assembly is called over the loud speaker as I'm walking to my locker. "All seniors please report to the auditorium."

We file into the auditorium and I take a seat next to Teddy, seconds later Evan sits next to me. "Dude, where'd you go?" he asks. I only respond with a shrug.

Mr. Wagner walks to the middle of the stage and starts talking about prom. Sitting back, I tune him out and think about Mr. Carlson and about those moments that we are given to prove self-love. I have to stop being a coward. I'm dragging my heart on the ground as it is—how much worse could it get? I have to believe I'm worthy of her and just ask. Her poem says she wants to know, so I'll tell her. Surprisingly, I stand and push by Evan.

"Where are you going?" he whispers, pulling me down between his legs and the chair in front of us.

"To fight for her."

He smacks my arm. "Finally!"

I peer at him with furrowed brows. "I'm not going to win."

"You might," he whispers. "They broke up Monday night."

"Are you serious?"

He nods.

Trace said they hadn't. That little prick! He was playing me the whole time. Saying he wanted to

351

know who she'll pick. Why didn't he tell me? What was that all about?

I glare at Evan. "Why didn't you tell me about this?"

"I just found out today, dude," he says, lifting his hands. "I tried to tell you in class, but you raced off."

"Stop thinking, bro," Teddy says. "Just jump!"

Staring at him, I start to laugh. He's like my own personal motivational speaker or something. Feeling ballsy, I sneak into the aisle facing the stage. "Wait, where are you going?" Evan whispers. "She's back there."

"Yeah, I'm going up there," I say, pointing to the stage. "I gotta jump, right?" They both grin approvingly and high-five one another.

Taking a deep breath, I stand tall and make my way to the stage. I made too many cowardly mistakes and now I have to put myself out there in a major way. Metaphorically speaking, this is a huge jump. I may very well fall on my neck and die.

CHAPTER 40

LIV

As Mr. Wagner talks about prom rules and graduation rehearsal, I think of Tannon. My poem didn't work. I thought it might get my point across, but he took it badly. Maybe I was harsh. I don't even know how to talk to him anymore. I'm desperate to know how he feels about me.

I feel so guilty feeling that way with Trace sitting next to me. He still wants to be my friend after all this confusion. I don't know if I deserve it, but I'm thankful he does. Gentle hands are suddenly on my knees, and then Cat asks Trace to move down a seat.

"Hey," she whispers after plopping down next to me. "I was in the bathroom. Don't ever eat the meatloaf here." She groans and I laugh.

A rush of whispers break out around the room and then I hear Evan yell, "You got this, TK!" My head pops up, wondering what's happening. Mr. Wagner sternly asks someone to get back to their seat.

"Please. Just two minutes," I hear what sounds like Tannon's voice beg. A mumbled back and forth follows.

"Thanks, Mr. Wagner," Tannon says in the microphone. "I'll be quick."

"You gonna sing again, TK?" someone shouts.

"Not today. I just have to get something important off my chest and then I'll get off the stage. I'll start by saying I was called a coward today and gutless the other day."

I cringe, lowering in my seat. *What's he going to do? Yell at me in front of everyone?*

"Did you kick their ass?" a guy yells. Mr. Wagner quickly reprimands him.

"Nope. Truth is, I am a gutless coward. Or at least I have been," Tannon says, and my heart sinks in my chest and my nerves prickle under my skin. "That's why I'm up here. I want to explain why. Thing is, I'm in love with a perfect girl, but I never thought I was right for her so I hid like a gutless coward. I never told her how I felt. Never told her that I've loved her since the first day I laid eyes on her." My body tenses in my seat. Cat grabs my hand.

"Is it me?" a girl calls out. The room roars with laughter. Tannon huffs into the mic.

"When I was fourteen I lost my favorite person in the world, my mom. I didn't think anyone would ever be able to fill the hollow pit in my heart. Then, first day of freshman year, I saw this beautiful angel sitting across from me. It honestly was love at first sight. It does exist," he adds. "I never met anyone like her. She was so sweet, so open, so full of life, and I was this sad kid."

He pauses and I squeeze Cat's hand as tears well in my eyes. "We all face challenges in life, some more difficult than others. The trick is to never give up. Never stop being real. Never turn your back on the one person that needs you the most, the one person you should always cheer the loudest for—yourself." He blows out a humorless laugh. "I unfortunately did the complete opposite. I threw in the towel the second things got hard. I let my challenges beat me to the ground. I let them make me feel worthless and ashamed. I let them spoil many years of my life. And I let them come between me and the one thing I wanted most—her."

He pauses again. The crowd is silent, hanging on his every word. The stage is far away and yet it feels as if he's right next to me and we're all alone in the room, just like it did during the talent show. Just Tannon and me.

A long sigh echoes through the speakers. "I got lost in all of it—the negative belief in myself—so much so that when she asked me who Tannon Keaton really was, I described a gutless coward. That was my answer because it was how I was living. I thought I was stupid, incapable, unworthy, and that's what I became, but that's not me. And I'm also not the cocky, carefree guy I've been hiding behind.

"God," he huffs into the mic. "It's an eye-opening day when you realize that the biggest bully you will ever face is *you*. That you would never let anyone talk to you the way you talk to yourself. That *you* are the enemy who stands in the way of everything you want. And that the only thing you have to do to beat the enemy is to show yourself some love." A quick, pained laugh escapes him.

"Guys, if you're like me, please stop listening to that negative voice in your head. Please know that the real you is good enough. Don't let your challenges win. Use what you got. And fight for what you want, no matter what your peers say. No matter what anyone says. Especially that negative voice. Just be you. Be real. Take chances."

I pull my lips into my mouth, trying to hold back the overflow of emotions he's unleashed.

"I made so many mistakes, but I'm ready to move forward, beat my bully, and fight for what I want. So I'm here to change my answer because I'm ready to be real. I'm Tannon Keaton. I suck at reading and I struggle in class, but I can write poetry, relate to Shakespeare, and tell you everything there is to know about Picasso, Monet, da Vinci, and O'Keeffe. I'm flawed, but my flaws don't define me. I have so much to stand on. So much to offer. And there is one thing I know for sure—I was born to paint, play hockey, and love this girl."

Everyone stays silent as they wait for him to continue. I realize I'm holding my breath but don't even bother to inhale. *Who needs air?*

Tannon fumbles with the mic and a loud thump follows. "Tannon, I need to get back to the announcements," Mr. Wagner warns.

"One more minute, please, Mr. Wagner," Tannon begs. "This moment is four years in the making and if I don't say everything I need to say, it will haunt me forever." His voice is getting closer to my aisle seat and then I feel his hand take mine. I flinch and instantly my pooled tears fall. "Liv . . ."

"Hey, you weren't talking about me?" a girl yells out.

"Sorry," he says. "There's only one girl for me. Liv, you are my favorite person in the world. I love everything about you. You're beautiful, smart, adventurous, bold, funny, and so damn sweet. I love you, Liv. I love you so much."

I sit motionless, still not breathing. I'm about to pass out.

"I'm so sorry I made so many cowardly mistakes. But I will never hide again. I will be real and open. I will do everything and anything I can to be all that you need. Please give me a chance to prove that."

CHAPTER 41
TANNON

My heart is drumming against my chest as I wait for her response. She sits, motionless. The dark lenses of her glasses and blank expression reveal nothing. All I have to go on are the tears that fall down her cheeks. Cat is smiling so wide that I can see all her teeth. I scowl at Trace for lying to me about them still being together. He raises a brow and shrugs.

The "always cool under pressure" dude. *Damn.*

"Liv," I say, "it took me a long time to get to this point, but I'm here and I know that we belong together. Give us a chance ... Maybe we can start with prom?"

All is silent as I watch her back straighten and ease out a long breath. "I don't think I can," she says and everyone within earshot gasps and sighs, feeling sorry for me. I fall back on my heels and stare at her. "I'm sorry. It's just Trace asked me."

Trace leans over Cat so he can whisper in Liv's ear. Liv shakes her head at whatever he told her. "I can't do that to you," she says back.

"What do you want, Liv?" Trace asks. "I don't want to be the reason you say no. Say it for your own reasons, not for me."

Wow, it actually sounds like he's on my side.

The room is silent again and I watch her play with his fingers as she holds his hand over Cat's legs. I peer at their connection. Here I am, kneeling before her with my heart lying on the floor, and she's holding his hand. I wonder how free she really is. Maybe she doesn't want to let him go. Maybe he's leaving and that's the only reason they broke up. Trace whispers in her ear, and whatever he says causes her to frown deeply. She whispers back and turns to me. "Okay," she says.

When her answer becomes clear to me, my soul smiles. Honestly, I feel it smile. "She said, okay!" I shout into the mic and everyone cheers. I go to take her in my arms but she stops me.

"No," she says, holding me back. "I need to let all you said soak in. You hid a lot from me. I need to absorb it."

"All right," I say. I deserve that. "I understand. I guess I have to go get a tux." *Jeez, where am I going to find a tux that fits me two days before prom?*

Her forehead wrinkles. "You really weren't going to prom?"

"Without you? No. It would've been torture."

"Mr. Keaton," Mr. Wagner calls. "Can I have my audience back now?"

I stand and walk down the aisle. A guy yells, "Jeez, TK, you just made my prom proposal weak in comparison." Everyone laughs.

Grinning, I hand the mic up to Mr. Wagner. "Thank you, sir. Really, thanks for everything."

He leans down and takes the mic and then my hand. "Who am I to get in the way of true love?" he whispers. "But don't ever steal my audience again." I nod at his seriousness and he keeps his expression unreadable until he winks and stands to address the seniors. *Damn I like this guy.*

I smile and turn to find Mr. Carlson standing with his hand out; I take it. "She's your Juliet," he whispers, so as not to disturb the announcements.

I shake my head and cringe. "Let's hope it doesn't end the same."

"Nah. You took that moment by the horns and won," he says, patting my shoulder.

"I still have a fight ahead of me," I say. "She's probably replaying four years of cowardly mistakes in her head. Though I do have a grand gesture up my sleeve."

His eyebrows lift as he nods. "A grand gesture should do it, but what you just did could pass for one." He pats my shoulder. "I'm proud of you. Everything you said . . . it brought a tear to my eye. I'm glad you finally see what we all see in you."

"I owe it to you," I say. He smiles and we shake hands again.

Glancing over Mr. Carlson's shoulder, I see Trace walking out of the auditorium and excuse myself to race after him.

"Hey!" I call to him outside the doors. The hall is empty and when the doors behind me shut, they seal us in silence. "You lied."

"Yeah, I did," he says, turning to me.

"Why'd you want me to think you were still together?"

"Because she's worth fighting for and . . . I guess I wanted you to put yourself on the line." He turns from me to continue walking and then looks over his shoulder to add, "And after all the times I found her in your arms, I think I earned the right to see you sweat."

I cross my arms and lean against the pole next to me. "I'm still sweating."

"I don't think you'll be for long," he says.

Wow, he continues to shock me.

"Are you looking to get into the sainthood or something?" I tease.

He turns. "Why, you think dealing with you will get me in?" he asks with a raised brow.

"Maybe."

"No, man, you can't fool anyone now. You poured your heart out in there for everyone to see," he says. "Besides, I think you need each other."

"Thanks, Trace," I say sincerely. "Really."

"Go in peace," he says, mocking my saint comment. I laugh. "Oh, and Tannon," he pauses. I lift my chin and wait. "You're one helluva painter and a damn good poet. Stand proud."

I watch Trace walk away and silently wish him the best. Just before he turns the corner, he says, "But that doesn't mean I like you."

I grin, shaking my head. "I still hate you too, man."

CHAPTER 42
LIV

The blow-dryer hums numbingly in my ears as Gabi, my hair stylist, dries it straight. It's officially prom day and I'm beyond nervous. It's my date who makes me so. I had no reservations when Trace was taking me, but now that Tannon is, I have butterflies in my stomach and a lump in my throat.

School was strange yesterday. I didn't know how to act around Tannon. He seemed really happy. Cat said he was smiling all day, which made me happy, but I couldn't help feeling so tense. *Do I hug him? Do I kiss him? What the heck are we now?*

And with Trace still around, I feel totally awkward!

Tannon went from being a complete mystery to me to sharing his feelings for me in front of the whole senior class. Even so, he hadn't tried to hold my hand yesterday or act like we were a couple. Actually, he didn't touch me much at all. I guess he's giving me the space I asked for to let this all sink in.

And he sure gave me a lot to absorb. For one, his feelings for me started freshman year, more so, they started the first time he looked at me—that's huge. And to think he didn't believe he was good enough for me. *How could he ever think that?* This guy he started revealing to me this year is amazing. He's kind and giving and talented and smart and protective. I wish he would've trusted me enough from the beginning.

"So Cat says your prom date is a real hottie," Gabi says over the humming dryer. I shake my head when Cat giggles in the chair next to me.

She's so fresh.

"He's all right." I hear Tannon's voice and stiffen in the chair. Gabi turns off the dryer.

"Tannon," Cat scolds, "what are you doing in our sacred girl space? You're not supposed to be here."

"Since when is prom like a wedding?" he counters. "I brought you ladies lunch."

"Oh, he's so sweet," Gabi praises then waits a beat and says, 'Hi, I'm Gabi. It seems your presence has rendered my favorite client speechless."

"Nice to meet you," Tannon says, and then he spins my chair and leans in. "Are you keeping your hair down, Boo?"

"Tan, I think I'm supposed to surprise you or something," I say, pouting, not knowing much about prom protocol.

Is there even a protocol?

"I hate surprises," he retorts. "And you promised me the day so technically I'm allowed to be here. But don't worry—I'm not staying. I was just next door getting lunch with Teddy and saw Cat's car. I brought over sandwiches."

"Thank you. Do you want me to leave it down?" I ask about my hair.

"I want it anyway you want it," he says, and I know he's smiling. "You always look beautiful."

"I'm nervous," I admit, my cheeks heat under his stare. I can always tell when his eyes are on me. He gives off such an intense energy.

"Good," he sounds pleased, "that means this means something to you."

Of course it means something to me. It means everything, actually.

"Thanks for the sandwiches, TK," Cat says. "Now leave our sacred territory before we place a hex on you."

"All right." He gives in easily. "Thanks for saying yes, Liv."

I ease into a smile and feel him push from the chair. "Tan?"

"Yeah."

"Do the faux hawk tonight," I request, liking the feel of it against my palms.

"You got it, Boo!" His lips press against my temple. "Nice to meet you, Gabi."

"You too, uh . . . Tannon," she stumbles.

"Side braid," he calls out while walking away. I laugh at his sly exit.

And then I receive a smack on my shoulder. "You lucky duck!" Gabi teases. "He's gorgeous and thoughtful. I'm happy for you, girl."

"He loves her," Cat singsongs.

"Cat, after all he said yesterday, I'm scared he loves an imaginary idea of me. Some perfect girl he fabricated in his head," I say. "What happens when he realizes I'm—"

"Don't even go there," Cat interrupts, "or I'll beat you with a blow-dryer."

"Liv, that guy is completely in love with the real you," Gabi says. "I've seen my share of guys walk into this salon and many of them have wandering eyes. There are a lot of eye-catching females in here. Tannon, he didn't look at anyone but you. He knows who he loves and it's you."

I shrug and paste a smile on my face. "Now what are we doing with your hair?" she asks.

"A side braid please." I laugh again, thinking of Tannon's hint as he exited.

"I think that's perfectly you," Gabi states.

"See? He knows you, Liv," Cat says. "You want your sandwich?"

I nod. We eat while talking about our guys in our sacred girl space.

***

After Cat and I get our hair and makeup done, we head back to my house. Cat's mom hasn't called or even texted since she moved in with us and I know Cat's been hiding how hurt she is. She hasn't said much about prom but I know she would like her mom to see her all dressed up, if for nothing more than to show her how good she's doing without her.

"When are you leaving for Evan's, girls?" Mom asks as we enter the kitchen.

"The gang's meeting at the Tullys' at four-thirty," Cat says, sitting at the table. The Tullys invited all the parents to come for drinks before the limo picks us up.

"My girls look beautiful already," Mom says, sounding as if she's holding in her tears.

"Mom," I laugh, "we aren't even dressed yet."

"Well, be prepared for water works when you are," she warns. "I'm so proud of you two and I love you both. Cat," she stresses her name, "I hope you feel it."

Cat pushes her chair back and walks around the table. Mom sighs and I know they're hugging. "I do. It would be hard not to. I love you too."

Smiling, I think of how true Cat's words are. It would be hard not to feel Mom's love. Almost impossible. And I'm so glad Cat lets herself be loved by Mom.

"Now sit your hinnies down," Mom orders and we obey. "I was thinking of what Tannon said in the auditorium."

I told her everything that night, but Mom needs to let things marinate. She's a marinator—she never states an opinion unless she's had time to really think it through.

"I always liked that Tannon," she starts. "It sounds like he's always been there for you. But I understand your concerns, Liv."

"He called me perfect. That's a huge concern. How do I live up to his idea of me?"

"I think what he means is there is nothing about you he'd want to change. You are exactly what he wants," Mom says. I hear it in her tone—she hopes she's right. "His passion makes me a bit nervous, though. He lost his mother and you fill that void. That's a lot to live up to." She continues, "Ask him what he wants in life. What his goals are. What makes him happy. Where he sees himself in ten years. If you are his only answer, then I would say he has all his eggs in one basket and you shouldn't even start this. But"—she draws out the word—"if he has his own goals and other passions, then he may very well be the greatest catch out there for you."

"Do you fear you will fall for him and then he'll change his mind or something?" Cat asks. I shrug. "Why, do you have secrets?" I shake my head. "Then what's he going to find out that would diminish his love for you?"

"That I'm far from ideal," I say. "That being with me won't be easy."

"First, that's bull. And second, you and Trace had no problems," Cat points out.

"But this is Tannon," I say. "I was completely attracted to Trace, but this is Tannon." I lift my hands and drop them. "Everyone's attracted to him. He—"

Cat huffs out a laugh. "Who thinks who's perfect now?"

Mom agrees. "You have him on a pedestal too, my dear. I think if he saw you as a burden, then he'd have stopped liking you four years ago, no?"

"I guess you're right," I say with a sigh. "I'm just scared."

"Totally understandable," Cat says, smacking the table, "but your fear is unmerited. If you turned into a frog tomorrow, that boy would still love you."

"Liv!" Gary calls, walking in the front door. "I found a big package on the front step for you." He places something heavy down with a thump at my feet.

"What is it?" I ask, reaching my hand out, feeling paper and following it around what feels like a large rectangle. A frame, maybe? "Who's it from? Is there a card?"

"Yeah," Gary says. "It's addressed to Cat, but the package has your name on it."

"Read it," I say. Within seconds the envelope is ripped open.

"'Hey Cat, TK here. Please have Liv open this before prom. Let her know she can touch it. Please don't give any clues. Let her *see* it for herself. Have her open it and then read more after she figures it out.'"

"Open it!" Mom exclaims, and her chair shifts.

I carefully tear the paper and feel a thick wood frame. I was right. The frame is big; if I stood, the top of the frame would probably reach my chest. Gary lifts it so we can get the paper off completely. And everyone gasps. "What?"

"Feel it," Gary says.

I reach my hand out and follow the frame down until I feel the canvas. I slide my hands over the top and believe I can make out small birds flying. "Birds?"

"Yes," Mom says, her chair moves again.

"How did he do this?" I keep moving down, sliding my hand horizontally as I go. Suddenly I feel what I assume is a head. Identifying the familiar outline of ears on either side helped me figure that out. Slowing down, I take my time, feeling all the details. The pads of my fingertips slide over what's sure to be arched eyebrows on a smooth forehead. My fingers move down, gradually. Sliding over closed eyes I can actually feel the strokes of tiny lashes facing down and then a long nose and a wide-open mouth. There is a distinct difference in depth inside the mouth from the rest of the face, as if he created a hollowness on a flat canvas board. Amazing. The head is tilted slightly up. I can feel the upside down "U" of the jaw. Following the lines of the stretched neck, I find shoulders, roundness of a chest, and arms turned in oddly. The fingers bend inward as if holding something. Both my hands move between the painted hands and feel something wide and flat. The paint strokes are smooth and then I feel a hard edge. I'm not sure what the flat thing is I'm touching so I move on. Expanding my touch, I feel curves in the paint strokes. Swirling circles ... Maybe. I backtrack and touch the area again. I can almost feel the motion of the swirls. Waves ... I think?

"Is this water?"

"Yes!" Cat says, she hops in place, landing with a thump.

I go back up and feel the face again. "Is this me?"

"Yes! What are you doing?" Mom asks, her chair shifting again.

I touch it all again, thinking of Tannon, and smile. "Wave boarding."

"Yes!" Mom shouts, hitting the table. "Oh my gosh, it must have taken him forever."

It must have. I can feel every brush stroke, every spray of the wave and outline of my face, like 3-D. I can even feel the emotion, the excitement, and the movement. And the best part is I can *see* it all. "Keep reading," I ask.

"'If you're reading this, then that means she saw it," Cat goes on. "She saw what she looked like to me on my favorite day. She saw the joy on her face as she rode that wave. She saw the girl I love. And hopefully she saw I spoke the truth about how she looked that day.'"

The words warm my heart as I continue to slide my hand over the large painting. I can't believe he did this for me. Well, now knowing the real him, I can, but still, it's amazing.

"This kid is making me look bad," Gary teases.

"He is," Mom agrees. I'm too stunned to move.

"'No more secrets, Liv,'" Cat continues reading. "'This is what's in my heart. This is all I have left to win you over with. My grand gesture.' It's grand all right," Cat says. "I had no idea he was capable of creating something so exquisite. This is museum-quality."

"One of his paintings won third place in state," I say, feeling the paint again.

"Well, this would win first," Cat assures. "Okay, last part. 'Now, Boo, what are you doing sitting around? Go get ready for prom. I can't wait to dance with you.'"

I laugh. "Did he really write that?"

"Yep!" she says. "So let's get ready for prom."

"Gary, can you hang this in my room?"

"How 'bout in the living room, over your piano? It's too beautiful to hide in a bedroom."

I smile ear to ear. "That would be perfect. Thanks."

Jumping with excitement, Cat and I make our way to my room. I can't wait to thank Tannon. And I can't wait to thank him in my dress. It's long and strapless with a beaded bodice and a sweetheart neckline. The pleated chiffon creates an empire waist before flowing, draped layers fall gracefully to the floor. I love it! I feel so feminine in it. Oh and it's peach, so I guess I look like a fruit. I don't know, but Cat says it looks good against my olive skin.

Cat's dress has sparkling silver sequins over a shimmering gold sheath with a straight, strapless neckline. Mom says it's elegant and very flattering on Cat's figure.

After slipping on my dress, I find my new peach-colored Converse in their labeled cubby in my closet. Cat starts laughing. "You're going with the Converse?"

"Yep!" I slip them on and stand. "You can't see them, can you?"

"Nope. Tannon will probably have his on too. You look beautiful, Liv."

"I know you do too," I say. And slide my aviators on. "Ready to knock 'em dead."

"Oh, these boys won't know what hit 'em," she says, hooking my arm. We walk back into the kitchen.

"Wow," Gary says, amazed. "Just wow!"

"Okay, now I'm gonna cry," Mom says. "Get the camera, Gar."

As he walks past me, he stops at my side and his hand touches my arm. "You are beautiful, Liv," he says and kisses my cheek. I'm touched by his words and smile so big. "And Cat, I can't wait to see Evan's reaction. He'll be dragging his jaw all night."

He leaves the room only to return a second later. "Babe, our girl is all grown up," he says to Mom. I can't stop beaming. My relationship with Gary has changed dramatically since our talk. He's definitely assuming the position of father. And I'm loving being his daughter.

"I know!" she cries. "It's horrible." We laugh as she cries harder.

CHAPTER 43
TANNON

"Dude, I can't believe how nervous I am," I admit to Evan while slipping my bow tie around my shirt collar. Since I have no idea what color Liv's wearing, I just went with a basic black tux. If Trace goes tonight, he'll probably match Liv. I'm sure they coordinated their outfits like prom dates do, and that's a bit unsettling. I didn't want to ask for that reason. What if she felt guilty about not going with Trace again and changed her mind? But I regret not asking now. Dates are supposed to match. Evan's bow tie and cummerbund are gold to complement Cat. I should've just asked Cat the color of Liv's dress.

Who would've thought something this insignificant would be what saddens me tonight? Hopefully this is the only thing that does.

I'm lucky I even found a tux that fit me. The guy at the store was really rude about me coming last minute. After I told him my story, he changed his tune and rented it to me half price.

I went with black on black—tux, shirt, tie, and cummerbund, all black. It looks kind of GQ. Maybe, with any luck, she's wearing black.

"Technically this is your first date with her, so of course you're nervous," Evan says, fixing his hair at his dresser mirror. "I'm so glad you're coming, man. It's gonna be a good night."

"I still can't believe I'm going." I stand behind him at the mirror and stretch my neck to button the top button of the shirt. "Maybe this shitstorm of a year will end with a rainbow."

Chuckling, he says, "You're such a sappy poet, TK. I'm glad it's almost over. I can't wait till graduation."

"What's the rush?" I ask, confused. Now that I almost, possibly, with any luck, have Liv, I don't want school to end.

"What won't Cat do until she graduates?" He stares at me in the mirror, his eyebrows dancing wildly.

"Oh yeah . . ." I smack his back. "That's right, stud. You better hope she forgives you after. You know you won't last five seconds."

"You're being too generous," he says. "It'll be a miracle if I get my pants off before I lose it." We laugh hard. He sits on the bed to pull his black dress shoes on while I try to tie my bow tie. "Guys should be here any minute," he says, glancing at his clock by the bed.

"Yeah." Honestly, I can't wait to see Teddy's big ass grin. He asked Laura to be his date and she said yes. He deserves this night.

The bow tie isn't cooperating and I feel myself getting frustrated. "I have to ask my dad to tie this thing."

"Why didn't you get a clip-on?"

"That old Italian guy told me no gentleman wears a clip-on and refused to give me one. I guess you're not a gentleman," I say.

"I guess not, but since mine's on, I look like one and you don't," he jests back.

"You got me there. I'll meet you downstairs." I find Dad sitting out on the deck with the Tullys. Mrs. Tully grabs her camera the second she spots me and starts flashing off pictures like a madwoman.

"Look at that boy," she says. "He's too handsome for words."

I shake my head, grinning. "I'm not ready yet." I point to the bow tie and Dad stands to work his magic.

"You look great," he says.

"Thanks."

Mrs. Tully takes a few shots of Dad and me. I notice a tear in her eye. Mom and her were good friends and I know she's wishing Mom were here. I do too. But I know Mom's watching.

She's been watching. Maybe even pulling a few strings for me too.

Evan's sister Kelly walks around the side of the house with Sparks and Tucker following behind. "Woo-hoo, TK, you clean up nice!" Kelly bellows. I can't even respond; my eyes are glued on Sparks.

"Holy sh . . ." I catch myself. "Wow! Look at you, Sparky!" He's wearing a powder blue tux and I'm so shocked I can't even laugh.

He smiles proudly. "How do I look?" he asks, spinning to model his blueness.

374

"Like a jackass," Tucker says, and Sparks frowns while punching him. The Tullys and Dad laugh as he models for them. I set my laugh free and can't stop. Tucker walks up the steps, shaking his head. He looks good in his black tux and hot pink bow tie with matching cummerbund.

"Where's Sam?" I ask as we bump chests in a manly greeting.

"She's coming with Robin."

Sparks asked Robin to be his date at the last minute. He was hesitant, but when he found out she was going alone because she only wanted to go with him, his opinion of her changed. I'm glad he asked her.

Evan walks out of the slider door, his eyes widen on little boy blue, and he falls back into the door. "What the fffu—"

"Evan." Mrs. Tully scolds, halting his curse.

"Sorry. Blame it on shock." He stares dumbfounded at Sparks and starts laughing hysterically.

"I look awesome!" Sparks boasts, holding his lapels.

Tucker's and Sparks's mothers come around back holding their cameras. Teddy strolls behind them, like a big bear in a tux. Laura walks beside him with her head down shyly. I hop down the deck stairs and hug the big guy before hugging her too. "You look very pretty, Laura."

"Thanks," she says. "You look handsome."

I wink at her and smack Teddy's arm. "And look at you, you stud." I hoot. "Damn, you're handsome." He smiles and Laura stares at his profile with a sweet grin on her face.

"Hey guys!" Teddy calls. "This is Laura."

Tucker's eyes bug out of his head when he sees her. "Wow, Teddy, who'd you pay . . ."

Evan punches his arm and walks down to greet Laura. "I'm Evan. And that knucklehead is Tucker. And the blue idiot is Sparks." She waves to them and Evan wiggles his brows at Teddy when she isn't looking, mouthing "Wow!"

Wow sure does describe her. The only skin her dress reveals is her arms and shoulders but, I tell you, both are great. Her long blond hair is styled in a fancy updo and her makeup makes her big brown doe eyes look even bigger. She's much smaller than Teddy in every way, but they look really good together.

"Okay, boys," Mrs. Tully says, "picture time." We stand in a line and wrap our arms around each other. I can't even believe this is it. I feel emotional just thinking about it. "Say . . . brotherhood!" she calls out and we all laugh while yelling it back at her.

"I think I'm gonna cry," Evan says, squeezing my neck.

Mrs. Tully asks us to look at the camera again when suddenly Cat and Liv appear around the side of the house. My eyes bug out of my head as my jaw drops to the ground, and it feels as if my heart is beating visibly outside of my chest like a cartoon.

Evan squeezes me tighter as he gawks at Cat. "Damn . . ." Evan groans and bites his knuckle.

Mrs. Tully turns around to see what we're gaping at. "Oh my heavens, you two are stunning!"

Liv smiles, looking absolutely breathtaking. I can't stop staring. I can't move. She looks like a Greek goddess. I want to move to her, but my brain isn't connecting with my limbs. Evan leaves me without a problem and walks to Cat. Kissing Liv's cheek before pulling Cat into a hug.

"Look at you! God, you're gorgeous," he says.

"And you're hot," Cat fires back, tugging his bow tie.

Liv's mom and Gary are staring at me. I catch their eyes on me. They look like they're waiting for me to say something, but I can't talk. Dad walks down the stairs and greets them before complimenting Liv. Teddy, Sparks, and Tucker all say hi to Liv and I've yet to move. Dad comes over and nudges my shoulder. "You all right?"

I shake my head and he laughs. I see Liv's head lower and a frown grow on her face. She must think the worst again. That pulls me out of my stupor and I walk to her, grabbing her corsage off the deck steps as I go. "Liv, you are the most beautiful girl I have ever laid eyes on."

Her head turns up and she smiles. "Really?"

"I couldn't even move. You took my breath away," I say and feel her mom's eyes on me. I swallow hard. "And I love the braid."

She lifts the hem of her dress and sticks out a Converse-clad foot. I laugh. "I have them on too. In black."

"Faux hawk?" she asks, lifting her hand high. I lower my head to it. Her fingers touch my spikes and she nods in approval. "Love it," she says. "I'm sure you look like a rock star."

Her hand grips my lapel and she shakes her head. "I can't find the words, Tannon." She tugs at my jacket while scrunching her nose. "Your painting is extraordinary. How'd you do it?"

"Four months, five tries, sleepless nights, a lot of paint, and . . ." I pause and move closer. "A desperate need to be understood."

"I'll cherish it always," she says.

I turn to Mrs. Sullivan to greet her and shake Mr. Sullivan's hand. "Tannon, the painting blew me away. And I love the hair and the black on black. Very GQ," Mr. Sullivan compliments me as his fingers make the okay sign.

"Thank you, sir," I say, grinning. "Liv requested the hawk. The tux was my pick." I turn to her. "I uh . . . I got you a corsage. It's white roses. I . . . I didn't know what color you were wearing." I can't believe how nervous I am. I'm actually stuttering. "I'm sorry."

"Sorry?" Liv questions, puzzled by my apology. "Tannon, I'm sure it's beautiful. White matches everything, right?" I agree and she grins, amused. "Is Tannon Keaton nervous?"

"Yeah, he is," I admit. "Big time."

"Good," Liv says. "That means this means something to you." She uses my line.

"It means everything," I say in a whisper and take the flower out of the plastic container. Taking her hand, I slide the band on her wrist.

"It's beautiful, sweetheart," her mom tells her. "It's perfect."

"Thank you, Tannon. I love it!" She squeezes my hand.

Seconds later, Cat pulls Liv away to take pictures, leaving me to Mrs. Sullivan's intense stare. Sweat beads under my collar. She's attractive and looks to be a couple years younger than the other moms here. She's shorter than Liv, but they both have big boobs—if I'm allowed to say that about her mom—

and olive skin. Liv shares a lot of her mom's traits, but I always wondered what Liv's biological dad looked like.

"You're a talented artist, Tannon," she starts. "The time it took you to create that painting lets me know how much Liv means to you. But tell me something, Tannon, what are your hopes for the future?"

I feel as if I'm on trial and I try to hide the distress it causes me. *Did she ask Trace this too?*

"I hope to make a living painting. I'm set to play hockey for the Metropolitan League after graduation. I'm not sure if playing hockey will go further than that, but I do hope to coach one day. And, of course, I hope to be with your daughter, if she'll have me, for as long as she'll have me." I answer truthfully. Her expression doesn't change. I glance at Mr. Sullivan. His straight mouth reveals very little as well. I'm forced to wait it out.

"And college?"

"I'm . . ." Crap. I swallow hard. "I'm not going to college."

Silence follows.

"Okay," she finally says, nodding her head. "Just checking to see if you have other interests besides my daughter."

My eyes widen. "Then I guess it's good I didn't say I plan on sitting on your front lawn until Liv says she'll be mine?"

She laughs hard. "Yeah, it's good you didn't say that."

"I like this guy," Mr. Sullivan says. I smile and pretend to wipe sweat from my brow. After touching my forehead, I realize I don't have to pretend.

"Tannon!" Evan yells. "Pic time, bro."

I wave at him and turn back to the Sullivans. "I promise to always protect her and respect her."

"Thank you, Tannon," Mrs. Sullivan says. "Go have fun."

I turn and jog over to the group waiting for me. Sam and Robin got here as I was talking to the Sullivans. I wave hello before slipping between Cat and Liv. All the cameras aim at us as we smile. I love this group, even Robin, who I hardly know. I'm just so happy I'm here. I wasn't planning on it and that would've sucked. I kiss Cat's cheek and tell her she looks beautiful before moving to pose with Liv as Dad and Mr. Sullivan take a few shots. Dad takes one of Evan and me and then the guys all pile on our backs for another shot. Teddy bear hugs us all and Dad gets that shot too.

Teddy's mom takes a few with him and Laura. Mrs. Todd, who is a petite woman—how she gave birth to Teddy is beyond me—is beaming over her son. She can't stop smiling at him and he keeps rolling his eyes at her, but I see his grin. He's a mama's boy. I was once too.

Teddy's parents are divorced and he sees his dad one weekend a month. His dad has a new family he spends most of his time with. I know it hurts the big guy, but he never talks about it. Laura's mom is here too. She keeps asking Laura to look up and I can see she worries over her timid daughter, but she smiles every time she sees Teddy lean down to talk to Laura because every time he does, Laura looks up at him and laughs. Laura looks so relaxed with Teddy and I know her mother sees that too. Again, how could anyone not love the gentle giant?

Looking around the yard, I notice everyone is smiling. This is what it's all about, finding things in life to smile about. Tonight I have a lot to keep me grinning and I hope Liv decides to be mine so it becomes my permanent expression.

I watch as Liv talks with my dad. He has her laughing about something, probably something embarrassing about me, but I don't care because he looks so happy. Mr. Tully gets in on it, adding to Dad's story every now and then. Mr. and Mrs. Sullivan are cracking up as they listen to the two go on and on. My curiosity gets the best of me and I walk over to find out what's so amusing. My dad grins mischievously when I stand between Liv and Cat.

"So Tannon and Evan walk in the house with blue skin," Dad says. "I mean *blue*, even their faces."

"And they stayed blue for about a week," Mr. Tully adds.

I shake my head and yell to Evan, "They're telling them about when we added food coloring to my kiddy pool."

"Traitors!" Evan shouts, shaking his head with a smirk. "Let's go before they share anything else."

"Which Smurf were you trying to be? Hefty?" Cat asks me.

"No. Brainy," I correct and her bottom lip pouts out, sympathetically. I just shrug it off. Liv hugs my arm. "Evan wanted to be Hefty," I add.

"Let's go, Hefty," Cat yells across the yard. He's grabbing our bags. We aren't coming home tonight. Tucker's having a huge after party and we—well, at least the guys—plan on staying the night. I hope Liv will stay, but I haven't even talked about it with her. I haven't dared do anything that may rock this boat.

"You got that right, baby!" Evan yells back. Mrs. Tully scolds him with a look. He walks over to her and juts his cheek out for her to kiss. "Love you, Mommy," he says.

"Love you too, baby boy. Be good!" She kisses his cheek.

I glance at Dad, missing Mom. "She's here," he whispers, knowingly. "Have a good time."

CHAPTER 44
LIV

We climb into the limo and the second the doors close, Tucker announces that the party is officially on and asks who wants a shot from his flask. Tannon places his arm over my shoulder and pulls me in close. I don't think he joins in the fun and wonder why.

"I love the dress," he whispers. "You look like a goddess. Did I already tell you that?"

"Thanks, and no, but hearing that would never get old." I lean into him more and his fingers slide over my shoulder.

"Liv, that dress is beautiful and the color is perfect on you," Sam says.

I turn my head to her. "Thanks, Sam. I know you look beautiful too." I sit back, hoping that didn't sound ridiculous to say. Saying it to Cat is one thing, but I feel awkward saying it to others. However, I have a hard time receiving a compliment without giving one back.

"My girl looks smokin' hot tonight," Tucker says, then lips smack in a kiss. "We all look frickin' awesome. Except Sparks. The jackass is wearing a powder blue tux."

"Is that bad?" I ask.

"Yep!" everyone says at the same time that Sparks says, "Nope!"

"Liv," Robin says, "never mind the color. His shirt has ruffles. Actual ruffles."

I laugh at that.

"I got myself a real hot date," Robin adds. I hear her amusement, but also her affection. She really likes him.

"That you did," Sparks agrees. "And so did I."

"Why thank you, Eddie," Robin says. I haven't heard anyone call him Eddie in years. Teachers even use his last name.

"Eddie?" Tannon teases. "You can't call him Eddie when he looks like little boy blue."

"Yes, I can," Robin protests. "And he looks handsome."

I can imagine Sparks smiling at that. "He's a sweetheart," I say.

"All right, girls, no need to fight over me. I have enough to go around."

"Ha . . . you wish!" Tucker mocks.

We make a few turns and then the limo picks up speed. Suddenly I feel uneasy. I don't know if it's from sitting sideways in a moving car, which I've never done, or from being squished between Cat and Tannon, but I don't feel right.

"Cat," I whisper, finding her hand and gripping it for dear life. "Something's wrong," I move forward. "I need air. I need to get out of here."

Everyone starts to panic, which makes me more anxious. Tannon knocks on something and yells for the driver to stop. *Oh my gosh, I can't be sick in a prom dress.* The limo stops and everyone piles out. I can hardly maneuver in the gown so Tannon lifts me into his lap and slides down the long seat and out the door. The warm air hits me and I breathe in deeply.

"I'm so sorry," I say, embarrassed. Everyone assures me it's all right and they try to comfort me. I appreciate it but need to be alone.

"C'mere," Tannon says, guiding me away from the limo. There are rocks under my shoes making for an uneven walk, and then he places my hand on a tree, grounding me. "You're probably car sick. Just take a minute."

"I'm sorry."

"For what? Stop." He shushes me.

"Where are we?" Cars zip by.

"The side of the highway. We'll sit in the back so we face forward. It's all right. I felt weird riding like that too."

I nod, touching his jacket. I stop at his bow tie and tug the sides and then slide my hands up to his handsome face. "This day has the potential of being another favorite."

"It's already made it on my list." He kisses my forehead and asks if I feel better. I nod and we make our way back into the limo, sitting in the back this time.

Tannon opens the window slightly and the driver drives on. I sit back, wanting to cry. Not from sadness or embarrassment, but from happiness. Everyone sounds happy. They all talk over each other, laughing and teasing, and it just feels right. This year was full of ups and downs and I'm so pleased everyone is on the same page tonight.

We make it to the banquet hall with no more glitches. Tannon opens the limo door and the music pumps in. It sounds like Paramore. I start wiggling in the seat with excitement. Tannon pulls me out of the limo and leads me to the music as Cat holds my waist from behind and sings in my ear, "'Ain't it fun . . .'"

People say hi as we walk by, offering compliments to one another. I hear Frankie ask Tannon to save her a dance. *Is she serious?* He actually laughs, and it's a "like that's gonna happen" kind of laugh. It's evil of me, yet I can't help tingling with satisfaction. How I feel about her is just below how I feel about Rita.

Evan wraps his arm over my shoulder as we wait for Tannon to hand in our tickets. He dances at my side—he has great rhythm, which I do not—so I let him move me. Cat's on my other side, describing the room. "The lighting's dim, room's decorated in our school colors, blue and gold, and it looks nice. Big dance floor, which is a plus."

"Let's go, pretty girl," Tannon calls. The noise coming from the room has my attention and I didn't comprehend what he said. "That's you, Liv," he laughs. "You're the pretty girl I'm talking to."

"Hey!" Cat exclaims. "I'm standing here too."

"Okay," Tannon says. "Let's go, pretty girls."

"Hey!" Evan exclaims. "What about me?"

"Like I said, let's go, pretty girls."

"Coming," Evan teases and walks forward. I reach my hand out and Tannon takes it as we walk to the table. We all get situated and Cat pulls me out of my seat the second I take it.

"No sitting tonight, girlfriend."

"Cat, I can't dance in front of these people."

"Like hell you can't," she snaps, pulling me. "Who cares what these people think anyway. The only ones I care about are at our table and they want us to dance."

Dancers bounce and bump into me as she drags me through the mob. Stopping short, she grabs my hands and swings them sexy-like. I can't stop giggling like a four-year-old. *Real sexy*. Robin and Sam join us, saying hi to me so I know they're near.

Suddenly I feel long fingers wrap around my hips from behind. "You look beautiful," Trace says at my ear. I spin and hug him.

"You came!"

"Yeah, I came with Jack and a couple dateless guys."

"Oh, I feel horrible." The thought of him coming stag fills me with guilt.

"Why? I'm fine," he says next to my ear. I touch the lapel of his tux and frown. "Liv, it's okay. All I ask is that you save me a slow dance."

"I promise. But I'm not a very good dancer."

He laughs. "Neither am I. Two left feet. I'll find you later." He kisses my cheek and just as soon as he came, he's gone.

Cat spins me and starts swinging my arms again. She pulls my hips to hers and does some crazy, completely embarrassing, gyrating hip action against me. I cover my face with my hands, squealing, as she sways us back and forth.

"Oh, you know you love it!" she shouts in my ear.

Wrapping my arms around her shoulders, I say, "No, I love you!"

"I love you more."

Heavy arms circle around us and then another set of arms wrap over them. A hard chest squishes me into Cat and she is squished back. Evan yells, "Yeah, baby!"

And Tannon replies, "Hell yeah!"

They sandwich us as they sway to the beat of the music. I lower my head to Cat's shoulder as Tannon's body presses very, very close to mine. His thigh muscles compress to the back of mine as he dips, forcing my knees to bend. Cat's laughing in my ear. The crowd is louder now. More people are dancing; I can feel their heat, hear their closeness. The stomping of many feet has the floor vibrating.

Tannon pulls me from Cat and spins me before squeezing me against his chest. He slides his knee between my legs as much as my long gown will allow and his hand is wide on my lower back as he moves me, swaying and dipping low then back up. "Chandelier" by Sia is playing. It's a sexy song and the way he moves me makes me feel desirable. His body rocks two beats to the left before swaying to the right for two, then he goes one beat left and back for two.

Oh my gosh, the way this guy moves feels sinful. But I start to get a feel for his rhythm and move with him.

I rest my head on his shoulder and just give in to the dance. Lowering his head, he presses his lips to my shoulder, keeping them there as he continues his sway. His fingers spread and then fist my dress at my back, pulling me even closer, like a desperate attempt to become one.

I slide my hands up his wide back, rising a little higher against him. Everything about Tannon turns me on—the way he feels, how good he smells, the way he moves, his touch, his words, the effortless way he wakes my desire. He's like an aphrodisiac. I can't get enough of him.

The song ends and Tannon changes his moves to fit the beat. I try to follow.

Without warning a big mitt grabs my arm. "Can I cut in?" Teddy asks and pulls me from Tannon before I even answer. He lifts me against his side and starts dancing, badly.

"You're crazy!" I yell as my feet swing inches from the floor.

His laughter rumbles through his barrel chest. "Can't be at prom and not dance with you, doll."

Laughing, feeling like a rag doll flopping around from his wild, haphazard moves, I ask where Laura is, and he says she's right next to him. I ask him to pull her in. Next thing I know, she's squealing next to me as he bear hugs us together.

He spins us and everyone yells his name. Next, Sparks cuts in. He's a better dancer than Teddy, that's for sure, but not as good as Tannon. "Hey, Sparky," I say.

"Hi, Livy." We dance until the song changes.

"Where's Tannon?"

"Break dancing with Tucker."

'No! What is that? Is he good?" I ask, yet another surprise about Tannon—he can break dance!

"He's okay, but not as good as Tucker. Its street dancing. Lots of spinning on the ground and stuff," Sparks says and I feel him pull someone next to us.

"Eddie, why aren't you breaking?" Robin asks.

"You break too?" I ask.

"I'm better than both of them," he boasts.

"Go!" Robin encourages him and he steps away. She takes my hand. I wish I could see this. "Oh my God," she laughs. "Teddy's trying to do the worm. He's going to bust his shirt buttons open."

I laugh trying to picture them one-up each other's moves—whatever those moves may be they sure involve a lot of thumping. Everyone's cheering their names and then they start chanting Sparks's name. "That boy's got moves," Robin says, squeezing my hand.

"Go, Sparky!" I cheer.

The song changes and I'm in Tannon's arms again. He's warmer. Breathing heavier. "You break dance too?"

"I'm a man of many talents," he teases.

Dinner is announced and we all take our seats at the table. Cat sits to my right, Tannon my left. The waitress pours us water and serves our salads. We eat and laugh.

Tannon pulls me to his side. "Having fun?" he whispers in my ear.

As I'm turning to respond, I hear Frankie calling his name. "You owe me a dance."

"Uh ... no, I don't," Tannon says, instantly irritated.

"Yes, you do ..."

"Frankie," Evan says, "you're drunk. Move on."

"Screw you, Tully."

"No, thank you," Evan retorts.

"Tannon didn't complain," she says, and I straighten in my chair.

"That's enough, Frankie." Tannon turns to face her behind us.

"Oh, I can be your first but you can't save me a dance?" she barks with her raspy voice.

All right, now I assumed he wasn't a virgin anymore, but never would I have guessed his first was Frankie. *Why her? Anyone but her.*

"Dance with your date. I'll dance with mine," he says. She starts to argue and he stands, his seat pushing against mine forcefully.

"Seriously? You aren't done with your charity case yet?" Frankie barks. "C'mon, you can stop the act. I know you just feel sorry for her."

"I feel sorry for me," Tannon retorts. "You're the biggest mistake of my life. You remind me of that every time you open your mouth. And I wish I could take that night back, but I can't. So I feel sorry for me."

"You don't talk like this when we're alone," she states with a slur.

"Really?" he sneers. "When's the last time we were alone?"

"Last night."

He starts laughing bitterly. "You're out of your mind."

Having had enough of this entertainment, I turn to them. "Please move on, Frankie, his charity case needs lots of attention," I say, and Cat and Sam hoot like my back-up girls. I go on, "You're disturbing the allotted time he must put in to reach his quota of good deeds for the day."

Tannon pushes into me and curses. Okay maybe he was *pushed* into me. A few grunts follow and I hear a bunch of commotion until—nothing. I reach out and come up empty. "Where'd they go?"

"He ... uh ... pulled her out the door," Cat says and I can tell she didn't want to tell me that.

"I'll go help him," Evan says.

"Tell her that, when I'm not wearing this dress that I really love, she's going to feel my wrath!" Cat shouts after him. And everyone at the table laughs.

"Your wrath?" Sparks teases.

"Yep."

My head drops to my chest and Cat wraps her arm around me. "What am I doing? This is crazy. I'm so not right for him."

"That's bull." She won't even entertain my sulking.

"Cat, be honest, what do we look like together?"

She turns me in my chair, holding my upper arms tight. "Liv, be honest, what do you feel like together?" I lower my head. I don't think I'm ready to admit how good I feel in his arms. "This is our senior prom, Liv. You're here with friends who love you. Don't you dare let that slutty lush ruin this night."

Long fingers touch my shoulders. "Can I have that dance now?" Trace says, leaning next to my head. I nod, pleased with his perfect timing. I don't want to be sitting here while Tannon is dealing with Frankie. Trace guides me to the dance floor. Holding me close and kind of swaying, he leads me, off beat. "Are you having fun?"

"I was. Then I wasn't. And now I am again."

"Sounds like an interesting night so far," he says. I rest my head on his chest with a sigh. Our relationship was so comfortable, so easy. I never had to wonder, never had to guess—he was safe.

Then there's Tannon. Everything about him, from his touch to his words, leaves me wondering. Is it dangerous to be attracted to someone who stands outside my comfort zone, causes emotions and sensations I've never had before, and leaves me wanting more? Tannon's obviously more experienced than me, but that's not what scares me. It's not his body's wants that concern me, it's his heart's need. I'll be eighteen next week, an adult, but am I still too young to handle Tannon's passion?

The song ends and we hug tightly before Trace walks me back to the table. He says hi to everyone, kisses my cheek, and then walks off. I feel Tannon next to me when I sit, but I don't say anything.

"I guess I deserved that," Tannon says.

"What?"

"You dancing with Trace."

"I told him I would. He's here alone because of me." I feel myself getting worked up and defensive. "Are you sure about this?" I ask wiggling my finger between the two of us.

"I'm going to pretend you didn't ask that," he says, leaning close to me so I can hear his angry whisper.

"Well, I did."

His chair pushes back and he takes me by the elbows, lifting me to my feet with ease. He pulls me from the table and doesn't stop until I feel the night air on my skin.

"She's drunk."

I guess he wants to start this with Frankie. "But is she a liar?" I ask.

"About my being with her one time? No, she isn't," he admits. "About everything else? Yes, she is."

I nod. "I don't care what you did with her. I danced with Trace because I care about him. I was supposed to be his date … He seems to think you and I belong together."

"Do you?"

"I have no idea." Shaking my head, I lift my hands and shrug. "I don't know what to think. I feel really blind tonight, Tannon. I feel like I'm missing a lot. Everyone's complimenting one another and I want to be a part of that, but I feel so ridiculous saying they look great. You guys were break dancing and I so desperately wanted to see that." I take off my glasses and turn my face to him. "Are you sure I'm not a charity case?"

The weight of his body bumps into me and his hands take hold of my face. "Yes, I'm sure! What are you doing? You think you can scare me away by taking off your glasses? I want them off. I hate those damn things." He huffs irritably. "You're gonna have to do better than that to get rid of me."

"Tan—"

"Don't you dare!" He groans and drops his forehead to mine. "Don't do this, Liv. You promised me a day. I know this must be hard on you— everyone dressed up, the dancing—I get it. But don't you dare try to convince yourself that I don't know who you are. Or throw the opinion of a drunk girl on me. Did you ever ask Trace if he was sure?" I don't answer. "Did you?" he asks, sterner. "Am I not enough for you, Liv?" His tone softens. "You believe nothing I say. Always think the worst. Am I not enough? Tell me now."

Reaching up, gripping his wrists, I hold them firmly. "Who do you think you love? The perfect girl you described isn't me."

"God, don't do this, Liv. Please don't do this."

"I'm not perfect, Tannon," I stress.

"You are to me! You're perfect for me," he says, and suddenly I feel his lips on mine. They move urgently. His hands on my face lift me to my tippy toes and he tilts my head. Kissing me ardently, as if his life depends on it, he causes my heart to beat wildly and my head to spin. I squeeze his wrists tighter as his tongue slides over my lips. I part them with a quiver. A tear falls onto my cheek and slides between our lips. The taste of salt hits my tongue. He cries while kissing me with more passion than I've ever felt. It's overwhelming. More than that, he kisses me with love and I never felt so adored. I grab his jacket and pull him closer to me. His hands drop from my face and wrap around my waist, lifting me against him, deepening our kiss. He spins us and presses his back to the side of the building.

"I love you, Liv," he whispers against my mouth. "Please don't question how I feel about you."

Kissing me again, his arm wraps around the back of my neck and he tilts my head up in his tight hold. His thumb pulls on my chin, fingers spread wide and slide over my cheek. He has an insatiable hunger and it's me he craves. The fact that I can feel this in his kiss makes me just as hungry. My knees weaken and I hold onto his jacket for dear life.

It seems he doesn't need words to convince me he's the right one. He ravishes my mouth and my mind spins woozily. I hang limp in his hold. The back of my head braced in the crook of his arm is all that supports me. My legs are useless. My arms are jelly. My back shutters as a sudden need to be touched—everywhere—races through me. All this from a kiss.

From an amazingly mind-blowing kiss.

If he lets me go, I will melt into a puddle at his feet.

If this is how Romeo kissed Juliet then I get it. I so get it now.

"You better believe I never kissed a girl like this before. Nor has a girl ever kissed me back like this," Tannon says against my mouth. My head lolls to the side. "Liv, hey, are you all right?"

"Who's Liv?" I say, as if coming out of a dream.

There's a silent pause and then he laughs. "Say you heard what I said and you believe me."

"I heard, I believe," I say, sighing.

"God, I've wanted to do that for so long." His fingers dig into my shoulder. "I never want to stop kissing you but we should enjoy our prom first."

I nod, still weak in the knees. "You may have to carry me."

Amused, enjoying the state he put me in, he says, "Two more hours. Then your sweet mouth is mine again."

"Okay," I say, still drunk off of whatever he stirred in me.

"You're doing wonders for my ego here, Liv." He laughs hard against my neck, then holds me to his side and walks us back in.

CHAPTER 45
TANNON

We eat our cold food and listen to Tucker and Sparks argue. Finally my requested song comes on and I ask Liv to dance.

"This is "I'm Yours" by The Script, and it goes out to Liv from Tannon," the DJ says.

I pull her against my chest and rest my chin on her head. The guys come out with their dates and dance by us. Even Teddy gets Laura in his arms. She lays her head on his big chest and closes her eyes. He looks down at her with a huge grin on his face. I wink at him when he glances my way. He nods and lifts two fingers off her hand he's holding to give me the peace sign. Evan and Cat come close to us and Evan squeezes us together, repeatedly saying how much he loves us. They spin away to tell the next couple the same thing. He took one too many swigs from Tucker's flask and now he's really getting sappy. I laugh as he hugs people he hardly ever talked to all four years of school. Cat hangs her head back and her laughter booms over the music. They are finally back as they were. Happy. Crazy. And a little weird.

Liv tilts her head up to me. "I like this song."

"I'm yours, Liv. I've been yours since the first day we met."

She drops her head back to my chest. I pull her closer, my thumb rubbing over the bare skin of her upper back as my other hand holds hers up against my chest, and I drop my head next to hers. "I love you so much. I've been wanting to say that for far too long and now I can't stop. Please don't make me stop."

A country song comes on next and it's the kind of song that can be danced to as a couple or alone; I choose to keep holding her. She doesn't protest. When Kid Rock's "All Summer Long" comes on, I turn her, press her back to me, and hold her by the hands, moving her with the music as Evan and the guys hold their dates the same way. We make a circle and sing every word. Hugging her arms around her body, I lean my head over her shoulder and sway her hips with mine.

We have the best time, laughing and dancing. Cat steals her away during all the girlie songs, but I always get her back.

So we had a little drama. What's a prom without a little drama? We got past it and it's all good now. Maybe even better since I got to kiss her.

And that kiss, that insane kiss … I've never experienced anything like it. I've kissed a lot of girls—they don't even compare. It was like an out of body experience, heaven on earth. It was the greatest kiss of my life, complete and utter perfection. And still my description doesn't do it justice. Take all I said and multiply it by infinity and that would be the equivalent of that kiss.

Un-effin'-believable.

Evan steals Liv for a dance and I pull Cat in. "She's scared," Cat says, one hand on my shoulder the other in mine.

"I know."

"Why do you think she's scared of you and not Trace?" she asks, looking up at me.

"Because he's her ideal," I groan.

She laughs while shaking her head. "No, you fool. Because you are."

"That doesn't make any sense."

"Oh really," she counters. "Why did you hide from her? Because you were scared right? Why?"

I smile down at Cat. "Because she's my ideal. But I hid fearing she wouldn't love me back . . . I love her and she already knows that."

"She thinks you love the idea of her. She's scared you won't like what you really get."

I look over at Liv with a frown. Evan has her laughing at something. Her mouth is open wide and she's smacking his chest playfully. He dips her and she laughs harder. "How could she think I don't know her?"

"You had four years to work out your feelings," Cat says. "Give her time to understand hers."

I look down at this little pixie of a girl. "You give good advice. Too bad you didn't give it to yourself nine months ago."

"I know." She rolls her big blue eyes. "We all seem to learn the hard way."

I kiss her cheek. "Love ya, Kitty Cat."

"I love you too, TK. And damn can you paint!"

The last song was voted in by the class, Bon Jovi's "Never Say Goodbye." We all form a huddle and sway. The girls cry, Teddy cries—gentle giant—and hell, I almost tear up just seeing the big guy cry. I pull him closer. "No goodbyes here," I promise him. "Never."

Evan leans in and rubs Teddy's head. "Never."

Teddy, Sparks, and Tucker all say, "Never," in unison. Cat and Liv hug in the middle of our huddle with Robin and Sam. I was blessed with this group, no doubt. If it wasn't for them, who knows where I'd be or what I'd be doing.

That's high school, right? You find people that help you get through it and hope they'll stick with you afterward. We know that the odds aren't in our favor. In a group of friends maybe only a few stay close, but I know we'll all do our damnedest to try.

I lift my head and notice Trace in his huddle with his friends. He lifts his head and we lock eyes. I smile and watch his mouth twitch at the corner—like he's fighting it—but the smile wins and I laugh. And then I notice Frankie coming my way and yell, "Incoming!" and push my way into the middle of the huddle and let Teddy and Evan close me in. I bear hug the girls and pray that Frankie keeps walking. She's a nightmare to deal with when she drinks and she seems to drink all the time lately. I slept with her once. Alcohol was involved. Lots of it. It was at Tucker's house during a party, and I regretted it as soon as it began. She's yet to let me forget it happened.

The song ends, the DJ says goodnight, and the lights turn up. Just like that, it's over. God, I hope that's not how Liv and me end tonight. *Thanks Tannon, it was a nice time, catch you at school on Monday. Wow, that would suck.*

We make our way back to the table to collect our jackets and things and follow the crowd out to the limos. Trace comes up to us, I shake his hand and he hugs Liv and then holds her to his side, rubbing his fingers over her arm. I eye him curiously. He starts to laugh. "Payback's a what?" he asks me with his hand to his ear.

I shake my head, amused. I guess he has me there. He kisses Liv's cheek and says goodnight before getting lost in the crowd. Our limo pulls up and Liv and I climb in last so we can sit in the back. I slip my arm over her shoulder and cuddle her into my side. It's dark except for the red track lighting above and it seems to sedate us all. Sparks plugs his iPhone in and music pumps through the long cab.

"Are you going to Tucker's?" I ask her hopefully.

"I don't know if that's a good idea," she whispers.

"Why?"

"I . . . just . . . prom night and all."

After decoding what she's saying, I realize she thinks I may try something. I start to chuckle loudly. "Liv, first, if you think I'd want to be with you like that at a party, then you don't get how I feel about you."

"What's second?" she asks, turning to me slightly.

"That's second too. I respect you. I respect us. If we have a first time, it sure isn't going to be at a party."

"What if I said it's not you I'm worried about?" After decoding that, I believe I'm mistaken and ask her to clarify who she's worried about. "Myself," she says.

401

My head snaps back. "You think *you'll* cross the line?" I whisper. She nods her answer, looking shy. "Wow, you have no respect for me," I tease. "Wanting to take advantage of me on prom night. What a cliché."

"I'm just saying, your touch is dangerous," she whispers.

Grinning ear to ear, I lean down and kiss her lips. "Good. But there is no way I would let that happen at a party. No matter how much you try to seduce me."

"Tan," she says with laughter in her sweet voice. "My bag's in the trunk."

"No way!"

"Yes way."

"Were you testing me or teasing me?"

"Both!" she says.

"Sneaky."

"Yep!" she agrees. I pull her back against my side and laugh.

All I want, more than anything else, is to lie next to Liv all night and wake up with her in my arms. If she gives me that, I'll be a happy guy.

The limo stops and Teddy opens the door to drop Laura off. We all say goodbye and he walks her to her door. Of course we stare out the dark windows to see if he gets a kiss. He does. A long one too. I tell Liv; she smiles.

The second he climbs in and shuts the door, we start smacking his legs and cheering for him. He actually blushes. "She's awesome," he says, beaming.

"I like her," Liv says. "She's very sweet."

The limo pulls up to Tucker's and people are already there. Limos are pulling in and out. The lights are on in his house and I wonder who let everyone in when I see Tucker's sister, Ana, standing at the door. Toby Slinger has his arm over her shoulder, kissing her, and Tucker loses his shit when he spots them. Toby's a good guy—big time lacrosse player, heading to Duke in the fall on a full scholarship. Good guy or not, Tucker thinks most guys are male sluts, just like him, and he's still holding onto this crazy hope that his sister will become a nun.

Tucker climbs over everyone to get out of the limo first. "No way, Toby," he shouts, walking to the steps. "My little sister's off limits. Move on or get out."

Ana turns and storms inside. Toby trots down the steps in his tux. "Dude, we've been dating for two months," I hear him say as I'm grabbing my bag from the back of the limo. "I had to go to the prom alone because she didn't want to tell you."

"What?" Tucker snaps. "You're dating my kid sister?"

"She's sixteen, a junior. And nothing's happened," Toby swears. "But I'm not moving on and I'm not leaving."

I grin at Toby's determination and yell for Tucker to leave him alone.

"Easy for you to say," Tucker shouts back. "She's not your sister."

"Toby's a good guy and you know it," I say, throwing Liv's bag over my shoulder and taking her hand.

Toby reaches his hand out to Tucker. "I'm falling hard for her and respect the hell out of her. This isn't a one-night thing."

Tucker peers at his hand for a moment and then takes it, wrenching him close. "You better not hurt her."

"Are you kidding me?" Toby says, amused. "It's her who will probably hurt me."

I smack Tucker's shoulder while walking by. "Me and Evan are putting our stuff in the spare bedroom."

"That's fine," he says, still peering at Toby.

"Is the pool warmed up?" Evan asks, walking by.

"Yeah."

Tucker finally turns from Toby when Sam walks up next to him. "Can I get changed in your room?"

"You think I'm letting you take that dress off without me?" Tucker asks. The music turns louder and I miss Sam's retort, but knowing Sam, it was a good one.

I walk Liv up to the spare room and Evan and Cat follow. "Tannon?" Liv says when I open the door.

"Yeah."

"I don't want to go in there."

Evan smiles behind her, being another protective brother, and Cat frowns. "Okay," I say. "I was just putting your bag down in here to let you change in private. I wasn't gonna pull a Tucker."

"C'mon, Liv, I'll take you in," Cat says. Pulling Liv in, she takes her bag from me and winks at Evan before shutting the door.

Evan turns to me with a shrug. "This all has to be scary for her. Don't you think?"

"Yeah. I just wish she would trust me."

"Give her time."

We drop our bags and get changed right in the hallway, hanging our tuxes on their hangers just as Mrs. Tully stressed before we got in the limo. It seems this instruction was more important to her than telling us not to drink or do drugs. "Be sure to hang those tuxes up properly, boys," she said as

Evan shut the limo door. Funny thing is, we're doing as we were told and share a knowing glance as we do.

"Gotta love her, bro," I say of his mother.

"We should take a selfie and send it to her. Look, Mom, we did good," Evan says. "Got piss drunk and screwed the whole cheerleading squad, but no worries, the tuxes are fine."

We laugh. "Seems she trusts us not to do that," I say.

"Yeah," Evan ponders over that for a moment. "Shit, that's cool."

We take the picture and send it before hanging the tuxes in the hall closet and tossing our bags by the closed door. Evan tells Cat through the door that we'll be downstairs and we head down.

I pour a few celebratory shots, but not wanting to scare Liv, I don't drink any. Cat joins us wearing a bikini top and sweatpants, and Evan adjusts himself in his shorts when he sees her. To his disgust, so do half the guys she passes. Her six-pack stomach is insane. She lets me know that Liv will be right down after she calls her mom. I nod and go back to handing out shots.

CHAPTER 46
LIV

"Hi, sweetheart. How was prom?" Mom says, picking up my call on the second ring.

"So good. I danced."

"Whoa!" she says. Yes, the news is shocking.

"I know. Cat pulled me on the dance floor before I could sit and then Tannon cut in. He's such a good dancer," I gush. "I danced with Teddy, who wasn't very good, but adorable. And Sparks—supposedly he can break dance like it's nobody's business. And I danced with Evan and Trace too."

"Sounds like a great time."

"It was. Then we all danced together at the last song and the girls cried. Teddy cried too. He's too sweet."

"He is. And Tannon?" she probes without asking a real question.

"He's awesome, Mom. There was some drama with a girl who called me a charity case . . ."

"A what? How dare she!" she snaps.

"Yeah, that put a damper on our fun, but then he kissed me. And Mom, it was the most amazing kiss."

"Whoa!" she says again.

"Mom."

"I'm absorbing," she states. "I really like him, Liv, but you lead this, okay? I don't know if you're ready for him to lead."

"I know I'm not, so don't worry," I assure her. "But I don't think he'd ever push me."

"I don't either. Are you sure you want to stay there?" she asks, sounding worried.

"I don't know. Can I call you if I decide to come home?"

"Of course. No matter the time."

"If I don't call, then I feel comfortable here," I say. "Don't worry, between Cat, Evan, Teddy, Sparks, and Tucker, I think I'll be fine."

"You didn't mention Tannon."

"Do I have too?" I laugh. "He's got my back, Mom."

"Have a good time, call if you need me, and be careful."

"Love you."

"Love you too. Wait, what?" she asks away from the phone. "Oh, Gary says he loves you and if Tannon gets out of hand, he'll kick his GQ ass." We laugh so hard.

"I don't think it's possible, but we'll let him think he can," she whispers into the phone. "What? I didn't say a thing. No. I totally know you can, you stud, you," she says to Gary.

"Tell him I love him too. And I have total faith in him. Give Hank a kiss. Bye." I hang up and make my way down the stairs wearing a sweatshirt over my swimsuit.

"Hi, Liv," a girl says, but I can't recognize her voice. "Tannon said to tell you that they're out by the pool shed getting the floats out. I can take you."

"Oh, thank you ... uh," I wait for her to tell me who she is.

"Lena."

Lena? I don't really know her very well. I think she's a junior.

She leads me out the front door, which is a weird way to get to the pool, but I don't question her. Maybe she knows an easier way? The kitchen sounds jam-packed. We walk down a gravel path and I follow closely behind with my white cane, and soon I hear people talking.

"They're in there," someone says. And a squeaky door opens and we walk in.

She steps away and then the door closes shut. Next thing I hear is a lock click and girls laughing. "Have a great night, Liv. We'll let Tannon know you changed your mind and had your mom come get you," Frankie says through the door. I'd know her scratchy voice anywhere. *That evil witch!* "Don't worry, I'll keep him company for you."

"No!" I shout and bang on the door. "Please, don't do this!"

Please. Oh my God, please!

I don't know where I am. It felt like we walked down the side of the house, but I don't think we made it to the backyard. The strong smell of motor oil and gasoline fill the air. It must be Tucker's tool shed. I feel for the door handle and pull. It doesn't budge. I scream and bang to no avail. How can anyone hear me over the music? Turning to find another way out, I hit my knee against something hard. Too scared to move around, fearing I may hit a saw or step on a nail, I walk back to the door and try banging again. I wish I kept my cell phone on me. I hear something scurry and then feel it flash over my foot. I jump up and scream. I hate that I'm so scared, but I don't know what's around me. And I'm obviously not alone in here.

I bang and yell for help, feeling more and more helpless as time goes on. I shouldn't have come to this party. I don't belong here. I wish Hank were here. Or, rather I wish I were home with him. *Hank.*

Someone help me!

CHAPTER 47
TANNON

The kitchen is completely packed with people and I have to sit on the counter to watch the door for Liv. It's been almost twenty minutes—could she still be talking to her mom? I want to go check but don't want to scare her into thinking I'm going up there with other intentions. I'd ask Cat to check if I could just find her . . . I don't see her or Evan in the kitchen anymore.

I'll give her five more minutes and then I'm going up. My eyes are on the door—big mistake—because I miss Frankie's approach from the other side. The girl is out of control. "Hey, Tannon. Can we talk?" she asks in a saccharine voice, as if that will work. Everything she says, anyway she says it, sounds like nails on a chalkboard to me.

"The answer is, and always will be, no," I say with steely eyes. She doesn't seem deterred and I look back at the door.

Her hands move to my thighs and she squeezes herself between them. Sitting on the counter, there's no way for me to move back away from her. "What are you doing?" I push her back and squeeze my legs together, not a comfortable position, but desperate times, desperate measures.

"C'mon," she begs, biting her lip as if it's seductive. It's not. "We don't have much time left before school's over."

"Why don't you get that I love Liv?"

"She left." I roll my eyes, like I'd believe her. "Honest. Lena said she helped her into her mom's car."

After pushing her to the side, I hop off the counter, forcing people out of the way as I rush by and race up the stairs two at a time. The bedroom doors open and Liv isn't in it. Neither is her bag.

I lean against the door frame, close my eyes, and suck in a breath. *Why would she leave without saying goodbye?* Next thing I know, a hand is sliding over my chest and I grab it. "Get the hell away from me, Frankie! God, don't you get it?"

"She left without even saying goodbye. She's not right for you. She knows it, I know it, you need to accept it."

I push her onto the bed and she laughs excitedly. She's completely delusional. "You're a fool!" Turning on my heels, I walk out, slam the door shut, and race down the stairs and out the front door.

I can't believe Liv left. Does she really not trust me?

I call her cell and seconds later I hear a phone ringing behind me, saying in a computer voice, "Call

411

from Tannon." Standing still, I listen and hear it coming from the bushes. I walk around the shrubs and see Liv's bag. I groan viciously, silently cursing Frankie as anxiety builds from the pit of my stomach.

Spinning in a circle, I start screaming Liv's name. Asking everyone I pass if they've seen her. I see Sparks and ask him to go question Frankie. I can't talk to that girl; she's crossed the line. I want to leave her tied to a tree in the middle of the woods and let the mosquitos have her.

I race back by the pool and shout for Liv. Cat hears me and comes running. After telling her what happened, we both race around in a panic. Tucker's house is surrounded by woods; she could be anywhere. Evan goes to check the dirt bike track in the back and Cat and I try the other side of the house.

"Liv!" I shout and hear a whimper and a few loud bangs. We spin in circles trying to figure out where it's coming from. Hearing it again, we race behind a row of evergreen trees and find a shed. I yell her name and she cries. The door has a bolt lock on it. Cat races to get Tucker, but I can't wait. I have to get to her.

There's a small window high on the sidewall and I ask Liv to stay by the door while I break it. I flip the garbage can over to stand on and break the window with a rock before pulling myself up to climb through the window, cutting my skin on the glass as I do and falling to the dirt ground in a thump.

"Tan!" Liv cries. "Oh my God, are you okay?"

I roll to my side, groaning from the pain in my shoulder. It's pitch dark in here. I call her name as I crawl toward the door, hitting my head on something hard as I go. Cursing loudly, I shake the dizziness from my head. Finding her foot, I reach up to pull her down, and she falls into my arms, crying and shaking. I wrap my arms around her and rock her gently.

I'm going to kill Frankie.

"I'm so sorry, Liv," I say, trying my best to soothe her. She's seriously trembling, causing my whole body to shake as well. I rub her back and whisper hushing noises in her ear. She cries on my shoulder. "I thought you were talking to your mom. Then Frankie said you left and I couldn't believe it so I called your cell and heard it ringing in the bushes. I put two and two together. God, she's crazy. I'm so sorry."

"I want to go home," she says through her thick sob. "I don't belong here."

"Yes, you do," I say. "You belong everywhere I am." I brush her hair back from her face. "But if you don't want to stay, then I'll take you home. It's okay. I'll take you home."

She nods against my shoulder. "Liv!" Cat yells through the window. "Tucker can't find the key. He thinks they must have thrown it in the bushes."

"Get Frankie to talk," I demand.

Loud commotion follows and then Evan sticks his head through the window. "We can't. Cat knocked her out cold," Evan says. "One shot. Out cold. Liv, we'll get you out through the window."

Tucker's head pops in next, and he knocks the excess glass from the frame. I lift her in my arms, one arm under her legs, the other at her back. Facing her feet out the window, I guide her through and hear Evan and Teddy helping her from the other side. I hop up and Teddy offers to help me out. I stand with a grimace—a group of people are standing watching and I'm annoyed by their stares.

Noticing Lena standing with a group of girls, I march up to her. "You think that was funny? You're as sick as Frankie. Karma's a bitch," I sneer, glaring at all of them before walking away.

Evan holds Liv tight, whispering in her ear and Cat hugs them both. Tucker looks me over. "Dude, you're bleeding really bad."

Liv lifts her head. "The glass."

"I'm fine," I assure her. "Get Frankie to pay for the window," I say to Tucker, and take Liv from Evan's arms. She squeezes my neck like a vice.

"Dude, your head is bleeding too," Tucker says. Liv squeezes harder and I mouth for him to give it a rest.

"Evan, can you get my bag. I need my keys." We dropped my car off here before going to Evan's to get dressed for prom so we'd have a car to get home with tomorrow.

"Liv, please don't go," Cat cries out. Liv doesn't answer. I carry her to the front and Teddy takes her from me as I grab her bag out of the bushes.

Evan races down the front stairs with my bag and yanks my passenger door open. Teddy sits her down as I get in the driver's seat. Together, Teddy and I get the seatbelt to click. "Wish you weren't going, doll," he says. Her hand squeezes his arm.

Cat sticks her face in from under Teddy's arm. "Give me a minute and I'll come too."

"No!" Liv exclaims. "Stay with Evan."

"Liv, I can't stay without you."

"Yes. I'll be sadder if you come."

Tucker sticks his head in next to Cat. "Frankie's never allowed here again." Liv nods in appreciation, but it doesn't make what happened go away.

"You really knocked her out?" she asks Cat.

"No one messes with my girl," Cat says proudly. I wink at her and she mouths for me to take good care of our girl. I nod.

"I wish I did it. I really want to hit that bitch," Liv says bitterly, shocking us all.

"You coming back?" Evan asks me. I shake my head. I think it's safer to go home then potentially deal with Frankie again. She's still wherever Cat knocked her out.

They shut the door with a slam and I drive off. Liv stays quiet for a few blocks. "You okay?" she asks.

"Yeah. Just flesh wounds."

"Battle wounds to tell the grandchildren." She uses my line.

"Yeah. Maybe your grandkids will be mine too and we can tell our stories together," I say and watch her back stiffen. Grinning, I say, "Now there's something to scare you."

She laughs. "Are you going back?"

I turn left after a light and proceed down her road. "No. I don't want to be anywhere you aren't. I don't even want to go home," I say, catching her raised brow before she turns her head. "I'm really scaring you tonight."

"Am I a baby for leaving?"

"No. Jeez," I say. "No, not at all." *Who wouldn't want to go home after a trauma like that?*

"I am. I'm doing exactly what she wants me to do," Liv argues. "I'm running away. And leaving you alone. Leaving you to see what a charity case I am."

415

I slam on the brakes right in the middle of the road and turn in my seat. "Don't you ever say that to me again. I don't give a shit what Frankie thinks or says. She's delusional." Taking Liv's chin, I turn her head to face me. "You are the girl I love. I'm supposed to take care of you."

"You have your superhero Underoos on tonight?"

Laughing hard, I say, "Of course, I'm wearing Spiderman tonight."

Her grin disappears as her chin pulls away from my fingers and turns into a frown quickly. "You don't have to take care of me."

"Yes, I do, and I'll always want to. Deal with it." Letting go of her chin, I slide my fingers through her hair. "You make your decision. Do you want to go home or back to Tucker's?"

She thinks a minute. "I want to go home. I'm sorry."

"Don't be." I pull into her driveway and help her out of my junkyard car. The house is dark but the light post next to the driveway shines bright on her face. "Thanks for going with me to prom. I had so much fun. And you looked so beautiful." A dramatic pout draws her face down. "Why are you pouting?" I ask.

"I just wish the day didn't end this way." Her hand rests on my chest as her fingers rub back and forth, right where the worst of my cuts is. I flinch and she notices. "Tannon, that's glass in your skin." Her finger runs over it again.

"I'll take care of it at home." I wince, feeling the piece of glass stuck in my skin.

"I'm going in," Liv says, stepping backwards. It upsets me instantly.

No hug. No kiss. Just "I'm going in."

416

"Go park around the street by Evan's house and come to the back window next to the deck. I'll let you in so I can clean your cut."

Okay, maybe I jumped to conclusions too soon. "Are you sure?"

"Yeah." She follows my car around and then walks to the stairs. I hop in my car when she gets inside the house and proceed to do exactly what she said.

CHAPTER 48
LIV

I tiptoe into Mom's room and tell her Tannon dropped me off because the party was crazy and that I'll tell her everything in the morning before heading to the bathroom to get the first aid kit. I quickly brush my teeth and then go to my room. Hank comes in, whining for attention, I pat his head and talk to him as I shut the door and open the window.

"You be good and don't bark, okay, boy?" Just as I say it, he growls and I know Tannon's here. "No bark," I say, hugging Hank's neck. "It's okay. Come in."

Tannon crawls through the window and pets Hank. "You don't have to do this, Liv."

"I want to. Take off your shirt," I order and smirk at my bossiness.

"Well, aren't you demanding?"

His shirt is removed with grunts and groans. We sit on the floor facing one another and I slide my hand on the smooth skin of his shoulder and work my way down. His muscles feel so powerful as I move my hand in a totally different direction than where I know the glass to be, taking the scenic route. I try to hide my enjoyment of the scenery by pulling my lips in tight.

"Feel free to touch every inch of me," he says, amused.

"Oh hush!" I snap, knowing he's on to me, and we both laugh. Getting back to business, I find the glass, lift the first aid kit onto my lap, and ask him to take out the peroxide. Holding a gauze pad under the cut, I pour the peroxide over the wound. Then I feel the glass, get a good grip with the tweezers, and pull. He stays stock-still and doesn't make a sound, not even when I remove the glass. "Are you okay?"

"Just biting my knuckle," he mumbles, it's obviously still in his mouth.

"Big baby." Shaking my head, I ask if he has any more glass stuck in his skin.

"I think that was the worst of it." I sense him scanning over his chest. "Just a few cuts." He takes the peroxide from me and uses it as I find a Band-Aid to put on the cut.

"My hero," I say, sticking the Band-Aid on his chest.

"I hope so. I'm sorry it even happened." He puts the peroxide back, and seconds later I feel him slide a soft towelette over my fingers, cleaning them.

"Thanks."

"No, thank you. I scored a hot nurse."

Knowing he's smiling, I reach up and feel his deep dimples. "I scored a sexy patient. How's your head?"

"It's fine." His head turns left and right in my loose hold. "I like your room."

"You do?" I scrunch my nose. "It's so basic, no?"

"No. Not at all. So many pictures and awards. You won a lot of awards."

"Displaying them is my mom's doing," I say.

"She's proud."

"Your painting's going next to my piano."

"In the living room?" he asks, puzzled or embarrassed—I'm not sure which.

"Yeah. Is that okay?"

"Yeah, I'm just shocked your parents want it there."

He has no clue how talented he is. "Are you kidding me? It's beautiful."

"I'm glad you like it."

"I love it! Can I kiss you?" I ask, not wanting to wait any longer.

"Liv, that's one question you never have to ask."

After moving closer to him, I place my hands on his face again. Dimples reveal his enjoyment and I grin. "Now I can't 'cause I'm going to laugh."

"I like your laugh."

He always seems to say the right thing. Always. I move closer still and Hank follows me so he can keep his head on my lap. He's jealous like that. Holding Tannon's head, I lean in and press my lips to his and laugh. His lips spread wide as he grins. Our teeth tap and I apologize. He playfully bites my lip and I shake my head. This is my lead. Trying to get control again, I hold his head firmly and kiss and laugh.

"Shh," I say. "You'll wake up mama bear."

"Me?! You're the one laughing," he points out with humor.

I smack his cheek lightly. "That's enough out of you. Now let me kiss you."

"Where've you been hiding this bossy girl? I like her."

I bust out laughing and have to let go of his face to muffle my hilarity with both hands. We both fall to the side and lie on the floor. His hand takes my neck, pulling my forehead to his. My laughter runs flat as my passion ignites, and I tilt my head to find his lips. I kiss him. He lets me set the pace and the movement. I push his back to the floor and straddle his hips, never breaking the kiss. His hands go to my legs, holding my thighs high where my hips bend. I'm still in my swimsuit and sweatshirt.

My hands roam over his chest and up into his hair. "Stay," I beg.

"What do you mean?" he asks, confused.

"Stay here with me. Tonight."

He sits me up on his lap. "You sure?"

"Yes." I pause, thinking I should make my intentions clear. "Well, just to kiss and sleep."

"No, I know, but are you sure?" Tannon asks again.

"I don't want you to leave me tonight." I really don't. I'm desperate to lie in his arms and feel safe as I sleep. "Stay."

"Does Gary have a gun?" he asks, and I laugh at the thought.

"Gary? No!"

"Does your mom?" he asks. I nod teasingly. "Okay, Liv McKay, I'll stay. Hopefully she's a bad shot."

A gleeful yelp escapes my mouth and I clamp my lips closed until he kisses them free. He lifts me with ease—and I have to admit I really love how strong he is—and he lowers me to my bed, pulling me up toward the pillows as he straddles my hips. Most of his weight sits on his heels at either side of me but I feel some of it heavy on my hips. I like it. He laces our fingers together and pins my hands over my head, and I like that too. We kiss for a long time. Sometimes it's fun and flirty and sometimes it's passionate and hungry. I love it either way, but I really love it most when it's the latter.

After receiving the longest, most mind-spinning kiss I've ever experienced, I come back to Earth and slide out of bed to turn off the lights. I find a T-shirt and pajama bottoms in my dresser and hide in my closet to change out of my swimsuit.

"I honestly can't see a thing," Tannon whispers, and I believe him but I stay in the closet anyway.

Slipping back into bed, he's lying on his side, still shirtless with shorts covering his lower half, and I curl against him, resting my cheek on his warm skin. He wraps his arms around me tightly.

"Thank you," he says.

"For what?"

"For this." He pulls me closer. "This is perfect. I've been wanting this, you in my arms, for four years."

At my side, he throws his heavy leg over mine and his hand moves to the side of my neck. His warmth surrounds me as he kisses every part of my face, even my eyes. I squeeze his wrists and exhale as his soft lips gently press against my closed lids, first the right and then the left. Then he moves to my lips.

His kiss is long and tender, and I sigh deeply when his lips leave mine. "Tan?"

"Yeah."

"Kiss me again."

He rolls on top of me and I love the feel of his weight on me. He kisses me deeply. "This was a good day, Liv. We hit a few bumps, but all things considered, it was a good day."

"Yes, it was. And I'm going to try very hard to erase all traces of Frankie from my memory of it so it can go down as a new favorite."

"Me too!" His lips meet mine again.

CHAPTER 49
TANNON

The girl of my dreams is asleep in my arms. With her soft cheek against my chest, I feel every faint breath she exhales against my skin. Her hands hold my back as if even in her sleep she worries I'll go, and for double security she has our legs tangled in a perfect web that would make it impossible to sneak out undetected.

Silly girl doesn't realize it would take an atomic bomb to get me away from her.

This—her in my arms—was all I wanted since I fell head over heels for her when I was fourteen.

I take that back. I want one more thing. I want her to love me. I want that more than anything.

My hand was under the back of her shirt before she fell asleep and it's still there sliding over her soft skin in lazy circles. I force my eyes to stay open.

Every time my lids fall, I pry them open again. I don't want to miss a minute of her in my arms. What if this is a dream or she changes her mind? I can't waste this time sleeping. The smile she caused by giving me this night grows bigger as I think of dancing with her at prom. When she danced with Cat, she bopped and hopped in all different directions like a sweet bunny hopped up on sugar, and I couldn't get enough of it. But when I pulled her in and she moved with me, good Lord that was heaven. She's so sexy-sweet with a hint of heat. No one has ever affected me like her. No model, no movie star, no internet chick—no one. She's all I need, nothing more.

***

I begin to stir from sleep and cuddle against the softest pillow I've ever slept on. As my head slowly rises and falls, I realize my pillow is moving. I cuddle against it, nudging my cheek to get more comfortable when I suddenly become conscious of where I am. A wide grin grows on my face as my hand slides over her stomach and I hug her tight.

Wow, what a nice way to wake up.

I open my eyes and see jeans beyond the phenomenal chest I'm lying on and slowly look up to find Gary looking down at me with an angry scowl. I thrash back and hit the headboard—hard.

Liv wakes up with a start and reaches for me. "Tannon?"

"Yeah . . . I'm here," I say.

"You should go before mama bear wakes up."

Her warning is too little too late. My eyes are locked on Gary's. "Papa bear is already up," he says, and Liv thrusts back against the headboard just as I had.

"Gary," she says and then stops. What could she say? We're guilty as charged.

"I opened the door to let Hank out and saw someone sleeping in your bed." He uses the words from the Goldilocks tale. Talk about mama bear and papa bear—the reference wasn't lost on me. I have a feeling I'll be running out the door in a minute, just as Goldilocks did. "This intruder was asleep with a smile on his face, which was displeasing given his position," Gary adds, staring right at me with steely eyes. "You better leave before mama bear walks in. She won't like finding someone sleeping in her daughter's bed. She will *shoot* you."

"I asked him to stay," Liv blurts out, taking the fault with a plea in her voice.

"What happened to you?" he asks, looking at my cuts. "You look like you got in a fight with a tiger."

"There was a slight problem last night ..." Liv starts, but he doesn't like how she's playing it down. Now in the morning light I can see that my torso is all cut up. Obviously there was more than a slight problem. I decide to tell him the truth.

"A girl that likes me was jealous of Liv and led her into Tucker's tool shed and locked her inside." Wow, there's no way to make that not sound horrible. "I couldn't find Liv, raced around the house like a madman, and when I did find her, the door was bolted shut. There was a high window—the only way I could get to her. She was crying and it was killing me, so I broke the window and crawled in."

"I wanted to come home after that," Liv jumps in. "Tannon brought me and when I felt glass in his skin, I asked him to come in to clean his cuts. It was a traumatic night, and he made me feel safe, so I asked him to stay."

"What happened to your head?" he asks me.

I touch it and feel the bump. "The shed was dark. I crawled into something while trying to get to Liv."

"And your shirt?" he probes.

"I . . . I . . ." I stutter. My shirt is in a ball on the floor. "It had blood on it."

He nods and turns his attention to Liv. "Mom's in the shower. You better say goodbye before she gets out or you're on your own with this one." He rubs his neck. "You had planned to sleep at the after party, so obviously the opportunity for you two to sleep in the same bed was there. Mom and I had to come to terms with that before we agreed to let you go. But you're going to be eighteen in a week. You're old enough to know what you want and make smart decisions. While coming home after something bad happened was smart, sneaking a boy in our house was not."

"I know. I'm sorry I snuck him in."

"Don't do it again," he says. "How'd you get out of the shed?"

"Tannon lifted me up and Teddy and Evan pulled me out through the window," she says.

"You have any cuts?" he asks her, full of concern.

"Tucker cleaned all the glass off before we sent her through. I didn't take the time to do that before I went in and that's why I look like this," I explain and he raises a brow.

"Don't disrespect us again, Tannon," he says.

"Yes, sir, I won't."

Mr. Sullivan walks out but leaves the door open. I jump from the bed and grab my shirt. It's all shredded and covered in blood. "I better go." I seriously didn't want her mother to find me. I was just making headway with Liv and didn't want anything to stop our progress.

Liv stands and reaches her hand out. I take it and pull her against my chest. "I'll call you after I shower. If that's okay?"

"You better," she says, lifting her face to mine. I kiss her forehead and turn to open the window. The second I start climbing out, I hear her mom call her name. Liv pushes me forcefully. One leg is still inside and I almost fall on my ass, but I make a quick save by grabbing the sill and pulling my leg out. In a panic, she slams the window shut right on my hand as I'm pulling myself up to stand. I yell out, jumping up and down with my hand stuck in the window. Her mom walks in with a robe on, I duck, and thankfully Liv's body hides my hand, which is throbbing in pain.

"Morning, sweetheart," her mom says. "I just have to dry my hair and then I want to hear all about your night."

"Okay," Liv says. She shuts her bedroom door and opens the window. "Oh my gosh, what did I do?" she whispers. I shake my freed hand, hopping around in circles.

"My hand was in the window."

She pouts and drops her chin to her chest. "I'm so sorry."

"It's okay. I have another," I tease to ease her guilt. "I'll call you in an hour." She nods and I sneak out of the backyard, holding my aching hand. I've accumulated more wounds in the last twenty-four hours than I have in a year.

CHAPTER 50
LIV

I wake with thoughts of Tannon already on my mind. We spent the day together yesterday. He picked me up after showering and we stopped to get bagels for everyone before heading over to Tucker's. The partiers were gone by the time we got there. Thankfully just the gang stayed, and I had a much better time without Frankie there. We swam in Tucker's pool, rode dirt bikes, ate barbeque, and talked around a fire while toasting marshmallows—it was another great day. Tannon dropped me off around eleven and we kissed in his car for a good twenty minutes.

Kissing Tannon Keaton is my new favorite thing to do.

I stretch and find a warm body beside me. Cat. I smile. "Hey, girl," I whisper, "you up?"

"No," she grumbles.

I laugh and hear my cell phone alerting me to a call from Tannon. "Morning," I answer, happier than I've ever been.

"Hey, Boo," he replies, sounding just as cheerful. "How 'bout breakfast?"

"Okay."

"I'll pick you up in twenty. Sound good?"

My head nods in response and then I giggle, remembering he can't see me. "Sounds good."

"Great. Be there soon."

I jump out of bed and hurry into the bathroom to get ready. Fifteen minutes later, I'm saying bye to Cat, who's still sleeping, and my mom, who's drinking coffee in the kitchen. I head out the front door. I sit on the steps, slide my sunglasses on, and lift my head to the warm sun.

Breathing deeply, I sigh against the railing and listen to the birds sing. Even in my relaxed state, I can't combat the tingling anticipation from coursing through me. I'm spending the whole day alone with Tannon. A gleeful smile lifts my cheeks and I giggle.

Jeez, what's with the giggling?

Oh, this boy! I'm in so much trouble. I sigh into a deeper state of bliss.

"Damn, you're beautiful," Tannon says, startling me. I flush with embarrassment.

"You're here!" I stand and his hands are around my waist instantly.

"Yep! I was going to announce it when you walked outside, but the sight of you in that sundress rendered me speechless. You were beautifully made, Liv McKay."

I rest my hands on his shoulders and smile. "You say the nicest things, Mr. Keaton."

His strong fingers squeeze my hips. "I mean them." He lifts me from the steps to the driveway. Tilting my chin, he kisses me. "Prom was kind of our official first date, but I had to share you with our friends and classmates, and I hate to share, especially you. Since we'll be alone today, I'm figuring this is our official, official first date."

I grin. "Official, official?"

"Yep. You ready for an incredible first date?"

My cheeks warm and it's not from the sun. "Yes. What do you have planned?"

"Not telling." He walks with me to the passenger side of his car and pries the door open. After shutting the door, I hear him jog around the car. When he gets in, he reaches over and clips my seatbelt and then sits there, motionless.

"You're staring."

"Yep."

I laugh. "At what?"

"You sure you want to know?" I cock my head, twisting my mouth. He laughs. "Your boobs," he admits. "That's right, I'm staring at your fantastic boobs."

I turn toward him and ask, "Are you a boob guy?"

He laughs once. It's short, more of a huff. "I'm a *you* guy. Everything you have, I want."

"Flattery will get you everywhere on this date."

"Really?"

I can actually feel his excitement. "Really."

"Well, be prepared to be sweet-talked all day."

After a short drive, we walk into a noisy diner and he tells the hostess that we're a party of two. A loud crash silences the chatter, and Tannon leans into my side, whispering, "Instead of waiting for a table, we can offer to eat off the floor."

"Yum. You sure know how to treat a girl."

He laughs.

After a minute, we are seated at a booth. The busy diner is buzzing again with people chatting and orders being called and silverware clanking. The smell of bacon, coffee, and maple syrup fills the air. A waitress comes to our table, popping gum. "What will it be, loves?"

I order pancakes and orange juice and Tannon orders a western omelet, rye bread, extra bacon, a toasted blueberry muffin, milk, and OJ. "Coming right up," she says, tapping the table and then leaving.

Wow, can he eat.

Tannon takes my hand and places it on a cool metal box on the wall. "What's this?" My hand roams over the box. There is a row of buttons at the bottom.

"A little jukebox full of 50's music. Pick a letter and number."

Without putting much thought into it, I reply with, "H6."

"'Mr. Sandman,'" Tannon says. A second later the song comes on. I smile.

"So Mr. Keaton, what are your dreams for the future?" I ask as the song talks about dreams.

I hear him moving against the leather bench seat across from me and feel his bare knees suddenly hit mine. He moves his feet to the outsides of mine and sandwiches my knees between his. The hairs on his legs tickle my calves. Well, now I know he's wearing shorts. Its warm out so I figured as much.

"My dream is to be successful doing what I love and marrying who I love. So basically, my dream is to marry paint and do you. Or is it the other way around?" he jokes with a sexy drawl to his voice.

I heat up. And I'd do it either way he said it. The first way, he's talking sex. The second, he's talking marriage. The first I get—he's an eighteen-year-old guy. The second I don't—he's an eighteen-year-old guy . . . Most guys can't even say the word marriage, even in the future tense, at this age. Maybe he's being flippant about it, but something tells me he's not.

"How do you know you'll still feel the same way about me in ten years? Or even ten weeks?"

His knees squeeze mine. "There's one thing you need to know about Keaton men—we are very loyal. When we love, we love hard and we love forever," he states this like a law. "We're like penguins—or is it swans that mate for life?"

"I think both."

Suddenly his knees are sliding away from mine and he takes my hand and pulls it across the table. "You're my penguin. I want you now, ten weeks from now, ten years from now, and until I die. Understood?" I nod, as my palm begins to sweat. Tannon releases my hand and assumes his earlier position. "Good! Pick another letter and number."

"A1."

"Steak sauce."

"That's the song?" I ask, puzzled.

"No, 'Unchained Melody' is the song. A1 is an actual steak sauce." We laugh and then settle back to listen to the song.

It's crazy that my opinion of him has changed so drastically in the last week. I thought he was a player. I was sure not to take anything he said seriously, and now I believe him to be the most serious guy I know. He means what he says and he believes it. I mean, who's to say if he'll love me ten weeks from now, but there's no doubt in my mind that he believes he will. He's not playing me; he's not out to score and run. He honestly wants a relationship. He wants me.

"You pick the next song," I say when the jukebox goes silent.

After a minute, music fills our little section. I throw my head back and laugh when I hear "Yakety Yak." My body starts bobbing, uncontrollably. It's such a fast, happy song.

We both sing, "Yakety Yak, don't talk back," and lower our voices like the singer does and then we laugh.

The food is served and I say, "Wow, doesn't this look good?" while facing my food. Tannon gets my joke instantly and his chuckle fills my heart.

After breakfast, we get back in Tannon's car and he drives without telling me where we're going. We park and the second he opens my door, I smell ... manure.

"Well, by the smell alone I'd say we're at a farm." I pinch my nose and he pulls my hand.

"C'mon, I have a surprise for you."

I extend my white cane and hold his arm. His very muscular, very sexy arm. We walk down an uneven dirt path and stop at a fence. "Hey, Mr. Ryler."

"Tannon, c'mon in," Mr. Ryler's chipper voice calls.

"I'm going to carry you, okay?" Tannon says to me. "There's too much crap to avoid."

I nod not wanting to smell like poop all day. I hop on his back and he carries me a few feet before

434

putting me down. A warm, rough hand touches my arm. "You must be Liv."

"Liv, this is Mr. Ryler. He's a friend of my dad's and the owner of the farm."

"Nice to meet you," I say politely, although I'm still not sure why we're here.

"Please, sit," Mr. Ryler says, and Tannon helps me to sit on a scratchy blanket on the ground. I can feel hay poking through the fibers. I can also smell it, along with the pungent smells of the farm. A moment later, a *baa* is cried out, and my smile is instantaneous, knowing exactly what's coming.

"This little boy was born three days ago." Mr. Ryler places a soft, squirmy baby lamb in my lap.

I pull him into my chest and hold him gently but securely. "Oh my gosh, he's so soft."

Tannon sits next to me and nuzzles his face between me and the sheep. "He's adorable."

"He needs a name. The missus and I have named so many we figured you two could name him." Mr. Ryler pats my shoulder.

My grin is actually hurting my face. "What about Otto?"

Mr. Ryler chuckles. "We never had an Otto here. I like it. Otto it is."

I hug the sweet boy against my chest and kiss his head. Mr. Ryler offers me a bottle and I feed Otto. Tannon kisses my shoulder and I turn my head into his.

Next Mr. Ryler brings out a loud, squealing thing . . . a piglet. "Now this little girl lost her mother during delivery. It was a sad day at the farm. We had Ginny for many years. This one's the runt and she's having a hard go of it. The missus spends as much

435

time as she can with her, but we have a lot to do around here. She also needs a name."

I hear squealing next to me and know that the farmer gave the piglet to Tannon. Tannon hushes her gently, patiently calming her down. Eventually she does when Mr. Ryler offers Tannon a bottle. I rest my head on Tannon's shoulder while Otto goes to town on the bottle, sloppily. Milk is all over my dress and I don't care one bit.

"You name her," I whisper to Tannon.

"Hey, little girl," he says softly. "You miss your mommy. I miss mine too."

I reach my hand out and pet her fuzzy, rough skin. The two animals feel so different but are both so sweet. "How 'bout Hope?" Tannon says to Mr. Ryler.

"Hope. I like it. I'll be back. I promised I'd tell the missus when you got here."

His steps fade away and I turn my head on Tannon's shoulder. Lifting my face to his. "Thank you for this."

His lips are on mine instantly. We kiss while feeding the babies. It's one of the most perfect moments of my life. Our kiss deepens and then we hear a throat clear.

"Hi, Mrs. Ryler," Tannon says, amusement in his voice. He doesn't seem embarrassed at all. I, on the other hand, am.

"Well, hello. How do you like our new additions?" she asks.

"I'm in love," I say, nuzzling the sheep. "Otto's such a sweet boy. And I think Tannon is smitten by Hope."

"I am. She stole my heart," Tannon admits. Mrs. Ryler claps and coos happily.

We stay a good hour with the babies. I can tell Tannon doesn't want to leave Hope. He promises her he'll come back this week and feed her again.

"Can I come?" I ask.

"Duh," he says. We say goodbye to the Rylers and get back in the car.

We're driving out of the driveway when my phone rings in my bag announcing a call from Evan.

I fish my cell out from the front pocket. "Hi, Evan."

"Hey, Liv. You with Tannon?"

"Yep."

"Well, tell that jackass to answer his phone," Evan barks, and I wonder what's bothering him. Since I have him on speaker Tannon answers, "My cell is off. I'm on a date, grumpy. What do you want?"

"Teddy's dad died," Evan says, softening his tone. "He won't answer his cell and his mom can't find him. I think I know where he is, but I think it's you that needs to go."

"Our skate hole," Tannon says, mostly to himself. "I'll find him."

"Yeah, call me when you do, okay?" Evan says and hangs up.

"Poor Teddy." He didn't have a great relationship with his dad, but he wanted one. I know he's hurting.

"Is it okay if I drop you home?" Tannon asks. "I think I should go alone."

"Oh my gosh, of course," I say and pat his arm. Heck with our date, this is more important.

CHAPTER 51
TANNON

The dirt path to the pond is long and riddled with potholes. I have to drive slowly and it's killing me to do so. I just hope Teddy's here. The end of the path opens to the pond. It's secluded and picturesque, and it's all ours, which is exactly why we love it. I spot the big guy sitting by our makeshift fire pit and my throat gets tight and my stomach twists into double knots. I have no idea what to say to him.

His car isn't here so he must've walked. Teddy hates walking. I text Evan and then approach Teddy slowly, trying to think of the right thing to say. Coming up with nothing, I opt for just being here. I sit next to him and stare at the empty fire pit. After a full minute, which seems like an eternity, I say, "I'm sorry, man."

He shrugs his big shoulders. "I don't even know why I'm upset. The guy left one family to start another. I wasn't good enough for him. He had me at his house once a month. I slept on the couch. I felt like a stranger every damn time. I hated him more times than I ever loved him. And yet . . . losing him . . . I feel . . ." He kicks the rocks around the fire pit. "I was waiting, man. I was waiting for him to love me like he loved his other kids and now . . . it's over. He's gone and I never got his love. I never will."

His head falls into his hands and he starts to cry. I pull him against me. Hugging his shoulders tight. I rub his wide upper back, but say nothing. All of a sudden he stands and moves around the pit. His finger points at me, anger in his eyes. "I'm just the fat kid he never wanted. I'm the stupid, fat kid. His other kids aren't fat like me. His other kids aren't stupid like me. He was ashamed of me. Ashamed and I felt it every time he looked at me. Every damn time," he spits out, venting all his anger, all his emotions.

"Do you know that they didn't call me to tell me that my own frickin' father died until three hours later? Three hours. They sat with him at the hospital. They got to say goodbye and I got a phone call from that skinny ass wife of his three hours later. I was an afterthought to them. Just like I always was to him. Well, screw them. Eff them all!"

He lifts his head to the sky and curses violently and then falls to his knees and drops his head. I rub the back of my neck, feeling so damn awful for him. "Teddy," I start and have to pause to compose my thoughts. "It's their loss. Their loss, man. You are the best damn guy I know. I love you like a brother. And the guys and your mom . . . God, your mom loves you so much. We all love you. You don't need that family. I know you wanted his love … Bro, I completely understand that. But you are loved and appreciated and admired and needed. I frickin' need you, man. And the guys need you. We're family. And you aren't fat." He looks up then and stares dumbfounded. "All right, you're kind of fat, but you're so damn tall it's all spread evenly. It's insulating all that muscle." I use hand motions that make him laugh lightly. I add, "You're a good-looking guy."

He shakes his head, grinning. "You always did look at me kind of funny."

Laughing, I say, "I have a thing for big chests."

His eyebrows rise high on his forehead and he laughs. "Really? Does Liv have a big chest? I haven't noticed."

Our laughter runs dry and my expression turns serious again. I say, "Teddy, I get the feeling stupid part. God knows I do. We'll never be scholars, that's for damn sure, but let me tell you something, quiet Teddy Bear, you have life down pat. There is no one I'd rather go to for advice. Seriously, man, I think you should be some kind of life coach or motivational speaker. You have a lot to offer. You can seriously help people."

He shakes his head again and looks back up to the sky. "Why couldn't he see me like you do?"

"Because he's the stupid one. How'd he die?"

"Heart attack."

My brows furrow. Kind of interesting that a guy that couldn't love his own son died from a failure of the heart.

"Aren't you supposed to be on a date?" Teddy asks, suddenly looking around for Liv.

"I was, but a brother needed me."

His big brown eyes round with emotion. "I appreciate ..." The words lock in his throat and he looks down. "How"—he clears his throat— "how was it going?"

"Good. I mean, she hasn't professed her undying love, but I have to keep remembering that I've loved her for four years and this is new for her. How's it going with Laura?"

He shrugs. "It's hard, you know, because she's a sophomore and she's so darn insecure, but when we're on the phone we talk for hours about everything." He looks down at his phone. "Someone must have told her about my dad because she's called at least nine times."

"She cares about you. I saw it at the prom. Every time she looked at you, she smiled. You're breaking her shell. She feels safe around you. That's huge, man."

Teddy stares at the picture of her on his phone. "Yeah, I want her to be strong, hold her head up high. She's too good a person to be so sad. But, when it comes to a relationship, she has two more years and she's so damn pretty, we really have no future."

"Are you forgetting you're a stud?" I remind him and he smirks. "Just take it one day at a time."

He nods. "I should call her."

I agree and he turns his back to call. "Hey. Yeah, I'm okay. I'm sorry I worried you. I'm with Tannon. You're at my house? Evan picked you up? Let me talk to him. Hey, man. We're at the pond. Yeah. Okay. Okay. Bye."

He turns and I wait. "Evan picked her up and brought her to my house so she could be with my mom. Poor thing's crying. Evan's coming here with her. He's calling the gang."

I nod. "You up for that?"

He shrugs. "It's fine. I have to call my mom." He turns his back again. I text Evan to pick up Liv and Cat and bring the big guy and me each a sweatshirt. If we stay after sunset, it's sure to get chilly.

"Hi, Mom," Teddy says and instantly gets all choked up. "I'm at the pond with Tannon. Yeah. I know. I know. I know. I love you too . . . so frickin' much. I know. It just . . . It hurts. I know you are. I'm sorry for you too, Mom. He left us both. Yeah. Okay. I'm gonna hang here for a while with the gang. Oh, give him my gray sweatshirt. I'll come home tonight. I promise. Okay. Bye."

He pockets his phone and wipes his face with his hands before turning around. I walk around the pit and go in for a hug, wrapping my arms around the big guy. After a pause, he hugs me back. "Thanks, TK."

"Anytime."

We skip rocks across the water while waiting for the gang to show. Ten minutes in and the cars all start pulling up. First Sparks and Robin, followed by Tucker and Sam, and then two minutes later Evan pulls up with Cat, Laura, and Liv.

I walk over and lift Liv into my arms. "Hey, Boo."

"Is he okay?" she whispers in my ear.

"He will be." I take her to him and she waits her turn to hug him. He lifts her to his height and holds her, feet dangling. He holds her longer than he held the other girls, but then again he hasn't held Laura yet. Her shyness is keeping her at the back of the line.

"I'm sorry, Teddy," Liv says, kissing his cheek.

442

"It's okay, doll." He puts her down, smacks shoulders with the guys, and then walks up to Laura. "Hey," he says.

She leaps into his arms and cries on his shoulder. "I was so worried. And I'm so sorry."

He walks, with her in his arms, along the side of the pond, a good distance away from everyone, and sits with her in his lap. She leans back and stares at him. He wipes her tears away. Leaning forward, she kisses him. My heart expands in my chest and I pull Liv against me. "Can I get a rain check for the rest of our date?"

"You had more planned for us?" she asks, surprised.

"I had us booked until about ten tonight. And don't ask because I'm not telling."

Tucker starts a fire in the pit and sets hot dogs on a rack. The camp counselor has arrived. Always prepared. Always willing to take the lead. All of us end up sitting around the fire well into the night. Girls lying back on their guys' chests while we talk and tell stories. We get Teddy to laugh a lot, and that was all we were after so the night went well.

When we're all ready to go, Teddy, Laura, and Liv get in my car. I drive Teddy home first. We all want to make sure he gets in his house, especially Laura. His mom greets him at the door and it eases our unspoken worry that he may head out again.

I look at Laura in the rearview mirror. Her phone lights her face—she's texting. I have a feeling she's texting Teddy already. When I pull in front of her house I say, "Tell the big guy I got you home safely."

She looks up and then smiles at me in the mirror. "I will. Thank you."

"Bye," Liv says, turning to face her.

"Bye, Liv. Thanks for letting me be with you guys again."

"You're always welcome," Liv assures her.

Laura walks into her house and I drive toward Liv's house. I don't want to drop her off but she seems tired. Hell, I am too. It was an emotional night. "School tomorrow," I say miserably.

"Ugh."

CHAPTER 52
LIV

At school this past week, Tannon would wait for me in the parking lot and walk me to homeroom and if he saw me in the hall, he'd always come up behind me and whisper "boo" in my ear. He came over twice for dinner, Evan too, and Mom loved having them. Thursday night I had dinner at his house with his dad. Mr. Keaton is a very funny guy and we laughed the whole time.

Tannon and I kind of sank right into being a happy couple, but he's sure not predictable. He keeps me guessing, not about his feelings—I know he loves me—but about what he'll do next. He's always surprising me. Yesterday, he stood up in English and recited another poem he wrote:

I feared my love would go in vain.
You are an angel and I am plain.
So I hid my love in a pool of shame
And prayed for the day you'd ease my pain.

That day is here.
My chance to obtain
The one thing in the world
I need to stay sane.

So I take this day by the reins.
Loving from the heart
Exposing every vein.
With nothing to lose
Only your love to gain.

He left me speechless. Mr. Carlson said he's so impressed with Tannon's poetry skills. Who wouldn't be? He writes from the heart. You can hear his emotion, feel his pain. He has more passion than anyone I know and I am falling deep.

All those emotions I was confused about now make sense. He pushes every button, leaves me all stirred up, fills me with anticipation and excitement, and makes me want to spend every waking moment with him. I wish he were here right now, cuddled against me, holding me tight.

This is how it's supposed to feel. Falling in love should be intense and untamed. It should make you feel alive. And I feel so alive.

"Wake up, birthday girl!" Cat sings, jumping up and down on my bed.

"I'm up," I say, flipping the covers off my head.

"The boys will be here in an hour to pick us up. So get ready. Wear a sun dress."

"Where are we going?"

"I've been sworn to secrecy." She jumps off the bed and starts singing the birthday song to me really loudly. Next Mom's voice chimes in and she jumps on the bed, kissing me eighteen times all over my face, plus one for good luck.

"Eighteen!" Mom bellows. "I can't believe it. Happy birthday, sweetheart."

"Thanks, Mom."

"I want her home by three sharp, Cat. Family's coming. Bring the gang back with you," Mom requests.

"Yes, ma'am."

"This was just dropped off," Mom says, placing a square box in my lap.

"What is it?" I ask. "And who's it from?"

"Who do you think?" she says, amused.

Tannon. I find the opening for the box and pop the top. It smells divine. "Crumb cake!" Shaking my head with a huge smile, I hand the box to Mom and ask her to break me off a piece. "It's from Burk's," I say happily after taking a big bite. I told Tannon in passing that my favorite indulgence was the crumb cake from Burk's Bakery. He pays attention!

"Yum!" I grin with a full mouth. They ask for some. I share, reluctantly.

We get ready and wait outside for the guys with Hank. I'm not told why he's invited but I'm so glad he is. A car pulls up and it doesn't even come to a full stop before a door opens and someone stomps up the driveway, and lifts me. "Happy eighteenth, Liv!" Tannon says, kissing my neck repeatedly. I knew it was him by the enthusiastic stomp alone.

447

"Thank you. And thanks for the crumb cake."

After placing me on my feet, he lifts my face and kisses me deeply. "That was nothing. I have a few surprises up my sleeve." He takes my hand. "C'mon."

He walks me and Hank down to the car and Evan shouts a birthday hello. I smile and climb into the back of his jeep, Hank sits tall next to me. "I feel like a hostage."

"I can tie you up to get the full effect if you want?" Tannon teases, sitting at my other side.

"I'll pass."

The four of us talk as Evan drives. I try to pay attention to every turn he makes, hoping to figure out where we are heading, but once he gets on the highway, I'm stumped. After about forty minutes or so, it becomes stop and go before he parks and we all get out. Our voices echo and I know we're in a parking garage. Hank leads the way along a crowded, noisy sidewalk. They still haven't revealed our location. However, the sounds of many cars and people echoing around me along with the smell of hot dogs, roasted peanuts, and pretzels every few feet makes me think we're in New York City.

After a short walk, we walk through a few doors and enter a large, open room. We walk down a long slope. Hank guides me slowly but confidently and I know there are no obstructions in our way. Curious, I reach my hand to the side and my fingers find a velvety soft chair. Putting two and two together, I know we are walking down rows of chairs. At the bottom of the slope, we walk up a few stairs and over a creaking wood floor. It's a theater. The echo of our many footsteps in the large, empty room, the rows of chairs down a slight decline, the steps up onto what feels like a stage—yeah, it's definitely a theater.

"Happy birthday, Liv."

"Mr. Tenley!" I stumble back, shocked to hear his voice.

"Yep. Do you know where you are?"

"A theater."

Tannon lifts my hand. "Not just any theater."

"No!" I say, squeezing his hand. "It's Carnegie Hall, isn't it?"

"Yes, clever girl, it is."

"Mr. Tenley, how did you . . ."

"No, Liv, it was Tannon."

My head snaps back to Tannon in shock. "How?"

"Mr. Franklin, the man who bought my painting at the banquet, called to set up an exhibit of my work . . ."

"Oh my gosh, that's huge, Tan. Congratulations!" I'm so happy for him I forget about everything else, release Hank's harness, and leap against Tannon's chest, hugging him tight.

"Yeah, it will be with ten other young artists, but it's a huge deal. Anyway, I told him about the grand gesture painting and he asked if I could paint more like them. He thinks I can tap into a new market and wants to help me. He asked about you and this place came up and it seems the douchebag you encountered was fired a month after the banquet for setting his claws on the daughter of his boss. He's a sleazeball," Tannon groans, and I can tell he still wishes he had hit the guy. "Mr. Franklin's good friends with the new director, a woman." He's pleased; I smirk. "You're here to audition for Mrs. Quinn."

"No way!" I grab his hand, feeling faint. He sits me on the piano bench. "Tannon, thank you! Oh my gosh, thank you so much!" He kisses me and I pull him in for another peck before he can move.

"Take a minute to get used to the piano and the sounds of the room," Mr. Tenley says. "Mrs. Quinn will be in shortly."

"Knock 'em dead, Liv," Cat says.

"Yeah, Liv, you got this." Evan hugs me from behind and I squeeze his arms.

"Tan?" I call out.

"Yeah."

"I love when you wear your Underoos," I say. His laughter fills the room. "Thank you, dream maker."

"This is your moment," he whispers in my ear. "Grab it by the horns."

They walk off the stage with Hank and I sit at the plush, leather bench. Breathing in the smell of the room, a mixture of wood polish and old, musky fabric. I slide my hand over the top of the piano. By its width alone I know it's a grand piano. My fingers move over the letters on the inside of the fall board—it's a Steinway.

Wow.

Taking in the grandness of this place and this moment, I stretch my fingers, content and ready to do what I was born to do—play. I think of the movie *Somewhere in Time*, of the corset tight on my waist, the long gown swaying at my feet, and I play. I play for Tannon.

And for the first time I don't have to wish for an all-encompassing love. I have it.

I have Tannon. And I love him with every molecule of my being. And he loves me.

I realize I've been playing a while and wonder when the audition will start. "When is Mrs. Quinn coming?" I ask, believing my friends are sitting in the audience.

"I'm here," a woman says, and a sudden swoosh of nervous energy flashes through my system. "I've been here for a while, dear. I didn't want to stop you."

I stand as heels click across the hardwood floor. "Mrs. Quinn, it's a pleasure to meet you."

She takes my hand. "The pleasure is mine. You are an exquisite pianist. I've been holding auditions for our Promising Artists concert scheduled for early September. I'd love to add you to the list. And I'm also looking for a backup pianist for a symphony concert in late October. Are you interested?"

"Yes. Yes, thank you."

"Wonderful. I will call you with the details. And happy birthday." I thank her and she leaves.

The others run up the steps. Cat gets to me first. Hugging me, we jump up and down like little girls, our squeals echoing off the high ceiling. Evan and Mr. Tenley hug me next. And then Tannon.

"You did it, Boo."

"I played for you," I say.

"It was beautiful."

We say goodbye to Mr. Tenley and Hank leads us back onto the busy sidewalks.

*　*　*

We end up back at my house. My whole family is here, the gang too. We barbeque and eat and laugh. The females in my family all gush over Tannon. The males tease him, threatening his life if he ever does me wrong. Tannon takes it all in stride. We have cake and eventually everyone leaves. Cat goes to Evan's to watch a late movie and Tannon and I head to his house so he can give me my final gift.

He sits me on his bed and excuses himself, leaving me alone in his room. I stand to explore—okay, snoop. My hand slides over the hairs of soft paintbrushes and the frame of a tall easel. I find a wall and then a frame, running my hand over the paint. I can't make out what it is. It's not three dimensional like the painting he gave me.

"That one's of my mom," he says from the door.

I pull my hand back. "Sorry."

"No, it's okay." He moves behind me and guides me a few steps to the left before leaning me over something. I place one hand down and realize it's a desk. He places my other hand on a canvas on the wall. "This is you. Just your face, sunglasses on and I'm reflected in the lens with my head down, wishing you were mine. I painted this last year. I was going through a dark period." He laughs.

He walks me to his bed and guides me on my knees over the mattress, lifting my hand to a painting over his headboard. "This is me and the guys. Evan, Teddy, Sparks, and Tucker sitting around the fire at the pond." He shifts me on the bed, facing the wall the mattress is pushed against. "And this is me and you. I've got you in my arms. Guess I was putting what I wanted out into the universe, hoping one day this would be us for real."

He's kneeling behind me on the mattress. I lean into his chest and turn my head. Our lips meet and we kiss. His hands move over my stomach and press me closer to him. I lift my hand to the side of his head and deepen the kiss, and his hand moves up, up, up. And I don't cower away or stiffen. I ease into him, gasping and kissing him more ardently.

I turn in his hold and pull off his shirt. He lies back, taking me with him. His rich, musky scent is all around me—from him, his covers, his pillow. I inhale as his hands move to my hips, lifting me to lie on top of him.

I'm not scared of him, his passion, or his need because mine is right there with his. I long for him. He has my heart and I trust him with it completely.

In the distance, as if in a dream, a door slams. Before I can even begin to comprehend what that noise means, Tannon lifts me off of him and rushes from the bed. He curses. Rustling follows and then a creak of wood. I sit up, throw my feet off the bed, and fix my hair. I'm adjusting my shirt when there's a knock at his door. "Yeah?" Tannon calls out.

The door opens. "Hey, Tan ... Oh, hi, Liv. Happy birthday."

"Hi, Mr. Keaton. Thank you."

"Party over?" he asks.

"Yeah, we came home so I could give Liv her present."

"Okay. Well, I'll be in my room. Oh, and Tan?"

"Yeah," he answers.

"Your T-shirt's on inside out and backwards." Mr. Keaton laughs and I hear the door shut.

Heat flushes my cheeks and I cover my mouth, mortified. Tannon curses and then laughs. He walks to the bed and lifts my hand to his shirt. The tag is exposed in the front. I laugh through my embarrassment. He kneels on the bed next to me.

"Tan, we shouldn't."

"Liv, we're eighteen. If he was pissed, he wouldn't have shut the door."

"I guess that's true, but the mood is gone."

He huffs. "I know. Relax. Here." He places a small box in my hand.

I run my finger over the velvety smooth top. "You've already given me so much."

"Open it."

I lift open the top and explore the contents with my finger. He helps me remove what I believe to be a bracelet from the box, securing the chain around my wrist. "It's a charm bracelet. I added a piano, dog, paintbrush, and a surfboard because it was the closest thing I could find to a wave board."

I explore each charm with my fingers, identifying each one easily. "I love it."

Lying back against his pillow, I continue to run my finger over the charms. "I see you now. I see the real you. I see a guy who loves a girl completely. A writer of poetry so honest and touching. An artist who found a way to get a blind girl to experience his extraordinary talent. I see a boy who let his struggles win and a man who is ready to fight past it. I see all your broken pieces and all your strengths. So many strengths. I see your Underoos, Tan—you wear them well."

He offers a faint laugh.

I breathe into a long sigh as he lies next to me. "I have five favorite days now. The day I got Hank, the day Gramps bought me my piano, the day at the beach with you, prom—especially that night—and today. The day I finally see the guy I'm meant to love. I've been waiting for him and he's finally here."

It's quiet. Only the rhythm of my heart in my ears fills the silence. "Tan?"

"Yes."

I turn and take hold of his handsome face. "I'm in love with you." His dimples grow deep under my fingers. "Madly and deeply in love with you."

The briskness in his movement startles me. Suddenly I'm on my back and he's straddling my hips. "Say it again."

"I love you, Tannon."

CHAPTER 53
TANNON

I think my heart is going to burst. "Please, say it again."

"I love you. I do."

I drop my forehead to hers. This isn't a dream. This is seriously happening. She's really speaking these words. To me. I've never been so happy in my entire life. My heart is going to explode. I want to scream. Jump on the bed. Run a frickin' marathon.

My whole body tenses, I'm so damn happy. "God, this feels good."

She runs her fingers through my hair. "I think I always have. It's always been you."

Lifting my head, I look down at her. "I'm going to kiss you. And this kiss is going to be long and memorable. This kiss is going to show you how happy you've made me. Do you understand?"

She laughs. "Yes, sir!" A snort escapes from her and she covers her nose, embarrassed.

"No hiding, Ms. McKay." I pull her hand away and kiss her palm.

"Well, I'm waiting to be blown away, Mr. Keaton," she says.

"Oh, the pressure," I joke. "Commencing in five . . . four . . ." I press my lips to hers at three. And she laughs around my kiss. Taking her head in my hands again, I turn her head and move up on my forearms to get a better angle. My lips slide over the lips of the girl I love. The girl who loves me back.

Finally, life doesn't suck anymore.

While deepening our kiss further, my thumbs roam up her face and over her forehead. I can't stop touching her face as our tongues tangle. There are other parts I wish to explore but not right now. Right now I just want to kiss this mouth and these lips that I've dreamed about for four long years.

"Holy crap." I lift up onto my forearms and laugh.

"What?" Liv asks, grabbing my face, looking both curious and concerned.

"I got what I wanted. I never get what I want. This is frickin' fantastic," I state. Her head tilts up as she laughs and I kiss her exposed neck. "I got my girl. Now what am I going to do with her?" I nibble down to her collarbone.

Her hands grab my face and she lifts my head. "You're going to love me good, Tannon Keaton. That's what you're going to do with me. Love me good. That's all I want . . . nothing more."

I smile. She's always stealing my lines.

Epilogue

TANNON VS. MR. CARLSON

"Mr. C!" Tucker yells when Mr. Carlson walks into his backyard.

"Hey, Tucker," Mr. Carlson says with a wave. "Nice pool."

I walk off the diving board and head over to shake his hand. "You ready?"

"Ready as I'll ever be," he says. "A deal is a deal. You made your B, now I get in the pool, right?"

"Ten laps," I remind him.

"Five."

"Seven."

He nods with a smirk. "Hi, Liv!" he calls to her across the pool.

She waves sweetly, calling back, "This is a good day, Mr. Carlson." I smile at her comment.

"She's right," I say. "You're grasping a moment."

"Are you going to take it easy on me?"

I consider him for a second, and then say, "Not a chance."

"I didn't think so." He groans.

"You didn't take it easy on me, did you?" I counter.

"Nope. You earned that B. It feels good, doesn't it?"

I nod. "Yeah, it feels really good."

"Kick his butt, Mr. C!" Cat cheers.

He smiles, rubbing at his neck. This is a huge moment for him and we all know it. "Okay." He pulls his shirt off and kicks his shoes to the side. "Let's do this!"

We set ourselves at the edge of the deep end and Tucker and Evan sit at the side, ready to count laps. Teddy and Sparks stand at each end to ensure we tap the sides before turning.

Mr. Carlson pulls a pair of goggles out of his swim shorts pocket and adjusts them to his face. I don't have any so Tucker hops up and digs through his pool supplies, eventually throwing me a pair. We get ourselves ready and Tucker yells, "Go!" I dive in and swim my fastest to the surface. There's no way I'm going easy on him. Win or lose, he needs to know I gave it my all, because if he does win, it will be that much sweeter. I push off the wall after the first turn and swim as fast as my arms and legs will take me, but swimming was never a strength of mine. I see him coming up, flip, and then push off the side. Back and forth we go, and he's always right there.

Last lap, I flip and kick with all my might, but the shark next to me passes without a problem and now my head is in line with his feet. I push myself and make it to his waist. I cup my hands more, flex my feet flatter, and hit the end. I thrust out of the water and find him already up and looking over at me with a huge grin on his face.

"Mr. C wins!" Sparks shouts.

"Woo-hoo, Mr. Carlson!" Liv and Cat cheer.

Shaking my head, I reach for the diving board and pull myself to his side of the pool. "Good race," I say, reaching my hand out.

He pushes it away and hugs me, smacking my back hard. "Thanks, Tannon. I would've never done this without your push."

"No, thank you for believing in me," I say. "You proved me wrong. Showed me I was capable. Worth fighting for."

"And you just showed me it's never too late. So who else wants to race?" he yells out, and we all laugh.

"Feeling good?" I ask, knowing he's feeling fan-frickin'-tastic.

"Yeah. I feel really good."

Tucker pulls his shirt off at the challenge and asks me for the goggles. They set up and I yell go . . .

THE END

Author's Note:

Tannon and I shared the same challenges; the same learning disabilities, insecurities, and negative mindset. Like him, I had a label placed on me and I became that label. Like him, I felt stupid, incapable, and unworthy. And like him, I hid in those small classrooms and I gave up on myself. The only difference between us was that Tannon hid behind his looks and I hid behind my laughter.

We both allowed our struggles to become greater than they were ever meant to be. They took over and became all we thought we were. As Paulo Coelho said: *"You are what you believe yourself to be,"* and he was so right. It's the power of the mind, and my belief that I was incapable didn't change until I was 37 years old.

It was then that I found the courage to face my challenges. Like a flip of a switch, I woke up one day and the dream in my heart was louder than the negative voice in my head, and it was so vivid and so complete that there was no mistaking it, no hiding from it. I experienced an extraordinary amount of courage, and with it, I forgot who I thought I was and stepped toward who I was meant to be. I had a story with characters that filled my heart, filled my mind, and blocked out that negative voice that said I couldn't long enough for me to try believing I could. I didn't question any of it, I just sat down and started writing. It was one of the most beautiful moments of my life because in it I realized I was capable of so much more than I ever imagined.

I now know I was given that moment because I was finally open to it. It was a time in my life when I wanted to believe that I was capable of more. I'll repeat the Paulo Coelho quote — *"You are what you believe yourself to be."* Crazy as it may be, in that moment, I believed I could be a writer, so I wrote. I guess I believed it because the ability was always hidden inside of me. Who knows? What I do know, is I'm so grateful for that moment, because I found my passion. To think it was hiding in my greatest challenge.

I still struggle with reading and writing, but now I know that the struggle doesn't make me incapable of following my passion, it just makes the road a little bumpier.

I'm sharing this because if you are trapped in that negative mindset, like me and Tannon were, believing you aren't good enough or smart enough or strong enough to face your challenges — whatever they may be — then I want you to know that I get how you're feeling, but I also know that you are enough — in every way.

We have to free ourselves from the lie and find our truth. We have to be open and willing to face our challenges because it's in our challenges that our true happiness lies.

It won't be easy. Challenges are designed to test us, and some days will suck, and you might fall down — a lot, and you might encounter haters — around every corner, and your doubts may overpower your will — often, and you might be tempted to quit — every day. There will be periods where you feel weak and scared and question everything because it's hard . . . it's so freakin' hard. But you can't quit because your happiness is just a step away. It's there . . . right there, in that fight, in that moment when you believe in yourself, when you show you are worthy of the time and effort, when you love yourself enough to push forward, when you face your enemies, when you're bold and true, and especially when you're dusting yourself off after a fall and you have the courage to try again and again and again. It's right there, right there . . . in that challenge. That's where you'll find true happiness. And it feels fan-freakin-tastic.

That's why I write. I write to experience that fan-freakin-tastic feeling of peace when passion overpowers fear.

I'll end this note with my favorite Tannon quote because I think he says it best: "It's an eye-opening day when you realize that the biggest bully you will ever face is you. That you would never let anyone talk to you the way you talk to yourself. That you are the enemy who stands in the way of everything you want. And that the only thing you have to do to beat the enemy is to show yourself some love. Guys, if you're like me, please stop listening to that negative voice in your head. Please know that the real you is good enough. Don't let your challenges win. Use what you got. And fight for what you want, no matter what your peers say. No matter what anyone says. Especially that negative voice. Just be you. Be real. Take chances."

Thanks for reading!
Best wishes,
Janine

P.S. If you enjoyed Nothing More, then please consider leaving a review on Amazon or wherever you bought the book.
Thank you!!!
And also look me up on Instagram and Facebook @janineolsson. I'd love to hear from you.

Acknowledgments:

I want to start by thanking you, my readers. You took a chance on me and that means the world to me. I hope you loved getting to know Liv and Tannon. And if there is a challenge you have yet to face, I hope they have inspired you to face it. Use what you got. You have all it takes to see it through.

Alison, my editor, thanks for all your hard work and dedication. I appreciate all the side research you did to assure this story was solid. It was comforting to know my baby was in such good hands. You are awesome!

To my husband, Steve, and our kids, Stephen and Savannah, I can't express how thankful I am for your unconditional love and support. Although the stories come easy to me, writing them out takes time and patience—and guts that I sometimes lack— and your unwavering love, support, and understanding keeps me striving forward. And knowing that you will love me no matter what, eases my fears. You fill my heart. I love you to the moon and back.

Dad, you have been rooting for this story since it was only a thought in my mind. Your love for these characters— especially Trace— kept me going whenever I got scared or discouraged. Thank you for loving my fictional world as much as I do. And for all your advice and support.

Mom, thanks for being a great cheerleader. You have believed in me my whole life and for that I am eternally grateful.

Ashlee, my goddaughter, thank you for reading this story in its rough draft and for all your notes. I still have the text you sent me at 2 in the morning telling me you just finished the book and how much you loved it. I took a snap shot of it and saved it in my photos it meant so much to me. I appreciate your help with cover ideas and for being as excited about this book as I am.

Kayla, thanks for being another teen perspective and assuring I did these teens justice. You offered your honest opinion and I greatly appreciate it.

Gwen, dude, thanks for all your advice on the story and the blurb. You never shot me down when I called with another blurb idea. You made me laugh when I wanted to scream with frustration.

Joey, for taking the time to talk about covers and blurbs and for being the best big brother there is.

Jeanette, my soul sister and sweetest person I know, thanks for being the first to read this book, way back when it was a mess of chapters. You've always been my kindest critic.

Renee, for being such a dear friend and always being there for me. Our conversations always end up with our faces hurting from laughter.

Megan, you know how much I love your mind. You never stop pushing me, challenging me to see things from a different perspective, and I love you for it. Thanks for all your help with this story, and for sharing your excitement and love for these characters. But mostly, thanks for being a wonderful friend.

Karen, Katy, Anthony, Joe, Carol, Kathleen, Tara, Denise, and all my friends and family who are always there for me. Thanks for your love, friendship and support. I had a lot of harbored feelings pop up when writing this book, thanks for letting me vent.

Made in the USA
Middletown, DE
09 March 2017